# The Burma Effect

Sometimes an obsession can become a death wish . . .

## MICHAEL E. ROSE

McArthur & Company
Toronto

Published in Canada in 2006 by
McArthur & Company
322 King Street West, Suite 402
Toronto, Ontario M5V 1J2
www.mcarthur-co.com

Library and Archives Canada Cataloguing in Publication

Rose, Michael E. (Michael Edward)
The Burma effect / Michael E. Rose.

ISBN 1-55278-601-3

I. Title.

PS8585.O729B87 2006      C813'.6      C2006-903344-7


Cover design & image/Composition: *Mad Dog Design*
Author photo: *Matt Dunham*
Printed in Canada by *Webcom*


The publisher would like to acknowledge the financial support of the
Government of Canada through the Book Publishing Industry Development
Program, the Canada Council for the Arts, and the Ontario Arts Council for
our publishing activities. We also acknowledge the Government of Ontario
through the Ontario Media Development Corporation Ontario Book
Initiative.


10  9  8  7  6  5  4  3  2  1

*The man stripped of all props except that of his spirit is sounding not only the depths he is capable of plumbing, but also testing the heights that he can scale.*

AUNG SAN SUU KYI, *Letters from Burma*

# PART I

Bangkok — April 2001

# Prologue

Nathan Kellner was a man of strict bohemian habits. He had moved to Bangkok to escape what he considered the excessive normalcy of Canadian life and to be free to indulge his drugs habit and his taste for young Asian women. But he had never truly escaped his need for order, routine, precision. Therefore, he took care to regulate and moderate most, but not all, of his interests, pleasures and vices.

He played badminton, for example, every Saturday afternoon, without fail, except when he was away from Bangkok on an assignment for his magazine or for his other, far less known, employers. He always wore his McGill University track team shorts and the Montreal Amateur Athletic Association T-shirt he had treasured for years and without which, he believed, he could never win a badminton match anywhere in the world.

He always smoked two large joints of mild southern Thailand marijuana before any badminton match, no matter who the opponent. Never more, never less. It was a routine from which he never wavered. The drug put his body and mind, he believed, into the same graceful, swooping rhythm as the badminton bird. He and the racquet and the bird and the net became one, when he was stoned on Thai marijuana, and the game became not sport but dance.

He usually won his badminton matches. He believed, modestly, that this was due to the magical properties of the drug rather than to any particular skill on his part. It may have also had to do, he acknowledged, with the poor physical condition and the drugged or alcoholic state of many of his opponents in the game. Journalists mostly, and most, like him, in their forties and based in Bangkok to nurse their various vices and obsessions.

He sometimes played against embassy personnel, who had other agendas and vices. And sometimes spies, though usually only those from Asian nations relaxed from their espionage endeavours by playing badminton in Bangkok. The Western spies preferred the harder, more aggressive challenges of tennis or squash.

Kellner never joined the others at the bar of Soi Klang Racquet Club after a match. He drank alcohol, of course, but he preferred to do this in the privacy of his own home, along with other stimulants and attractions that can so enhance the pleasures of strong drink. He drank nothing but Nemiroff vodka from Ukraine — the best, he believed, in the world and somewhat difficult to obtain in Bangkok. He drank this with shaved, purified ice, and slices from tiny Thai limes. Two ounces, exactly, at a time, poured over the ice and the fresh-cut lime in a favourite tall glass.

He intended to have three of these when he got home on this particular Saturday evening, as usual. He intended to smoke one more joint and then to have sex with Mai, his almost perfect Thai girlfriend who had lived with him in his peaceful and immaculate apartment at the end of a small *soi* off Thanon Sathon boulevard for almost 11 years. Unlike many older Western men who come to Thailand for women and drugs and drink, Kellner had, after the usual random couplings of the first years, settled with one woman and now went with no other.

It was never difficult to get a taxi outside the racquet club on Thanon Sukhumvit. Kellner had in fact varied his routine slightly in recent years, now preferring to use the clean, quiet Japanese taxis that had slowly been pushing out the noisy *tuk-tuk* motorized rickshaws once so emblematic of Bangkok. Perhaps a sign of age, he thought, as he settled into the freezing back seat of the car. Perhaps a sign of weakness that he no longer wished to endure the screaming engines and noxious fumes of Bangkok traffic from anything other than the inside of an over-air-conditioned Japanese car.

The taxi coursed through the traffic easily, the young driver an expert and, with Kellner speaking to him in reasonable Thai, not bothering to try to go the long tourists' way around. Getting to Kellner's apartment required a heart-stopping U-turn on Thanon Sathon. Sukhumvit and Sathon were not the classic tourbook back streets of Bangkok. They were broad modern thoroughfares, almost highways, which bisected the city in neighbourhoods of modern high-rises, hotels and embassies.

He always enjoyed the freezing ride home from the racquet club late on Saturday afternoons. He enjoyed the sensation as the effects of the marijuana gently faded from his brain. He enjoyed the warmth of the grey sweatshirt he always wore after sport, as the sweat dried on his skin. He enjoyed watching Bangkok slide past, through the green tint of the taxi windows. He enjoyed the muted sounds of the traffic and the Thai music playing low on the driver's radio.

Kellner's apartment on the *soi* off Sathon was not far from the United States Information Service compound. Four stories, owned by some wealthy Thai general who had built it, or so it was said, with the proceeds of various dubious timber and gem deals. It was a modest building, from the outside, but well constructed, well managed and safe. As Kellner got out of the taxi, the watchman, always there, lay under a tree in the courtyard on a rough wooden single bed with a straw mat. One sandalled foot lay perched on the bent knee of the other leg.

From this position he gave Kellner the traditional Thai

welcome sign of the *wai*, palms pressed together at chest level. He did not get up, because he had seen Kellner come in and out of the building so many times, at all hours of the day and night, that they had mutually decided to forego the strict application of Thai etiquette. Kellner, sports bag on shoulder, returned the *wai*.

"You win?" the watchman asked in English from his bed.

"Of course," Kellner said.

"You not too fat?"

"Not too fat."

This was a routine Kellner also enjoyed. The watchman was allowed to observe that Kellner had thickened around the middle in recent years, that his once powerful frame had sagged slightly, that his hair was thinning fast. He was allowed to do this only because he knew that Kellner was still solid, still worked out with weights, that he had survived many dangerous assignments in war zones and that he could still very much take care of himself. And that he still had the lovely Mai in his bed.

"Mai waiting for you, *Khun* Nathan," the watchman said with a massive grin. He knew Kellner's routines.

Mai was watching a Hong Kong Chinese soap opera on Kellner's big screen TV. She spoke fair Cantonese but really just liked to see the shoddy costumes and the false goatees and pigtails of the characters, supposedly from some distant Chinese era or other. Always in the Chinese period soaps there was drama, disappointment, shock and outrage. Always there was shouting, reedy music, drum beats, gates slamming, messengers coming and going.

She looked up as Kellner came in and clicked off the TV using the remote. This wasn't movie night.

"You win?" she asked.

"Of course. You ready?"

"Always."

Kellner stayed with Mai not just because she was beautiful, but because she was smart and loyal and funny. Each time they came out of his bedroom after sex, he thanked whatever gods might be responsible for his extreme good fortune. Mai was not a former bar girl, like so many of the Thai girlfriends other expats maintained, but from a family of shopkeepers who had tried to prevent her from going down that path. And from going down that path with expats like himself.

She was young, of course, roughly half Kellner's age, but no teenager, and she was full of ideas and energy and promise. She was taking high school courses at night. And she was a dream in bed. So Mai was almost, but not quite, perfect. Perfection in women, in one woman, Kellner was still seeking, in his methodical way.

Kellner and Mai always wore identical sarongs of plaid Karen cloth after they had sex and a bath. Kellner wore his pulled firmly around his Western expat stomach. Mai wore hers draped fetchingly from almost perfect breasts. She watched Kellner as he rolled another joint; the last, she would know, that he would have for the day. Alcohol from now on.

"Out tonight?" she asked.

"Press club," Kellner said as he lit the joint. The vodkas from earlier had already given him a substantial buzz.

He was a vice-president of the Foreign Correspondents Club and tonight he would moderate a panel discussion about the safety of correspondents in war zones. Too many media companies still had to be convinced to provide battle gear and survival training to their staffers. Kellner, the senior man in Southeast Asia for *Defence Monthly*, was a respected voice. Some of his other professional activities would be less respected in media circles.

He smoked, and looked dreamily through the haze at Mai as she fed her goldfish. Her bare feet made small slapping sounds as she moved to and fro on the waxed tile floor.

It was fully dark when Kellner went back outside. He loved

the velvet Asian nights, heavy with humidity and heat and the intense scent of many flowering plants. The marijuana was working its magic. The watchman, also a dope smoker, was already asleep.

A couple of motorcycle taxi drivers usually waited at the end of the soi. Kellner didn't always use them much now, only when he was late for an appointment and did not want to walk down the long dark street to the main road to get a taxi. And he no longer enjoyed hanging onto the back of a hurtling motorcycle in Bangkok traffic, no matter how quick and efficient the ride might be when compared to a car.

Tonight, however, he was late and the Dusit Thani Hotel where the press club was located was not far away. He climbed onto the back of the Honda and the driver started the engine, popped out the clutch and raced the bike forward with what seemed like a single split-second operation. In another split second, they were between the high walls of residential compounds that lined the soi. Large trees blocked the lights from windows. Far down toward Thanon Sathon, miniature with distance, gas lamps flickered on food vendors' carts.

The big car that lunged out in front of them a split second after that came from an alleyway to Kellner's right. The motorcycle driver made an expert panic stop, and then died as a passenger in the car leapt out of the back seat and shot him once in the neck. He fell heavily to the left and the bike clattered to the ground, engine racing crazily and rear wheel spinning at great speed.

Kellner managed to jump away from the bike and to stay on his feet, seeing all this happen from a drug-induced distance and detachment. He had been in trouble before, he had had people try to kill him before, and he was not a man to panic, especially when stoned on Thai marijuana on a balmy Asian night. *Robbery*, he thought. His mind worked languorously. *Robbery. How much do I have on me?* Then his brain and the marijuana and the vodka bounced the thought slowly back the other way. *Robbery? Maybe not.*

There was no one around. The gunman approached Kellner slowly. He was small, but wiry, tough, professional. Kellner thought he could be northern Thai, or Burmese. It was too dark to really tell. The driver had sunglasses on, despite the hour and the darkness. The car was a black Lexus, with a heavy grey tint on the glass.

Before the pistol butt crashed onto the side of Kellner's head, his brain had started to work slightly faster. *Who have I pissed off now?* he wondered. He just had time to think of all of those people, all those many possibilities, before he hit the pavement and heard the trunk of the Lexus popping open. He felt arms trying, with difficulty, to drag him to the back of the car, then two more blows to the head, then nothing.

# PART 2
## Montreal and Ottawa — April 2001

# Chapter 1

The spring, after an overlong Montreal winter, smells like thawing earth and gritty pavement newly exposed to the sun, with a whiff of months-old dog shit. Frank Delaney, journalist and spy, was enjoying the sharp smells and the faint warmth of early spring as he sanded and painted and otherwise pampered the sailboat *Natalia*.

He had been ignoring his mobile phone all morning when it rang periodically somewhere below deck. There was much to be done on his boat before the next April rain blew in across the Saint Lawrence River and before the next sailor had his day in the club's dry-dock berth. The boat was Delaney's first priority, as always, and the telephone could wait.

But eventually he could bear it no longer. He put down his paintbrush, wiped lacquer from his hands with an old rag and moved below to rummage for the phone as it rang again. He suspected it would be his editor, nervous because no column had yet appeared and angry that the weekly deadline had been once again ignored.

It was not the newspaper. It was Rawson, calling from Ottawa and pumped up.

"Francis, can you tell me why you have a mobile phone at all if you never bother to answer it?" Rawson said.

Rawson was one of very few people who still called him Francis. It was Frank now for almost everyone except those few who were close when he went off the rails and who knew the reason why. Rawson knew the reason better than most.

"I'm on the boat," Delaney said.

"I knew you would be on that damn boat," Rawson said.

He, and some others, felt that Delaney's continuing obsession with the boat was somehow unhealthy, a sign that Delaney had still not quite left the past behind. For Delaney, who had lived almost full-time aboard in various Caribbean ports and backwaters for more than two hazy years in the aftermath of his first disastrous leap from investigative journalist to spy, the *Natalia* had been a refuge, had kept him almost sane.

Rawson at first was Delaney's enemy, and was now his friend. Rawson was the CSIS man assigned to unravel what had gone so overwhelmingly wrong after Delaney had first agreed, and then reneged on that agreement, to help the Canadian intelligence service sort out a little problem with Polish and Vatican agents apparently undertaking covert operations on Canadian soil.

When all of that exploded, trailing bodies on two continents, and when Delaney had crossed crucial lines both professional and personal, Rawson gradually moved from spymaster and debriefer to friend. Still spymaster, yes; but still, five years later, friend.

Rawson had known who the real Natalia was, had seen her body and the gunshot wounds as she lay in the snow of a Quebec winter. He came to know that Natalia was the only woman, even counting his first wife, that Delaney had every really loved without holding back and that in killing her killers in Europe many months later Delaney had gone down a path from which there could be no return.

Delaney, after a sailing trip that lasted two years, had emerged far more spy than journalist. CSIS now used him periodically, in Canada and elsewhere, when Delaney's cover proved useful. At other times, Delaney polished his boat, wrote a vaguely focused column for the *Tribune* and worked, very occasionally, on a book aimed at exposing certain methods of rogue members of the Vatican security service, which he still insisted was the real force behind Natalia's murder.

The column usually made it into the newspaper with minutes to spare. The book might never see the light of day.

"Kellner's missing," Rawson said.

"Not for the first time," Delaney said. "He'll turn up when the party's over."

Delaney knew Kellner from the old days, when they were both much younger journalists, with much less personal and professional baggage. He knew that Kellner, living a very *louche* lifestyle for years in Bangkok, was also a handy occasional resource for CSIS. He knew almost nothing about what sort of assignments Kellner actually took on, but had never really bothered to ask. CSIS people were still coy about such foreign intelligence operations, many of them, pretending such operations never took place, were still not actually allowed to take place.

"Not sure about that, Francis. Not this time," Rawson said.

"What's happened?" Delaney said.

"Not for the phone, OK? Can you come up?"

Delaney did not consider a trip to Ottawa an inviting prospect at the best of times. He was behind on his boat maintenance and substantially behind on his column.

"Not a good time for me, Jon," he said. "I'm up against it this week."

"This is urgent, Francis. Really." Rawson rarely used the word urgent.

"OK, Jon. But not tomorrow. I can't tomorrow. Friday maybe."

"Tomorrow night?" Rawson must be really worried. Keeping Canada safe from the forces of evil usually did not extend to weeknights. Spymasters, Canadian spymasters in any case, had wives and children and handsome homes in the inner suburbs.

"OK, tomorrow night," Delaney said. "Where? When?"

He would have been astonished if Rawson had invited Delaney to his home.

"Press club?" Rawson said. He had always clearly liked the faded surrounds of the bar in the National Press Building across from Parliament Hill. Some journalists of a certain vintage still met their contacts there.

"Fine. You'll owe me one. Ottawa on a Thursday night."

"I'll add it to the list."

Delaney climbed back on deck and carried on with his painting. He realized as he worked that the appointment in Ottawa would mean missing yet another Jung Society meeting. *Just as well*, he thought as he worked. The whole idea of his ever having joined such a group was ridiculous in the first place. More fallout from the Natalia days; a link, slowly fading, between him and the psychologist's life she had lived so intensely.

The Jungians found him an odd fish, and one who had never, so far, delivered the paper he had been promising them to write and to deliver before one of their meetings. They had found his contributions to their dream workshops stimulating, however, if sometimes alarming. His personal unconscious, his journalist's unconscious, was a maelstrom, a war zone that many of the well-to-do and well-grounded Society members entered with more than a little trepidation.

Natalia would have found all that very amusing. Delaney knew this. Whether she would find his other interests and other recent professional activities outside journalism amusing was another question altogether.

When the light started to fade, Delaney cleaned up and went to let the club staff know he would try to get back the next day to finish. That was the last day possible, before the next sailor with an obsessive compulsive disorder hoisted a beloved vessel into the dry dock.

Stan, the old guy employed by the club to manage such things and to ferry people in a small outboard out to where their boats were anchored, was a no-nonsense sort. He lived in a small trailer on the Royal Saint Lawrence Yacht Club grounds. He usually smelled of Player's Mild smoke. He had a ruby red rum-soaked nose. No one had ever seen him sail.

"No way we can let you have that berth for more than another day, you know, Mr. Delaney," Stan said. His faded T-shirt said: "Barbados Goombay Summer. Share the Experience." Short grey chest hairs bristled at the frayed neck.

"I'll be finished," Delaney said.

"There's a crowd of them waiting, all this week and next," Stan insisted. "You still got lots to do?"

"Yeah, I'll manage."

Stan would talk weather next.

"Weather's been OK," he said.

"Yeah," Delaney said.

"Should be good sailing this weekend. But cold, probably. Blowy. The river'll be pretty choppy. You going out?"

"May do," Delaney said.

"I can run you out," Stan always ran him out; he ran everyone out to their boats. He did little else.

"OK, Stan, thanks," Delaney said, wondering how many times they had had precisely this conversation since he bought the boat. Stan shuffled out toward his trailer looking ever so slightly crestfallen, as he usually did. Delaney went to get his car.

He headed back slowly from the West Island to downtown, going against rush-hour traffic. On his way up to the highway, he saw older women and a few older men in the fading light, raking suburban lawns flattened and browned by a winter's weight of snow, only just gone. All of Montreal would soon come out of hibernation, pretending for a few precious months that summer actually existed and that grass and flowers could actually thrive in their city.

Delaney planned to work on the column that night and try to get a full day's work in on the boat on Thursday before the two-hour drive to the nation's dreary capital late in the afternoon. He hoped his aging Mercedes, in dire need of a tune-up, would make it.

The answering machine light was flashing, as it always was, when he got back to his Sherbrooke Street high-rise. Delaney had a theory that the answering machines of those who live alone always seem to be more heavily used than those in couples or families. He had no empirical proof, but it seemed to him that the many loose or fraying ends of a single person's life all seem to come together on an answering machine.

The opinion pages editor had called again. Patricia Robinson. Agitated. Never amused.

*Frank, Patricia here. Not sure what's happening again this week but we really need that column in now, today. Got to figure out the illustration and one of the subs is off sick. Please give me a call as soon as you can. I'll try your mobile, thanks.*

The column was called "Delaney at Large." He'd always hated that name, had seen similar column names in a few newspapers around the country. Such columns were almost always the domain of journalists of a certain age who had had very successful careers, usually as political or economic or war correspondents, and then had either crashed and burned, or dropped out for a while, to resurface later and look for work. Delaney had done both, actually; crashed and dropped out, but the public version was that he had only dropped out.

Now he was to write eight hundred words each week on any aspect of Canadian, but particularly Quebec, life that interested him. Usually, the editors expected political comment. Sometimes they liked a bit of colour, a so-called people column. Always, they liked it on time.

This week, Delaney was trying to write something about whether Canada could still consider itself to be above the international fray, beyond the reach of terrorist attacks. He knew from both sorts of work he did now that it was only a matter of time before another major attack took place. There had been Nairobi and Dar es Salaam so far that year. The question was, where next? And who now could ever hope to be exempt?

But despite several Molson Export Ales and a very large Jameson's, Delaney had been unable the night before to make any headway on the column at all. He would try again tonight, maybe with less alcohol and more resolve.

O'Keefe had also left a message.

*Yo Francis, it's O'Keefe. I need a drink badly and my friends and admirers say I should not drink alone. I think they are mistaken on this, but it would be on your head if they are correct. I will be at Grumpy's this evening, in the usual place. You are cordially invited to attend.*

O'Keefe's marriage had foundered again, on the same shoals as always. His wife didn't like him. And she didn't like journalists. It was as simple as that. But they had so many years together, so many tumultuous years, and a son now almost ten years old, that the final break did not come. Just periodic breaks, more frequent than in the past but never, as yet, final.

O'Keefe was living in a spare room the sports editor kept ready for him. He was drinking more than usual, which was saying a lot. He did not like to drink alone, because when he drank alone he tended to beat people up. Karen, his wife, was still living on the dilapidated farm O'Keefe had bought for them once when he was somewhat more unstable than usual. She beat people up in a different way, even when sober.

Delaney avoided drinking sessions with O'Keefe if at all possible, but at such times felt a strong obligation because when Delaney's own marriage had foundered, O'Keefe had given him a bed and a glass. Then, when Natalia was killed, O'Keefe for once in his life dropped the facetious persona that had always put so many people off and allowed himself to actually feel Delaney's pain.

Delaney called O'Keefe's mobile.

"Brian, it's Francis," Delaney said.

"I know who it is," O'Keefe said. Bad humour before a night out. A very bad sign.

"Where are you now?"

"Just coming in from a day at the news boutique. Rewarding as always. Five hundred words on a drug bust in Point St. Charles. Going out again shortly to give the cops something else to do."

"Bad day."

"Yup. You coming?"

"Brian, I . . ."

"When you start out every second damn sentence with 'Brian' or 'Brian, I' you are not in the mood for drinking. OK, no problem."

"I've got to finish up my column," Delaney said.

"No problem. We all have our crosses to bear."

"On the weekend, OK? I've got to go up to Ottawa tomorrow."

"State secrets."

"Right."

"You are a devilishly handsome and interesting young man, you know that, Francis? What a life of intrigue we lead."

"On the weekend, OK?"

"Yup."

There was also a message from Kate, the woman who thought she was Delaney's girlfriend. She was a Mountie, RCMP, doing criminal analysis now in Montreal—a specialist in credit card fraud. She had even spent a couple of years on and off travelling the world on RCMP time researching a book on card fraud—

now seemed to know everything there was to know about the subject.

About men, she seemed to know, or understand, far less. She could not fathom, for example, why Delaney was still refusing to fall in love with her, why he still seemed under the spell of Natalia, dead now almost five years.

She knew a little about that story, but far from all of it. She knew that Natalia had been murdered, but she did not know by whom. She knew that Delaney at the time had been working on something very secret and very dangerous, but she did not know that it was his first assignment as a CSIS spy. The phrase *investigative journalist* covers a multitude of sins.

She had strong views as to how much time a man needed to get over a loss, to move on, to get on with the next phase of his life. Sometimes Delaney seemed about ready to do that. Sometimes he moved in Kate's direction. Sometimes they had good times together, or good sex, or both. But Kate still felt threatened by and jealous of a dead woman and this, more frequently now, made her angry. Her anger made Delaney want to go live on his boat.

*Hi Frank, it's Kate. Not sure where you are. I'm thinking of going up to Sue's cottage this weekend the weather's so nice and I think you should come. Let's go up there and relax and see if the weather turns really warm, OK? Call me when you get this, all right? It's, um, three-thirty on Wednesday. I'm at work. Bye.*

Delaney listened to that message a second time, listening closely for tone, subtext, delivery. Nothing obviously amiss. A straightforward proposal, or so it seemed. Still, as always lately, Delaney was wary, particularly about excursions that required overnight stays. Things were at a delicate stage between Kate and himself and, as with everything else in his life, he preferred to avoid complications.

It was almost 7 p.m. He dialled Kate's mobile. She answered right away. Someplace noisy.

"Hi Kate. It's Frank. Where are you?"

"Crescent Street. The Winston Churchill. Just moved in from the tables outside. They put them out this afternoon for the first time this year. It's getting a bit cold now. You want a drink?"

"I'm just back in. I was at the boat."

"What else is new."

Kate seemed as jealous of the boat as she was of a woman with the same name.

"Spring spruce-up."

"Come over," Kate said. "I'll buy you a drink."

"I better not," Delaney said. "I'm behind on the column."

"Too much time on the boat."

"Yeah, maybe. I better finish it, though."

"Your deadline's Wednesday afternoon, no?" Police. Observing everything, remembering every detail.

"I'm late again this week."

There was a silence. Delaney let her fill it; his strategy in such matters.

"You get that message about the weekend?" she said.

"Yes."

"What do you think? Could be nice. It's nice up there in the spring."

"I'd better pass. I've got a lot to do."

"The column's for Saturday's paper, Frank."

Delaney let that go. Kate didn't.

"The column's for Saturday, no?" she said.

"The column is not all I do, Kate," he said.

"Oh really? So what's to detain you this week? Sandpapering the boat or failing to write the book?"

Delaney did not want to let this go any further. It was all too familiar.

"Let's drop this, OK?" he said. "I can't make it this weekend. You go. Have a nice time and we'll get together next week some-time."

"I'm tired of this, Frank," Kate said. "I'm really tired."

"You putting too much stock in this sort of thing, Kate. Don't worry about the small stuff. I've always told you that."

The line went dead. Fuck, Delaney said out loud.

Kate was still at the bar when Delaney got to Crescent Street about half an hour later. There was the usual Montreal hubbub of French and English, spoken interchangeably. She was handing a credit card to the waiter. Two glasses with beaten-up lemon slices sat on the smudged table along with Wednesday's *Tribune*.

"Don't let that card out of your sight," Delaney said. "They have a way now of recording all the data on the magnetic strip."

She looked over, surprised but obviously pleased. Her face was lovely when she was pleased—soft skin, not ruined by the sun, and green eyes that shone. Laugh lines around the mouth. Disappointment and resentment did not come naturally to her. It was something she was having to learn from him.

Her hair was expensively streaked in golds and bronze, but tied back tightly, so she would look more like a cop. It wasn't working tonight.

"We're closing," she said.

"They know me here," Delaney said.

"It's a young crowd. No fortysomethings here, usually," she said.

"Nasty."

"You too."

"Not always."

"Usually. Lately."

"Sorry."

They looked at each other over the tabletop. The waiter looked over.

"Gin and tonic?" Delaney asked Kate.

"Depends."

"Depends on what?"

"Are you my lover boy?"

They both laughed out loud. The hard thing about Kate was that no matter how much Delaney tried not to like her, he failed.

"Drink?" he asked again.

"And afterward we go back to your place and fall hungrily into each other's arms? Have passionate sex. I drag myself to work at the last possible moment tomorrow, looking worn out, eliciting knowing glances from colleagues. I am distracted from my important police work. A whispering campaign starts. My reputation is ruined. Yours is ruined. It doesn't matter. We have each other. Like that?"

Delaney ordered a gin for Kate and a Molson for himself.

"Do you need a heart-to-heart talk or something?" he asked her.

"We've had those."

"Then you know what's what. A little."

"I know what's what," she said. "I've seen this all before. The man needs space, the man needs more time to get over her, the man is not sure what he wants. But the man is pushing fifty and he is shorter than I am, by almost two inches."

She was trying hard not to smile or laugh. It was hard for her to be tough.

"I enjoy your company, Kate."

"When you want company."

"I'm here tonight."

"I want to go back to your place tonight, Frank. I want to wake up in your bed. I want to drink the last of the skim milk in your fridge. I want to see what else is on the shelves. I want a normal, standard, passionate love affair with you. I will refrain from saying I love you. But I need you to fall for me, Frank. I can get company if I need it."

Delaney rarely invited Kate, or anyone else, male or female, to his apartment. Before the events of five years ago, it had been an austere, ordered, almost antiseptic place. Now there was

24

disorder, dissonance, which he did not like to share. Items brought from Natalia's apartment were now in his space. Her favourite reading chair and lamp were in his space. Most of her books. Some of the paintings that had been on her walls. Her diaries, full of Jungian thoughts and sketches. Not for sharing.

Delaney had no satisfactory reply to make to Kate tonight, or any other night. He sat in silence.

"Invite me back to your place, Frank," she said. "Would you please do that? Let someone else in besides a woman's ghost?"

"Don't do this tonight, Kate. OK?"

She stood up and put her phone in her bag. Delaney could sense the eyes of other men in the bar locking onto her, as always.

"Call me when you've figured out what you want to be when you grow up, OK Frank?" she said. She did not even seem particularly angry. "Maybe get yourself some therapy. That's what Natalia would have suggested, isn't it? For an obsessional difficulty?"

Then she was gone.

*Someone died because of me*, he wanted to say. He wanted to run after her and say: *Someone died because of me.*

Of course, working on a newspaper column that night was no longer in the cards. But going over a couple of blocks to meet O'Keefe was a very dangerous idea. So Delaney went home with some takeaway Vietnamese and six bottles of beer. George, the omniscient doorman, was not at his post for some reason. No knowing looks to endure.

Delaney dreamed that night. It had been a while since he last had the classic Natalia dream. But the dream came again that night:

*She is lying in the snow in the Laurentian woods, with the horrific bullet wounds to her head and to the fingers of her hands that she had used to cover her head before the gunshots came. It was snowing, as it was then, and always would be in that dream, and after a while*

25

*the snow covered her up and all went peaceful, in a way. The dream then hovered like that, like it always did, for a very long time. Still. Quiet. The body in the woods, the snow falling steadily, silently down. Delaney watching, watching.*

Chapter 2

Delaney detested Ottawa with unusual ferocity. This was not entirely to do with the fact that his ex-wife lived there now with an ambulance driver. He had hated it even when he first worked in Canada's capital as a journalist in the parliamentary press gallery. He had hated the incestuous, parasitical nature of the work he had to do then, cultivating contacts among politicians and politicians' aides and their various consultants, hangers-on and flunkies in order to have anything to write about at all.

He hated the look of the place, except for the grand sweep of Parliament Hill itself, with the elegant sandstone Peace Tower and the neo-Gothic House of Commons high about the Ottawa River and directly across from Quebec. Except for that one landmark, he found the rest of Ottawa an uninviting hodgepodge of architectural styles, treeless malls, inward-looking neighbourhoods and dismal near-empty restaurants.

He hated the chattering crowds of civil servants who poured out of buildings everywhere at lunchtime, parka- or anorak- or sweater-clad, depending on the season, desperately seeking sandwiches and soup and takeaway coffees in oversized cardboard cups. He hated the vibrations they exuded, of job security and tidy lives and weekend yard work, and the odd *frisson* of disquiet about pension entitlements.

He hated any city described as having good bicycle paths or as a good place to bring up kids.

Delaney's mood darkened as he approached Ottawa from Montreal that Thursday afternoon, the way it darkened anytime he was forced to make that drive. But he had left Montreal already well into a dark mood, generated by the combined effects of Kate, of alcohol abuse, of yet another editorial dispute and the inflexible rules at certain suburban sailing clubs.

After he had eaten his Vietnamese dinner from its plastic container the night before and after he had finished the six beers he bought to go with it, Delaney was little inclined to complete any newspaper columns about the global terrorist threat. He drank some Jameson's whiskey, too much, and some more beer and flicked through news channels and movie channels on the TV until sleep and the Natalia dream came.

In the morning, his journalistic skills were not up to standard and the writing had gone badly, or so his editor had told him soon after he delivered the required eight hundred words. She must have read it seconds after it landed.

"Frank, Patricia here," she said when she called.

Delaney's heart sank.

"What's up?"

"Quite a bit, actually. Sorry, but I'm going to have to ask you to have another whack at this column. I just can't see where it's going, to be honest. What are you trying to say, actually, that Canada is a potential target or that it is not?"

"I'm saying it is not clear at this point," Delaney said wearily.

"Well, that is what isn't clear, in the column. It's confusing. We're not clear what stand you are taking."

"I am taking the stand that the next attack could be any-where. New York, Washington, London, Paris, even Montreal or Toronto. That's the point. Canada is no longer automatically exempt. No place is anymore."

"I think we already know that, Frank."

"Damn it, Patricia, people already know almost everything they read in the paper anyway these days, don't they? Not every piece breaks new ground."

"It's an opinion piece, Frank. It should try to break new ground. Give a new perspective."

"Every goddamn week."

"Yes. Ideally."

"Well, not this week, I'm afraid."

"Can you work on it?"

"No. I'm on my way up to Ottawa to meet a contact. The paper's going to have to live without a new perspective this week."

"I think I'll show it to Harden, see what he thinks," Patricia said.

"Fine."

"It would be much better if you filed earlier in the week, Frank. We'd have more time for changes."

"We would. Yes."

"I'll say that to Harden, too."

"Do that."

"I will."

Delaney tried to call Kate after that, on her mobile. There was no answer. He left no message. He called her office. A cop-like male voice answered.

"Kate Hunter's phone."

"Is Kate around?" Delaney said.

"Who's calling?" the cop voice said.

"It's a personal call."

"Who's calling, please?" the cop voice said, obviously a natural-born detective inspector type.

"Frank Delaney. I'm a friend of hers."

"Right. OK. She's not here at the moment."

"When is she coming back?"

"Not sure, I'm afraid."

"Today?"

"Not sure."

"Is she working today?"

"That's not something we usually tell people on the phone. Security reasons."

"Security reasons," Delaney said.

"That's right, sir," the Mountie said. "Can I take a message?"

"Tell her lover boy called, OK?"

There was a dignified coplike pause.

"Will do. Have a good day."

In the lobby of Delaney's apartment building, the doorman was back at his usual post.

"The mailman's been, Mr. Delaney," he said.

"Thanks, George."

"You got a lot."

"Right."

George spotted Delaney's small overnight bag, as he usually did.

"Away tonight? I'll watch your place."

"Thanks, George. Ottawa for one night. Maybe." Delaney always found himself feeding the doorman's insatiable hunger for bits of news.

"Right. I'll watch your place. Better get that mail."

Delaney obediently opened the mailbox. Bills, lots of them, magazines, junk mail, and a letter from his publisher in Toronto, probably asking again for a delivery date for the overdue Vatican book. A postcard from his sister in Los Angeles. She was the only family Delaney had left. She sent two or three postcards a year.

*Hi Francis, really hope you're well. Sorry I'm so bad at staying in touch. I will write a proper letter soon, or will call you, OK? The kids say hi and Justin says hi. When are you coming down to see us? Running out of space, got to go, bye for now. Helen.*

George watched him read the card.

"Nice when people stay in touch," he said.

"Yeah," Delaney said.

By the time Delaney got to the sailing club it was almost 3 p.m. The wind had come up and there were short bursts of cold rain. Stan was waiting for him at the dry dock in a filthy windbreaker.

"Not much time for working left," he said.

"I know that, Stan," Delaney said.

"The next guy wants to put his boat up this afternoon, so he can get started right away."

"I've got till what time?" Delaney asked.

"Till five, tops. That's the rule."

"It's only about three."

"The guy's here already," Stan said, pointing to the clubhouse. A young stockbroker type in a white V-neck tennis sweater was having a coffee and talking on his mobile phone.

"Fuck," said Delaney.

"You going to try to get a little done?" Stan asked. "You need a hand, maybe?"

"No. No thanks. I guess I'll just tidy up and put some things away and let that guy get his damn boat in the berth. What's he got anyway?"

Stan pointed to a pristine 40-footer bobbing at the dock. It was called *Overdraft*. It made the *Natalia* look like a beginner's boat, despite it being 30 feet.

"That thing doesn't need any work, Stan."

"He wants to examine the hull."

Delaney climbed onto his boat and started stowing paint cans and sandpaper and steel wool. He felt a strong urge to lie down in one of the bunks and sleep until five o'clock, but he knew Stan wouldn't let him do that and he suspected the stockbroker would raise a fuss.

He thought for a moment about how he could arrange things to live on the boat again, but knew this was impossible in Montreal. In the Caribbean climate, yes, but not in Montreal.

He thought it might be about time for another long sabbatical. He could feel a change coming, something coming.

As Stan was winching the *Natalia* back into the water, the stockbroker came out to watch.

"Nice little boat," he said, brushing a hand over his thick auburn hair to show Delaney the Rolex on his wrist.

"What would you know about that?" Delaney said.

"Hey," said the broker.

"Easy does it," Stan said over the noise of the winch.

Delaney arrived early at the press club, at ten minutes to seven. Rawson had said he'd be there between seven and seven-thirty. He was usually late for such meetings, so Delaney settled down at one end of the bar with a copy of the *Globe and Mail*, a draft beer and a bowl of the club's world famous stale peanuts.

There was only a small crowd. No one he knew from the old days was there and no one he cared to know from the current crop of press gallery types. Kenny the Indonesian barman was still there, still wearing the same tight royal blue vest and crooked glasses he used to wear when Delaney and a crowd of young reporters used the place just about every night. He probably recognized Delaney but didn't bother to say.

The same framed front pages of newspapers lined the narrow section opposite the bar. The wider main area of the club had tables and big ashtrays and low stuffed chairs. Usually, at this time of night, people preferred to sit or stand near the bar. The TV was on with the sound down. CNN faces mouthed journalistic wisdom.

Delaney hadn't given much thought to what Rawson had told him on the phone the day before about Kellner being missing. He considered that now as he waited at the bar for the CSIS man.

He knew that Kellner, like himself, was an occasional operative, mostly overseas, for the Canadian security service types, or the ones who acknowledged that this sort of work was being done. On paper, CSIS was still forbidden to undertake foreign intelligence work overseas, but most people in the game knew, or suspected at least, that the CSIS mandate was being slowly but surely extended, in fact if not in law.

Delaney himself had done four or five jobs for the spy service, and had taken to the work, just as Rawson predicted he would. Even in that first disastrous foray into the world of Polish and Vatican spies, Rawson had said Delaney was a natural. On subsequent assignments, in Sudan, Sierra Leone, Kashmir, Delaney was tougher, far more careful, far more professional.

CSIS found his journalistic cover handy. The agency apparently found Kellner's equally so. Delaney had gathered useful information for the Canadians about groups thought to be a threat to Canadian domestic security or to Canadian business interests abroad, or both. He occasionally did some investigative work closer to home and he assumed Kellner was doing the same from time to time, and for the same exceedingly high pay, from his base in Bangkok.

The problem for Rawson and Company, Delaney suspected, was Kellner himself, or, rather, his personal lifestyle. He suspected that Kellner had got himself into some kind of jam, had gone to ground, and CSIS needed to know where and with whom. They would want to know how reliable Kellner could now be seen to be, if at all, and whether to sever their ties with him altogether.

And that would be their biggest problem. Severing a mutually advantageous arrangement with, for example, Delaney, would be relatively simple and not terribly unpredictable. With a man like Kellner, one could never know. Presumably CSIS had bothered to find out all about Kellner's weaknesses and appetites before they reeled him in, Delaney thought.

Delaney had worked with Kellner for a time at the *Tribune*, and had contributed the odd piece to Kellner's short-lived magazine before he headed to Asia a few steps ahead of his creditors. Even before Kellner hit Bangkok, however, he was known around the media hangouts in Montreal as a very loose cannon.

He had been a good reporter once and an outstanding political feature writer. As the dope and the booze addled his brain, his material became unfocused, less sharp. But even stoned or coming off a bender, Kellner could produce material that made people want to read on. Newspapers often put up with such behaviour because they need the high-energy jolt that characters like Kellner can bring to their pages.

But no one, in the months before Kellner quit Canada for good, wanted to drink with him anymore.

His idea of a night's entertainment in that period was to drink as much vodka and smoke as much Lebanese hashish as he possibly could, and then to roam wild-eyed around downtown Montreal literally howling at the moon and accosting locals and tourists alike. Often he would then head into the newspaper office to hang around with the printers as they put the paper to bed and drink beer with them till daybreak in late-closing workman's bars in the East End.

His former girlfriends, and there were many of these, told harrowing tales of his mood changes, his violent outbursts, his utter unpredictability. The only time he seemed to settle down was on frequent visits to his aging mother in lower Westmount. Kellner adored her, spoiled her, could never do enough for her. She was old when Delaney had met her and must be ancient now, he thought, if she was alive at all.

Delaney hadn't seen Kellner for years. He'd stopped in once to visit on the way through Bangkok just after Kellner had set up shop there. But that had been it. Kellner must have developed some exceptionally valuable contacts in Asia in the years since then for CSIS to take a chance on using someone like that, Delaney thought.

When Rawson entered a room, impeccably dressed as he always was and with his salt-and-pepper hair impeccably close-cropped, people never failed to look up. They all apparently assumed he was someone important or powerful or a carrier of secrets of state.

He was in top shape, a fitness man. Tall, straight, about ten years or so older than Delaney but wearing it well. Delaney wasn't sure he himself would be able to look that good as he pushed 60.

"Whiskey one ice cube, thanks, Kenny, and another draft for my friend Delaney," Rawson said. He wasn't a journalist, wasn't a member, but he made the club his own. He folded his navy cashmere topcoat carefully inside out, perched it on a bar stool and sat down next to Delaney.

"Sorry I'm late, Francis," he said.

The barman brought over a fresh bowl of nuts.

"Not for me, Kenny, thanks very much," Rawson said. "I stay away from those."

He looked over at Delaney, who had helped himself to another handful.

"You should too," he said.

"Why?" Delaney said.

"They'll kill you eventually. All fat, cholesterol, just junk, nothing else in there."

"Spare me, OK, Jon? And please don't tell me how many kilometres you ran this morning."

"Twelve. All along the canal and back."

"Congratulations. Can we talk about something else?"

"How have you been?"

"OK. Hassles with the paper, as always."

"Keeps you out of trouble, that paper, no? What would you do without that? Except work for me occasionally."

"I'm starting to think that would do me fine."

"You can't live on what we pay you, Francis."

Rawson usually took on the father figure role in any meeting.

"I could manage. My Cuba book's still selling OK. I got another one on the go."

"You almost done with that one? You still want to go ahead with that?" Rawson had never liked the idea of Delaney writing about Vatican matters. CSIS was no promoter of spy service exposes.

"It's coming along."

"Too bad," Rawson said with a half-smile. "You know my feelings on that, Francis."

"It's not about CSIS, Jon. It won't be. You know that."

"Try to spell my name right, all right?" Rawson said.

Rawson never got directly to the matter at hand without at least a little of what he considered light, polite conversation. Delaney knew the rhythm, expected the chit-chat was about over. He ordered another beer. Rawson declined another whiskey, took a Perrier instead.

"Kellner," Rawson said.

"Ah, yes. Kellner," Delaney said.

"This could be a little tricky."

"I expect it will be. Because it involves Kellner."

"Yes." Rawson looked around the bar to see who was standing near.

"What's he got himself into this time?" Delaney said.

"That's what we want to know. He's just dropped out of sight."

"It wouldn't be the first time. I told you that on the phone. He used to do that here in the old days."

"I know that, Francis. This one has a different feel."

"How would you know that, I wonder? You wouldn't be watching your part-timers when they're off shift, would you?"

"Guys like that, yes."

"Guys like me?"

"No comment," Rawson said with a smile. He raised his glass of Perrier in a toast.

"I never figured out why you would use a guy like Kellner anyway, Jon. Not worth the grief to use a guy like that, in my view."

"Sometimes he has been very much worth the grief for us, Francis. He's absolutely plugged in over there. Knows an awful lot, really an awful lot. Knows where to find out what he doesn't know. Gets stuff we can't get and gets it for us very discreetly."

"I find it hard to imagine using the words *Kellner* and *discreet* in the same sentence," Delaney said.

"Oh you would be surprised, Francis. The guy knows when to play it close to the chest."

"When he's not under the influence, maybe."

"That's a risk we have been willing to take. The very fact that he is, what would I say, a bit of a bohemian in fact makes him an unlikely person for people to think of as an operative, no?"

"I'll need to ponder that logic for a bit, Jon."

"Well, the fact of the matter is that he has been useful for us. And now he's dropped out of sight and we need to know why."

"What was he working on?"

"Nothing. Not for us anyway. Not for a good while."

"What was his last assignment for you guys?"

"I can't tell you that, Francis. I wouldn't tell many people what you work on for us either."

"Makes it pretty hard to know where to start. What do you want me to do anyway? I have no idea where a guy like that would go. No one over here would."

"Over there, yes."

"You want me to go over to Bangkok?"

"Yes."

"Why can't your guys find him? They know the drill over there just as well as I do. Better, probably."

"They've tried. But we can't be seen to be trying too hard."

"Get the Yanks to look for him. They're all over the place there. Everywhere. They don't work under the same constraints as you guys."

"We don't want to involve any other services on this one, Francis."

"You think they don't already know what you're up to? What Kellner's been up to for you? Bangkok is like a small town as far as spooks go. Everyone knows what everyone else is doing."

"I'm not so sure about that, Francis. But the fact of the matter is we want you to go over there and find out what's going on. Where he is, what he's been working on."

"You don't know what he's been working on lately? Even as a reporter?"

"We read his stuff. Just like everybody."

"I don't. What's he been writing about lately?"

"His usual stuff. Defence purchases in the region. He's been covering a few arms fairs. Routine stuff. Did an article about maritime security recently, a while back now—that one, actually."

"And for you, what?"

"I told you, Francis. I can't share that."

"Give me a general idea. What countries?"

Rawson looked annoyed.

"If you want me to go all the way over there and figure out what the guy's got himself into, I can't go in totally blind," Delaney said. "I know what that can lead to. If you want me to go over there, you've got to give me a bit more of an idea where this might have come from."

"It might have nothing at all to do with what he has done for us," Rawson said.

"If you really thought that you wouldn't be asking me to find out what's what," Delaney said.

"We would be," Rawson said.

"I'm not going to go in totally blind," Delaney said.

Rawson put down his glass. "Look, he does the odd job for us, just like you. He goes up north for us sometime, into the Golden Triangle, looking for Canadian connections up there, drugs. He's been over to Vietnam a couple of times, again, looking for Canadian connections, links to the Viet expats here. He's had a look once in a while at who's been sneaking around our companies working over there, who's asking them to do it. Industrial espionage. That sort of thing. Cambodia once, a while back. He's very good on Burma. And he talks to people for us about the Islamiyah al Jemayah movement in Indonesia. Risk assessment stuff, counterterrorism. That's what we do."

"Does he do spook work for anyone else?"

"Possibly. I hope not."

"You're not sure?"

"No. We'd be very pleased if you found out for sure."

"How long's he been gone?"

"A month. About a month."

"How'd you find out?"

"Come on, Francis. If you disappeared, we would find out."

"Who else knows?"

"His girlfriend. Some of his mates in Bangkok. The local police. Now you."

"His family in Montreal?

"His mother died about a year ago. His father went a long time ago. His sister's around. I very much doubt she knows."

"Kellner's girlfriend told the Thai police?"

"Yes."

"She knows what he does besides journalism?"

"Not sure. We doubt it. Girls like her don't ask their men many questions, usually."

"She's been with him a long time, that one, if it's still the same one. She'd have to have an idea what he was up to in his life."

"In a general way, yes. Sure. Not sure how much she would really know, or even care. Nice little lifestyle for her, so who cares where the money comes from? Ask her yourself."

"What does she say happened?"

"We haven't talked to her directly. The police told our

embassy people that Kellner was heading out one Saturday night to the press club and never showed up. Passport, everything, still back at his place."

"A month is a long time to be on a bender, even for him."

"Precisely."

Delaney munched peanuts, drank some beer.

"How much are you not telling me, Jon?"

"A bit. Nothing major."

"If it was minor you'd have told me."

"If it was something you needed to know to stay safe, I would tell you, Francis. You know that."

They both sat quietly for a moment, Delaney thinking about Natalia and staying safe. Rawson almost certainly thinking the same. They had become close after Natalia died for a variety of reasons. One was that CSIS had not told Delaney enough for his lover to stay safe and Rawson was a man of conscience, a man of regrets.

"OK, I'll have a try," Delaney said. "I'm getting sick of things at the paper again anyway. I like Bangkok."

"Good one, Francis," Rawson said. He called for a second whiskey for himself and another beer for Delaney. "Can you get away all right? When could you go?"

"I can write that column from anywhere, Jon. And I've always got an emergency one hidden away. I'll go as quick as I can. Monday probably. Tuesday."

"Go as quickly as you can," Rawson said. Delaney looked over at him.

"There's nothing else you want to tell me about this, Jon?"

"Nothing else I can tell you, Francis."

They eyed each other carefully.

"Cheers," said Rawson, holding up his glass. "Your health."

"My health," Delaney said, holding up his beer bottle.

There was something else Rawson wanted to talk about.

"How are you on speechwriting, Francis?" he asked.

"There is no way I'm writing any speeches for CSIS, Jon. My patriotic fervour does not extend to that. No way."

"No, no, I don't want you to write anything. Just have a look over this for me, would you?"

Rawson pulled a folded sheaf of papers from his inside jacket pocket and flattened it on the bar. The text was covered in arrows, crossed-out lines, marginal notes.

"The chief is giving a speech in Vancouver next week, to a convention of intelligence types. He's asked me to give him a hand with it."

"What do you know about speechwriting?" Delaney said.

"Nothing. But they think I'm a clear writer. They like my reports."

"Report writing and speechwriting are two very different things."

"Have a look at it would you, Francis? He's worried about this one. He wants to, you know, give these guys a bit of a peek at what we've been trying to do overseas lately. Generate some debate, see how it flies."

"That's a bit of a risk isn't it? Operating outside your mandate and telling people about it in a speech?"

"Oh, a few years ago, yes, sure. When you and I first started working together, yes. But slowly, slowly, people are starting to come around, I think. The politicians aren't stupid."

"You're talking to a former political reporter here. I still always assume the worst," Delaney said.

"Just have a look at it, would you?"

Delaney read the first few lines aloud: "Many of Canada's security preoccupations originate abroad, making it imperative to identify and understand developments that could become 'homeland issues' for residents or citizens of this country. The Canadian Security Intelligence Service continues to adjust its method of investigating threats to national security in response to the changing geopolitical environment and the emergence of threats against the Canadian economy, information infrastructure, proprietary information and technology."

He looked over at Rawson. "Pretty dreary. Annual report stuff."

"Well spotted, Francis. A lot of that draft is from annual reports, documents like that. Not too exciting."

"No. The audience will fall asleep. If they are already in this sort of game."

"I know. Have a look at this section, though." Rawson flipped a couple of pages over and showed Delaney a typewritten section that had been pasted into the text:

Delaney read aloud again: "Foreign sources of threat-related information have become predominant. Events have increasingly required us to operate abroad."

Rawson looked somewhat furtively around the bar.

"That's getting better," Delaney said. "Any reporters going to be listening to this?"

"Yes, probably. Or maybe we will leak it to someone here."

"This will get some play, I would imagine. I wouldn't mind covering this myself. Or leak it to me," Delaney said with a grin. "Your guys would love to see my by-line on something like this, wouldn't they?"

"Behave yourself, Francis," Rawson said. "Read on."

Delaney read: "Canada's enemies respect no barriers, either international or moral. The situation calls for an integrated approach to intelligence collection that is not bound by artificial administrative barriers. Accordingly, working covertly abroad has become an integral part of CSIS operations . . ."

"Jesus Christ, Jon. This will set the cat among the pigeons. There's a headline if I ever saw one."

"You figure? That's mostly from me. And Smithson."

"Of course. No one's ever said this in public before, as far as I know."

"This might be the time," Rawson said.

"Is your guy going to buy into this for a speech?"

"Maybe."

"Some of the politicians across the road from here are going to go apeshit."

"This might be the time."

"Or you might be looking for work."

"I'm not giving this speech. The chief is giving it."

"You're helping to write it."

"Me and a cast of thousands. Hundreds anyway. Dozens."

"The MPs across the road, a lot of them anyway, are going to take a very dim view of you guys operating way beyond your mandate. You always told me that and I always thought that anyway. What are you going to do next, tell them about people like me and Kellner? Why don't you just take out a full-page ad in the *Globe and Mail*?"

"We want to generate a little bit of debate about our mandate. Some of us are sick and tired of sneaking around, doing what needs to be done abroad and fussing about legislative mandates. You of all people know that."

"Well, you'll generate some debate with this, Jon. No doubt."

Delaney finished reading the speech, making a few notes in the margins as he went. Rawson drank his whiskey slowly and appeared to be pondering his fate. Kenny the barman stood idle.

"It's good," Delaney said when he had finished. "Except for the bureaucratese in the first couple of pages, it gets pretty good. You'll have reporters ringing your phones off the wall."

"If our guy delivers it like that," Rawson said.

"Exactly."

"Maybe he'll figure the time is not right."

"Exactly."

"We shall see," Rawson said glumly.

The bar was starting to fill up now, as print media reporters and editors and hangers-on came in after their day's work. The TV people would start coming in soon as well. Kenny started scurrying around making drinks. He had turned up the sound on CNN.

"Put it on CBC," someone called out. "The news is almost on."

"Fuck that," said someone else. "Leave it on CNN."

Kenny ignored everyone and went on about his business. CNN prevailed.

"I've got to go," Rawson said.

"OK," Delaney said.

"You staying?"

"No. Not with this crowd." Delaney said.

They took the elevator down together and came out of the National Press Building onto Wellington, all but deserted as usual on a weeknight. Across the street on Parliament Hill a TV reporter, standing in a circle of intense light, delivered a stand-up to camera. The sound man hovered with a giant microphone the size of a mortar covered in furry grey felt.

"Sources on Parliament Hill have told CTV news that the second reading of Bill C-78 may have to be postponed for at least a week," the reporter said, with a stylish toss of her heavily permed hair.

Delaney and Rawson exchanged glances.

"Hard-hitting stuff," Rawson said.

"She'll blow this town wide open."

They got to Rawson's car, a brown government issue Ford.

"You going back tonight?" Rawson asked.

"Yeah, I think so."

"You'll head to Bangkok on Monday?"

"Tuesday latest."

"It'll be our usual arrangement. Let us know where you want the money sent."

"I trust you guys, of course." They both smiled. "You're always good with payments. Payments yes. Information not always."

"Watch how you go over there, OK Francis?"

"I know Bangkok," Delaney said.

"It's not the city I'm talking about."

"I know that."

"How have you been anyway?" Rawson asked suddenly.

"You asked me that already. In the bar."

"How's the Mountie?" Rawson asked.

"No comment."

"Troubles?"

"No comment."

"You all right these days? How have you been? Seriously."

"I'm seriously all right."

"Francis, I often wonder . . ."

"No, Dad, I'm not over Natalia yet. No. You usually ask me that earlier in the night."

"It's a long while ago now, Francis."

"Yes. And you think it's time for me to move on."

"Yes."

"Move on where?"

"Hook up with that Mountie, maybe. See how that turns out."

"I don't like surprises, Jon. You know that."

"You're getting into the wrong business if you don't like surprises, Francis."

Delaney watched as Rawson's car moved off down Slater Street. He watched until Rawson signalled left and turned onto Laurier. Then he walked on down to where he had parked his own car, across from the Westin in an outdoor lot. For a moment, he thought about checking in and ordering a room-service meal and a good bottle of wine. But then he thought about how many hotel rooms he had done that in, in how many cities, and he unlocked his car instead.

It was just after 10 p.m. He sat in his idling car and felt an urge to just drive anywhere, any direction, except Montreal. It was Thursday night. He could be in New York for breakfast if he left now. He could be in Toronto sooner than that. Then the urge passed. He could check into the Ottawa Westin instead. He could pick any hotel in Ottawa, put down a credit card, stay for a week, more if he wanted to, live on room-service meals, watch movies, news channels, game shows on TV.

The car idled quietly, ready to go anywhere. Delaney pulled out his mobile phone and dialled Kate's home number. No answer, no answering machine. He looked for a long while at her mobile number in his own mobile's memory. Then he tossed the phone onto the seat beside him and pulled out of the parking lot, heading for the only place that ever felt remotely like home.

# Chapter 3

As always, there were a few loose ends to tie up before Delaney left on any assignment, whether as reporter or spy. He usually declined to think of how few loose ends he actually had left. Light duties now for the newspaper, apartment and related matters, an on-again off-again book project, a few friends, mainly O'Keefe, maybe Kate.

He decided he would see Kellner's sister before he left. And he decided he would go to Bangkok via London, to see some of the people Kellner worked for at *Defence Monthly*. He spent most of Friday morning setting things up: plane ticket for Sunday night, emails to the London magazine trying to make appointments, reading some of Kellner's recent articles on the Internet. Kellner's sister said she could see him that afternoon.

He tidied up one of his emergency columns for the *Tribune*, a stand-up piece about whether the Quebec separatist movement had now, once and for all, lost its way. *Patricia will think this doesn't break any new ground*, he thought grimly as he called her just before noon. It would have to do for the next week. The one after that, if he was still away, he would write in a hotel somewhere or other.

"Patricia, I've got some good news for you," he said when she answered. "Two bits of good news. I'm going away for a week or so, so I won't drive you crazy for a while. And I'm filing next week's column early, today. It's in the system now. Your lucky day."

Nothing ever made Patricia truly happy.

"You're going away again?" she said

"Yeah, I'm going to chase up some columns in London, maybe a few other places."

"The focus is supposed to be on Canada and Quebec," she said.

"The column is called 'Delaney at Large,'" he said. "I'm at large for a few days. I've always got the Canadian angle firmly in mind, Patricia. It is lodged firmly in my mind. Have no fear."

"You clear this with Harden?" she said.

"Not yet."

"You going to?"

"Probably."

"You'll need to for the travel money," she said, apparently sensing an obstacle that would prevent the trip from taking place.

"I'll keep my receipts. Claim when I get back. Cash on delivery."

"I think you better have a quick word with Harden, Frank. I had a meeting with him yesterday. About your column. Where it was going, maybe trying to refocus it a bit."

"That was good of you Patricia. Looking after my career like that."

"To be honest, Frank, we don't think you're giving that column your full attention. We think it shows sometimes."

"We?"

"Yes. Harden is concerned too."

"Before or after you pissed in my pond?"

"I think you'd better have a word with Harden before you go anywhere, Frank," she said.

"Delaney is at large," he said.

"I'm serious," she said.

"Me too."

He tried not to slam the phone down too hard. A minute later, it rang. It would be Patricia, he was certain of that. Five minutes later his mobile rang. The tiny screen told him "Patricia, office." He let it go.

Cynthia Kellner lived a life of suburban Montreal ease. She had, as the saying used to go, married well. Her husband was in the rag trade, ran a big women's wear operation in Montreal's East End. Ladies' blouses, skirts, cheap jeans with brands no one had ever heard of. Lots of Quebecois and Vietnamese and Haitian staff manning the cutting and sewing machines and the loading dock.

When business had been very, very good, before Asian factories started chipping away at the trade in Montreal and New York, Cynthia's husband, Josh Rabinowitz, had made serious money. He spent a lot of it on a giant house in Côte Saint-Luc —a split-level number with a three-car garage and perfect hedges. They had several children, apparently; rarely seen.

Delaney had met Cynthia a few times; he could barely remember when or where or why. In the old days when he and Kellner had run in approximately the same circles, probably at a party somewhere, or at a bar. She was about 35 or 38 or so now. He had never been to her house.

She was impeccably and expensively dressed for a weekday afternoon—black cashmere sweater, designer leather pants, black also, and what looked like fake snakeskin boots. Very black hair, very expensively done up, probably that morning. Cynthia had not wanted to meet him downtown. She was epileptic and didn't drive. Kellner remembered that much about her.

She kissed Kellner elegantly on each cheek in the European way. Her perfume smelled of money and order and calm as she led him through the cavernous entry and living area of the house to the backyard to where some weak April sun was making it just

possible to sit outside on what was still known in such neighbourhoods as the patio.

The outdoor table where she poured Perrier and sliced a
lemon was the requisite wrought iron and heavy frosted glass.
The chairs, wrought iron with the requisite cheery blue cushions
and cheery yellow piping.

"It's been years," Cynthia said as she spooned ice from a
small stainless steel bucket. "I always wondered what happened
to you and some of the old crowd."

"Still plugging away," Delaney said, wishing the vacuous part
of the conversation could be dispensed with altogether.

"I don't see your articles in the paper much anymore."

"I have a column now. On the opinion page. On Saturdays."

"Oh," she said. "I don't usually look at that page."

"Not many people do. Not enough, or so they tell me."

"I'm sure your column's fine," she said.

Fine is not a word anyone had ever used to describe his column, even when it actually was fine. He decided to save them
both a little time.

"Look, Cynthia, I wanted to talk to you about Nathan for a
few minutes."

"So you said on the phone."

"Have you heard from him lately?"

"No."

"Is that unusual?"

"No, not with him. Not since he moved to Thailand. I saw
him last year when our mother died. He came in for two days
only. He stayed downtown, not with us. Josh had to lend him a
suit and a yarmulke for the funeral."

This seemed to be a capital offence.

"What's he got himself into now?" Cynthia said, sipping her
Perrier. "And why should I care? Why should you care all of a
sudden, for that matter?"

"I'd like to talk to him about something I'm working on. I

haven't been able to reach him at all. I'm going over to Bangkok next week and wanted to touch base."

"I would imagine he is still living with that teenage girl he hooked up with," Cynthia said. "My mother detested that girl."

"She met her? She's not a teenager, you know."

"Nathan brought her over here once. On some kind of holiday. God knows why."

"They've been together for a long time," Delaney said.

"Maybe she doesn't charge by the hour anymore," Cynthia said.

"I don't think she was like that. I'm pretty sure she wasn't a bar girl," Delaney said. "Nathan made a point of telling everyone that."

"Why would anyone believe anything my brother ever said? He usually couldn't think straight, he smoked so much dope."

"He handled it pretty well when I knew him. He was a lovely writer. Very strong. Everyone thought that. And he's made a bit of a name for himself now in Asia. He's a real specialist on the region."

"He squandered his talents. My mother said that and I said that. Most of you used to say that, too. He could have gone far."

"Get himself a Saturday column at the *Tribune*, for example. That no one reads," Delaney said.

"Yes, why not? Better than wasting his life over in Bangkok, taking drugs and living with some little Thai tart."

"Shall I put you down in the 'no comment' section?" Delaney said. They both smiled.

"Sorry, Francis. It just makes my blood boil, that's all. I don't talk about him much anymore. I never see any of the old crowd anymore."

"Nobody?"

"Oh, I still used to see that character Cohen, Mordecai Cohen, once in a while. You remember him. He and Nathan went to Côte Saint-Luc high school together. Hippies. They always stayed in touch. Mordecai was the man to see for dope in the neighbourhood; he was dealing even in high school. His mother lived around the corner. He used to come in once in a while to see me and Mum when she was still alive. He's over in Bangkok now, too, I think. Still there probably. Fancies himself an artist. Paints. Takes pictures. Used to, anyway. He's there for the dope too, I'd say."

"How long's he been over there?"

"I don't know. A fair while now, I think. His mother's still alive. She came to the funeral. He didn't."

"That's interesting," Delaney said.

"Why would that be interesting?"

"Well, it might help me track Nathan down."

"Maybe. Unless they're off on some crazy escapade or other. You know what they used to do? Maybe they still do? Nathan told me when he was here for the funeral. You know what's their idea of fun, a little light entertainment? Mordecai, believe it or not, or maybe it was Nathan's idea, got some little stainless-steel pea shooters made, somewhere over there. He got them made up by some local gunsmith, god knows how, and they got them rifled inside, I think that's the word, got them fixed up inside like little rifle barrels so the peas would fire straight and go far. So you know what they like to do over there? They get stoned and or drunk and they go hunting the neighbourhood cats, scaring the poor things with rifled pea shooters. Like a couple of crazy boys. In their forties. Nathan bothered to tell me about this when he came home for my mother's funeral. They chase the neighbourhood cats around, scaring them with steel pea shooters and probably laughing themselves sick. At night. In Bangkok."

"A victimless crime," Delaney said.

"Francis, please," she said. "It's not normal."

"Do you know how I could get in touch with Mordecai Cohen when I get over there?"

"No, not really. I could ask his mother for you maybe."

"Would you mind doing that?"

"No. That's OK. I can call you."

"Thanks, Cynthia."

They sat in silence for a moment.

"You never got married again," she said. "After the first time."

"No. That was enough for me."

"Was it bad?"

"At the end. The break-up was bad."

"They always are."

"Not that bad. Not always."

"You seeing anybody?"

"Sort of."

"It's always 'sort of' with guys like you."

"Guys like who?"

"Oh, I don't know. Journalists. I don't know. Guys who don't settle."

"I'm still here in Montreal."

"You've been everywhere. Foreign correspondent, war correspondent. Investigative journalist. You've written books. You're off to Bangkok next week. Big-time guy."

"Not anymore. Even you don't read my column."

They laughed together, one last time.

"More Perrier?" she said, looking at a heavy Tag Heuer hanging loosely from her wrist on a steel bracelet.

"No, thanks. Time for me to go."

"Me too really."

The European kiss good-bye, a jolt of expensive perfume. Delaney couldn't be sure if it was the perfume that left him edgy as he drove back downtown, or something Cynthia had said.

Patricia had left two terse messages on his answering machine, giving him some career advice. Nothing from Harden. A good sign. Delaney didn't think the editor was as troubled as Patricia had said. Harden was an old pro. He was used to little problems with columnists, feature writers, malcontents. He had bigger fish to fry, putting out Montreal's only English daily in a tough Quebec market.

From Kate Hunter there was nothing. From O'Keefe, there was another invitation to drinks. Word, it seemed, had already got round the paper that Delaney was off to London and parts unknown. Patricia was a natural storyteller. O'Keefe always insisted on seeing him off before trips.

Delaney surprised himself by going to the gym. He hadn't been in weeks but he usually tried to go before a major assignment or a trip. For this one, since it was a CSIS assignment, he never knew what sort of shape he would need to be in. One session at a gym would not be enough, but it was his routine to at least go before any important departure.

At least at the gym he was sure to never meet any of the people from the paper. The younger reporters of course would frequent gyms, but not this one, an old and expensive and quite unstylish one right downtown. The scribes of approximately his age would not know what the inside of a gym looked like.

He sweated for about 20 minutes on the rowing machine, working far too hard on something he used to find easy. He tried the weight machine and the Stairmaster and essentially just punished himself as much as he could. Sometimes a workout was a sort of meditation for him. Today it was penance. But he wasn't sure what for. He had to assume it was something to do with Kate.

The trainer, a young McGill University health sciences student named Vernon, came over as he was slowing down.

"You ought to do some stretches now, Frank," he said. "Your muscles are going to seize up. I was watching you go."

"Geriatric aerobics," Delaney said.

"You're still in pretty good shape," Vernon said.

"For a guy my age."

"Yeah. You got to keep active. Keep those legs moving."

"Fuck off, Vernon."

"Will do, Frank," Vernon said with a grin.

Another reason for the workout was that Delaney fully expected to get drunk that night with O'Keefe. Not because he wanted to but because it would be almost impossible not to. So the workout would somehow compensate for a night of excess, before the fact. Or something like that.

O'Keefe suggested they start out at Darwin's, once a trendy Bishop Street bar and now well past its prime. O'Keefe preferred them like that. He claimed to detest yuppies, claimed he could not be responsible for his actions in a yuppie bar. The yuppies had long since moved on from this establishment and the drinks were now reasonably cheap.

He was standing at the bar when Delaney arrived, all six feet four inches of him. Hunched over the bar, drinking San Miguel from a bottle into which the waiter had forced a wedge of lemon.

"That's a girl's drink, isn't it Brian?" Delaney said.

"No, it is permitted at this time of the night. It is for hydration purposes, before the festivities begin. It is cold and it is cheap and it goes very nicely with my rum."

A short glass with melting ice cubes sat near him at the bar.

Delaney surprised himself by ordering a double whiskey. Early in the night for him. The bespectacled boy behind the bar looked impressed.

"Now what have we here? Young Delaney drinking a large Jameson's and it's just gone eight o'clock," O'Keefe said. "Is everything all right at home?"

"Is this where we're settling in for the night?" Delaney asked. He felt his Air Canada tickets in his jacket pocket and wished he had left them at home. It was going to be a night to lose things, he thought.

"I have many fond memories of this place, my lad," O'Keefe said. "I grew up here."

Delaney remembered that O'Keefe used to enjoy picking on university drinkers here years ago, flashing his Quebec Provincial Police press card so fast that it looked like a police pass, confiscating small stashes of hashish from terrified youngsters and smoking it in the men's room.

They drank in silence for a moment.

"You have been avoiding me, Francis. You have decided I am a bad influence," O'Keefe said.

"Correct," Delaney said.

"The rule, established and etched in stone over the years, is that we get drunk together before you head off on a big bird somewhere. Is this not our unshakable rule? Am I not your next of kin, God knows, maybe even your only kin, possibly the executor of your will, trusted confidante, former colleague, et cetera, et cetera and so on and so forth? Have we not been somewhat remiss? Would this meeting have taken place without my insisting it be thus?"

"We have been remiss," Delaney said.

"We will make amends," O'Keefe said. "My heart is heavy with grief, this night, and there shall therefore be festive times. Or something."

"Shall we exchange tales of woe?" Delaney said.

"Me first," O'Keefe said.

They drank for hours, moving from bar to bar, slowly but surely moving eastward. They ended up on Saint Lawrence Street, south of Saint Catherine, where the Anglo yuppies rarely went. The language now was almost entirely French, the entertainment tacky, tending toward end-of-the-world striptease and pole-dancing bars. They had not been in such bars for years.

They talked much less than one would have thought. There was very little to say that had not already been said over the years, through various shared disasters personal and professional. The city spoke for them, said enough, said what needed to be said.

Late, very late, they made their pilgrimage to Schwartz's for smoked meat sandwiches. In the crush and noise of the place, under neon, elbow to elbow with strangers, intoxicated, O'Keefe said: "We've patched things up, Karen and I. I have rented a van for the transportation of my necessaries. Tomorrow."

"Ah," said Delaney. The room swam slowly around him.

"Too too much water under the bridge. This particular bridge."

"Yes. Possibly. I would say."

"Yes."

They drunkenly munched sandwiches.

"Your love life, of course, is, as always, in splendid condition, correct?" O'Keefe said. "Soon to be a feature story on the *Tribune* lifestyles page?"

"Yes, absolutely."

"RCMP. They always get their man."

"Not quite."

"She's OK, you know. Kate is," O'Keefe said, suddenly made serious by drink.

"Ah. Advice."

"She is OK. You are not. We know this. She is the only one who will have you. All other women everywhere, in every nation, have seen you for what you are. Especially your first wife. They will not have you. Et cetera. Then of course there was Natalia, a possible exception. But Natalia is dead, still dead. She will not wake up. Et cetera."

Even seriously intoxicated, Delaney and O'Keefe knew there were lines dangerous to cross. O'Keefe crossed this one anyway.

"I am allowed to say that," O'Keefe said. "This is the rule. We have rules for this sort of thing. We get drunk, I advise you to let all of that go. You refuse, your life goes nowhere, we do it again some months down the track. We have rules governing this sort of thing."

"Yes."

"You go off on another little assignment. Not for the newspaper this time, right? You leave all of the hard stuff behind. Yes?"

"My business, Brian," Delaney said, the alcohol suddenly lighting his aggression fuse.

"Wrong, brother. My business too."

Delaney stood up unsteadily. O'Keefe stood up too, put a large hand on Delaney's shoulder and sat him firmly down again. The other diners carried on with their sandwiches. This was Saint Lawrence Street, after 2 a.m.

"Wrong, my brother," O'Keefe said. "My business too."

The taxi let Delaney off in front of his place just before three. O'Keefe had walked back to the sports editor's house, for the last time until Karen threw him out again. Delaney barely managed to get his door open without an instruction manual.

He sat in Natalia's chair, with her reading light on. He drank a litre and a half of bottled water. He took three aspirins before sleeping. He did not call Kate until the morning.

He dreamed this:

*He is sitting in a barber's chair in a comfortable, safe old-fashioned barber shop. An avuncular, apron-clad barber is slowly and expertly cutting his hair, occasionally massaging his scalp and shoulders. It is a wonderfully soothing and pleasant experience. The barber then somehow tilts the chair so Delaney is completely upside down, suspended completely upside down so that his hair hangs away from his head, straight away from his head. The barber cuts the tips of his hair like that, somehow standing below him and reaching up. Delaney watches the world from this position, as the avuncular barber snips and combs and shapes his hair from below. There is a sudden dizzying return to upright, some final snipping and combing and then the proud barber's moment with mirrors front and back. Delaney has been transformed. He has the thick, wavy, perfectly combed hair of a very young man, the fresh beardless face of a much younger, a much more hopeful man.*

It was late morning, in fact, before Delaney was able to call Kate. He woke at 10 a.m. fantastically hung over, suffering for his sins. The scalding shower was penance. He could not look at food. His head was still spinning ever so slightly as he dialled Kate at home.

There was no answer. There was no way to avoid the mobile number any longer. She answered after two rings. She was clearly outside. He heard the sound of something like a chain saw far off in the background.

"Frank," she said. The mobile screen had told her.

"I've been trying to call you," he said.

"Not on this phone."

"I left a message for you at work."

"I took a couple of extra days off. I'm up at Sue's cottage."

"How is it?"

"You and I refuse to indulge in small talk at such times, remember Frank?"

"At which times?"

"Times crucial to the future of our relationship."

"Ah." His head was aching horribly. "Are hangovers an excuse?" he asked.

"Now we are sharing details from our private lives. How interesting," she said. "The man is actually telling me what he does in his private times."

"I'm going to London tomorrow. Then Bangkok."

There was a moment's silence. *Good*, he thought.

"Oh," she said. "What's come up?"

"Assignment." She knew nothing of his CSIS work.

"I see. How long?"

"A week or so, probably."

"I see."

"I called to say good-bye."

"I'm glad."

"Are you?" he asked

A pause.

"Of course, Frank."

A pause.

"We'll sort something out when I get back," he said.

"Will we?"

"Yes."

"Like what?"

"We'll come up with something. OK?"

"Are you my lover boy again, Frank?" He could sense the wry smile all the way down the phone line.

"Something like that," he said.

RCMP Officer Kate Hunter did not consider herself a sentimental woman. She did not normally fall under the spell of just any man she met along life's way. She did not consider herself, in fact, to be under the spell of one Francis Delaney, journalist at large. Or, more accurately, she did not allow herself to believe that to be the case. However, as she put down the telephone after her last conversation with Delaney before he left for Europe and Asia, she felt the unmistakable tug, what she would in another mood have called the adolescent tug, of longing.

Delaney, to be sure, was a most infuriating man. Kate knew this, had known this from the first minute they had been introduced at an overcrowded, overheated party almost a year earlier. There had been the requisite drunken heart-to-heart on a rainy balcony, the escape for a late-night meal, the return to a downtown apartment, the fumbling for belts and buttons in the early hours, the drawing together and the moving apart.

Then, this infuriating, months-long stasis. This now so Delaney-like reluctance to fall in love, his reluctance to give up ghosts of the past, to give up on one female ghost in particular. Kate Hunter did not normally allow herself to waste time like this on conflicted males of the species. Certainly never with police males of the species nor, until now, media males.

So why, she asked herself as she pretended to read magazines in a friend's sunny cottage backyard, was she compelled to think again and again about this infuriating journalist at large, to wonder if he by now was packing a bag for his latest assignment, what he might usually bring along on such a journey, what he was actually going to do while away.

Instead of simply reading and drinking summer lemonades, instead of relaxing as planned from the rigours of her police work, she found herself imagining what sort of person Delaney would be while abroad, what he would be like as he did his journalist's work, how he might look at a desk somewhere in some hotel, writing up the day's events somewhere in the world.

She very much looked forward to his return.

Kate Hunter did not usually allow herself to indulge in such adolescent musings. It was unsettling and, she told herself sternly, unbecoming to a usually sensible, usually two-feet-on-the-ground member of the Royal Canadian Mounted Police financial and high-tech crime squad. Not a job for hopelessly sentimental daydreamers.

Better, she thought, far better, to stop all this nonsense at once.

# PART 3
## London and Bangkok

# Chapter 4

London swallows up a visitor faster than almost any other European city. The maelstrom begins at Heathrow Airport, where masses of travellers and family members and airline staff and cleaners and security personnel and police stream endlessly across each other's paths in a fantastic unchoreographed dance of travel.

There is no let-up on the roads outside the airport or on the aging mass transit system that thunders cityward from there. Fleets of buses and taxis sweep in and out of all four terminal areas at all hours of the day. Private cars letting off and picking up passengers queue in gigantic metal snakes. Baggage carts lie abandoned everywhere. Haggard police in yellow reflector vests try in vain to restore order, with rare success.

The only respite comes, and this for precisely 15 minutes, on the fast, quiet, direct and highly overpriced ride on the Paddington Express train from the airport to West London. Unlike most British trains, this one usually runs regularly and on time. Delaney, a veteran of too many London traffic jams and Tube disruptions and taxi shortages, always went downtown this way.

He had learned as well to always stay at the Four Seasons Hotel on Park Lane, convenient to most places he would want to go, but more importantly not so close to Paddington Station that Cockney cab drivers would grumble about setting out for too little return, and not so far that the fare would give even a veteran traveller a nasty jolt.

London was chaotic, crowded, faded and maddening, but Delaney loved it all the same.

He was not someone who needed hours of recuperation time after a long flight. His routine for dealing with fatigue and jet lag was to rest after arrival for 20 minutes on an expertly made hotel bed, then to shave and shower and plunge directly into the business at hand.

Kellner's section editor at *Defence Monthly* was Jeremy Winton. He didn't want to meet Delaney in the magazine's office at the lower end of Regent Street. On the telephone he suggested the Groucho Club, in Soho, the trendy private hideaway for a certain monied media elite. Delaney knew there was very little chance of private conversation anytime at the Groucho, and suggested the Foreign Press Association's stately Georgian building in a square near Piccadilly instead. Winton said he would be there by noon.

Delaney walked to the club along Piccadilly and then down streets past shops selling absurdly expensive handbags, pipes, tableware, designer draperies, wine. Miraculously it was not raining, but in London in April this did not mean the sun would shine. The sky remained steely grey, refusing to give up either moisture or any decent light.

Winton climbed out of one of London's rotund black cabs just as Delaney arrived. Leaning through a half-opened window in front to pay the driver from the street, Winton was short, bespectacled, very intense, very Oxford or Cambridge and, Delaney soon learned, hungry and very thirsty. They shook hands on the club steps.

"Nice to meet you, Delaney, so glad we could do this," Winton said. "They serve a nice lamb couscous here at lunchtime. The chap who does the catering is from Tunisia, his whole family seems to be with him at lunch. I would suggest we avoid the FPA wine at all costs. I suggest we stick to the beer."

The small dining area on the main floor was still empty. They chose a table near the door. A couple of what appeared to be superannuated foreign correspondent types sat at the small bar, nursing pints of bitter. Winton ordered a bottle of Beck's, Delaney a local pale ale. The couscous idea was confirmed. The menu was not large.

"We have been doing everything we possibly can to locate Kellner, you must understand that straightaway," Winton said after the waiter had poured his beer. "British embassy involved, the Canadians as well. The local police over there are useless, of course."

Delaney decided to let him roll.

"But now perhaps with you going over there, a friend of Kellner's on the case, as it were, we might have some better luck. The editor-in-chief says to thank you very much for your efforts in this, by the way. He says to give you his best regards."

Winton raised his glass, drank deeply. Delaney thought it would be interesting to time how long that first beer would last.

"We're very worried about him, of course. All of us at this end," Winton said. He blinked at Delaney through his round glasses. "Gravely worried now. More than a month has gone by."

"Long even for Kellner, I would imagine," Delaney said.

"Quite," said Winton, looking intently at Delaney. "Exactly so."

"Shall we assume we both know Kellner and his idiosyncrasies well enough to talk frankly, Jeremy?" Delaney said. "That would save us a bit of time."

"It would, yes, I quite agree," Winton said.

"We both know he is a bit of a wild man, can be a bit of a wild man, at times," Delaney said.

"Not quite how I would have put it, but, yes, I do know what you're getting at," Winton said. "A first-rate correspondent, however. First rate. Amazing contacts. He has done some very fine work for us over the years. Very good stuff."

*Defence Monthly* was, essentially, a trade magazine. Its trade was war, and particularly arms. Who wanted them, who was buying them, who was supplying them and how, who would buy advertising space for at least some of them in *Defence Monthly* magazine. This required people in the field who knew that world very well indeed.

"Tell me something, Jeremy, just so we can eliminate possibilities right away," Delaney said. "Do your people think Kellner has just gone off on some jaunt to abuse substances or that he is in some kind of serious trouble?"

Winton looked uncomfortable with this.

"I don't think it would be right for me to start speculating about what Kellner does on his own time," Winton said. "Much as we would all like to help. It's true he sometimes worked to what I suppose you could say is an unusual schedule. Of course he did take rather more time off than most of our correspondents and sometimes he wouldn't tell us exactly when he was going and when he was coming back. But it has never been like this. A day or so, maybe, and then he would call in from somewhere or other or he would be back in Bangkok. And when he was on assignment we might not hear from him for a while but he would often be in obscure places, where the mobile network was not good, for example, or where he might simply have not wanted to be seen to be calling. So we were used to that, to a certain extent. But now, this time, it's different, I would say. Too long. Far too long this time. His girlfriend is very worried too. That tells you something. She calls us from time to time. Asking what we have been trying to do."

The food came and they started to eat.

"What was he working on lately?" Delaney asked.

"For us? Anything he liked, really. We gave him a lot of leeway. He would sometimes work on several things at once, for weeks at a time, and then suddenly something would come to fruition and he would file a solid piece," Winton said. "He assigned himself, most of the time."

"Was he particularly interested in anything lately?"

"Well, Thailand of course. The Thai military. The border situation, refugee movements, people trafficking, what that means to arms movements, people who need guns—regular army, militias, others. He was keenly interested in Burma lately as well, for similar reasons. Myanmar they officially call it these days, as you know. There's lots to interest a foreign correspondent there. Warlords, the drug trade, a huge drug trade. Opium for heroin, lots of that, amphetamines more recently. And timber, gems, construction contracts, trading of all sorts across the border with China, casinos on the Chinese border, prostitution, forced labour, forced relocations up in the Shan State. Hundreds of democracy campaigners and dissidents are in jail. Aung San Suu Kyi is still under house arrest in Rangoon, as you know. There are all sorts of quite unpleasant things going on in Burma as we speak, and that means a lot of very good stories. Investors, those who can stomach doing business with the generals, want to know what's going on, so they want to read as much as they can. There is money to be made in Burma, Delaney, enormous amounts of money, but the regime is vicious, absolutely corrupt. It runs on drug proceeds, mostly, but also on big bribes and kickbacks from foreign businessmen. The government has an awful lot of cash to spend on guns and equipment as a result. So do the various militias up north. Kellner was interested in all of that. Very much so."

"Was he in Burma lately?"

"Not lately. But he was going to try to go in, I think. It's very hard to get visas for journalists to go in. The regime is very careful who it lets in. They were not too happy a few years ago with some of the stuff we were running, some of it was Kellner's stuff, about the regime. They made that very clear through their embassy here." Winton paused for a minute, looking slightly ill at ease for some reason. "I'm not at all sure they would let Kellner in again if he tried to go. There's a rather large blacklist, as you know. An Australian reporter was banned for life not too long ago. A TV man."

"Would Kellner have bothered to tell you if he was trying to go in?"

"On something like that, yes, he would have to. He would need letters from us here in London to get a visa. Their embassy would be involved. He couldn't just go in. Unless he didn't bother with a visa at all. Which would be very, very unwise. Some correspondents have been treated rather unkindly if they are found inside the country illegally. Insein Prison is a nasty place, I'm told. Not the most attractive address in Rangoon, I'm afraid. Some of them have ended up in there for a while before they get thrown out of the country."

Winton was onto his third Beck's, couscous finished. The dining room was now almost full, people well on their way through lunches and the dubious wine.

They ate for a while in silence. Winton looked around the room, apparently checking for people he might know. He smiled at Delaney from time to time.

"Do you know if anyone would want to harm Kellner?" Delaney asked suddenly.

"I've told you I don't feel comfortable delving into Kellner's personal life or that of any of our correspondents," Winton said, ever so slightly aggressive now. The small British smile was not enough to conceal that.

"Maybe you should sometimes," Delaney said.

"We have nothing to apologize for in the way we deal with our people in the field, Delaney," Winton said.

"How do you know that, if you don't try to keep up with what they are doing?"

"I'm not sure I see where this is going," Winton said.

"Well, it's so much easier, isn't it, for the magazine to always be able to say you had no idea what sort of things a reporter was up to in his personal life than to address that before something came up."

"Like what?" Winton had started looking at his watch.

"Like if they disappear on you, for example. Like if they piss someone off badly, for example."

"If it has to do with their work for us, we want to know about it," Winton said. "We would want to know, for example, if they piss someone off, as you put it. But if it has to do with their personal lifestyles, that is certainly not our business at all."

"Convenient for everyone," Delaney said. "If you ignore someone's lifestyle you can't be expected to intervene if it gets risky or complicated."

He realized this would have to apply equally to how CSIS dealt with its freelancers in the field. How they dealt with Kellner, for example.

"What would you have us do, Delaney?" Winton said, looking at his watch again. "Trail after our people in the field as they go into various press clubs around the world, and count their drinks? Choose their friends and girlfriends for them? These people are adults, professionals."

"Most of the time," Delaney said.

"I don't want to have conflict with you on this, Delaney," Winton said. "We all want to find out if Kellner is all right."

"I want to find out if he is all right and what it is that might have made him not all right," Delaney said. "Do you want to find out both of these things too?"

"Of course," Winton said. "We want precisely the same things. We are working toward the same goal."

Lunch ended somewhat more abruptly than Delaney would have wanted. Winton waved for the waiter and paid for the meal with an American Express Corporate card. They shook hands again on the steps.

"Good of you to come over and try to help out, Delaney," Winton said. "Much appreciated. Do call us from over there if you need anything at our end."

He set off down the steps past Carleton House walking quickly in the direction of Green Park. Delaney watched him go, and then headed back up the way he had come, on foot along Piccadilly to the hotel.

He had a couple of hours to kill before he met some Reuters people he knew. They were Asia hands, now beached on the agency's World Desk in London. They knew Kellner from their Bangkok and Singapore days.

Delaney checked for emails on his laptop back in the hotel. Rawson had messaged, using a commercial email address. He never used CSIS email to contact freelancers.

*Hello Francis, hope you're well. Just to let you know, some people have been around to see M at NK's apartment. Or so I'm told. Asian appearance. Civilians apparently. That's all we've got for the moment. Two days ago. Bests, JR.*

Delaney did not bother to reply. Instead he sent an email to Mai in Bangkok, reminding her that he would be arriving late the next night and that he would see her on Wednesday. He thought it best not to use the phone for this sort of thing now.

From the Montreal chapter of the CG Jung Society there was an email asking for a progress report on the paper he had been promising for months. He was to write something about war reporting and conflict zones, from a Jungian perspective. He was to look for archetypal elements and images in any aspect of the conflicts he had witnessed. Working title: "Mars and Mercury—Jungian Reflections from a Messenger of War."

He had absolutely no idea how to begin such a paper, bitterly regretted ever having been persuaded to try and had been delaying matters for months. He was a stray the Jungians had picked up, as a service mainly to Natalia. She had been one of their star members. He messaged Willa Mackenzie, the Society's president, apologizing yet again.

*Hi Willa. Thanks for your message. I'm on the road again, London now and Bangkok next, so not at all sure I will be able to get my paper ready in time for the May meeting. Hope this is no trouble. Can you possibly slot someone else in? I will try my best for June. Can't promise, though, as really pressed these days with work and some other personal things. Apols once again. Best regards, Frank.*

O'Keefe had sent him a press clipping about a former colleague of theirs who had been fired from the *Toronto Star* and another about the Thai government campaign to promote condom use.

The Reuters men were in their usual supper break places at the rundown Calthorpe Pub on Gray's Inn Road. It was 6 p.m. and they were on the agency's four-to-midnight news desk shift. They were, like Delaney, in their late forties, very experienced, very well travelled and, most of the time now, very fed up with their jobs, with news agency work and with journalism.

Ron Cranwell was from London originally, had lived in Asia for years and was back mainly to give his daughter a chance to finish school in the British system. He was known as a rock solid agency deskman, unflappable under the intense pressure when major stories broke and a good clear writer of news breaks. His thick crop of wiry hair had gone entirely grey since Delaney last saw him.

Ed Stanton was an American who had lived outside the U.S. for almost 30 years. He never expressed any interest in going home. He had covered most of the big stories in Asia and had lived with a series of Asian women, never for more than a couple of years at a time. He had run into trouble with a senior Reuters editor in Singapore and found himself dispatched to London for a spell on the World Desk. His drinker's face had reddened substantially over the years and his paunch had expanded substantially now that he had come in from the field.

"Kellner is an absolute nutcase," Stanton said after fresh pints were fetched from the bar and Delaney had been brought properly up to date on the latest Reuters gossip. Lately, this gossip usually involved journalists of about their age who, whether willingly or unwillingly, had left the game, usually to be replaced by people half their age, or less.

"That's saying something, from a bloke like you, Ed," Cranwell said. He was tucking into a very large plate of steak, eggs and chips. The chips were blood red with cheap ketchup and malt vinegar. An ashtray brimming with cigarette butts produced spirals of smoke at Cranwell's right hand.

"No, fine, OK, we all like a drink," Stanton said. "But Kellner's brain was addled with dope as well. None of us were into the dope like Kellner. The guy was floating around the region in a purple haze most of the time. Seriously."

"Nice writer, though," Cranwell said. "He still does some nice stuff from out of there."

"Sure he does, yeah. Of course he does," Stanton said. "But Delaney's trying to figure out where the guy's gone and all I'm saying is with someone like that there's no way of knowing. Word was he was into all sorts of stuff. Little bits and pieces on the side. You never know how stuff like that will end up, especially in Bangkok."

"What was he into on the side?" Delaney asked. "Does anybody know for sure?"

"It's just gossip," Cranwell said. "Bullshit."

"I don't know, I don't know about that," Stanton said. "You kept hearing stories."

"Press club bullshit," Cranwell said. He drained his pint, got up to get three more. The Irish publican and his waiflike wife darted to and fro behind the heavy oak bar. The place was jammed with locals from a nearby housing estate and a sprinkling of

Reuters and commercial TV types from the big office block down the street. A tremendous roar erupted from time to time as tiny soccer players on a TV screen made particularly dramatic moves.

"What was he into on the side, do you think?" Delaney asked again when Cranwell was back.

"Well, he was the guy a lot of them went to for smokers' supplies, for example. A lot of them didn't want to deal with Thais and he was a contact for that. Nothing major, just a little service for the correspondents club guys who didn't want to deal with locals. Nothing big time as far as I was told."

"What else?"

Stanton lit up a small cigar. Cranwell lit another cigarette off the end of his previous. His ashtray badly needed changing.

"Well, he had a deal with some guys up north to bring furniture down and sell it on to Australia or somewhere. Or New Zealand."

"Furniture?" Delaney said.

"Yeah, chairs and tables, things like that."

Cranwell snorted. "Bullshit. Who told you that?"

"That was the word, Ron."

"The word around the Bangkok Press Club isn't worth shit and you know it, Ed. Furniture. Who cares anyway?"

"He also was a sort of consultant for businesspeople who wanted to know the score on how to make deals in the region. He told me that himself one night," Stanton said.

"Now that would be a nice little earner in that part of the world," Cranwell said. "That would be something I would want to get into."

"There's a lot of people wanting to do business with the Thai military, and the Burmese military who'd pay big money for the inside story on any sort of big project, any big deals coming down the pipe," Stanton said. "Timber, for example, the Thai military guys are big on timber. There's a lot of road construction contracts up for grabs. Thailand and Burma both.

Building contracts. Tobacco even. Some of the Australians are pretty keen on Burma around now, for example. Kellner could have made a lot of money just introducing people, giving them briefings, maybe going in to various places with groups of guys."

"Was he doing that for sure?" Delaney asked.

"The guy was always flush with cash. He always had a lot more dough than he should have had with a job like his. It's what I heard," Stanton said.

Cranwell snorted again. "When?" he said.

"A while back," Stanton said.

"You've been in London for fourteen fucking months."

"Yeah, OK, but I'm just telling Delaney what I heard."

"Don't believe a word this guy tells you, Frank. He doesn't know what he's talking about. Never did." Cranwell raised his glass with a big smile. "A usually unreliable source."

They all laughed and drank their warm beers, blinking in the haze of cigarette smoke. The crowd in the pub was now far too large for the space. It would be almost impossible to move through the throng and to get close enough to the bar to order another drink. Cranwell and Stanton would have to get back to work soon in any case.

"What do you think's going on, Frank?" Cranwell asked.

"No idea," Delaney said. "He just fell out of sight."

"Fell. That'd be right."

"You going over soon?" Stanton said.

"Yeah, tomorrow," Delaney said. "I'll go see his girlfriend, try to find out what's what."

"Now she is a real fox, a beauty," Stanton said. "I've met her. A foxy lady."

"You working on a piece, Frank?" Cranwell said.

"No. Just checking out what's what for his family."

"I thought he wasn't close to his family," Stanton said.

"His sister's still around."

"She ask you to check things out?" Stanton said.

"Sort of," Delaney said.

"What are you really working on, Frank?" Cranwell asked.

"Don't start playing journalist on me now, OK, Ron?" Delaney said with a smile.

"Pretty hard not to," Cranwell said. "Not much happening around here." He looked at the seething, increasingly loud pack of drinkers and smokers. "I better get back. There's a fair bit of copy to move tonight."

"I'm going to have one more," Stanton said, looking over at Delaney. It was Delaney's round.

After Cranwell had left, Stanton said, "Is Kellner in real trouble, do you think?"

"He's been gone for month," Delaney said. "No one has heard a word from him for a month and it's Southeast Asia."

"I think he's bought it. I think someone's probably snuffed him," Stanton said.

"How do you figure that?"

"Oh, just a feeling. I've worked with guys like that on and off over the years. Someone eventually snuffs them or maybe they get killed in the field or in a car accident or whatever. They're hiding out in Asia but they usually end up dead. Even an over-dose, or whatever. Or some deal goes wrong or the guy puts his nose in a story he should have left alone or it's to do with a girl. There's a lot of ways to piss people off in that part of the world, Frank. I've done it myself."

Delaney raised his glass in a toast.

"You need a hand over there, Frank? A fixer? A driver?"

"I've got one lined up, Ed, thanks. A driver I used to use whenever I went over. He's good."

"OK. If Kellner's pissed off the military you're going to need a local guy with you."

"Yes."

"What are you actually working on, Frank?"

"I'm a Good Samaritan, Ed."

"Right. Of course."

Delaney walked down Gray's Inn Road with Stanton to the office. It was 7:20 p.m. A camera crew was coming out of the giant revolving doors. Cabs idled at the curbside. After Stanton went in, Delaney ran for the 19 bus. It was an ancient Routemaster, with an open area at the back to hop on. He was not in a hurry and the slow swaying ride down to Piccadilly on the old double-decker would give him time to think.

In some ways, the situation already seemed obvious. Kellner had run afoul of someone, somehow, and they had taken him out. Delaney was almost sure his assignment now would be to find out where Kellner's body was and who had killed him. But Stanton's talk about business deals and consultant work left open the possibility that Kellner had simply run off to avoid debts or a bad deal or an unhappy client. But would he have left Mai behind? Kellner was not the sort to ever be without a woman, no matter where he was.

The giant Jamaican bus conductor was panting heavily after climbing up the stairs to the second level to collect fares. On the old Routemasters after a certain hour, the older conductors preferred not to bother at all with the second level. There were very few passengers upstairs. This would be his only sweep of the upper deck for an hour or so.

Delaney gave him a five-pound note. The Jamaican stood on the swaying floor, his substantial weight braced against a seat behind.

"What the fuck's this, man?" the conductor said. "Coins, man. One pound."

"I've got no coins," Delaney said.

"I don't want no notes on my bus, man. I don't want no folding notes on my bus."

"I've got no coins," Delaney said again. It had been awhile since he had had the Routemaster tourist treatment.

"One pound," the conductor said again. "Coins only, man. I want coins."

"Leave him alone, you old bastard," said a ginger-haired Irish teenager in an LA Rams sweatshirt. "He's a Yank tourist, isn't he? He's got no fucking coins. Leave him alone."

The conductor pressed a rubber strip above his head, twice. A bell clanged down below and the driver stopped the bus with a great lurch.

"Off my bus. You both," the conductor said.

"Fuck off," said the ginger-haired kid. A Japanese couple up front looked back, alarmed.

"Off," the conductor said. "This bus going nowhere tonight, man, till you both get yourselves off."

"For Christ's sake," Delaney said, regretting he had chosen to put himself in the way of this particular London Transport experience. He got up and moved to the narrow bus stairs.

"I'm not going anywhere," the Irish kid said.

Delaney got off somewhere in the theatre district, amid a small Monday night crowd of tourists and young drunks in from the suburbs. The argument on the top deck of the bus raged on as he moved away. The driver got out and lit a cigarette, leaning against a huge red fender in the fading London light.

Delaney ate in Chinatown, at a place he remembered on Gerard Street. It was full of Asian families and other large groups. He was the only one eating alone and the waiters seemed perplexed. He caught himself thinking that Kate would like London, would have liked the scene on the bus, would like the Chinese food he was eating by himself. He resisted the impulse to call her on his mobile phone.

When he got back to the hotel, the message light was flashing. Winton had called, had left a mobile number. Delaney called him right after opening a miniature bottle of Johnnie Walker from the bar fridge and pouring it over ice.

"Winton here," the editor said when he answered. He was in a noisy place, probably a bar, probably the Groucho Club, Delaney thought.

"It's Delaney," he said. "You left a message." He was still annoyed and impatient with Winton after their lunchtime conversation.

"Yes, quite," Winton said. "Look Delaney, there's something I neglected to tell you this afternoon."

For some reason, Delaney did not find this surprising.

"I had a word with the editor-in-chief, Rodgers, and he thinks we should tell you that we had a little visit recently from some officials at the Burma embassy here. They came in to the office. Saw Rodgers, then Rodgers and me together. Asked about Kellner's work."

"Why didn't you tell me that this afternoon?" Delaney asked. His annoyance increasing.

"Wanted to get the OK from Rodgers, I suppose. Wasn't sure it was anything terribly significant,"

"You must be joking," Delaney said.

"Seemed rather routine to me. I mentioned to you, I think, that the embassy had not been happy some while ago with a couple of things Kellner had written. They watch the media very very carefully. It was just a matter of a few lines, a way of describing the regime, the way they were handling the Aung San Suu Kyi issue. Nothing major.

"Why did they come in again? When was it?"

"About three weeks ago now."

"Just after Kellner disappeared."

"Quite."

"What did they want?"

"They wanted to know if Kellner had been working on a piece about Burma. Whether he had filed anything on Burma recently. We very politely told them we couldn't help them. No comment. None of their business. That was our view."

"Had he filed anything?"

"No nothing at all. I don't think he was even working on anything about Burma before he disappeared."

"You said this afternoon he assigned himself. How would you know what he was working on? You said you thought he might try to go in again soon."

"I just didn't get the sense he was very far along on that project, Delaney," Winton said. "Rodgers agrees with me on that. In any case, we told the Burmese nothing. We very politely showed them the door."

"Is there anything else you have forgotten to tell me, Jeremy?" Delaney said.

"Look, Delaney, I'm afraid I don't like your tone. I didn't like it this afternoon at lunch either. We are trying to help you. We are under no obligation."

"One of your people is missing in the field," Delaney said.

"We are taking steps to find out what has happened to him. We have set the wheels in motion."

"That's the very least you could do if one of your reporters goes missing, Jeremy."

"What more would you have us do, Delaney?"

"You could tell me everything you know, for example."

"I have just done that. And I really do not like your tone. You are sounding more like a policeman than a journalist, Delaney."

"And you are sounding more like a bureaucrat than an editor with a missing colleague," Delaney said.

"I see no reason why I should have to listen to this," Winton said.

"I'll give you some reasons after I get to Bangkok, how does that sound?" Delaney said.

"We have nothing to apologize for," Winton said.

"I'll get back to you on that," Delaney said.

# Chapter 5

Benjarong Yongchaiyudh was as proud of being a professional driver as other middle-aged men in Thailand might have been if they were doctors or lawyers or Buddhist priests. He was particularly proud that life had dealt him the hand of being driver to a series of international journalists. His little business card said it all:

BEN YONG, Media Driver.
Experience in all areas of Thailand and environs.
References available—CNN, ITN, VisNews, Reuters,
  AP, New York Times, etc.
War zones OK.
Day rates, fuel extra however.
Tel/Fax 0 2467 0811.

The *Tribune* was not on his list of references. But Delaney had used Ben Yong many times, on many assignments, not all of them safe, not all of them for the newspaper and not all of them successful. And Delaney was always thankful when Ben's wife, who handled most of the telephone requests for his services, answered in her singsong affirmative that Mr. Ben would, easy, no problem, be available once again for Khun Frank when he arrived at Bangkok airport.

Ben spent any waiting time polishing his immaculate Toyota

Crown station wagon with a selection of soft cloths he kept in a special metal box in the back. Sometimes wax was applied, but Ben usually caressed the aging vehicle's turquoise and white two-tone paint job for the sake of it, for the love of it. Delaney had known many media drivers, in many countries—Sierra Leone, Nigeria, East Timor, Haiti, Cuba, Nicaragua, just about everywhere there was a story and where he had been on assignment. And the good ones always, without fail, took loving care of their vehicles, no matter how old. These cars represented their livelihood, their badge of honour and, very often, their last refuge when the going got tough.

The good drivers, the ones who knew how the media operated and how journalists needed to work, elicited affection, admiration and respect from the reporters who often entrusted them with their lives. When a well-known, experienced and reliable driver died or left the game, word would shoot around the world's press clubs and news desks at a speed approaching that achieved when a veteran foreign correspondent died on assignment.

Ben had gained weight, and lost hair. He was one of the few Thai men with a balding problem. He gave Delaney a slow, elegant wai, and then rushed over to shake his hand at the entrance to the airport terminal building. There was the usual chaos at the doorways and Ben extracted them from it expertly—negotiating the crowded sidewalk, fending off other drivers and tourist touts and sliding Delaney's small suitcase and equipment bag into the back of the car. Ben had long ago made a deal with the parking police and he was always able to wait just at curbside, sparing himself and his clients a long hot trek to the jammed airport parking lots.

"Too long now since you are in Bangkok, Frank," Ben shouted over the headrests, grinning happily as he manoeuvred the Toyota through impossible tangles of cars, buses and motorbikes heading for the airport approach road. "What's up, you need to buy some shirts?"

Delaney always sat in the back of the car, no matter how many times he used Ben's services and how well he got to know him. Ben preferred it that way. It left the front passenger seat empty and available to store anything that might be required immediately to hand and, Ben had always said, it could elicit respect for the passenger in back, sometimes, when police or soldiers stopped the car for paper checks or to demand bribes. Only greenhorns and aid workers rode in the front seat with their driver; this was Ben's theory.

The car's aging air conditioner was beginning to kick in, but it was a noisy system and conversation had to be at high volume. As always in Thailand, conversation also had to battle with local music scratching its way out of bad loudspeakers and aging tape players.

"I'm still working through my shirts from the last trip over, Ben," Delaney said. "And the paper's not sending me to Asia like it used to."

"Everywhere is the same," Ben said. "All the guys, the same now. No travel like before, bad budgets, even for TV. Bad for me, guys like me."

"I'll need you for a few days at least, Ben," Delaney said. "At least."

"Good, good, very good," Ben said. "Where we going?"

Ben didn't mean which hotel. He knew that Delaney always stayed at the venerable Royal Hotel, in a teeming neighbourhood near the Democracy Monument. It was aging badly but had a long history with media people and locals alike. Delaney and Ben had been sitting together in the hotel's famous lobby bar in 1992 when Thai soldiers chased in a crowd of pro-democracy demonstrators and shot a few of them behind the check-in counter.

"Not sure where we're going this time, exactly," Delaney said. "Stick around Bangkok for a while, maybe have to go outside later on."

He wanted to wait until they were sitting down to a couple

of cold Singha beers before telling Ben about Kellner and asking for a rundown on what he had heard around town.

The lobby of the Royal was quiet. A few Thai businessmen in dark blue suits sat in the lobby bar, as did a few taxi drivers in brightly patterned short-sleeved shirts. The prostitutes had not yet shown up for the afternoon shift. The ceiling fans turned lazily as they had for the past 60 years, still in service if only because of the hotel's ramshackle and notoriously unreliable air-conditioning system.

Delaney got the room he had requested, in the hotel's original building and not in the so-called new wing, which had actually been around since the bad old days of 1970s hotel décor. He asked Ben to give him an hour. He wanted to perform his postflight ritual of 20 minutes sleep and a long hot shower. Ben said he would sleep too, in the car where he had parked it behind the hotel out back, in perhaps the only reliable patch of shade for kilometres around.

Ben was waiting for him in the bar exactly an hour later, with two cold Singhas already poured and a small wooden bowl of mixed nuts at the ready. Ben had never once in Delaney's experience been late for anything, except when detained by police or soldiers. Even then he always managed to extricate himself in record time from whatever the problem might be.

"What we working on, Frank?" Ben said, always eager to get started.

"Nathan Kellner," Delaney said.

"He coming too?" Ben said. "Haven't seen him for a long while. I don't think Khun Nathan is around."

"That's what we're working on, Ben. Kellner's gone to ground. I'm looking for him."

"You not doing a story?"

"Might be. Depends what Kellner's up to. I've been asked to find out where he's gone."

"He's in trouble maybe. Like that?"

"Yeah."

Ben was eating nuts one by one, as he always did. He drank beer very slowly and ate peanuts as if time had stood still.

"I never see him now. Never drove for him much anyway. He used another guy. I could ask a few people maybe."

"OK. I'm going to go see his girlfriend. She's Thai," Delaney said.

"All your guys have Thai girls here, Frank. You would too, in Bangkok," Ben said with a smile.

"They've been together a long time," Delaney said. "Not like with the other guys, I would say."

"Maybe not," Ben said. Not convinced. "Bar girl? Used to be?"

"No. I don't think so."

Ben was clearly not convinced.

"Let's take a run over there so I can talk to her."

"Sure, OK."

"His place is on a little soi off Thanon Sathon."

"Near U.S. Information Service?"

"That's it."

"I know where," Ben said.

The traffic was dense, but not as dense as Delaney remembered from the last time he had been in Bangkok. It seemed to be getting ever so slightly easier to move around the city each time he came. Perhaps because of the Skytrain that had at long last been built. Perhaps because Bangkok, like so many Asian cities, was becoming more and more Westernized, adopting Western trappings such as traffic lights that worked and driving schools for young people and policemen who, occasionally, refused to look the other way when confronted with egregious infractions of the traffic rules. Perhaps.

The watchman in the dirt courtyard of Kellner's apartment block stood up when Delaney arrived. He had watched from a reclining position on his wooden bed when Delaney got out of Ben's car and had sat up when Delaney turned to come onto the property. He stood up only when it was clear Delaney wanted to go inside the building. He offered the Western visitor no wai, a rare failure in Thailand and one that Delaney noted with interest.

Delaney offered the wai and said: "Nathan Kellner's house."

No smile from the watchman. Another rare failure in Thailand.

"He is not here," the watchman said, looking past Delaney's shoulder to the car where Ben was already reading his newspaper.

"I know. I am here to see his girl," Delaney said.

"You are a friend?" the watchman said; dubious.

"Yes."

"Whose friend? Mai or Khun Nathan?"

"Both."

The watchman looked at him closely.

"Canadian?"

"Yes."

"I'll go see," the watchman said.

He slid into his sandals, classics with soles made from old automobile tires, and headed through an arch into a ground floor corridor that led to a line of doors painted maroon. Delaney remembered that Kellner's apartment was on the ground floor. He turned around to look at Ben Yong, who gave him the thumbs up and an interrogative shrug. Delaney shrugged back.

From far down the corridor, Delaney heard quiet words in Thai, then the slap of the watchman's sandals as he came back. Now the wai was offered.

"So sorry, my friend. Mai is waiting for you now. So sorry."

"Any troubles here?" Delaney asked.

"You know," the watchman said, looking intently at Delaney. "Mai will tell you if you don't know."

"Lots of visitors for Mai now?

"Yes."

"People you know?"

"Some of them."

"People Mai knows?"

"Some."

Delaney could see Mai through the screen door of the apartment as he removed his shoes and placed them on a low stand in the corridor outside the entrance. She was sitting on a large Thai reclining platform, resting against triangular upright cushions and stroking two tiny kittens. A big-screen TV flickered CNN images silently in a corner. The place was very dim. Even in the dim light Delaney could see she was as heartstoppingly beautiful as ever. She did not get up.

"Kuhn Frank," she said.

"Mai, my friend." Delaney pushed open the screen door and moved across the coolness of the shining waxed floor to shake her hand. She offered up a cheek and he kissed it, feeling a breath of fine silky hair on his own cheek as he did so. The cats scattered.

"Where is Nathan, Frank? Where has he gone?" Mai immediately started to cry softly. "He has never been away so long without calling me."

"I know that, Mai."

"Have you come to give me some news?" she asked.

"No. I've come to find out where he has gone," Delaney said.

"Oh good. Good," she said. "I miss him, Frank. I am worried this time."

"We'll find out what he's doing," Delaney said.

"Please."

Mai made him tea. The cats chased her bare feet and legs as she padded around the apartment getting things ready. Delaney could not keep his eyes off her. She moved with fantastic grace. That alone would capture any Westerner's eye. She was older than most of the girls living with Western correspondents in Bangkok, at least the ones Delaney knew. Late twenties, thirty maximum, or so Delaney had been told. But looking far, far younger.

There was a lot to discuss. Mai told him that Kellner had not appeared worried or distracted in the days before he left. He was always working on something or other, she said, and often he did not tell her much about what that might have been. Kellner and Mai had a quiet lifestyle in their dim, immaculate apartment, she said. Visitors often came from embassies, particularly Asian embassies, often people who went into Kellner's study with him and closed the door. Usually men who carried with them cartons of cigarettes and bottles of Johnnie Walker as offerings when they arrived.

But these visitors did not stay to eat or drink after such meetings. Occasionally another Western correspondent would come, usually with a Thai girl like Mai. There would be food on those occasions, prepared by Kellner's housekeeper before she left for the day, and then lots of marijuana. And vodka and beer for the men. There would be much talk of journalism and Asia and travel and there would often be video movies on the giant TV screen and more marijuana and vodka and beer. Sometimes the guests would sleep in the guest bedroom, sometimes not.

Kellner worked from home. Delaney wanted very much to look closely at what was on his desk and in his desk and in his appointment book if that had been left behind. He had not decided whether to ask to do this later that day, on the first meeting with Mai. He wanted first to hear everything she had to say about how Kellner had disappeared.

"He went out to play badminton that day," she said. "He came home and we smoked some Thai stick and he drank his vodka. We went onto the bed."

Delaney always marvelled at the sexual frankness of young Thai women.

"After we had our bath he got ready to go out. He said he had to say something at the press club."

"Say something?" Delaney said.

"Like a speech maybe," she said. "He got ready to go out, like anytime, and then he went out. And he has not come back."

Mai hugged her knees on the reclining platform. Her sarong fell away slightly. Delaney cursed himself for the *frisson* her slender thighs elicited. He thought suddenly of Kate, remembered the last time they had had sex. A languorous Thailand evening was working its magic with his senses. He wondered how intense that might be for someone like Kellner, in a deeper, drug-induced trance that he never, apparently, quite allowed to end.

"Do you think he might be dead, Frank?" Mai asked.

Delaney thought about it for a while before answering, before deciding how much of an answer he wanted to give to this sad young woman sitting before him.

"It's too early for us to talk like that," Delaney said finally.

"You are a good man," Mai said. "Nathan liked you."

"We didn't see each other much," Delaney said.

"He liked you. He liked Montreal and he liked you."

Delaney didn't push her too hard on the first meeting. He knew, from all his years as an interviewer, to circle the subject slowly in a case like this, to allow Mai to remember things at random and then to slowly ask for clarification, amplification, explanation. He knew that too many questions, too early in a case like this, would be counterproductive.

He had already decided that there was no way Mai was hiding anything from him. He knew there was no reason for her to do that and he knew, he sensed, that she was telling him as much as she possibly could. They talked for a long while.

"Who would be angry with Nathan, do you think?" Delaney asked eventually. "Were people complaining about his stories lately?"

Mai looked up at Delaney.

"You know there are stories he wrote that made people angry," she said.

"No, I really don't anymore," Delaney said. "What was he working on?"

"He would only tell me after, most times," she said. "He liked to show me his stories when they came back from London by fax. Mostly gun stories, big weapon stories. Tanks. In lots of countries."

"What lately? Before he went away." Delaney was avoiding the word *disappeared*.

"Not so much lately. Less than before. He was working from here more lately. Less travel. Lots of phoning. Lots of time in there." Mai pointed at Nathan's study.

"Who was angry at him, Mai?" Delaney asked again.

She sat quietly, stroking one of her cats. Delaney began to wonder if she was indeed hiding something now or whether she was just trying to remember.

"There were some Australians who were mad once," she said. "Two or three Australians. But a long while ago now. Months ago."

"Australians."

"Yes."

"What were they angry about?"

"One of Nathan's articles. He wrote about Australian rich men, you know, businessmen. What they were doing in Burma. He had other people in the story saying they should not be in there, that it is a bad place and that they shouldn't work with the generals. Something like that."

"What sort of work were they doing over there?" Delaney asked.

He knew that the answer, for Burma and for northern Thailand near the Burma border, could be any number of lucrative things. Timber, tobacco, construction of roads, casinos, the gem trade, the people trade, the drug trade—it was wide open if you knew the right general. But a very tricky part of the world to do business.

"Building, I think," Mai said. "Maybe a road. Hard to remember now."

"Have you got the article?" Delaney asked.

"Probably in there," she said, pointing again at Nathan's study.

"I'll look in there soon," Delaney said. "Will that be OK?"

"Nathan would say OK, I think," she said.

"Good. What did the Australians do?" he asked.

"Many telephone calls. Nathan said they were yelling on the phone. Not happy."

"Did they come here?"

"No. I think Nathan met them, maybe. But this was a long time ago now. Months now."

Delaney wasn't sure it would be so unusual, or even potentially dangerous, for a journalist to have upset a few foreign businessmen trying to make a fast buck in Thailand and Burma. Despite the world condemnation of the Burmese military regime, businessmen from Australia, Europe, all over, were quietly going in to make deals and to make big money. It was not so unusual. The regime was utterly corrupt and utterly ruthless and needed a lot of money just to keep the lid on things, especially with the democracy movement simmering away and its leader Aung San Suu Kyi under house arrest in Rangoon again. Making a couple of businessmen angry was one thing; making the generals angry would be quite another.

"People have been coming to see you since Nathan went away," Delaney said.

"How can you know that?" Mai said.

"I'm a reporter," Delaney said, smiling.

Mai smiled too. "That's what Nathan always said when I asked him how he knew things."

"Who has been coming?"

"Mordecai. Other *farangs* from the press club. Their wives and girls. My family."

"Mordecai Cohen? From Montreal?" Delaney said.

"Yes. Nathan's good friend. He has been trying to help me. He comes, with his girl. He brings me smoke. Other guys visit from the press club sometimes. It's like that."

"Who else?" Delaney remembered the email in London from Rawson saying two Asian men had been at the apartment.

"A Canadian embassy man. Thai police."

"Who else?

"Two men. Last week. Thai. In suits. They said they were police too but they had no uniforms. They were wearing suits. Nice Western suits."

"Thai? You sure?"

"Yes. But northern-sounding, I think."

"Did you ask them for ID?"

Mai looked at Delaney as if at a child. "That is not how it works here, Frank."

"What did they ask?"

"They asked what Nathan was working on, just like you. Just like everyone asks now when they come. I told them I couldn't remember. That is what Nathan would have told me to say."

"Did they ask about Burma? Or about the Australian story Nathan wrote?"

"Not about Australia. About Burma, yes."

"What did they ask?"

"They asked if Nathan had been in Burma, if he was going to go to Burma."

"You sure these guys were not Burmese?"

"I would know this, Frank," Mai said quietly. "But they asked about Burma. They asked if Nathan was going to be writing about the democracy people there. Aung San Suu Kyi's people. The lady."

Everyone in the region simply referred to Suu Kyi as "the lady." The daughter of General Aung San, the independence hero, now herself a hero whose party won elections in 1990. In and out of house arrest for years and even while detained, staging famous rallies every Sunday afternoon from over the fence at her rambling rundown house in Rangoon.

"Was he writing about Suu Kyi?" Delaney asked.

"I don't think so. He wrote about guns and business. Not people so much," she said.

"People who buy and sell guns need to find people to carry them and shoot them, Mai," Delaney said.

"I don't think Nathan wrote about that part so much," she said.

Delaney could see it was time to have a good look through Kellner's papers.

"Nathan liked the lady," Mai said. "He has pictures of her in his working room."

"Pictures of Aung San Suu Kyi?"

"Yes. On his board."

"But he wasn't writing about her."

"I don't think so," Mai said. "But he liked her. He said she was very special, very beautiful. Important. Sometimes I felt a little jealous." Mai looked embarrassed, and then smiled. "Like a foolish girl, maybe."

"Can I look in Nathan's study now?" Delaney asked.

"OK. But I have to go out soon. To my classes. I am going to be a teacher. Did you know that, Frank?" she said.

"No. That's terrific," he said.

"I study only part-time. Nathan helps me. It is very slow."

"That's terrific."

"My brother has been taking me to my classes since Nathan went away. He is probably waiting outside now."

"Why wouldn't he come in?" Delaney asked.

Mai again gave him a patient look.

"Because that is not how it works here, Frank," she said.

"How would he know I was here?"

"The watchman watches," she said. "And you have a driver, like always, probably."

"Yes."

"So my brother waits outside."

She stood up, scattering cats.

"I will go out to tell him I'm coming. Then you can look in Nathan's room."

"Let me meet your brother," Delaney said.

Mai looked uncomfortable.

"Frank, my brother doesn't like Western guys."

"I see."

"He doesn't think Thai girls should should go to bed with farangs and live in their houses."

"I see. So he didn't like Nathan either?"

She hesitated, but only for a moment. "No," she said.

"What about the rest of your family?"

"For my mother, it's OK. She is happy Nathan is nice to me and helps me to be a teacher. My father is dead. My other brothers, not so happy."

"This brother outside, what does he do?"

"He works in a hotel."

"Let me meet him."

"OK, Frank."

Mai got a bag and some books and got ready to go. She found Delaney a spare key.

"You stay here, OK? Don't stay in a hotel. Nathan would have invited you too," she said.

"I'm OK. I'm at the Royal. I'm OK, really," Delaney said.

"Stay here. It's lonely here without Nathan. Sleep with me in my bed. Nathan wouldn't mind. You can hold me. Nathan wouldn't mind. Just holding."

Delaney, despite all his travels in Asia, was still always taken aback by such frank suggestions.

"I don't think so, Mai," Delaney said. He felt, however, an intense jolt of sexual energy.

"You have a girl?" Mai asked

"Sort of," he said.

"Would she mind? Just holding?"

"I'm not sure." He really was not sure.

"OK, Frank. But you stay anyway. In the other bedroom. Very nice in there too. Maybe I come in to hold you in the morning."

They went outside into the early Thai evening. It was still very hot. The watchman and Mai's brother were sitting together on the watchman's wooden bed frame, smoking cigarettes. They both stood up when Mai and Delaney approached. The brother offered no wai. Ben was reading a newspaper in his car across the street. He folded the paper and got out when he saw Delaney, but waited where he was.

Mai said something in Thai to her brother and the watchman. Her brother looked sullen. He turned as if to go. Mai touched his arm and he stopped.

"Frank, this is my brother, Thaksin. He speaks only a very little bit of English." She said something else to her brother in Thai.

Thaksin stood for a moment and then took Frank's hand. Thaksin's small hand was rough and hard in Frank's. A hand that had done much manual work.

"I'm a friend of Nathan's," Frank said. "I'm helping your sister find out where he is." Mai translated this.

"OK," Thaksin said finally, not smiling. Mai said something else in Thai. The watchman spoke in Thai as well. Ben started to walk over, apparently thinking something was wrong.

"Everything OK, Frank?" Ben said.

"Yeah," Delaney said.

Mai spoke to Ben in Thai. Ben looked at Frank, and then spoke to Thaksin in Thai. There was a burst of Thai among the group of four locals, and a series of looks over at Frank. Finally, Thaksin said, looking at Frank: "OK. OK."

Thaksin touched Mai's arm and gestured toward a very beat-up Mazda parked near Ben's car.

"I go now, Frank," Mai said. "You stay in the apartment." She came away from the group and said to him much more quietly. "You stay tonight too."

"I think I will go to the hotel now instead," Delaney said, loud enough for all to hear, not at all sure he would be understood. Staying in the apartment now, and especially overnight, would clearly not be a good idea. "We will look at papers tomorrow. Ben, let's get going."

"Sure Frank," Ben said.

Mai spoke again in Thai to her brother and to the watchman, and then came over to give Delaney a light kiss on the cheek. Her brother's face darkened.

"Thank you for coming to help me, Frank," Mai said. "We will find Nathan, right?"

"Yes, Mai," Delaney said.

"Thank you, Frank." She walked over to the Mazda with her brother. Delaney shook the watchman's hand.

"I'm coming back tomorrow," Delaney said. "To see Mai again."

"OK," the watchman said. "Daytime is better."

Ben said something in Thai to the watchman, who said nothing in response.

"Let's go," Delaney said.

He walked to Ben's car and got in the back.

"The girl's brother is not a happy guy, Frank," Ben said. "He doesn't like farangs."

"So I'm told. Didn't like Nathan very much at all, I'm told."

"So? He doesn't like any Western guys."

"So Nathan's disappeared."

"No way, Frank," Ben said. "No way. That's not how it works.

These guys are not stupid people. Guys like him. They don't like the farangs who sleep with their sisters but the whole family gets something. Directly or indirectly. Always. They would not break that."

"You sure about that, Ben?"

"Sure," Ben said.

Delaney was not convinced.


They headed back to the Royal. Delaney filled Ben in, trusting him totally and relying on his insights into regional politics, business, social relations. Then Ben waited in the lobby with his newspaper while Delaney went upstairs. Despite his post-flight nap, Delaney was feeling the effects of the long trip from London.

He checked emails on his laptop computer. Another one from Rawson that simply said: *What you got? JR.* Frank emailed back, saying: *On the ground in BKK and on the case.* Rawson was not usually so inquisitive so early. Something important was going on, something potentially important.

Another message from the Jung Society, expressing disappointment that, again, Delaney had failed to deliver his promised paper. No message from Kate. But one from Harden.

*Dear FD. Would have appreciated a bit more of a discussion with you before you headed out this time. Call me ASAP. Need to talk column, assignments, logistics, chains of command. Thanks and regards, Harden. (Editor-in-Chief).*

That Harden had bothered to remind Delaney of his position and title was a worrying sign. Delaney looked at his watch, calculated that Harden would still be at his desk and decided to wait before calling. Best to hit voicemail for something like this. He would make the call later. The opinion page editor had been at work and Harden would need soothing.

Delaney called Mordecai Cohen's mobile phone. The photographer answered immediately. It sounded like he was on a construction site.

"Cohen," he shouted over the din.

"Mordecai, it's Frank Delaney. Where the hell are you?"

"I'm in a tuk-tuk on Khao San Road. It's fucking hot and noisy. You in town?"

"Yeah," Delaney said. "Not far from Khao San. At the Royal."

"I figured you'd be through eventually. Kellner's still AWOL."

"I know. I saw Mai today."

"Drinks? Too noisy for me to talk anyway," Cohen said.

"When?"

"Half hour, more or less. Depends on traffic and this tuk-tuk. It's an antique. Say an hour. At the press club."

"Not here?"

"Nah. I hate the fucking Royal."

"OK," Delaney said.

Delaney realized that he was very hungry. He hadn't eaten since breakfast on the plane. He went downstairs and ordered some *pad thai* in the bar and more beers for himself and Ben and they talked over what Delaney had gathered so far.

Ben thought, after hearing what Delaney told him, that Kellner had gone into Burma on some secret assignment. A lot of Western reporters tried periodically to go in, usually on tourist visas, but the regime was tough on the foreign media and turned most reporters back. Those who got in without official approval risked arrest and, if discovered, at best a short stay in Rangoon's Insein Prison and a fast deportation back to Bangkok. Such reporters would usually be barred for life from entering Burma again.

Kellner, however, was an old hand. If he had gone into Burma without a journalist's visa he would probably have gone in by road, with plenty of U.S. dollars for bribes. Through Mae Sot on the Thai side into Myawadi on the Burmese side. Then by very bad road anywhere else in the country until he got caught. Or so Ben thought.

"Why would he not tell Mai where he was going?" Delaney asked.

"He didn't want to worry his woman," Ben said.

"He always worried any woman he has ever been with. That was no big deal for him."

"Maybe he's softening up," Ben said.

Delaney was not convinced. He saw the Burma connections firming up but saw also that with a man like Kellner, those connections could go wrong outside Burma as easily as inside. It could also be any number of other connections gone bad, other stories and other deals gone bad. Delaney wanted to pump Mordecai for information and knew that the press club would be the place to do it. It risked, however, being a very long night.

Ben dropped Delaney off in the crowded parking lot of the Dusit Thani hotel. The press club, improbably, was located at the very top of the high-rise, a deal made years before with the hotel management. The club drew in many reporters, of course, but also hangers-on, VIP speakers, diplomats, girlfriends, wives, spies. A mutually advantageous arrangement for the hotel and the press club executive board.

Delaney insisted that Ben go home. He would be drinking with Mordecai and his crowd for hours and Ben had young children. Delaney remembered once having had the rare privilege of going to Ben's modest little home on the outskirts of Bangkok. He had watched as Ben's boy, about 10, and his daughter, maybe 12, had raced across a dusty field to leap at their father and hug and kiss him as if he were the best and most important man in the world. The children, and his wife, were intensely proud of Ben, of his profession, his friends from around the world, and of his lovingly maintained little car.

Delaney always tried to prevent Ben from staying out too

late, especially if it was just to wait outside some drinking establishment of dubious reputation. They always had the same argument, but in the end Delaney always prevailed.

"Family, Ben. It's important," Delaney said.

"Yes, grandfather," Ben would say, smiling. "Yes, grandfather." But Ben would always go home in the end, in such circumstances, except if there was real work left to do or if Delaney really needed help. Delaney, no family man, had other priorities. He wondered, as he watched Ben's car disappear into the humid Thai night, just what these had come to be. He needed someone to remind him.

# Chapter 6

W hen Delaney emerged from the Royal Hotel the next day, he was in extremely ragged shape. Ben Yong just shook his head sadly and took Delaney's equipment bag from him.

"Was I not wise in advising you to avoid the press club last night, my friend?" Delaney said. He ordered a litre-and-a-half bottle of mineral water from the barman and a foil packet of aspirin that the bar staff always also kept in stock. Ben was drinking tea.

"Not so very wise, it looks like," Ben said. "What time you finish?"

"It seems like a very few minutes ago, Ben," Delaney said.

The night, as expected, had been a classic Asian press club night. Delaney had run into Cohen in the crowded lobby of the Dusit Thani. Cohen, as always, looked like he had just stepped off a helicopter in from a dirty, dangerous war zone. He wore the regulation combat green photographer's vest with many pockets, battered khaki pants and sturdy hiker's sandals. He did not, however, have a giant Nikon or Canon camera dangling from his neck, not so much because he was off duty but because he was rarely on duty and not a very good photographer at all.

Cohen, like some expats of a certain type in Asia and elsewhere, had energetically adopted the freelance news photographer lifestyle, dress and attitude without actually having paid his dues on the job. He got the occasional assignment from minor magazines, and sometimes played second or even third string to other more respected shooters, but it was common knowledge that he had neither the technical skill nor the experience to make it big.

In fact, word was that he very much preferred things that way. He used the photography to finance his rundown apartment, his dope smoking, his girlfriends and his painting. No one among the Bangkok expat crowd quite knew if Cohen was a better painter than he was a photographer. No one had seen his paintings and no one really seemed to care. Cohen was amusing to have around in a drinking session and he was a solid, reliable contact for soft drugs. Occasionally he produced a news picture that appeared somewhere in the world's media.

Cohen was arguing with the hotel's impeccably dressed night manager about where he had left his car. He had parked the filthy old Ford directly outside the glass entrance doors, under the hotel's sweeping awning. It was unmistakably his because it still had the letters *TV* applied in various places to the pocked window glass and the roof with heavy tape—*de rigueur* in battle zones, less so outside downtown five-star hotels. Cohen had not been anywhere vaguely resembling a battle zone for a very long time, but left the TV markings on his car as a badge of honour.

"Fuck it, man, that's where I always leave my car. I could be called out again at any moment," Cohen was saying to the manager, pushing his long unruly hair back from his eyes. "I'm a press club member. I may need to get to my car in a hurry."

The hotel man was patient, polite, very Thai.

"Please, you must remove this car. We have many guests arriving tonight. Tour buses also," he said quietly.

"No way. I may need it at any time."

Cohen spotted Delaney and said to the manager: "Here is

my colleague now, from the *Tribune*. Frank, could you please explain to our friend here that you and I may at any moment be called to the frontline?" He grabbed Delaney's hand and shook it furiously. Obviously stoned, well on his way to being drunk as well.

The manager gave Delaney a slow wai.

"Gentlemen, please, that car cannot remain there tonight."

"Mordecai, just move the car, OK?" Delaney said. "It's bad for property values."

Cohen hesitated, then fished his keys out of a vest pocket and handed them to the hotel man.

"OK, fine, OK," he said. "But tell your valet we may need this vehicle at any time. Urgent business."

The manager took the keys and handed them to a uniformed doorman, who looked decidedly unhappy about having to get into such a disreputable vehicle with fresh clothes on. Cohen pulled Delaney toward the elevators.

"Cocktails," Cohen said. "On the *Tribune*, I would imagine."

Delaney had spent a lot of time that night greeting reporters and cameramen he had known from previous assignments or other newsrooms. The press club, and its crowd of regulars, never changed. The focus was, of course, the bar. People tended to crowd around it rather than sit at any one of the 20 or so small tables they could have used at any given moment. The tables in the press club were almost always empty while the bar stools and bar area teemed with people. An adjacent small dining room was where people usually sat if they felt they had to or if they wanted ed to eat instead of simply drink.

"No idea where Kellner's gone, no idea," Cohen said much later, after he and Delaney had gone through the social niceties, if they can be called that in a bar where journalists congregate. "He just, like, disappeared."

Cohen had been useless all evening, in his customary haze

and never clear at the best of times about what Kellner might have been working on at any given moment.

"What were you guys up to lately?" Delaney asked again.

"Us guys? Kellner, you mean," Cohen said through a mouthful of beer nuts.

"You were often working on stuff together, no?"

"Nah, not much anymore," Cohen said. "When I first came over maybe, the odd picture for his mag, the odd thing together upcountry around Chiang Mai when I first came over. Not now."

"Surely you've got some idea what he's doing, where he's gone."

"Honest to God, Frank, I've got no clue. The guy was supposed to come over here a few weeks back, to do another version of his wonderfully boring do-gooder speech about safety training for corros in war zones. He never showed up. That's it."

"Have you pissed anyone off lately?" Delaney asked.

"What, me personally?"

"You guys. You two. You ran together."

"Not so much anymore."

"Dope?"

"Ah, minor stuff, man. We did the odd minor deal together, nothing heavy. He fronted me a bit of cash for deals sometimes, but it was small stuff, very small stuff. Recreational use, a little on the side for friends. Third- and fourth-hand deals. Westerner-to-Westerner stuff. Nothing."

"You burn anyone lately?"

"Frank, come on, we're talking small stuff here. Friends and family. No rip-offs. The generals are the big players in Thailand. We're nobodies."

"What about Burma?"

"What do you mean? Dope?"

"No. Was Kellner going in on a job?"

"I don't know, Frank. Maybe. He liked that Suu Kyi broad, I know that. The lady. He liked what she was doing over there."

"Did he have an interview set up?"

"She's under house arrest, Frank. She's not talking to the press. You know that."

"Mai says some guys were at their place, asking whether Kellner was going to Burma, whether he had been in."

"Aha," Cohen said. "The plot thickens."

"Mordecai, you really don't seem to be taking this seriously," Delaney said. "Kellner's been out of the game for more than a month. You don't seem to give a shit."

"He'll turn up. I'm sure he'll turn up here any day now. He's off on some adventure somewhere. What's your angle anyway? You guys weren't such close pals. What you doing over here looking for him anyway?"

Delaney found himself getting more and more exasperated. He knew he was battling through Cohen's deepening late-night trance, but had expected more information, more concern. Delaney didn't answer. He ordered more beer. Cohen was going to be dead end. That night, in any case.

More journalists had rolled in to the club. Delaney's information gathering ceased.

Ross Laverton was there, holding court. In Delaney's view, one of the most insufferable specimens that Canadian journalism had ever produced. A weekly newsmagazine man, under no particular pressure to produce, and under no particular pressure to produce anything other than matchers for breaks in the newspapers. Laverton had been in Bangkok for too long. It showed in his sallow complexion, his rumpled tropical weight suit and expanding beer gut.

"My round," he shouted to no one in particular. This news did not stop the intense buzz of conversation.

"Delaney," Laverton shouted. "Surely you must allow me to buy you a glass of beer. And Cohen, come on. Dost thou think because thou art virtuous there shall be no more cakes and ale?"

Delaney and Laverton had been at odds, if not enemies, ever since they had started out together on the *Tribune* a lifetime ago. Laverton had seen Delaney as a competitor. Delaney had never seen Laverton as anything more than a modestly talented middle-class boy from Montreal's western suburbs.

Beers were purchased; pleasantries, near-pleasantries exchanged.

"I read your column regularly, Frank, of course," Laverton said eventually. "A new beat for you, really, isn't it. Political trends."

"Not really, Ross," Delaney said.

"Well, I mean, the analytical side of things," Laverton said.

"Don't use words of more than two or three syllables maximum with this dickhead," Cohen said drunkenly. "Delaney gets confused easily. But he thanks you for the beer. Right, Frankie?"

"No really, I mean, it is quite a departure for you, isn't it Frank? A weekly column? No?"

"I was actually quite used to filing every day, Ross," Delaney said, not yet drunk enough to be offended, not sober enough to completely let things go. "I find the weekly rhythm very easy to take, actually. Quite relaxing."

"Touché," shouted Cohen. "Touché, you weekly fucking magazine scumbag. Still your round, Ross."

More rounds of drinks were bought, many more rounds, by a series of other reporters, hangers-on and knaves. More stories were exchanged; more complaints about the media game were aired. Ferocious little arguments started and stopped. Colleagues and competitors were slandered or praised. Plates of Thai food were consumed very late. Then, for Delaney, a jumbled impression of the gently spinning hotel lobby; handshakes, embraces, exchanges of business cards, exchanges of notes. Backslapping, handshakes, cars.

Then a freezing air-conditioned taxi ride back to the Royal, a long slow fumbling for keys, and a cool pillow rushing up to meet Delaney's face. He woke, in his clothes, to the warble of the room telephone. Ben Yong was waiting for him downstairs.

Ben dropped him off at the end of Kellner's soi. Delaney told him he would call if he needed a ride toward the end of the day. The watchman was neither friendly nor unfriendly. He offered Delaney a brief wai and then went back to reading a newspaper on his wooden bed. He didn't go down the corridor first to announce Delaney's arrival as he had done the day before.

Mai didn't look good when Delaney pushed open the screen door. She had been crying again, it appeared. She was feeding goldfish in a small tank. She looked very tired.

"Mordecai Cohen was no help last night, Mai," Delaney said.

"He would know where Nathan is, Frank. If anybody would know," Mai said sadly. Neither of them had much more to say for the moment.

The key thing now was Kellner's study. Delaney went in right away. Mai watched TV in the living room, kept company by cats.

The first thing that struck Delaney was the pictures. Ten or more, pinned up on the big bulletin board over Kellner's old wooden desk. Aung San Suu Kyi in a variety of poses, at various stages of her career. The biggest one, a reprint of an Associated Press news picture, showed Suu Kyi standing on a platform behind the fence of her house in Rangoon, addressing party supporters and democracy campaigners. Hard-looking Burmese soldiers looking on uneasily. The fence was decorated with images of dancing peacocks, symbols of the student democracy movement and of Suu Kyi's party, the New League for Democracy, the NLD.

The picture was dated November 2000, about six months ago—and a few months after Suu Kyi had been placed under house arrest for the second time by the military regime. She had been free, or relatively free, for about five years before that. She'd been under house arrest for the first time in the late eighties, Delaney recalled, until about 1995.

Other pictures showed Suu Kyi looking very attractive in other settings, in wide Burmese woven hats with flowers in her hair or at the nape of her neck. A charismatic, Oxford-educated beauty, whose fate it was to return to Burma to visit in 1988, just as the democracy movement was taking flight and as the generals panicked and cracked down. Now the leader of the strongest pro-democracy political grouping in the country and a thorn in the side of the regime. She had an open invitation from the generals to leave Burma, but she did not leave, even when her husband was dying back in England, saying she feared she would never be allowed back in to her home country again.

Under the pictures, Kellner—Delaney had to assume it was Kellner—had pinned slogans and quotations, written by hand on pages from a reporter's notebook.

*"The work of our national movement remains unfinished. We still have to achieve the prosperity promised by the dragon. It is not yet time for the triumphant dance of the peacock."* Suu Kyi.

*"Some people in Burma spend the period of the Thingyan spring water festival in April in meditating, worshipping at pagodas, observing Buddhism's eight precepts, releasing caged birds and fishes, and performing other meritorious deeds. Children are told that <u>Sakya</u> comes down from his heavenly abode to wander in the human world in the days of Thingyan, carrying with him two large books, one bound in gold and the other bound in dog leather. The names of those who perform meritorious acts are entered in the golden book . . ."* Suu Kyi

Kellner had underlined, in red, the word *Sakya*.

The final quote was not attributed. It said: *"To turn Aung San Suu Kyi from a martyr into a saint could only further harm an already-tarnished image of the military regime."*

Delaney found it hard to imagine Kellner, a veteran foreign correspondent of the most cynical and hardened kind, pinning up inspirational quotations about any democracy movement, anywhere in the world. Kellner was not the type to idolize movements, or ideas. Women, perhaps. Not movements or ideas.

The bulletin board also contained a mishmash of business cards, receipts, postcards, memorabilia—none of them immediately noteworthy. Cohen's business card was there. Another for the military attaché at the Taiwanese embassy. One for the Canadian consulate's press officer. A schedule of court times for Kellner's badminton club.

Delaney started looking methodically through Kellner's drawers. The usual pens and paperclips in the top right. Cassette tapes, with names of interview subjects and dates. He would have to listen to those, perhaps, but later. That would be a long job.

The second drawer down was full of reporter's notebooks, tossed in a jumble but quite well labelled on the back with story subjects, interviewees' names, dates. It looked like Kellner had been at an arms fair in Singapore about two months previously. Lots of notes from interviews conducted there. Nothing that stood out.

In notebooks from the period prior to that, a series of interviews and story subjects one would expect for the correspondent for *Defence Monthly*. Possible heavy equipment purchases by the Thai military. Maritime signalling equipment possibly being bought by the Taiwanese. What looked like notes for various political features. Nothing at first glance at all about Burma, or Suu Kyi, however. Delaney found this odd.

Then he spotted a slightly larger notebook, the kind university students use in class. It was in Kellner's jammed in-tray on top of the desk. This one had the word *Oz* written in the top-right corner in felt marker pen. It was full of densely written notes about what appeared to be a construction contract in Burma, for an access road to a casino complex being built in Mongla, in northeast Burma near the Chinese border. Australians were involved, the notes indicated, providing engineering support and subcontracting services for equipment and materials. And, Kellner had indicated, for project security. Kellner had written in the margin in that section, apparently later, with a different pen, the word *mercs*. Delaney wondered if this meant Mercedes or mercenaries. In that part of the world, it could well be either.

Mongla used to be just another backwater Burmese village, in the Shan State. Now it was a notorious drug-running and people-smuggling centre, and also a place where thousands of Chinese tourists poured in on tour buses from across the border in Yunan Province to gamble and watch seedy transvestite sex shows and get drunk. Mongla was the turf of one of Burma's most powerful ethnic Chinese drug warlords, Min Lingxian, who had long ago cut a deal with the Burmese military regime to share profits from the opium trade in the wilderness bordering China, Laos and Thailand.

There was huge money to be made in Shan State, most of it of dubious origin, but some, as it appeared for the Australian consortium working the road deal Kellner had become interested in, more or less legal. Legal, but dangerous, financially risky and impossible to conduct without a nod from the military regime, the local warlord, and probably both. Impossible to conduct without protection of various sorts, military and political.

The area was awash with weapons—another reason Kellner and his magazine would have been keenly interested. Min Lingxian was reported to have more than three thousand heavily armed militiamen looking after his interests there. No foreign company could ever hope to operate in Mongla without dealing, directly or indirectly, with Lingxian's people. Construction companies from Thailand had built many of the roads in the parts of Burma run by drug traffickers. Now, it appeared, an Australian company was getting a slice of that business too. And Kellner was onto the story.

Kellner put the big notebook into his equipment bag to study further at the hotel. He didn't bother to tell Mai. She would surely be unaware of the details of Kellner's journalistic activities, and probably of much of his other activities as well. She would never miss the odd notebook or sheaf of papers.

Kellner's deep bottom drawer was even more interesting than the rest, in a much different way. This was where he kept some of his stash of marijuana and smoker's paraphernalia. Small plastic bags of dope. Other smaller quantities in grey-plastic 35-millimetre film canisters. Also small chunks of black resin wrapped in bits of aluminum foil, almost certainly opium or possibly Afghani hashish. No hard drugs apparently, no tablets or cocaine or heroin. Just smoker's supplies and various pipes, rolling papers, matches, lighters. There were also DVDs, with Chinese-language labels showing pictures of naked women.

Delaney fired up Kellner's laptop, hoping it would not need a password. He would want to read files on that computer later on. No password was requested. Delaney put one of the DVDs into the proper slot and clicked on the play function. Hard-core pornography poured across the laptop screen; young Chinese girls, obviously heavily drugged, having gynecologically explicit sex with rough-looking Chinese young men. No plot, no dialogue except moans and grunts; just plain old hard-core porn.

"Nathan and I used to watch those together," Mai said quietly from the doorway. She had apparently heard sound from the film and come in to see what Delaney was doing.

Delaney found himself blushing; a small boy caught looking at naughty pictures. He turned off the show.

"Nathan liked to watch that before we went to bed together," Mai said. "You like that?"

"Not my thing, Mai," Delaney said.

"You are finding all there is to know about my man. His little secrets," she said. "Now you have to find out where he has gone."

"I'm trying, Mai," Delaney said.

She looked past him at the pictures of Aung San Suu Kyi.

"And you see the pictures of his other lady," she said. "No picture of me there. Just Suu Kyi. With clothes on."

"I see that," he said.

She gazed at the pictures on the bulletin board for a while.

"Did you see Nathan's scrapbook?" she asked. "Is that the word? Scrapbook, where you collect things on paper?"

"Scrapbook?"

"Yes."

Mai reached up onto a shelf near the bulletin board and pulled down a ragged scrapbook with a floral-patterned cover— the type any school kid would use for special projects or to collect pictures. Kellner's was full of clippings about Aung San Suu Kyi. They went far back. Some as far as her release from a first period of house arrest in 1995, then through her increasingly important pro-democracy activities and her struggle to force the military regime to recognize the results of the 1990 election that her party clearly won. Then house arrest again in 2000.

On one recent clipping about Suu Kyi's daily, almost monastic, routine in her secluded house on Rangoon's University Avenue, Kellner had written in felt pen: "From martyr to saint."

"What does he mean by that?" Mai asked when she saw Delaney looking at the inscription.

"I'm not sure," Delaney said. "The two words are quite similar in some ways, in English."

"I thought martyr meant a dead person," Mai said.

"I thought so too," Delaney said. "The word *saint* also."

"Nathan always said Suu Kyi was a caged bird. He said she shouldn't be in a cage like that, in Rangoon. He seemed angry about that sometimes."

"Angry."

"Yes. At the generals, for keeping her in her house like that, for years."

Mai went back into the other room and sat down on a rattan chair. Her hands shook and she tried very hard not to cry again. She fought back her grief and her fear, and also her shame at what Delaney had had to learn. She tried hard to believe that this nice Canadian man, this friend of Nathan's, would help end this nightmare and allow her to resume her little life again. She tried hard to believe that because she believed, with all her heart, in men.

She had believed in Nathan when he picked her out, for reasons she still could not quite understand, to be his woman. She was not a bar girl, not as pretty as some Thai girls, not as experienced in the ways of pleasure that brought so many Western men to Bangkok, to Thailand, to Southeast Asia. But he had picked her and, to her own very great surprise and delight, he had been kind and loyal and caring to her now for years. She allowed herself to believe he loved her.

He was not like most of the other Western men in Bangkok, who took young girls when they felt the urge and kept them like exotic sexual pets for a time and then threw them aside. She had been with some of those men, had known their aggressive desires, had seen them use their bodies against Thai women like weapons.

Nathan was not like that. He was a different man. He liked women—he told her that often—he liked their presence around him. He liked her presence around him, he liked her. He did not say he loved her, but Mai did not need that very much, she did not need to hear that. She just wanted to be with him, to feel his presence in their space, to yield to his intense, but never aggressive, desires.

And now he was gone. Now she knew she was not his only lady—that in his mind there was another object of his intense desire. Mai did not understand that desire, where such obessional desire came from and where it was meant to lead. It was beyond her comprehension, beyond all comprehension.

Mai sat in her rattan chair in the ordered dimness of her man's space, the space they had shared for years, and she fought back her grief and fear and shame. The air was hot and still. She felt a sudden intense desire herself, her skin tingled with desire. She felt a sudden need for sex with her man, for the sort of sex that could leave no doubt, no possibility of doubt, about anything whatsoever.

Delaney had put away the pornography and resumed his searches. He wanted to know more about Kellner's apparent obsession with Aung San Suu Kyi. He wanted to know much more about this Australian business deal in Burma. He wanted to know if somehow, according to some convoluted logic, the two issues could somehow be connected, if only in the mind of a man like Kellner, a mind clearly not always functioning on a rational level. Delaney himself, however, knew what it was like to be guilty of obsession with a woman. He considered that for a while as he sat quietly looking at the pictures of Suu Kyi.

Delaney found Kellner's 2001 agenda book, such as it was. There were various entries for interviews, meetings, badminton games. One page per day. But surely too few entries on any given day for a busy reporter like Kellner. He probably failed to enter much of what he was doing on any particular day or week. Or perhaps preferred not to record certain things. But certain recurring entries caught Delaney's eye. Periodically, a short stretch of two days, three days, would be blocked out with a line running from top to bottom of the pages. These entries said simply: "House." Earlier in the year, some entries said "House preps."

Delaney rummaged around on shelves and found other agenda books going back a few years. In late 2000, there were more "House" and "House preps" entries. In the 2001 book, one recent entry, from March said: "Stefan et al at the house. With gear."

It was possible Kellner referred to his apartment as the house, but Delaney thought this unlikely. He wondered what "gear" could mean. Drug slang, in some countries, but usually referring to hard drugs and the related paraphernalia. He went outside with the books and showed them to Mai.

"What do you make of these?" Delaney said, showing her the house references.

"What does it mean?" she said.

"I don't know. Does he mean this house? This apartment?"

Mai looked at some recent dates.

"Why would Nathan write down that he was at this house? He was here a lot. He doesn't need to write that down. It is not a house anyway."

"Did you have another house somewhere? A house at the beach?"

"No, Frank," Mai said, looking up at him. "No other house."

*That you know of*, Delaney thought. He sensed Mai was now thinking the same thing.

"Do you think Nathan had another house, Frank?" she asked quietly.

"I can't say, not from this. Maybe it was another guy's house. Where he went for visits. Did he ever mention something like that?"

"We never went to visit people's places, hardly ever," Mai said. "In Bangkok maybe, but not very much. And they were apartments. Not houses."

"Maybe he went alone somewhere," Delaney said.

"Yes. Maybe alone," she said.

"Do you know someone named Stefan?" he asked.

"No," she said.

"You sure?"

"Yes. I never heard a name like that."

Delaney realized he was straying into territory where Mai had never been, and where he should probably not attempt to bring her. He went back into the study and began making notes of his own, on one of Kellner's big pads. Mai said she would make them a late lunch.

He heard her moving around quietly in the kitchen, heard the classic Asian hiss and sizzle and scrape of food and oil and metal spatula in a wok. Suddenly he felt the urge to just spend the rest of the day at ease. To rest on Kellner's bed, to enjoy the safe domesticity of a quiet tidy home where he could share hot lunches with a beautiful young woman, or share quiet nights on a balcony where breezes always blew. Somewhere he belonged, where he truly wanted to be.

They ate together at a little table on the balcony. Delaney drank some beer. Mai mostly sat watching him eat and drink, saying almost nothing, taking little food for herself.

"Nathan would speak about you sometimes. And about Montreal," she said finally.

"What would he say?"

"He said you were good at being a reporter."

"That was nice of him," Delaney said. They both smiled.

"He read your newspaper on the Internet. He liked to know about Montreal, even though he lived here."

"We Montrealers can never really leave our city," Delaney said. "Not in our minds, in any case."

"Nathan was like that too," she said.

She sat looking dreamily at him for a while, probably thinking of her lost man. Then she stood up.

"Let me get something," she said.

She moved off into the house and into Kellner's room. She was gone for a few minutes. Then she came back carrying a large brown envelope, apparently bulging with papers.

"Letters," she said, putting the envelope down on the table.

"Whose letters."

"Nathan's," she said. "Love letters. In a way."

"You want me to look at these?" Delaney said.

"They weren't for me," she said. She sat down and waited. Delaney looked at her for a long time and then picked up the package, pulling out a few letters in slim white envelopes. On each was written the words: "Suu Kyi." No address, no stamps.

"You can read them," Mai said.

Delaney opened one. A single page, apparently like all the others. It began: *My beautiful, beautiful lady* . . .

He looked at Mai.

"My beautiful, beautiful lady. Most of them start like that. When I first found them, I thought they were for me."

Delaney read on: *How can I tell you what I feel when I see your face? How can I tell you? One day I will tell you. And one day the world will not only have to see your face through the bars of a cage. This I promise you, my lady* . . .

Delaney would have dismissed the words as the ramblings of a lovesick adolescent or a very bad poet. Except that he knew they had been written by Nathan Kellner, a man nearing 50 and one with years of experience of the real, hard world.

Delaney skimmed a few other letters, satisfied himself that they were all approximately the same. None carried addresses or stamps. He put them back in the bigger envelope, closed it, pushed it toward Mai.

"Nonsense," he said.

"For the Burmese lady," Mai said.

"Yes. I would say so," Delaney said. "Bizarre. But never mailed anywhere. Not intended for mailing."

He could imagine Kellner writing any number of things at

his desk in the tropical night, hatching wild plots or recording secret activities, illicit or otherwise. But love letters to Aung San Suu Kyi? This did not seem possible. Only drugs, or a truly profound obsession, could explain it.

Mai looked very sad indeed.

Later, they smoked some mild marijuana in the dying light of the day. Delaney had not smoked for years. The drug put him instantly in a quiet, gentle other space. Mai and he sat in the cool breeze on the apartment balcony, saying nothing, thinking nothing.

Much later, she undressed him in the guest bedroom. Gentle assistance with his clothes. He floated on a warm sea of tropical air and the marijuana trance. Mai dropped her sarong to the floor. They climbed into the cool sheets of the guest bed, together. She held him from behind, knees bent up behind his knees, breasts against his back. Her skin was fantastically cool and smooth. Every pore of his own skin was burning, alive to her touch. The merest touch of her hair was electric. He did not remember if they made love, he would probably never know.

He dreamed and dreamed:

*Kate rides toward him on a perfect chestnut horse. She is naked. Her right hand is raised in a small sign of greeting, of expectation. Natalia walks elegantly behind Kate in the robes of the dead, a little to the left of the horse. Natalia's right hand is raised in a small sign of benediction. There is an emblem of a caged bird on the breast of her garment. Delaney watches in the dream as the two women approach, approach, approach; but they never get any nearer. Somewhere behind them or above them or off to the side is danger or a darkness, but still very far away. A danger that is as yet impossible to discern clearly or to combat.*

# PART 4
## Bangkok and Mae Sot

# Chapter 7

Just before the attack came, Delaney sensed something was wrong. He was not able to articulate quite what afterward, but he knew in his gut that if he had just been a little more watchful, a little more attentive, he might have been able to avoid it.

Ben was waiting for him outside Kellner's apartment building. Delaney had gone to see Mai another time, after his meeting—a daylight, sober one this time—with Cohen at a place called Chivas Bar. Ben pulled his car out from a shady spot into the late-afternoon Bangkok sun. Delaney was in the back as usual. Immediately, a black Lexus with heavily tinted windows pulled out of an entrance a short way up the soi and blocked their path.

Ben had been in the business a long time and had been in bad spots before. He had no formal training that Delaney knew of in defensive-driving techniques, but he knew exactly what to do and he did it fast. When a stocky Asian man in a dark blue tracksuit got out of the back of the Lexus and took aim with a pistol, Ben threw his Toyota into reverse and stomped on the accelerator. The aging station wagon rocketed backward amidst a screech of tires and an acrid haze of rubber smoke.

"Down, Khun Frank, down, down, down," Ben screamed as he threw his arm over the passenger seat and peered wild-eyed backward to guide the slip-sliding car out of danger. Delaney plunged sideways onto the rear seat.

The first shot punctured the windshield just below the rearview mirror. Delaney didn't see the hole in the glass, but he saw Ben hunch even lower, as low as he could into the back of the driver's seat, his eyes squinting tight as he anticipated the next shot. Two more rounds came in quick succession, this time taking the windshield glass out completely. Shards exploded over Ben's shoulders and cascaded into the rear over Delaney.

Ben yanked the steering wheel left, a true expert, and the car rocked and heaved backward into the short driveway and then the walled dirt courtyard of Kellner's building, all the while screeching and heaving up smoke and dust and stones. It came up against something hard and stalled dead.

"Out, out, out, out," Ben shouted. They both flung open the doors on the driver's side and rolled into the dirt. The watchman's wooden bed was now a pile of timber under the Toyota's rear wheels. The watchman himself was nowhere to be seen. Delaney and Ben picked themselves up and raced into the open air corridor on the ground floor.

"Have you got a gun, Ben?" Delaney shouted.

"No, no. Never," Ben shouted back.

"Run," Delaney said.

Some instinct made Delaney turn right instead of left, away from Kellner's corridor and the apartment where Mai would be watching TV as she was when he left her a few moments earlier. He prayed she would not have heard the gunfire and come out to see what was happening. He ran with Ben to the end of the right-hand corridor and began climbing stairs to upper floors. Each dim corridor ended with a windowless archway that kept the building breezy. On the third floor they could see over the wall and trees out onto the long soi where the Lexus had been waiting. It was gone.

They stopped, panting heavily, and looked at each other for a moment.

"Up?" Ben said.

"They may be in the courtyard. He may have parked it there," Delaney said. They listened intently, trying to control their breathing so they could hear.

They could hear no steps, no voices, no car.

"Gone," Ben said, slipping down against the end wall of the corridor, knees against his chest.

"Maybe," Delaney said, still listening, still ready for flight. "Don't sit, Ben. Be ready."

"Ready. Ready," Ben said. He looked all in. His flowered shirt was wet with sweat. Delaney remembered that he must be almost 60.

Delaney put his head cautiously out of the archway and looked far up the soi to where it met Sathon Road. He thought he saw a black car turning right, joining the river of traffic on the huge main boulevard, but he couldn't be sure. There were no other cars in the soi. Far up, a lone food vendor pushed a wooden cart in the direction away from Kellner's building. Delaney wanted to ask him what he had seen. But not yet.

He slumped down beside Ben below the archway and rested his back against the wall, knees up.

"I think they're gone," he said.

"Me too," Ben said.

"You all right?" Delaney said.

"Tired, Frank. Scared."

"Me too."

"Tough guys," Ben said.

"Yeah."

"My car. Wrecked now."

"We'll get it fixed," Delaney said.

Ben pulled a small piece of windshield glass out of the front pocket of his shirt and sat staring at it. He looked up at Delaney, as if waiting for some kind of cue.

"Tough guys," Delaney said.

"Yes," Ben said.

They waited for a long time, sitting in the dim coolness of the corridor. A light breeze wafted in through the archway. Delaney thought for a moment that Ben was going to fall asleep. Neither of them spoke for some time.

"I think we can go down now," Delaney said eventually.

"OK, Frank," Ben said.

They headed very cautiously down the stairs, stopping and listening often. They heard two low voices, speaking Thai. When they peered around a wall into the brightness of the courtyard, they say the watchman and a gardener standing together near the car, both looking extremely grave. They turned when Delaney and Ben emerged from the shadows.

The watchman immediately launched a torrent of Thai, talking loudly to Ben and waving his arms and pointing at the car, the apartment, Delaney, everywhere. Ben poured back his own torrent of Thai. Delaney could only stand and let it flow.

"What did he see?" Delaney said eventually.

"Nothing, he says."

"Where was he when we rolled in here?"

"At the other side. Helping the gardener, he says."

"He didn't see anything? He didn't hear anything?" Delaney knew the watchman spoke English, but today he seemed to be able to speak only Thai. "Did you hear anything?" he asked.

The watchman looked at him angrily and turned to Ben to reply in Thai.

"Nothing, he says," Ben told Delaney. "Nothing."

"Why won't he speak to me?"

"He's angry. Scared."

"We'll pay for his damn bed," Delaney said. He knew he was being understood. Even the gardener seemed to understand.

"He isn't angry about the bed, Frank. He says he doesn't want you around here anymore. He says things are better without farangs around. Better even that Khun Nathan is gone now."

"What does he mean by that? What does he mean about

Kellner?" Delaney said. He turned to the watchman, addressed him directly. "What do you mean by that?"

"I call police," the watchman said.

"And what will they do?" Delaney said.

"Take you away," the watchman said. "Back to Canada."

"And who will find Khun Nathan?"

"No one. He is gone," the watchman said.

"Where?" Delaney said.

"Anywhere. Not here," the watchman said.

"Don't you understand that someone tried to kill us here today?" Delaney said.

"He knows that, Frank," Ben said.

The watchman started talking again in Thai to Ben. Ben spoke to him quietly, pointing from time to time at Delaney. The watchman seemed to calm down.

"He says if we pay him for the bed and get the car out of here right away he will not call the police," Ben said.

"Fine, fine. But make sure he's clear we are not afraid of the police," Delaney said.

"No point, Frank. No point," Ben said.

"How much for the damage?" Delaney asked.

"He says one hundred U.S. dollars," Ben said, with a knowing look. "Pretty expensive bed."

"I'd say," Delaney said. He reached for his wallet. "Make sure he understands we are not afraid of the police, OK?"

He knew the watchman understood that and a lot more besides. Delaney handed him a hundred-dollar note. He decided to give the gardener a twenty.

Ben was looking sadly at his car. But aside from the shattered windshield and a flat rear tire, it did not seem to be too badly damaged. Ben squatted to look underneath at the back.

"Not too bad maybe," he said. "Crown is a very strong car. Toyota is OK."

"We'll get it fixed, Ben. We'll be needing it," Delaney said.

"You still want to drive for me?"

"Yes, Frank. Sure. Always," Ben said. "Media driver."

"Maybe a different sort of story this time, Ben," Delaney said. "Maybe not for media."

"Everyone needs a driver, Frank. All you guys. Any kind of story."

Ben called for a tow truck on his mobile phone. Delaney headed down the left-hand corridor of the building to Kellner's apartment at the end. Mai looked very surprised to see him back so soon. When he explained to her what happened, her face darkened and tears came.

"This has to do with Nathan," she said.

"Yes, I'd say so," Delaney said.

"They have guns."

"Yes."

"What do they want? Where is Nathan?"

"I'm trying to find out."

"Please find out fast, Frank. OK?"

"I'll try."

Mai looked for a fresh shirt for him while he cleaned up. His own was dirty and torn. When he came out of the bathroom, Mai was waiting. She gave him a shirt for Ben as well. They were too large. Kellner's shirts.

"Stay now, OK?" she said. The light was fading outside.

"No, I'd better not," he said.

"I'm scared and lonely," Mai said.

"I will make sure the watchman is careful tonight. He's got a cell phone. You lock the door and don't let anyone in but me. You've got your cell phone right there. We'll check the number for police. Your brother can come to stay."

For a bad moment, he remembered the last time he had assured a woman she would be safe if he went away. The image of Natalia lying dead in a snowy Quebec wood flashed through his mind.

"Stay, Frank. We can smoke and hold," Mai said. "It was good last night."

"No, Mai," he said. "We can't."

Delaney very much wanted to go back to the hotel and simply think things through. The game in Bangkok had changed dramatically, he could see that now, and he wanted to think about possible players, possible next moves. On their part and on his. Mai would have to rely on someone else to get her through the night. He wanted to stop feeling it was his job to take care of women any time things got complicated.

He thought he might call Rawson in Ottawa, to see what was happening at that end. He surprised himself by thinking of also calling Kate. He allowed himself to like the thought that there was someone to call, somewhere in the world, after danger, stress. But he knew he would tell Kate nothing about the afternoon's attack even if he decided to make the call.

He asked Mai suddenly, "What kind of car does your brother drive?"

"What?"

"What kind of car does your brother drive?"

"Why?" she said. "A Mazda. You saw it the other day. Why are you asking that?"

Delaney knew it was almost impossible anyone in her family could own a high-end Lexus like the one he had seen today. He also knew it was highly unlikely that Mai's brother, any of her brothers, would be angry enough to try to kill him. Or Kellner. But he had spent his professional life seeking certainties, not likelihoods.

"My brother wouldn't do anything like that to you, Frank," she said sadly.

"To Nathan, maybe?" Delaney said.

"Never. Never, never," she said.

Ben was supervising a tow-truck driver when Delaney went back outside. The watchman and the gardener were carrying away pieces of the smashed bed. The watchman looked sullenly Delaney's way but said nothing.

"It doesn't look too bad, Frank," Ben said, peering underneath his beloved car as it was winched off the ground. "They can put a tire and new front glass on tonight. Good as new."

"You need cash?" Delaney said.

"We figure things tomorrow," Ben said.

They shook hands. Ben was smiling again. He got into the tow truck alongside the driver. Delaney walked slowly toward Sathon Road, looking for a cab that would take him to the Royal.

Not all bars in Bangkok cater to men who like to see young women gyrate and pout and offer themselves for sex. There are some bars in Bangkok where there is no pole dancing, no gynecologically explicit displays complete with flashlights, no end-of-the-world girlie shows involving vibrators, cigars, ping-pong balls, whatever comes to hand.

Chivas Bar, on a quiet street tucked behind the worst of the Patpong Road sex and rip-off strip, was one of these. It had no shows at all. It was dark, American-style, with a long bar and a combination of booths and smaller round tables for serious drinking, by men who could arrange sex for themselves when they wanted it or who had made longer-term regular arrangements.

There were women in the Chivas, of course, some of them prostitutes, but not the insistent kind. They were only a few of them, hand-picked by management, and they sat quietly at one end of the bar smoking cigarettes and drinking Cokes. Other young women came in, too, with an assortment of Western middle-aged men. These women sat quietly also, while their partners swapped stories with buddies or simply sat and drank.

It was a place where younger, tougher-looking men also came for a quiet drink. U.S. military types, some of them, and a core of South Africans, and some Australians and New

Zealanders, former soldiers who had pitched up in Bangkok and decided to stay. Many were still soldiering, but for much better pay and in much less public campaigns. Some of these mercenaries had been coming to the Chivas for years, and recruiters knew where they could be found.

There were also a few journalists and cameramen at the Chivas Bar usually, mainly those who did not like the press club for daytime drinking. Mordecai Cohen was one of these, and he had suggested meeting Delaney there on the afternoon before the attack on Ben's car.

Most regulars at the Chivas ordered beer or straight spirits. It was not a bar where elaborate cocktails were considered appropriate. Cohen did not accept that philosophy. He was drinking a bright yellow-red Tequila Sunrise when Delaney came in and stood peering around through the dimness from the doorway.

"Over here, mate," Cohen called out from the back. He had spent a lot of time with Aussies and liked their banter. "Behind the yellow sunrise, mate."

Delaney sat down and ordered a draft beer.

"You find Nathan, yet?" Cohen asked, sipping his cocktail through a straw. He offered a large gently-buzzed-in-the-daytime smile.

"Still AWOL, Mordecai. Any ideas?"

"None. I avoid ideas when I am drinking."

Delaney was instantly irritated.

"You really don't give a shit where Kellner might be, do you?"

"I told you the other night, Frank. The guy is on some bender somewhere. Some particularly potent weed may have arrived from somewhere or other and he's gone off to smoke it with a pretty young thing. He will surface when he's done."

Delaney decided to control his irritation. He drank some more beer and said nothing; he was not sure, now that he was there, how he expected Cohen to be of any real help.

"Didn't see you atop the Dusit Thani tower last night, Frank.

The guys were asking for you. Your round, apparently. We were all concerned as you slouched off the other night. Thought you might be in need of medical attention."

"I pulled through," Delaney said.

"Find any company last night, mate?"

"In bed with my book at nine," Delaney said.

"Ah, the palm sisters. I only use picture books when all else has failed, Frank. I can fix you up tonight, however. This afternoon, even. Couple of possibilities at the bar as we speak."

"No thanks. I've never liked soldier boys," Delaney said.

"The other end of the bar, of course. Direct your gaze to the other end, if you would. All but one of those young women are over the age of 18, I would guess. From here. In this poor light."

"How's business in here these days anyway?" Delaney said.

"Who for. The girls or the soldier boys?"

"Soldiers."

"Not too good, as far as I hear. A lot of the lads have shoved off. Africa's the place just now. Equatorial Guinea is supposed to be good now. And Ivory Coast. Nice little rebel thing developing up north there, and the government's looking for what they so quaintly call instructors. Some of the guys have gone over there. A thousand U.S. a day I hear. Plus expenses. Over in Ivory Coast."

Delaney looked over at a crowd of what were almost certainly mercenaries. One Thai girl of about 16 sat among six or seven burly young men.

"No local work?" he asked.

"Oh, there's always the odd job for some of them upcountry," Cohen said. "For expat businessmen, mostly, who sleep better at night with young strapping Western lads outside the compound or watching the warehouse. That sort of thing. Routine stuff. No real bang-bang. I'd be up there if there was."

Delaney doubted that. He doubted any newspaper or magazine would hire Cohen to shoot any serious action unless the entire Bangkok photographic corps had been killed or deported forever.

"Where do they go these days, around here?" Delaney asked.

"Burma border, mostly, these days," Cohen said. He held up his empty cocktail goblet for the bartender to see.

"Burma seems to be on everybody's mind these days," Delaney said.

"How do you mean?"

"These guys over at the bar, or so you say. Other guys who turned up at Kellner's place, asking if he had gone in. Kellner himself, or so Mai says. And his editor in London. And you."

"Ah, I was just talking about Suu Kyi. The lady. Kellner was obsessed."

"So I hear."

"Who from?"

"Mai."

"I see."

"You been in Kellner's place lately? His study?" Delaney asked.

"Not lately. Not really. Why?"

"The guy has pictures of Suu Kyi everywhere. Bits of quotations. Clippings. All kinds of stuff."

"I told you. He was obsessed. He wanted to get into her drawers."

"Come on, Mordecai. Come off it."

"He had stuff like that at the other place too."

"What other place?"

"Fuck," Cohen said.

"What are you talking about?"

"Fuck," Cohen said. "Kellner's going to kill me. I've got to quit drinking and smoking dope during the day."

Cohen looked genuinely worried. He quickly slurped up the rest of his cocktail, lit a cigarette, looked for a waiter.

"What are you talking about, Mordecai?"

"Don't tell Mai, OK?" Cohen said. "Kellner will kill me."

"Tell her what? Come on, Mordecai. Kellner's been missing for a month. What have you got?"

"He has a house," Cohen said quietly.

"A house."

"Yeah."

"Where? He has another place?"

"Yeah."

"Where?"

"Upcountry. In Mae Sot."

Delaney had been to Mae Sot only once. It was a dusty little Thai town on the Burmese border. Main industry: black market trading across the frontier. Lots of jade and gems. The place was filled with Thai army rangers, Burmese exiles, Hmong and Karen hill tribespeople, and a world class assortment of ne'r do wells and thieves. Once in a while a stray mortar from the Karen rebels on the Burmese side would land in the town, adding to the ambience.

"Kellner's got a house in Mae Sot," Delaney said.

"Yup. Don't tell Mai."

"What's he got a house up there for?"

Cohen looked pityingly at Delaney.

"What do you figure?" Cohen said.

"What?"

"It's a holiday house. For little getaways, little rendezvous. A little weed, some nice local girls. No interruptions, no stress."

"That's mainly what he did down here," Delaney said.

"Yeah, but it's different up there. More buzzy. Different scene. Edgy, like. Plus Mai wouldn't be around."

"You've been there?"

"Only once. It was Kellner's private little deal. He didn't want guests, usually."

"How long's he had it?"

"Oh, not long. Six, eight months. I helped him drive some

stuff up there not long after he got it. Got him set up. Our big secret. He's going to kill me for telling you."

"What's it like? What's he got in there?"

"Oh, nothing special. A local-style house, but quite big. Couple or three bedrooms. Two stories. Off by itself near the river. You can see the Burmese side from the roof terrace. A little gentleman's hideaway. There's a sort of fixed-up barn with more sleeping space up top. Not that he wanted many guests, as I said."

"Christ," Delaney said.

"He's put a lot of Suu Kyi shit in there, too. That's what made me think of it. A big picture of her, some other stuff. Her books and articles. Plus books about her. Kinda weird. Like a shrine. He's obsessed. I figure he gets high and deflowers virgins in front of Suu Kyi's picture. Way the hell up in Mae Sot."

Cohen laughed out loud.

"You think that's where he is?" Delaney asked.

"I can't think of any other place he'd be," Cohen said. "Not for this long."

"Why doesn't he let people know?"

"No idea. Stoned. In love. Both, probably."

"Mai's worried," Delaney said. "He should call her to say he's all right."

"That's a 1950s concept, Frank. A suburban North American concept, in my humble opinion. Around here anyway. Ask some of the guys at the bar if they remembered to call their sweethearts today to say they were OK."

"You truly are an asshole, Mordecai, you know that?" Delaney said.

"I know that," Cohen said. "Drinks?"

Ben Yong was waiting for Delaney outside the Chivas sometime later, as arranged. Then they almost got themselves killed in the backwater little soi outside Kellner's apartment.

After Delaney had left Mai and got back to the hotel, he realized how tired he was. His muscles were aching from the exertion and the adrenaline rush of the afternoon's violence. As always after a dangerous episode, Delaney needed absolute quiet, calm, solitude.

He had a shower and put on the hotel bathrobe. He felt better not wearing Kellner's shirt. He stood looking at it, a multi-coloured tropical number from Robinson's, the big Thai department store near Patpong Road. A dead man's shirt? Maybe. Delaney had started the day thinking Kellner was dead. Now he was not so sure.

He pulled a big yellow legal pad out of his bag and sat at the room's desk. This, too, was his pattern when things got complicated on an assignment. Sitting quietly, thinking, writing elements of the story down as they came to him, underlining particularly odd or important items. He had spent a long time as a reporter developing these habits. They were useful now that he was in another line of work.

What did he know? What was emerging? The major element, he could see clearly now, was Burma. And, for reasons which were still absolutely unclear, Aung San Suu Kyi. But, in the Kellner story, there might be no direct link, or at least no logical link, between those two particular pieces of the puzzle.

Delaney wrote "Burma" at the top left of the legal pad, and then drew a line down the middle. He wanted links, patterns.

He wrote: London–Burma embassy questions. Kellner plans to go in? Editors cagey.

Then he filled the page, over the next hour or so, with many items, some linked with arrows, some underlined: Australian businessmen, angry about a Kellner story—Burma connection? Burmese men (officials?) visit Mai in Bangkok apartment. Burma materials in Kellner study. Suu Kyi pictures, texts. Suu Kyi love letters?? Mae Sot house; near Burma, plus more Suu Kyi items . . .

The list also included: Drugs, dealing small time—moving

136

into bigger time? Guns?? (Delaney crossed that out eventually). Mercenaries?? (This, too, he crossed out eventually). Other business deal?? Consultancies? For foreign deals?

He wrote: CSIS. Why Canadian interest? Kellner on CSIS assignment?? Kellner working for another agency?

He wrote: Domestic. Mai brother/brothers. Foreigners with sister. Kellner/Delaney out? Gun attack?? In a Lexus?

Delaney pondered these last points for a while. The gun attack outside Kellner's place had come the afternoon after he had spent a night with Mai. The watchman's attitude had changed suddenly. Mai's brother clearly did not like foreigners sleeping with his sister. But to shoot at Delaney for that? And at another Thai? Those were not warning shots, Delaney was sure of that. Would Mai's family, her brothers, actually try to kill someone, kill Kellner and Delaney, for hooking up with Mai? He thought not.

Clearly, Delaney decided, he was being watched. At least when he moved in and out of Mai's. If it was government or police, or Burmese agents, her phone might not be secure. Delaney himself had said little of substance on the phone in any case.

Then he wrote, suddenly: Cohen. Watch Cohen.

He wondered if Cohen was feeding someone information, or if Cohen knew far more than he was letting on about what Kellner was actually up to. He seemed completely unworried about his old friend Kellner having disappeared. This seemed too nonchalant, even for a man like Cohen. Even if he knew all about Kellner's habits and his Mae Sot love nest. If that is what the house was truly used for.

He wrote again: Suu Kyi. Obsession? Obsession with one woman?

Delaney pondered that entry, too, for a long while. It sent him into other areas, some personal, some usually taboo. He thought of his own apartment back in Montreal. What would an investigator or a journalist make of that, of what could be found there in desk drawers and hung up on walls? What would this tell people about Delaney and his relationship with a woman called Natalia?

Delaney eventually decided on several things, several whiskies into his evening of journalistic analysis and deliberation. He would now make it known that this was all too hard and too dangerous and that he was no longer looking for Kellner anymore. He would perhaps play tourist for a while. And he would, at all costs, go up to Mae Sot to find Kellner's house, maybe even Kellner himself. But discreetly, very discreetly.

Delaney looked at his watch. Friday morning in Ottawa. Rawson would be in his office, almost certainly. Delaney dialled his mobile number. The CSIS spy handler answered immediately.

"This is Jonathan Rawson."

"Mr. Rawson, this is Mr. Delaney."

"Francis, excellent. I was wondering how you were getting on. Where are you?"

"Bangkok. In my hotel. The Royal."

"Right. What phone are you on?"

"Cell."

"Right. Hmm. So. How's your little trip coming along?" Rawson said, more guarded now.

"Complicated. Very complicated," Delaney said. "Some little setbacks."

"I see," Rawson said. "Anything really worrying?"

"Yes. For a little while this afternoon. Some very, very unhappy locals. I seem to have upset someone over here. Very badly. They made that clear to me, and to my driver, a little earlier today."

"I see," Rawson said. "Everything came out OK, though?"

"Just," Delaney said. "Just."

"Right," Rawson said.

"I'm not sure where this is heading, Jon. Not sure at all. I think I may head to the beach for a few days, and think it all over a little. Koh Samui is nice this time of the year. I might bring Kellner's lady along with me. She needs a change of scene."

"The beach. Right," Rawson said. "Right. Whatever you think wise, Francis. Can you email me, perhaps. With details of your plans?"

"I will."

"When?"

"Soon. As soon as I can," Delaney said.

"Do that please."

"Will do."

"Any sign of our long-lost friend?" Rawson asked.

"Some. Maybe. I'll get back to you."

"Right," Rawson said.

Delaney dialled Kate's mobile phone number next. She also answered right away.

"Oh, Frank, it's good to hear your voice," she said, speaking very low. "I'm really sorry, I'm in a meeting now. Can I call you later?"

"It's late now, Kate. Quite late here. It's good to hear your voice too. Go back to your meeting. I'll call you another time. I'll leave a message on your tape at home, to let you know what's up. I'll call you on the weekend maybe."

"Good," Kate said. "Good. Sorry, lover boy. I'm in a meeting. I really, really have to go."

"Police business," he said.

"Mountie stuff," she said.

"Bye."

He wanted to say: *It's late here. I'm tired and sore because some-one tried to kill me and my driver today and we ran for our lives and I feel like someone needs to know that. Someone. Probably you.*

He called her tape at home and then immediately regretted it. After her greeting message he was left with a large opening to fill and he wasn't sure what to say, or how much, or whether he should have called her at all, on any phone. He had simply wanted to connect with someone. He had spent too many long nights in too many silent hotels in the middle of the world, and he wanted only to connect. An outdated, 1950s concept. A suburban North American concept, according to some.

"Hi Kate," he said to the silence of the tape. "It's me again. Sorry I disturbed you at work. I just wanted to say I was OK. In case you were wondering. Not sure when I can call you next. I'm going to go south of Bangkok for a few days. Still on this crazy assignment. I'll call you."

He paused, with a tape running in an apartment ten thousand kilometres away in Montreal.

"This is getting a bit complicated," he said. He wanted to add: *You and me.* He said instead: "This assignment."

Of course he dreamed heavily that night. In his giant hotel bed in a silent hotel in the middle of the world. He dreamed the Natalia dream:

*As always, she was lying dead in the snow in the Laurentian woods. The body in the woods, the snow falling steadily, silently down. But in this dream Kate and Mai were in the woods, too. And Aung San Suu Kyi. And other unidentifiable women. The snow falling steadily, silently down. He wasn't sure what they were all doing there, what they could all be expecting from him. Delaney watching, watching.*

# Chapter 8

Delaney slept in very late the next morning, exhausted by the events of Friday and by a night full of dreams. He knew also that this would be a transition day and so rest might be wise before heading into what would very likely be an uncertain and dangerous situation.

He decided against meeting Mai again at Kellner's apartment, certain as he now was that the place was being watched. He needed to get her over to the Royal and he needed Ben and his car. Ben, as Delaney had hoped, was waiting for him outside the hotel lobby around noon, even though they had fixed no meeting time. This was the style of the best Thai drivers. They sensed when they would be needed and they didn't mind a wait.

The old Toyota Crown looked as good as ever. Ben was polishing the new windshield glass, picking off a sticky label and looking very pleased with himself as he worked. The left rear tire looked much newer than the others.

"Quick work on the car," Delaney said.

"My cousin's got a garage over near Siam Square," Ben said. "Ready now to go again."

"Good," he said. "Ben, I've got some ideas for us and I want to make sure you're on board."

They went into the lobby for coffee and Delaney told Ben

about his plans. Ben was to go get Mai that afternoon for a meeting with Delaney at the hotel. Delaney had decided not to use phones anymore if possible. Ben was to be very sure he was not followed on the way back across town.

Then Delaney would explain to Mai that they were going to travel by train together to Surat Thani in the south, like friends, lovers or tourists, depending on who might be watching. Delaney would slip away at Surat Thani and fly back to Bangkok to meet Ben. Mai would carry on by ferry from Surat to the beach bungalows of Koh Samui and rest for a day or two there before very discreetly coming back to stay with one of her sisters until word came from Delaney, Ben or, possibly, Kellner himself.

Delaney and Ben would drive up to Mae Sot, find Kellner's house and figure out, if at all possible, exactly what was going on. Even Ben, a normally very optimistic and stoic specimen, saw several ways Delaney's plan could go badly wrong.

"You sure about this, Frank?" he said. "You think you can go to ground like that? Those guys yesterday were professional people, I think."

"We have to try, Ben. We can't keep walking around Bangkok with everybody knowing our business."

Ben did not look convinced.

"And Mae Sot is a tough place, Frank. We don't know what is what with Khun Nathan's house. Who might be there. We have to go easy, easy."

"We'll go easy, Ben," Delaney said. "What is it? You worried about your car?"

"Not just the car, Frank."

Mai was also unconvinced, decidedly unconvinced. She did not want to leave the apartment in case Kellner came home. She did not want to leave her cats. She did not see the logic of going at that point on what appeared to be a holiday with a Western man. She did not want to anger her brothers or upset her mother. But mostly she did not want to miss seeing Kellner if he came home.

Delaney used the same arguments with her that he had used with Ben. But he did not mention the Mae Sot part of the plan or anything about Kellner's secret house.

"We can't just keep on walking around Bangkok with everyone knowing what we are doing," he said in the hotel's wood-panelled lobby. "Once we are clear of whoever's watching us I can look better for Nathan. Someone is watching your apartment. Someone is probably watching us here, now, in this hotel. We have to get ourselves some room to manoeuvre. And I want them to think I have given up, that I'm just taking it easy on the beach. I want them to think they have scared me off."

"I think maybe they have scared you off, Frank," Mai said sadly. "We still have to find Nathan."

"I will look for Nathan. That's what I'm trying to do, Mai. When we shake off whoever is on top of us first."

Mai still looked unconvinced. Ben just stirred his coffee and tried to mask his own misgivings.

Eventually, however, Mai came around to the idea. They would meet the next evening at Bangkok's main intercity train station, and get overnight berths for Phun Phin, the closest station to Surat Thani. Somewhere there, Delaney would slip away and head for the airport and a flight back north alone.

Ben dropped him off at the Chivas Bar on his way to take Mai home. Delaney wanted to make sure Cohen, and therefore all of expatriate Bangkok, knew he was heading south on holiday. Ben would make certain the watchman, and therefore another circle of potentially interested parties, knew Mai was off to the beach with this new Western man.

Cohen of course, was in the bar, in the same booth as the previous day.

"So it's off for a little R&R then, with the lovely Mai," Cohen said when Delaney had explained his plan. "I have always admired how the Thai ladies generously share their charms with friends of friends. I'm sure Kellner won't mind a bit, you jumping on her bones on the beach train."

"She needs a break, Mordecai. So do I. This whole thing is going nowhere. Nathan will come back when he's good and ready. I think he's up at that house in Mae Sot anyway, like you said. I think he's probably OK."

"A wise course, the wisest possible course," Cohen said. "Let things unfold as they will. Get laid if you can. Try not to piss off your friends. My philosophy exactly."

Delaney got up to go.

"Yes, a beach holiday with, Mai," Cohen said. "Just the thing." He paused, looked at the end of his cigarette. "No little side trips planned up north, I would assume? Mae Sot is not good this time of year."

Delaney spent Saturday night worrying about his plan and about what he might encounter in Mae Sot. He tried to call Kate but got messages on both her mobile and her home phone. He also worried, but only for a few minutes, about his next newspaper column, due by Wednesday. Delaney at large. With a Canadian angle. He was not at all sure how he could find eight hundred words for the *Tribune* editors that week. Canadian journalist missing in Bangkok? Possible small-time drug dealer or business fixer or womanizer not seen for over a month? Girlfriend worried. Who cares? Why would *Tribune* readers care? Canadian Security Intelligence Service worried? Now that, maybe, was a story.

Late on Sunday morning, Delaney checked out of the hotel and threw his bags into the back of Ben's car. They drove to various places picking up the things any self-respecting Western tourist would need for a beach holiday. Some light shirts from Robinson's, shorts, sandals, a beach towel. Standard issue stuff. Then a long touristy lunch with Ben at a barge restaurant moored in the Chao Phraya River not far from the end of Khao San Road.

Eventually they ended up at Hualamphong Station, teeming as always with locals, Asian business types and tourists. The train to Surat Thani was due to go at 6 p.m. Ben stood watching for Mai as Delaney bought more travel things from one of the crowded little shops on the concourse. Sandwiches, nuts, fruit, bottled water, and a litre of mild Mekong whiskey.

Mai arrived looking very much the part, smiling broadly. Wide-brimmed sun hat, pink T-shirt, straw bag, leather satchel. She looked very good indeed. Delaney hoped he would be able to remember this trip was business, not pleasure. At least for the next 11 hours on the train.

"Have a good trip, Khun Frank. See you soon," Ben said, shaking hands gravely with Delaney. "Bye bye, Mai."

"Back soon, Ben," Delaney said.

Their second-class carriage was full. In a few hours, teams of young State Railway staff would scramble all over the car, unfolding ledges, reversing seats, hanging curtains and making up narrow beds—transforming the seating area into a long series of snug bunk-style sleeping compartments. Travellers would perform ablutions at open sinks at one end, and then retire to their little enclosures. An armed watchman would doze at the other end while all slept.

While they waited for the compartment boys to arrive, Delaney and Mai sat quietly, sipping Mekong from plastic cups and munching peanuts. She was far more relaxed than the last time they had seen each other. After several small whiskies, she insinuated herself under his right arm and rested her head on his shoulder.

"Nice here," she said.

They could have been any of a hundred such couples on the gently swaying southbound train.

Sometime after midnight, Delaney was reading in his little upper bunk. A crack in the drawn curtains let in some of the passageway light. Occasionally he saw the green-clad railway guard walk by, this way and that. He very much sensed the presence of Mai below him. He was glad the sleeping arrangements were single. This simplified matters a great deal. Mai had retired very much in her "smoke this and hold me" mode.

His mobile phone rang. It was Kate, apologetic for the late hour.

"Where are you now?" she said.

"On a train," he said quietly. "In a berth."

"Alone, I hope," she said with a laugh.

"Of course. They are very narrow berths in Thailand."

"I wish I was there with you tonight, Frank. I like trains. Don't quote me on this, but I think I may actually be missing you. Despite your lack of social skills."

"Abstinence makes the heart grow fonder," he said.

"Something like that," she said. She paused.

"Where are you headed? What are you actually writing about over there?" she said.

"Nothing yet. Working on a sort of feature story."

"About what?"

"Complicated. You'll have to buy the *Tribune*."

"I wonder about you sometimes, Frank."

"What do you wonder?"

"I wonder if I know as much about you as an alert policewomen ought to know."

"Sergeant Kate of the Mounted."

"Yes."

"I'm a journalist."

"Sometimes. When it suits you."

"Yes. Self-assigned."

"Lucky."

"In some ways."

"I look forward to reading your story," she said.

"Working on it," he said.

Phun Phin Station was fantastically crowded with tourists, other travellers and touts. It is a crossroads for people heading out to islands in the Gulf of Thailand and those heading back up north. Others changed trains there to head even farther south, toward Malaysia.

Delaney was quite sure no one had watched them on the train. Ben had been certain no one had followed his car to the Bangkok station. But Frank looked around carefully as he got off the train, fending off taxi touts and ferry boat touts and trying to spot anyone who didn't fit properly into the scene. He saw nothing that made him worry.

He picked out an older-looking taxi driver with a decent-looking older Mercedes and they went to the ferry quay, also teeming with travellers. In the confusion, he would get Mai settled on a crowded boat to Koh Samui and then take another taxi out to the airport for an 8 a.m. flight back to Bangkok.

Mai kissed him several times as he stood next to her on her outside deck seat.

"I don't think I like this idea anymore, Frank," she said.

"It's best, you'll see. I'll see you back in Bangkok soon. Rest and swim for two or three days and I will see you back in Bangkok. It's best," he said.

The deck was strewn with brightly coloured backpacks. Delaney picked his way past them just before the boat was to cast off. The quay was still extremely crowded. A line of taxis waited nearby. At the last possible moment, he headed quickly back down the gangplank and directly into an ancient Mazda.

"Airport," he said. He didn't look back at the boat, knowing that Mai would be too tempted to wave.

The flight from Surat Thani was just 70 minutes. Ben was waiting for him at the Bangkok arrivals gate. Delaney was sure now that no one had followed him, that no one could have followed him. He was convinced that those interested in his movements would have completely lost his trail.

They headed out right away. Traffic outside the airport was heavy, as always, but it thinned a little once they were on what passes for the highway north toward Nakthon Sawan, Tak and then west toward Mae Sot. Delaney would share some of the many hours of driving with Ben. The major challenge would be staying out of the way of the fleets of belching, overloaded Thai trucks and buses that always dominated the road.

Ben's scratchy tape deck played Thai and Chinese tunes. His wife had packed sandwiches and sweet fizzy orange drinks for them. She didn't like Ben drinking beer while on a long road trip. Too dangerous, she said. Ben told Delaney this with obvious pride. He was a happy family man.

They pulled into Mae Sot just after nine that evening, tired and sore from the long hard drive. On the way into town they passed one of several refugee camps that had sprung up for Burmese Karen people fleeing the fighting between Burma's army and KNU rebels across the border. Delaney's journalistic instincts tugged him in that direction for a moment as they passed, but this was not the story he was after this time.

The pedestrian and bicycle traffic became heavier and more exotic the closer they got to Mae Sot's small town centre. Burmese men in traditional *longyi* sarongs walked alongside the dark and rutted road, illuminated by dozens of dim yellowish headlight beams. Hill tribesmen and their wives also wore traditional dress. There were a lot of soldiers, Thai Rangers, sitting in small roadside beer parlours, drinking and smoking cigars. Western hippies and backpackers occasionally appeared in the light.

Ben said he knew a good guest house where they could wash, eat and get to bed. Their problem the next day would be to try to find Kellner's house without raising any alarms. But tonight they needed rest.

Ben pulled the car into the courtyard of the three-story Mae Thep Guest House, not far from the central square, and parked it under a massive mango tree. The aging engine of the Toyota clicked quietly as it cooled. Some small tables were set on the hotel's wide covered balcony and a mix of Western and Asian travellers were eating by the light of small oil lamps.

"This is the place, Frank. Nice here," Ben said. "I know the house lady. Clean rooms, hot water usually."

"Perfect," Delaney said, climbing stiffly out of the car.

Half an hour after that they were drinking beer on the balcony, late suppers ordered and bags stowed in tidy single rooms. Delaney felt the glow he always felt on a warm Asian night, with the smell of bougainvillea all around and the humid air soft on the skin.

"Perfect," he said again as plates of pad thai arrived. "Perfect."

"Tomorrow we start," Ben said, squeezing limes onto his meal. "Beers tonight."

"Beers tonight."

The next day they realized how hard their task would be. Finding Kellner's house without actually telling people what they were doing would be a delicate matter. Delaney realized also that there was a reasonable chance, unless Keller was actually hiding out, that they would simply run into him in the street somewhere in town. After all the effort he had made travelling to Thailand, Delaney was not actually sure what he wanted to ask Kellner if he found him alive. Rawson could eventually help him with that. Maybe.

They took a preliminary drive around town, in the hope that something would indicate a house owned or rented by a foreigner. Delaney wished he had asked Cohen more about what the house looked like or where it was located. Mae Sot was a typical northern Thailand outpost town: a hodgepodge of small shops, guest houses, dubious-looking banks, depots and warehouses. In this part of the world, near the Burma border, there was also a jumble of Buddhist temples, mosques for the

Burmese Muslims and a couple of small Christian churches.

"Could be anywhere, Frank," Ben said as he steered carefully between bicycles, motorized rickshaws, beeping taxis and walkers.

"Cohen said it was off by itself somewhere. Near the river."

"That river runs all through town, Frank. And way past."

They stopped outside a couple of places almost at random, looking for signs at least of foreigners living inside. But those houses could not be described as being off by themselves and none had any outbuildings. Cohen had mentioned a barn fixed up as sleeping quarters.

In the afternoon, Ben went into a real estate agency on the pretext of trying to find a house to rent for the foreigner in his car. Through the glass shop front, Delaney watched him talking intently to the young woman sitting behind an aging computer screen. Then Ben motioned for him to come inside.

"Mr. Delaney, this kind lady says there is nothing suitable just at this moment but she would like more information about exactly what you are looking for. She says a very nice place was rented to a foreigner about half a year ago that might have been good for you. Rented now, but she may find another one like it possibly soon."

The agent's name was Somchay "Mary" Vechiraya. It was inscribed in full on a small plastic badge pinned to her blouse. Her long black hair had one enormous wide streak of white, apparently the latest in Mae Sot fashion statements.

"I'm a writer," Delaney said. "I need somewhere quiet to work, with rooms for guests that may come in from overseas sometimes. Maybe three or four bedrooms and a good place to work. Quiet. Not in town."

"Yes, yes. We have such houses sometimes in this agency," Mary said. "Usually owned by army generals but coming for rent sometimes."

"What was the one like you rented last year? When was that?" he asked.

"That was in September, I think sir. Last September. To a tall foreign person like yourself. He also wanted quiet."

"Too bad that one is gone," Delaney said. "Would it be available sometime soon, perhaps? Where would that one have been?"

"I do not think it will be free soon, sir. No. The foreign man liked it very much. It is not actually in Mae Sot. It is on the road to Huay Bong, actually. Maybe 10 kilometres from here. You have to first drive as if you are going to Mae La Lao and to the national park. Then a road goes off to Huay Bong. But it is not good maybe for one person. No one around. Too big for one. Better in town for you, I think."

"That one sounds perfect," Delaney said. "Does it have a parking garage?"

"A small barn, sir. Parking downstairs and some extra bed places upstairs. Too much for one man."

"That is the sort of place I need," Delaney said.

"Not available sir," the agent said, putting her palms together in a graceful wai. "I will look for another for you, beginning today."

"Thank you very much."

Delaney and Ben looked carefully at a big-scale local map during lunch. There was not much between Mae Sot and Huay Bong. Nothing much shown at all. The Mae Nam Moei River flowed near there. It sounded like the right spot.

Ben proposed driving up there later that afternoon, but going right past if they sighted a house that looked right. He wanted to go back at night for a better reconnaissance if they decided it was the house they sought. Delaney was not sure about operating at night anywhere in that part of Thailand.

They drove slowly out of town and headed east and then north toward Huay Bong. The road became very bad after they turned off the main road, Route 105. They saw only small peasant houses once in a while, with chickens scratching in the dirt outside and small fires going. Occasionally a local kid waved and shouted. But it was far from a main thoroughfare. They saw no other cars, parked or otherwise.

After about 20 minutes heaving along the bad road, they saw a big copse of mango trees to the left and in the distance behind them, visible only through a break in the trees, a two-story house. A small barn lay behind the house. As they drew closer, with no break in the trees, the place was completely out of sight.

A rutted driveway wound away from the road and through the trees. They pulled closer and Delaney motioned for Ben to stop.

"Not sure it is good to stop here right now, Frank," Ben said. "We come back later maybe. I will go up and circle back and we go past another time, OK?"

"Stop just for a second, Ben. Just for a second. We won't go up just now."

Ben looked very dubious, nervous. He stopped where the driveway met the rutted road and looked in his rearview mirror.

"Not good, Frank," he said. "We don't know who is up there. Later, maybe."

Delaney got out.

"Two seconds, Ben," he said.

He went over to the driveway. It was in very bad shape. It would be four-wheel-drive terrain in the rain. The drive wound through the trees and no house was visible. There was no mailbox. Just a single post stuck in the ground near the road, leaning over at an angle. No number, no name.

Delaney looked more closely at the post.

"Let's go, Frank," Ben said. "Back later when it's dark, OK?"

Delaney saw that someone had stuck a very small rectangular Canadian flag lapel pin into the top of the rotting post. A tiny pin, not visible from the road or from a car. That was all. The most subtle of signals.

"This is it, Ben," he said.

"Please get back in the car now, Frank. Let's go."

Ben seemed annoyed. He never usually got annoyed about anything. He was clearly frightened. The shooting in Bangkok had left him rattled and he obviously wanted no more troubles like that.

"I'm sorry, Ben. But now we know it's Kellner's place," Delaney said as they drove back.

"Just because of a little flag."

"It's the place, Ben. I know it. We'll have to go back."

In the end, Delaney was able to persuade Ben it was better to go back in daylight. If they were caught snooping around the house at night, it could be very bad. If they were caught by day, they could feign innocence, claim to be house hunting, potential renters.

That gave them another night to relax and eat another excellent meal and drink more beer and Mekong whiskey.

After dinner, Delaney walked along Prasit Withi street and turned left into Sri Phuant past a mosque. There was a little Internet café there, Cyber Sot, run by a couple who in another era might have decided to launch a late-night grocery store or run a little taxi service. Their café was immaculate, their computers in excellent condition. An assortment of backpackers and local kids peered intently into glowing screens. Keyboards clacked gently.

Mr. Khongkaew and his wife showed Delaney all around their establishment and offered him tea before he was able to sit down at a screen. He was by far the oldest customer in the place, by at least 20 years.

"Best Internet café in Mae Sot. Best, best," Mr. Khongkaew said proudly. "Always high-speed connection, never problems here."

Delaney first sent an email message to Patricia Robinson, opinion page editor, with some bad news. *Tribune* readers would have to try to live without his column this week. Frank Delaney is away this week. Delaney is at large. Unavoidably detained.

"Try to deal with the grief, Patricia," he wrote, somewhat fuelled by a series of drinks with dinner. "I will file something next week. Will try to break new ground."

He copied Harden into the message; however, Harden was a different problem. Delaney knew the editor-in-chief was losing patience with him, but they had a long history together. Delaney was confident he could weather this latest newspaper storm. Harden was of the old school. He knew that every journalist, certainly every columnist, had fallow periods, distractions of various sorts.

Next, he emailed Rawson, filling him in a little about what he had found. As always with Rawson, not telling him the full story, if only because he rarely gave Delaney the full story himself about any freelance spying assignment.

"In Mae Sot up north now and think I may have found Kellner's secret house," Delaney wrote. "I'm with my driver, Benjarong Yongchaiyudh. We'll go back to have a look tomorrow, and see if Kellner is there."

He finished with a question: "There is a Burma connection that keeps coming up in this, Jonathan. What more can you give me from your end on that angle?"

*Nothing much*, Delaney thought, as he paid for his computer time. Rawson will be holding something back, as always.

On the way back to the guest house, Delaney kept his eyes open for the Burma Border Press Club. He had read about the place, where dozens of exiled or refugee journalists from Burma gathered to talk politics and exchange information. He had read that they met regularly in a Chinese restaurant near the centre of town.

He doubted there would be a sign indicating where they met. The Burmese military regime managed the media with an iron fist. They would not take too kindly to gatherings of journalists anywhere, even in Thailand, where sedition was the lead story. Mae Sot was full of informers and spies. Some of the members of the press club were stringers for the BBC and Voice of America, and their reports could be heard inside Burma on shortwave. It was risky business.

Delaney and Ben went back about their own risky business early the next day, heading directly to what they now agreed had to be Kellner's house. Ben was still not happy, but absolutely loyal and dependable, as always. This was a job he had been hired to do and he would never let Delaney down. But he was silent, dead silent, as they made their way back up the bad road toward Huay Bong. The same local peasant kids waved and shouted at the car as it went past.

The house hove into view through the break in the mango trees and then disappeared again as they drove on. At the driveway, Ben stopped. He pulled the car off the road under the trees.

"Maybe I should block the driveway, Frank," he said.

Delaney thought about that for a moment.

"We're supposed to be here looking for a house to rent. Nothing to hide. Would we block the driveway?"

"We'd drive straight in if we weren't expecting trouble," Ben said.

"I don't want to do that either. I don't think we should do that," Delaney said. "Let's go up slow on foot, see what we can discover as we walk in."

"OK, Frank."

Ben carefully locked his car and they began to walk up the overgrown driveway toward the house. The drive twisted a couple of times and then they saw the house in the distance. The barn was out of sight from there. There was an uncovered balcony at the front of the house, extending to both sides of the open front door. A table and one chair were set out. Delaney wished for binoculars.

"What you think, Ben?"

"No car. Maybe in the barn. Door to the house is open. Someone is there."

"Yeah."

"Maybe Khun Nathan."

"Maybe. If it's him, no problem. If it's someone else, we may have a problem."

"I know that, Frank."

They moved quietly a little closer, praying for no dogs. All was silent. The day was very warm. Ben was sweating heavily, his forehead beaded with perspiration.

They came into the clearing before the house. The barn was now visible behind it. No cars in sight. The door to the house was wide open. On the small table on the balcony was a large beer bottle, a portable radio and what Delaney thought might be a pistol. He motioned to Ben to move closer along with him. He reached into his pocket for the real estate agent's card, in case questioned.

They moved up the few steps onto the balcony and stood beside the table. Delaney was right; it was a pistol, a chrome 11-millimetre Colt. The bottle was half-full of beer. Suddenly, a tall figure in full camouflage fatigues and black military boots appeared in the door frame, almost filling it. He was a Westerner, very muscular, very red in the face and very angry. Delaney thought: *Mercenary.*

"What the fuck?" the soldier said. He lunged for the gun on the table.

Delaney saw that coming. He grabbed the gun himself and pointed it at the soldier, who stopped dead, crossing his flattened palms in a menacing X sign, either a martial arts stance or some other clear warning that he was ready to fight.

"Easy," Delaney said. "Take it easy."

The soldier stood stock-still; wary, waiting for Delaney to make a move.

"What the fuck you doing up here?" the soldier said in a

South African accent. "You guys get out of here right now."

"We're looking for a house to rent," Delaney said.

"Bullshit," the soldier said. He spat at Delaney's feet. "You know how to use that gun, you little scumbag? You sure the safety's not on? You know where the safety is on that thing?" He spat again.

"Easy, friend," Delaney said. "We're just looking for a house to rent."

Ben looked terrified. Delaney was still holding the real estate agent's card in his left hand. He tossed it onto the table.

"The agent sent us here."

The soldier looked over at the card but made no move to pick it up.

"Bullshit. You guys better get the fuck out of here. Right now. You better hope I don't ever see you around here or in town again or I'll rip your damn heads off."

"We'll go. We'll go. Just take it easy," Delaney said.

"Who you working for, you little scumbag?" the soldier said, hands still in marital pose.

"Let's go," Delaney said to Ben.

"OK," Ben said.

"You better leave me my gun," the soldier said. "You try to take that gun, I'll rip your damn head off."

"I'll leave it out front at the road," Delaney said.

"No way," the soldier said. He made a massive airborne lunge at Delaney and came crashing down on top of him. The gun went off but hit no one. They both fell. Then the soldier was on his knees, pummelling Delaney where he lay, hitting him hard in the face and head with both his fists. Delaney was stunned by the blows. The soldier tried to reach over to where the gun had fallen on the balcony floor.

Ben picked up the metal chair and smashed it down over his head. Then another time. Blood rushed from two bad cuts in the soldier's clean-shaven scalp. He looked up, bellowing, and stood to face Ben. Delaney got to his feet and picked up the chair to hit him again on the side of the head. The soldier staggered, his ear gushing blood, and turned toward Delaney again. Ben hit him from behind, this time with the beer bottle. Beer and blood ran down the soldier's face and he slumped to his knees.

"I'll kill you both, you scum," he mumbled, about ready to topple over. "You scum." No one else appeared. No one ran out of the house. It appeared the soldier was alone.

Delaney hit him one last time with the chair and he collapsed onto his side, still conscious but badly stunned. He was bleeding badly from his series of head wounds.

"We'll have to tie this guy up," Delaney said. His lip was cut and blood trickled from an eyebrow.

"We should go," Ben said.

"No. We've got to look inside the house. There's no point otherwise. Then we go."

Ben ran over to the barn and came running back with some clothesline he found there. They pulled the groggy mercenary off the balcony and up against the side of the house, and then ran the clothesline around his wrists, ankles and knees—a couple of amateurs tying up a hostage.

"Make sure you've got him very tight, Ben. This guy is very, very pissed off," Delaney said.

The soldier was coming to his senses. Delaney gagged him with a dishtowel he found in a sink. They wedged the dazed soldier in the angle where the balcony met a wall and watched as he came around.

When the soldier found he had been bound and gagged, he went into a frenzy, violently shaking his arms and shoulders and head, kicking out against the knots, moving himself in all possible directions to get free. He ground around in the dirt, banging himself against balcony and wall. Even through the gag, they could hear his dire, very dire, threats.

# Chapter 9

t was still early, not yet midmorning. Rain had been threatening since sunrise and it started at last to fall. *That would make the driveway difficult-going for cars,* Delaney thought. It would also further enrage the trussed-up mercenary outside. Occasionally they could hear him lunging around in the dirt, trying to free himself from his bonds and cursing through his gag.

They were in the open main floor of what appeared to be a recently built house. Many Thai generals, many generals all through Southeast Asia, had made themselves very wealthy by building a series of such houses, usually for rental to foreigners. Many of these landlords demanded a year's rent in cash in advance and then used this to build their next house, and the next, over and over again.

Ben sat down on one of the straight-backed wooden chairs that surrounded a very large rectangular table made of teak. He looked badly shaken. Delaney went to the sink and rinsed his face. He looked at himself in a small mirror and saw that he had been cut in several places, but not seriously. His split lip was sore and there was a big welt on a cheekbone. His eyebrow had stopped bleeding.

He stood leaning against the sink and looked out at a very large, high-ceilinged room that served as kitchen, dining room and living room. It was furnished with heavy local wooden furniture and big local mats and cushions.

"We're going to have a good look around and then get out of here fast," Delaney said.

"Yes, Frank. That guy out there will kill us if he gets loose."

"I've got his gun," Delaney said. He had stuck it in his waistband, gangster-style.

"I don't think he needs a gun to kill us, Frank. Not that guy," Ben said. "And other people will be coming back maybe. Maybe soon."

"It's morning, Ben. If they were here today, they have gone off somewhere else for at least a little while. It's still early in the day."

There didn't appear to be evidence of a lot of people staying in the house, or at least having stayed there the previous night. The table was clear, except for some large local vases and baskets. In fact, the whole place looked unnaturally neat, in military order.

"I think that guy was here alone. A guard," Delaney said.

"I hope so," Ben said.

"We'd better look around. Maybe you go out to the barn and start there, Ben, and then let me know what you find. Then maybe stand by in the driveway in case someone comes. Let's go as fast as we can."

"OK, Frank."

"You want the gun?"

"No way, Frank."

Ben went out and down the stairs off the balcony toward the barn, walking fast through the soft tropical rain. The enraged soldier lunged about and shouted muffled curses at him as he passed. Delaney turned his attention to the main room.

There was nothing remarkable about it, except perhaps its extreme order. There was no sign either of whose house it might be. He saw nothing that told him Kellner had been there. An open plan space, with a small bathroom off to one end. Kitchen cupboards full of dishes, cutlery and food. It looked as if a small stockpile of food had been laid in; many bags of rice, lots of oil, sugar, salt, spices. The fridge was jammed with beer but also with a wide assortment of goods that indicated someone who cooked, who knew how to cook.

In the bathroom, there was shaving gear on the sink, one toothbrush and a traveller's bag full of men's items that anyone would bring on a trip. Thai labels on most things, with international brand names on the rest. No clues there.

The upstairs area, however, told a very different story.

There were three large rooms up there, all approximately the same size, and a large bathroom. Delaney could see that two of the rooms would have windows facing the back and sides of the house, as would the bathroom between those two rooms. The third room was to the right of a small vestibule at the top of the stairs and would probably have windows facing the front and the right side.

All doors were closed. Delaney went to the left-rear room first.

It was like an upmarket hotel room, furnished in stylish, expensive Thai designs. A huge bed sat in the middle, with two fluffy towels and a face cloth neatly folded on the cover. Small bars of hotel-style soap sat on the facecloth. There were dried flowers in vases, small dishes of fragrant flower petals and spice. Magazines on a small round table. *Time, Newsweek, The Economist. Defence Monthly.*

There was a desk with an old black Remington upright typewriter. Inside the drawers, fresh stationary, envelopes, notebooks, rulers, pens, sharpened pencils, erasers; all unused. On the shelf above, a small selection of books, mostly political titles. Most were about Asia. Several were by Aung San Suu Kyi. The Penguin paperback edition of her *Letters from Burma* lay face up at one side of the bottom shelf. The cover showed Suu Kyi looking splendid in a peach-coloured cotton tunic and an enormous

Burmese-style straw hat, with peach-coloured roses gathered fetchingly at the nape of her neck.

There was a silk bookmark inserted. Delaney opened the book at that page. A line had been highlighted in yellow. It read: *"The names of those who perform meritorious acts are entered in the golden book."*

On the wall between the bottom shelf and the desktop was a small black-and-white photograph in a wooden frame. Delaney recognized the picture immediately as Suu Kyi's decaying colonial house in Burma. A world famous address: 54 University Avenue, Rangoon, from behind the fence of which she staged increasingly popular political rallies despite being under house arrest. Her home and prison, both at once.

*Kellner is insane*, Delaney thought. *This is his house and he is insane.*

He went back out to the vestibule and then into the bathroom. More hotel-style comforts. A fluffy white bathrobe, wrapped in plastic, on a hanger behind the door. A wide selection of women's creams, oils, shampoos on a shelf. All new, never used. Drawers full of tissues, cotton wool, makeup pads, nail files, hairpins. Bottles of perfume. Every need anticipated, everything in intact packaging, ready, it appeared, for an honoured guest to arrive.

There was a door on either side of the bathroom. The left-hand one opened onto what could only be called the woman's room, the hotel room. The right-hand one was bolted. Delaney slid the bolt and walked into what he saw immediately was Kellner's room. It looked very like his study in Bangkok, but in this case a small bed was pushed against the far wall, near a side window that overlooked part of the yard and the barn.

On one wall was a poster-sized picture of Suu Kyi. *Obsessed with this woman*, Delaney thought.

He went to Kellner's desk. Again, on shelves above it, political books, and Suu Kyi books. Not in such careful order as in the other room. There were also papers, files, folders, notebooks in the shelves. This was a room that was in use.

The desk drawers were also jammed with papers, notebooks, files. As in Bangkok, the bottom drawer held marijuana, hashish and opium. Lighters, matches, rolling papers, pipes. The shallow middle drawer was locked. Delaney looked around for a key.

He found it in a small lacquerware box near the bed. Another key lay inside, beside it. Delaney pocketed that one and went back to the desk to open the drawer. Inside he found an 11-millimetre pistol not unlike the one now tucked into his jeans. Two boxes of bullets. And a couple of large coil-bound notebooks. On both, the word *Burma* was written in felt pen.

Delaney knew he should not linger and that he could read the notebooks later, after they had left the house. But he skimmed the contents quickly, unable to contain his curiosity despite the danger.

The notebooks were a combination of record keeping, planning documents, agenda and inventory. As Delaney read, he became more and more convinced that Kellner was at best delusional, at worst insane.

Entries had begun about a year earlier. They recorded, as a journalist might, meetings with contacts. Businessmen, in this case, at first. Facts, numbers, place names, bits of interview quotes. It appeared that Kellner had been meeting Australian businessmen, to discuss construction and road projects in northern Thailand and Burma. Perhaps for a story. But then it became clear from the entries that Kellner, as Delaney had suspected, was acting as consultant and fixer to a consortium with big ambitions and big anxieties. They wanted advice on security, on doing business with the Burmese generals, on which industries and activities were open to foreigners who were willing to work with the regime.

Delaney knew that the Burmese military, and particularly the powerful military intelligence people, were fully fledged criminal entrepreneurs, making huge amounts of cash from drugs, people trafficking, prostitution and gambling. But, bizarrely, they also had recently received instructions from the highest level to branch out into quasi-legitimate businesses to help fund their activities and the regime itself. So, or so Delaney had read, military intelligence ran such things as a prawn farm and a printing business. Another division of the military had cornered the country's concrete industry. Another, trucking.

Often these activities involved foreign partners, often from China, but increasingly from other Asian nations and Australia. Western businesses, however, wanted more security, certainly more than was usual in this part of the world and mercenaries were sometimes hired by them to do guard duty, to escort shipments or to protect executives, usually with at least tacit consent from the generals.

Kellner's notebooks, after a very quick reading by Delaney, indicated he was involved in a complex deal to help protect an Australian-backed road project in the virtually lawless area around Mongla on the Chinese border. Warlord country.

Then things became very murky. Delaney would need to study the notebooks more slowly to get a real sense of what Kellner had in mind. But it appeared he also planned to use the big proceeds from his mercenary support deal with the Australians, and possibly with the Burmese generals themselves, to finance some other operation in Rangoon itself, possibly linked to Aung San Suu Kyi or to her NLD party.

*Idiot*, Delaney thought. *Surely Kellner was not going to involve himself in Burmese politics.* He began to understand why the Canadian intelligence service had started to get nervous, if they had got even the slightest hint that a Canadian citizen, let alone one of their own operatives, was even considering a foray into Burma's domestic affairs. Kellner had prepared a sort of timeline, a cryptic timeline, that showed something very complicated and very risky, was about to happen.

*Weeks 1 through 3 or 4: Mercs assemble, Mae Sot house. Briefings.*
*Week 5 (latest): Cross border ex Mae Sai. Payments. Truck ex SPDC.*

Delaney recognized SPDC as the acronym for the State Peace and Development Council, the name for the Burmese military government that had recently replaced the even more ominous former name, SLORC: the State Law and Order Restoration Council. By any appellation, still the same band of unpredictable, utterly corrupt and murderous thugs.

*Week 6: Mongla divert and sting. Pullout/payoffs. Fixed wing ex Kengtung. Regroup N. Rangoon.*
*Week 7: Payoffs, final. Gen. Thein facilitates trucks/logistics for next feint. Mercs wait Rangoon safe house.*
*Week 8: Thein out. Institute Plan B for the lady. Chopper ex Mae Sot. Return Mae Sot house.*

What on earth, Delaney asked himself, could this crazy planning really be about? Kellner's game could not have been more dangerous, no matter what the final objective, if he was even pondering a deal of some kind with an SPDC general. Surely, Delaney thought, Kellner could not have planned to bring a band of mercenaries right into Rangoon itself?

Delaney heard Ben calling him through the side window. He went over and looked out. Ben was standing in the yard, looking up through the gentle rain. His thin hair was plastered over his scalp and the big bald spot on top glistened.

"We better go soon, Frank," he called up.

"What's over in the barn?" Delaney asked.

"I will tell you as we go," Ben said.

"Just tell me what you've got. I'm almost done up here."

"Looks like a small barracks, Frank. For about 10 or 12 guys maybe. Bunk beds in three rooms upstairs. Really messy. Beer bottles all over the place. There's a sort of kitchen. Bad smells."

"No cars downstairs?"

"Two motorbikes. Trail bikes. That's all."

"Weapons?"

"No. Frank, I think we should go now," Ben said. "Please."

Delaney knew Ben was getting really frightened. He was a gentle man and the fracas on the balcony earlier would have left him very rattled.

"OK, Ben. I will just have a fast look in the last room and then we go. You wait in the car. If you see anything, give a quick honk on the horn and I will come out fast and we go. OK? Park so we can head out quick."

"I think you should come now, Frank. I have a bad feeling now."

"Five minutes," Delaney said. "Take this gun." He held the pistol out the window. "I will come down."

He raced down the stairs and out on the porch. The mercenary was lying prone now, on his side, exhausted and soaked. His blood-red eyes told the story however. The only thing that separated them from his murderous wrath was the thin line around his wrists and ankles. The soldier didn't move; he just watched Delaney go around the side of the house carrying his gun.

"I don't want that thing," Ben said.

"Take it, I've found another one upstairs. You'll never use it. Just show it to anyone who comes along. It will give us a few extra minutes maybe. I don't expect you to use it."

"I don't like guns, Frank. Even just holding them."

"Take it. I'll leave the safety on. Take it."

Ben very reluctantly took the gun, and held it stiffly by his side, pointing directly at the ground.

"Go on out to the car. I will be there in five minutes. Then we'll go straight back to the hotel and think things through, OK?"

"OK Frank. OK." Ben headed slowly off through the yard toward the driveway. Delaney ran back up on the porch and upstairs. He stopped outside the third room and tried the second key he had found. It opened the lock and he went inside.

This room was very different from the other two. It smelled of machine oil and wood. A big tarpaulin had been spread on the floor and three rectangular crates were laid out on top. On a rack like those found in clothing stores were hanging a few field uniforms in military camouflage.

There was a heavy blue flak jacket in the corner. A word on the front had been taped over. Delaney tore off the tape, revealing the word *PRESS*.

He went to one of the crates. There were no labels on any of them. The lids were loosely nailed shut. Even without a crowbar, Delaney was able to loosen the lid on the one he was examining and pull it up. Inside, AK-47 assault rifles, six of them, not new but in good condition and well oiled and polished. The same number of guns in the two other crates.

In a smaller wooden box, Delaney found ammunition, smoke bombs, stun grenades, flares, tear gas canisters and a launcher. Other gear lay here and there in boxes or in small piles. Handcuffs, batons, a few helmets, originally NATO or UN issue probably; some first aid kits, ropes and rigging. Enough gear for a heavy defence or minor assault. But against which enemy or to be directed at which target?

Delaney looked at his watch. He had spent almost an hour inside the house. Time to go. He left the room without bothering to close cases or lock the door. He ran into Kellner's room, grabbed the pistol from the desk and then ran down the stairs, through the kitchen and out onto the balcony. Then down to where the mercenary lay in the mud.

He squatted down, reached over and carefully pulled away the gag. The soldier immediately let loose a volley of curses and threats.

"You are dead, you're dead, you scumbag. I will kill you when I get clear. You're dead. Dead."

"Who are you working for? Kellner? Where's Kellner?"

"Fuck you. You're dead."

The mercenary redoubled his efforts to free himself of his bonds. Delaney pulled at the barrel of his pistol, cocking the mechanism and making it ready.

"You'd never use that, you faggot," the merc said.

"Only if I have to, friend," Delaney said. "Where is Nathan Kellner? I'm a friend of his from Montreal. He knows me. I'm looking for him. That's the only reason I'm here. I don't care what you guys are doing."

"I am going to make it my mission in life to kill you. I'll kill you slow. You're dead," the mercenary said.

Delaney looked at his watch and stood up. Conversation was not what the South African military man wanted at this stage.

Suddenly, from out at the main road, Delaney heard the sound of car horns. Several long blasts, followed by a much more feeble short blast from another car. Ben's car. Then two bursts of gunfire. One burst, almost certainly an automatic rifle, then another. Then silence.

"My Christ," Delaney said and started running for the driveway and the trees.

"You're dead, you're dead," the soldier shouted after him. "My buddies are back and you're dead. You're both dead."

After he left Delaney, Ben decided he would walk down the driveway instead of going through the trees. Eventually, he would have to come out to the road anyway, he thought, and into possible danger. So there was no use trying to prolong things by creeping through the trees. He walked slowly, enjoying in an odd way the quiet of the drive, as if it were an oasis of safety in some way.

He trudged slowly, carrying the pistol at his side and wishing he could be out of this now, back in the quiet of the hotel, sipping beers and talking quietly with Frank or, better still, sitting in his own crowded living room in Bangkok with his wife and children, sipping beers and talking quietly. Quiet was one of the things Ben valued most in life, despite the crazy job he had done for years with foreigners. Sometimes there had been bad times and even dangerous times. But he tried to avoid them now, more than he ever had.

*Getting older now*, he thought. *Driving for these guys is a job for a younger man, maybe.*

Songbirds were still in voice despite the rain. The birds stopped as he moved under their trees, and then started again as he passed on by. Ben had birds in a cage at home, small yellow and green finches that he and his son would feed together. He wished he could be there now, instead of in this difficulty in the rain.

His feet were soaking wet and his old leather sandals squeaked and squelched as he walked. When he got to the car, he put the gun on the passenger seat in the front. He walked farther out into the middle of the road and looked carefully south to where he and Frank would be heading very soon. Nothing. *We will get out of this*, he thought.

He backed his car out from where he had left it under the trees and stopped it, facing Mae Sot. He backed it down the road a little farther and then shut it off and left the driver's side door open. He wished he had some lunch. He wished he could be opening one of the nice lunches his wife always made for him before he left on a long drive. He wished he could open one of the fizzy orange drinks she always packed for him and sit there having a nice little picnic in his car, maybe with the radio on low. With no troubles. *Why have troubles?* he thought.

Suddenly he sat up very straight. He was sure he heard a car in the distance, maybe more than one. The noise grew louder fast, something coming. Now there was no doubt; at least two cars were coming fast toward him on the bad road.

Two grey vans swung into sight up ahead, slipping and slid-ing in the mud and gravel. Headlights on in the middle of the day. The driver of the first one must have spotted Ben's car because he gave a loud blast of the horn. The vans came closer and the lead driver leaned on his horn again, again, again.

*Maybe they want to come straight through*, Ben thought. *Maybe they are not going to Khun Nathan's at all.* He reached for the gun and put it on the dashboard. *Just let them know I have one, like Khun Frank said*, he thought. For some reason, he decided to sound his own horn. He wasn't clear even in his own mind why he did that. He started the engine and waited as two tough-look-ing men in American-style T-shirts got out of the front of the lead van, carrying rifles.

Ben reached for the pistol with his right hand, and then held the gun and steering wheel with that hand as he shifted gears with his left and looked back over his shoulder to reverse away from trouble.

"Gun!" one of the van men shouted.

The first burst of their gunfire smashed out Ben's new wind-shield and tore into his left shoulder and side. His pistol went off as his body stiffened involuntarily and slammed back against the seat. The second burst from a stranger's rifle ended his troubles forever, put him somewhere still and quiet forever.

Delaney ran straight toward the trees, not taking the driveway. The rain had made everything slick, slippery. Sweat and rain poured into his eyes. He brushed clumsily through undergrowth and vines, keeping away from the driveway but heading toward the entrance as best he could. He heard two cars powering up the driveway now, obviously slipping around in the mud but moving fast. He thought he glimpsed one of them through the trees before he hit the ground. A grey van.

He lay still, listening. In the distance, near the house, he heard shouting. Ahead, from where Ben had parked, he heard nothing. His heart pounded in his chest and he fought the panic that gripped him.

"Jesus Christ," he said quietly.

He stood up cautiously, dripping wet, covered in mud and leaves. No matter what his next step, no matter what he might find, he had no choice but to head to the road to find out what had happened to Ben.

Suddenly he heard shouts again. Then voices in the trees behind him. The mercenaries were coming back after him from the house. He began to run clumsily toward Ben's car. When he got to the edge of the woods, he stopped, looking out from the heavy shadow into the clear area at the start of the driveway.

Ben had parked the car at the side of the narrow road, almost blocking it, but about 25 metres past the driveway so that cars coming from Mae Sot could still turn in toward the house. He hadn't tried to hide his car. He had just moved it out of the way and positioned it so he could speed off down the road past the driveway when ready.

The windshield was shattered on the right-hand side. Ben's body was still upright behind the wheel but slumped back against the driver's seat. Head way back. His mouth was open. His chest and one shoulder a glistening mass of ruby arterial blood.

"Ben, Ben," Delaney shouted out as he ran for the car. "Ben."

A burst of gunfire kicked up mud and stones in front of Delaney's feet and he stopped running and turned, not even thinking of raising his own gun.

"Stop there or I'll kill you," shouted a tall black man with a West African accent. He pointed an AK-47 directly at Delaney. He was wearing jeans and a T-shirt stretched tight over his muscular shoulders and chest. Rain ran from his shaved head. He shook droplets from his eyes.

"Get rid of that pistol," he said.

Delaney dropped it on the ground.

"My driver," he said. His heart was pounding and grief was gripping his guts.

"Gone," the West African said. "He's gone. Move here toward me now."

Delaney instead moved toward the car, wanting a closer look at Ben. A burst of gunfire tore up earth in front of his feet.

"Last chance," the gunman said. "Move here toward me now or I'll kill you. You'll go where your driver's gone."

Delaney stopped where he was, turned to face the gunman. A group of four other men now emerged from the driveway, all running, all carrying assault rifles. All were wearing jeans and T-shirts; none in military fatigues.

"I got him, I've got him, no qualms," the West African said. "Under my control."

The small band of gunmen lowered their rifles and stood staring at Delaney in the rain.

"Check him out, Abbey," said one of them in a heavy Afrikaner South African accent. "Get his gun. I'll give you cover." He had spiky blond hair and wore one small loop earring. There was a small spiderweb tattoo on his neck, just below his left ear.

"OK, Stefan, you watch him good."

The black man walked warily toward Delaney as Stefan pulled the AK-47 expertly to his shoulder and sighted down the barrel. The three others who had run with him from the house stood by, guns cradled downward.

"You killed my driver," Delaney shouted, numb with grief and shock. "Why would you kill my driver?"

"Shut up, shut up," Abbey said. "What you got on you, man? You kneel now, we check you out."

He shoved Delaney to his knees, picked up the pistol from the road and put it on top of Ben's car.

"What else you got?"

"Nothing," Delaney said.

"I find another gun on you, I'll beat you good," Abbey said. "You got a knife?"

He shoved Delaney over into the road, pushed him flat on his face and kicked his legs apart with a foot. He began to pat him down, looking for weapons. Then he pulled Delaney's wallet out of his pocket and began looking through it as the others watched.

As he pulled out credit cards and papers and Thai and U.S. banknotes, Abbey called out to his colleagues who stood watching and waiting.

"Gold American Express card, Francis J. Delaney. Green Am Ex card, corporate. Francis J. Delaney." Abbey dropped both cards into the dirt. "Quebec driver's licence, looks like, all in French. Monsieur Francis Delaney. Canadian Red Cross Society blood donor's card, Francis Delaney, Blood type B Positive. That's good to know."

He pulled another card out.

"Fuck, man," Abbey said. "We got trouble here, my friends. This guy's a fucking reporter. International Federation of Journalists, Member in Good Standing, Frank Delaney, *The Montreal Tribune*. My sweet Jesus, we got a reporter here."

The others walked over to where Delaney lay in the dirt. Abbey pocketed the cash from Delaney's wallet, had a quick look through the rest of its contents and threw everything into Ben's car through the side window.

Stefan walked up to Delaney, put a stylish Reebok trainer on the back of his neck and pointed the AK at his cheek.

"What's your deal, reporter man?" he said.

"I'm a friend of Kellner's," Delaney said. "From Montreal."

"Who's Kellner?" Stefan said, grinding his shoe harder into Delaney's neck.

"You know damn well who Kellner is," Delaney said. "You're living in his damn house."

"Are we now?" Stefan said. "Well, maybe we are at that, reporter man. You seen your friend Kellner recently?"

"I'm looking for him."

"You're looking for him," Stefan said.

"For Jesus sake, Stefan," said one of the other mercs, a short Brit who looked like a weightlifter. "Let's get in out of the rain. Let's question this cunt inside somewhere instead."

"This be British weather, Clive. You used to this British weather," Abbey said.

"The hell I am," Clive said.

"OK, let's do this inside," Stefan said. "Clive's right. Why should we stand here getting soaked because some reporter man has come to see us? We'll let Bobby find out what's he's up to, inside. Bobby's not too happy with reporter man right now. You realize that, Francis J. Delaney, reporter man? Bobby tells me you hit him over the head with a metal chair. He is not the sort of man who likes that sort of thing. He's not used to that. He is going to have an attitude meeting with you, Francis J. We are all going to watch."

Stefan prodded Delaney with his gun barrel. "Up," he said.

"What about my driver?" Delaney said.

All five of the mercenaries laughed as one.

"That is a dead man in the car," Clive said. "He won't be needing anything."

"You can't just leave him there," Delaney said.

"We bury the dead. Usually," Abbey said. "We are civilized people. When the rain stops, we get civilized and bury the dead."

Stefan, the man in charge, said: "Tom, Sammy. One of you get a tarp over that car. Get a tarp from the barn."

"After the rain," said one of the mercs in an American accent. He was wearing a red baseball cap.

"Now, Tom," Stefan said.

The small group headed back down the driveway to Kellner house, Delaney going first. He took a last look back at Ben, sprawled backward against the seat of his car.

"That man dead," Abbey said.

# Chapter 10

When Delaney emerged from the driveway into the clear area in front of the house, Bobby was sitting on the porch steps, despite the rain. Inside the doorframe stood another mercenary, this one also tall, sporting an old-style, flat-top, military haircut. He wore wire-rimmed glasses, military issue.

Bobby now had small bandages on his head wounds. He spotted Delaney and let out a roar. He leapt up, rushed off the steps and tackled Delaney hard, sending both of them flying into the mud and gravel. The other soldiers formed a loose circle around them.

"Lucky we got a medic with us," Clive said. "Hey, Dima, come down out of there and watch that no one gets hurt."

The bespectacled soldier in the doorway moved out and down the stairs. His faded khaki T-shirt had Cyrillic writing on it and an elaborate military crest.

Bobby was sitting astride Delaney's chest, pummelling him with his fists. There was no real defence against an enraged attack like that. Delaney only tried to shield his face with his hands and forearms.

"Move your arms out of the way, you little faggot," Bobby shouted. He pulled Delaney's arms back and began slapping him in the face, slapping methodically back and forth.

He jumped up and started kicking Delaney in the side, legs and arms with his military boots. Delaney rolled around trying to protect himself, trying to protect his head and neck. Bobby stomped on Delaney's chest with a boot.

"Lie still, scumbag," he shouted.

"Don't kill him, Bobby," Stefan said.

"Why the fuck not?" Bobby said, pausing for breath. Delaney was bleeding from various cuts and almost unconscious in the dirt. "Why not?"

"We've got to talk to the cunt, that's why," Sammy said, another stocky Brit.

"Nothing to talk about. We don't need this guy," Bobby said, panting heavily. He delivered another kick to Delaney's ribcage.

"Don't kill him, Bobby," Stefan said. "That's enough."

"Payback time is over," Tom said.

"Fuck off, Tom. I'll tell you when payback's over," Bobby said.

"It's over," Stefan said. "Dima, see if you need to fix this guy up. Some of you guys help Dima put him in the barn."

A couple of mercenaries pulled Delaney to a sitting position. He was barely conscious. They half-carried, half-dragged him to the barn. The two vans were parked outside. The men pushed him into a sitting position in a space clearly used as a garage. Two motorbikes stood on their stands to one side.

Dima peered at Delaney through misted glasses, holding his head up with one hand and pulling an eyelid up with the thumb of the other hand.

"He's OK," Dima said in a heavy Russian accent. "He's not nearly dead yet."

Dima grabbed an old rag from a shelf and wiped blood and rain from Delaney's face. "You will live, my friend. You are not even nearly dead. You are a lucky man. Bobby would kill you if we let him."

The others stomped up a staircase. Through the haze of pain and shock, Delaney could hear them moving around on the wooden boards overhead. He heard the sound of bottles clinking, cupboards being opened and shut. Someone turned on a radio to a Thai music station. He heard cutlery and plates.

Dima the medic gave Delaney some water to drink from a bottle and pulled him into a corner to prop him up. Then he went back toward the main house. Delaney rested his head back against the garage wall, knees pulled up, forearms on knees. The room swam before him. He could not see clearly through one eye.

Dima came back, carrying a syringe. He pulled up Delaney's sleeve, wiped a spot expertly with a swab and jabbed him quickly with the needle. Instantly, Delaney's pain evaporated. He felt a warm glow and all was well. He was floating on a lovely gentle summer breeze. All was well. Then everything went warm and dark.

Delaney dreamed about Ben and about Natalia:

*Even the drug could not mask the pain he felt about how they had died, how they had died because they had been somewhere dangerous with him. As always, Natalia lay under a thin blanket of Quebec snow. Ben was partly covered in leaves and humid Asian earth. In the impossible logic of dreams they were in the same woods, in a climate that allowed for snow and tropical heat at the same time. The bodies lay still, not far from each other, and Delaney thought his heart might burst with grief and guilt. He called out wordlessly to them but they did not stir. I'm sorry, I'm sorry, I'm sorry, he said to them, over and over again. The words made no sound. He wanted them to hear. He wanted to bury them both properly, with proper gravestones and epitaphs and flowers. He looked in vain for a shovel, for caskets, for stones. But there was only the deep woods and the leaves on the ground and the heat and the silence and the snow. Even the drug could not mask his pain.*

When Delaney woke up it looked like morning. Brassy sunlight was streaming into a small window. He was lying on a bottom bunk bed, naked under a rough blanket. Somehow he had ended up on a bunk bed somewhere in the barn. Someone had taken off his wet clothes and put him into a bed.

He was dazed, groggy and incredibly stiff and sore. He lay looking up at the slats and mattress above him. He raised one hand to a series of small bandages that had been taped to the worst of the cuts on his face and head.

Someone said quietly: "The sleeper awakes." A South African accent.

Delaney turned stiffly on his side. Stefan was sitting on a lower bunk on the opposite side of the room, drinking coffee from a large mug.

"Dima always gives a very large shot when he's playing medic. The Russians don't play around when they're giving people needles," Stefan said.

Delaney said nothing, still too dazed to speak. He ached everywhere.

"You've slept almost 20 hours," Stefan said.

"What day is this?" Delaney managed to say.

"Thursday."

Delaney said nothing for a moment. Then he said: "Ben."

"We buried him yesterday afternoon," Stefan said, sipping coffee.

Delaney lay quiet.

"You guys are amateurs," Stefan said. "Your driver reached for a gun. Bad move. My man shot him."

Delaney closed his eyes.

"You better get up. We need to talk. Figure out what to do with you," Stefan said. He stood up and threw some camouflage pants and a black T-shirt on the bed. "Your clothes are finished. Soaked and wrecked. Wear these. I'll be back."

Stefan walked out of the room, carrying his coffee. He left

the door open. Delaney struggled slowly into the clothes, every muscle aching from the exertion of yesterday and the beating. His ribs were very sore. He drank some water from a bottle on a table, and then sat back down on the bed with his head spinning.

Stefan came back in with Dima. The medic looked him over briefly and pulled up one of Delaney's eyelids again.

"He's fine," Dima said.

Stefan and Dima sat on wooden chairs. Delaney sat with his back against the wall, knees up and bare feet on the blanket, watching them from his bottom bunk. He could hear voices from other rooms and from the yard outside. He smelled eggs and bacon cooking and suddenly felt very hungry.

"We figure that you are a friend of Kellner's," Stefan said eventually.

"I am a friend of Kellner's," Delaney said. "I told your guy that. Bobby."

"Why are you looking for him?" Stefan said. Dima sat watching the conversation as he might a slow tennis match. Not terribly interested but waiting for the game to heat up.

"I'm his friend. He's gone missing."

"Someone asked you to find him?"

"Yes, his editor. And his girlfriend."

"So you come all the way over here from Canada to try to find him."

"That's right."

"You're close friends."

"Yes. Pretty close. His editor asked me to come."

"You see Kellner a lot?"

"No. He lives in Bangkok, I live in Montreal."

Stefan paused, looked over at Dima, said nothing for a while.

"Do you know where Kellner is?" Delaney said.

"He's late," Dima said.

"Late?"

"Yes," Dima said.

"What do you think we are all doing up here?" Stefan asked. "Guys like us. What kind of people do you think we are?"

"Soldiers, obviously," Delaney said.

"Seven of us, here, at Kellner's place," Stefan said. "Two South Africans. One Nigerian guy, two Brits, a Yank and a Russian. All together in a nice little Thai farm, just visiting Kellner for a while. Right?"

"Mercenaries," Delaney said. "I don't care."

"Reporter man," Stefan said.

"You tell me Kellner's OK, I'm gone," Delaney said. "I will tell his girlfriend and his editor he's OK and that's that."

"Just like that," Stefan said. "And what about your driver? What would you tell his wife and family? And the police."

"I wouldn't tell the police," Delaney said.

Dima lit a cigarette. "You don't know where Kellner is?" he said.

"No," Delaney said.

"You know a man named Mordecai Cohen?" Stefan said.

"Yes. He's also a friend of Kellner's. Do you know him?"

"Cohen is worried about you," Stefan said.

"About me?"

"Yes. He thought you might get into some trouble on your trip up here. Reporter trouble."

"I didn't tell him I was coming up here," Delaney said.

"He said we should expect you. He is not so sure you are a friend of Kellner's. A real friend. That got us worried, as you can imagine. That made us cut short our little R&R trip yesterday to come back here to see what the hell you were up to."

Delaney's concentration was improving, but his body still ached badly. Cohen had some connection, too, it was clear now, with this band of soldiers. Almost certainly with Kellner's knowledge.

"Why wouldn't you tell Cohen you were coming up to Kellner's house?" Dima said.

"Because it was none of his business. He's an asshole, drugged out half the time. Unreliable."

"He's a friend of Kellner's too, no?" Dima said. "Why wouldn't you tell him where you were headed?"

"Because it's none of his business what I do. What Kellner does."

"But it's your business," Stefan said.

"Yes," Delaney said. "If someone asks me to make it my business."

"Reporter man," Stefan said, getting up. "You worry me."

"I can see that," Delaney said.

"Let's go and eat," Dima said.

They all went out to a sort of communal kitchen, Delaney walking slow and stiff. Still barefoot. Tom, the American, and Sammy, one of the two stocky Brits, were sitting at the long table, eating kids' breakfast cereal from large bowls. The package sat near them: Cocoa Puffs. They both looked up but said nothing as Delaney came in. This morning they were wearing fatigues and black combat boots.

Dima spooned out some scrambled eggs from a pot on the stove and took some bacon and sausage from a pan. He sliced bread and motioned for Delaney to sit and eat. Delaney ate quickly and hungrily. Dima and Stefan ate with him. No one spoke.

From outside he heard low voices in the yard. There was a sense of people killing time, waiting. Delaney knew that they must be waiting for Kellner or word from Kellner before embarking on something together.

Tom and Sammy got up to go, putting their bowls in a sink piled high with dirty dishes and glasses and cutlery. As they walked past, Tom said: "Lucky man."

Stefan and Dima lit cigarettes.

"We've got to figure out what to do with you," Stefan said eventually.

"Yes," Delaney said.

"Kellner would be upset with us if we killed you," Stefan said.

"Yes."

"If you are his friend."

"Even if I'm not. Kellner's not the type to just sit around while people he knows get shot."

"You're quite sure about that."

"Yes."

"Tell me then, reporter man. Tell me what you know. We know you were looking around in Kellner's room. Bobby tells us so. You might as well tell me straight what you know, because you're not going anywhere and maybe, maybe, you can persuade me what's best to do next."

Delaney told them most of what he had discovered upstairs in Kellner's house. He told them that he thought they were all about to go on some sort of mercenary assignment to help protect an Australian business project, probably construction, probably in Mongla.

He told them he could also see there was another plan, much less clear, to go into Rangoon, maybe after a big change in the first plan, maybe a double-cross of some sort. And he told them he could see some connection with Aung San Suu Kyi throughout Kellner's planning, throughout much of what he had discovered in Bangkok and now in Mae Sot.

"And what do you make of this Suu Kyi thing?" Stefan asked.

"Kellner was obsessed with her. I'm not sure why. I'm not sure what all that's about. Nothing probably."

Stefan and Dima looked at each other for a moment.

"It's about Rangoon," Stefan said eventually.

"I could see that in Kellner's notes, a bit of that," Delaney said. "But to do what in Rangoon? And why with you guys? Protecting Aussies up on the Chinese border, maybe, if the generals or the warlords agree and you make it worth their while. But Rangoon's a different game. For mercenaries."

Another long look between Stefan and Dima.

"You know what I think I'm going to do, Delaney?" Stefan said. "I think I'm going to tell you what exactly it is we're planning to do over in Rangoon. Then you can tell us what you think and why you think Kellner is late like he is. Where you think the man might be. I have worked with him before and he has never been late like this. Never."

"We've got to figure out what's happened to him," Dima said.

"Me too," Delaney said.

"For his editor and his girlfriend," Dima said.

"Yes."

"That sounds a little like bullshit to me," Dima said. "Reporter bullshit."

Another pause. Delaney knew they were nervous about telling him too much but he could see that they, like him, were stumped for a next move. They clearly thought that he in some way could help them move forward.

"Kellner is a strange one," Stefan said. "I know him. I like him. He's got balls. He's no soldier but he's got balls."

Delaney said nothing.

"We work together sometimes," Stefan said. "He's a deal-maker, a fixer. He doesn't mind a little risk. He likes a nice adventure sometimes. And he makes big money, sometimes. And we do too. And that little junkie friend of his, Cohen."

"This time, Kellner had something really big big big in his head," Dima said.

"It would take a lot of money just to pull off," Stefan said. "Trucks, chopper support, lots of gear, bribes for some of the generals, safe places to wait and regroup. Lots of money. But the Aussies had lots of money. They were going to make lots and they were ready to spend lots. So Kellner was going to rip them off. He was going to take lots of their money and get us all in position across the border and then he was going to use the Aussie money to do something else. Something big that they had no idea about. Something the generals had no idea about either. The generals were going to think we were setting up to help them out with one thing, in Rangoon, with the Aussie money, and we were going to pull off something else entirely."

"A robbery," Delaney said.

"*Nyet, nyet, nyet*," Dima said. "You watch too many videos."

"We are not robbers, Delaney," Stefan said. "Mercenaries are not usually robbers. We work for fees, very big fees. And we do the work because we don't give a shit, because we all like a big laugh."

"What is it then?" Delaney asked. "In Rangoon? What?"

"The lady," Dima said.

"Suu Kyi?"

"Right," Dima said.

"What about her?"

"We take her out," the Russian said with a smile.

"What, kill her?"

"No, no. Imbecile," Dima said. "You think Kellner would let us kill Suu Kyi? No, we take her out of Rangoon, out of Burma. Bring her here. To the nice room over in the house. Kellner has it all ready for her. Nice."

"You're crazy," Delaney said.

"Kellner's crazy. We get paid to have adventures," Stefan said.

"You are going to kidnap Aung San Suu Kyi," Delaney said.

"That's the plan," Stefan said.

"From Rangoon. Right out of her house in Rangoon."

"Correct."

"You're crazy," Delaney said. "You'd never get near the place."

"Oh, getting near the place isn't hard," Dima said. "Not when the generals think we are working for them on something else. Getting out with the lady is going to be a little hard. But with chopper support, it works."

"Helicopter support," Delaney said.

"Correct. We know lots of interesting guys."

"Suu Kyi's house is wide open, most of the time," Stefan said. "A couple of sentries at either end of the street, except on weekends, when she has her rallies. They don't expect her to go anywhere. She doesn't want to leave Burma. They don't need a lot of people there to keep her inside. They would never think someone would go in to take her out."

Delaney could not believe what he was hearing.

"This is Kellner's plan?" he said.

"Correct. And ours. The details, the tactical portion," Dima said.

"It's crazy. It can never work. People are going to get killed. Maybe Suu Kyi herself."

"We are professionals," Stefan said. "The very best that U.S. dollars can buy. We can get her out. And anyway we want people to think she has been kidnapped or killed. You see? We want people to be worried. Or Kellner does, anyway."

"Why would he want people to think she was dead? Or missing?" Delaney asked.

"Kellner said he would turn a martyr into a saint. He said when the people in her party find out she is dead, that maybe the generals have killed her or taken her away, they will go into the streets like they did in 1988. This time they will bring everything down," Dima said.

"You can't be serious," Delaney said.

"Kellner was serious," Stefan said. "So we're serious."

"You guys are going to try to start a revolution in Burma," Delaney said.

"Correct," Dima said. "The people go onto the streets. The generals crack down again like they did in '88 but this time the people are really, really angry. They think the lady has been killed or hurt. They think they will never see her again. The people will go out of their minds. Foreign governments will get upset. Other countries aren't going to let the generals crack down like they did last time. Everything will fall down. The regime will fall. They always fall when the people get angry enough. Iran, the Philippines. No one thought those governments would ever fall."

Stefan said: "Suu Kyi lives here for a while, in her nice little room. Kellner gets to help out his lady. He's a hero. He makes a martyr into a saint. Then, when everything is done inside Burma, we bring her back in. Presto. She reappears. She is alive, after all. Takes power. My, my, my. A happy ending."

"That is absolutely the craziest thing I have ever heard in my life," Delaney said. "It is dangerous, wild, too wild for words. It puts a very important world figure at grave risk. Hundreds of people are going to get killed if a new revolt starts. Thousands maybe. It's crazy."

Stefan and Dima smoked quietly.

"Suu Kyi will never agree to this," Delaney.

"She will not be given a choice," Dima said.

"You can't be serious," Delaney said. "The regime will kill you all. You'll all be arrested and end up in jail and executed."

"We don't think so," Stefan said.

Sometimes, when faced with an event or an idea so far-fetched, so utterly wild in its conception or execution, the only sensible response is silence. Delaney was dumbfounded. He sat staring at the two mercenaries, who calmly smoked their cigarettes and stared back.

They brought him back to the room where he had slept, and left him for a while. He sat back against the wall on the lower right-hand bunk. Through the doors of the other three rooms he had seen signs of soldiers' life. Duffle bags on more bunks, gear strewn around.

Delaney lay on his bed, thinking of Ben, and also, this morning of Natalia. And of Kate. And, for some reason, of O'Keefe, of Rawson, even of the old doorman in his apartment building in Montreal. Something in this dangerous situation made him think of everyone he knew, of snatches of conversations he had had or might one day have. His head ached and he slept again for a while.

When he awoke he heard voices, some of them raised, from outside. He got up stiffly, with no idea how long he had slept or what time of day it was. He looked out of the window into the yard. The mercenaries were gathered on the porch of the main house, sitting and standing, some smoking cigarettes, some drinking beer. He could hear the ones who were talking loud.

"No fucking way. No way, Stefan," Bobby was saying.

Delaney couldn't make out what Stefan and some of the others said in reply.

"Not that asshole. No," Bobby said.

It appeared the mercs were having a meeting of some kind, a discussion, probably about next steps and what to do with Delaney. He could hear only a little and he did not want to be seen at the window. He sat down again on his bunk and tried to decide what he could do next.

Escape would be almost impossible. He didn't even have shoes, let alone a weapon. And these people were professional soldiers, possibly professional killers. They had killed Ben and so they would not hesitate to kill Delaney too if necessary. The only thing saving him now, probably, was his connection with Kellner. If they believed him about that.

He thought, just for a moment, of trying to find a gun in the other rooms of the barn. Then he realized just how foolhardy that would be. One man, an amateur, with a pistol against seven professional soldiers with AK-47s. He let the idea drop.

There was nothing to do except wait. He would have to wait to see what fate they decided for him. It was a position he had rarely been in, allowing his fate to be decided by others. He believed, throughout his professional life as a journalist, that he had been in control most of the time. That decisions about his life and his safety and his future were his alone to make. Except for a very brief period of detention by some irregulars in Bosnia while he was covering the war there, he had never been anyone's prisoner.

Eventually the mercenaries' meeting ended. The voices stopped, or at least the arguing stopped. He went to the window again and saw most of the group sitting on the porch or the porch steps. Three of the others were coming toward the barn: Stefan and Dima, clearly the two leaders. And Abbey, the man who had shot Ben. Abbey was wearing a pistol in a shoulder holster over his camouflage T-shirt.

They climbed the barn stairs noisily and came into his room. There was not much space for three to stand. Delaney stayed where he was on the bed.

"We think you should come down to talk to the men," Stefan said.

Delaney said nothing.

"Before you come, Abbey has something he wants to say to you," Stefan said. "Abbey?"

The big Nigerian looked uncomfortable, almost angry.

"If you be a friend of Kellner, man, I am sorry I killed your driver," he said. "The man went for his gun."

"That man would never go for any gun," Delaney said. "He never wanted to carry a gun. I told him to bring it with him to the car just for show. He would never use a gun."

"He picked it up and I shot him," Abbey said.

Delaney said nothing.

"If you are going to be with us, we have to clear this thing up," Stefan said.

"I am not going to be with you," Delaney said.

"Yes, we think you are," Dima said.

"I am not going to be with you guys," Delaney said, knowing as he spoke how ridiculous the statement was. If they wanted him to stay, he had no choice whatsoever.

"Come on down to the yard with us," Dima said. Abbey looked distinctly unhappy as he headed back downstairs.

They brought Delaney over to the main house. He stood in the yard with his three escorts while the others sat or stood on the porch or the stairs. The scene had the look and feel of a people's court, some sort of bush tribunal.

"We've decided you will come in to Burma with us," Stefan said. "We took a vote and you're coming in."

"Five to two," Bobby said darkly, spitting off the balcony. "Not unanimous."

"Easy Bobby," Clive said.

"This scumbag's going to be trouble. We're going to have trouble with this piece of shit all the way down the line," Bobby said.

"Easy," Clive said.

"It was a group decision," Stefan said to Delaney. "So you're coming. When we find Kellner, he can tell us really what's going on with you. If you're his mate, then we'll fix something up. If not, we decide what to do at that stage."

"What's the point of bringing me into Burma on some kind of wild operation like this?" Delaney said.

"Exactly my point," Bobby said.

"You got no choice, dickhead," Sammy said to Delaney.

"Too right," Clive said.

"We cannot leave you here," Dima said.

"And we need a witness," Tom said.

"A witness?" Delaney said.

"Yeah," said Tom. "We're making history. We're liberating Aung San Suu Kyi. We're cool, we're heroes. We need a witness. A scribe. You get us on the cover of *Newsweek*."

Tom struck a pose for an imagined photographer. Sammy and Clive laughed. Bobby, Abbey, Stefan and Dima did not.

"This is getting crazier by the minute," Delaney said. "You're all going to get killed or arrested. Lots of people are going to get killed."

"You too, then," Tom said. "You go out like a hero. If not, you've got a hell of a story."

"I don't want this story. I don't want anything to do with this," Delaney said.

"You're in," Stefan said. "For a while. At least until we find Kellner."

"And how are you going to find Kellner?" Delaney said. "This is the only place he would be."

"Something's come up. He's late," Dima said. "He'll probably meet us on the Burma side. He knows where. Upcountry or in Rangoon."

"We're too far along in this operation to let it drop now," Stefan said.

"Kellner could be dead," Delaney said. "The Burmese could have got wind of this and killed him already."

"Who would have told them?" Stefan asked.

"I don't know. Anyone along the way. Cohen maybe."

"Not Cohen," Stefan said. "He's Kellner's man."

"Maybe," Bobby said.

"Kellner could be dead," Delaney said again.

"Then you in deep shit, man," Abbey said.

Delaney found himself eating lunch in an isolated Thai barn with a band of mercenaries about to cross into Burma to double-cross an Australian business consortium and an array of Burmese generals, all with a view to kidnapping one of the world's most prominent democracy advocates.

Sammy and Clive cooked. Steaks sizzled in iron pans, and potatoes and fried onions. Cartons of beer were opened. The lunch took on a somewhat festive air. Only Bobby, Abbey and Delaney put a damper on proceedings. Delaney ate, however, hungry again as he recuperated from his ordeal. Knowing also that he might need the strength in the days ahead.

"The condemned man ate a hearty meal," Tom said, punching Delaney on the shoulder. "Eat up good."

"Who knows what kind of rubbish we'll get to eat over on the other side," Clive said.

Afterward, Dima and Stefan went back with Delaney to the room it seemed he had now been assigned. Stefan cleared a few of his own things off the opposite bunk and moved them out. Delaney was to be alone, it appeared.

"When are we going to go?" he asked.

"Soon," Dima said. "Tomorrow night, maybe Saturday. Sunday latest. We go soon. Rest up. It is a long drive."

He threw a book on Delaney's bunk. *Letters from Burma* by Suu Kyi. "Something for you to pass the time," he said.

The mercenaries had a party that night. Perhaps they had one every night. Delaney was not invited. It started in the kitchen late in the afternoon. Delaney had read for a while and slept again. Loud voices and the clink of beer bottles woke him.

As the light faded, the party spilled out of the kitchen into the yard. The soldiers did not use the main house at all, it seemed. Someone put a tape in a cassette player in one of the vans and turned it up loud. Rolling Stones. Through the window, Delaney heard shouts, curses, laughter, snatches of increasingly drunken conversation.

Eventually, after dark, he heard a van engine start up. He went to the window of his room and looked down into the yard. Six of the mercenaries piled into the van, carrying beer bottles. They were all in civilian clothes now. Dima, it appeared, was to stay. He stood in the yard watching his comrades get ready to go.

"No women back here after," Dima called out.

"Absolutely not," Stefan called from inside the van, drunk too, despite being leader of the group. "These men are under my command."

"Bullshit," Sammy shouted.

Abbey was driving. He pulled around in the yard and slowly headed out and down the driveway. The headlights of the van cut long beams in the steamy tropical night. Delaney saw the beams bounce and glance through the trees and then disappear.

Dima stood watching them go. Then he walked over to the porch of the main house and sat outside on a metal chair near the table, under a light. An AK-47 was propped up near the doorway. A pistol lay on the table, along with beer bottles and a book. Sentry duty.

Delaney stood watching from the upstairs window of the barn. Dima looked up, saw him and raised a beer bottle in salute.

"Don't even think about it, my friend," he called out to the prisoner across the silent yard. "Don't even think about it. You would not get three metres out of that doorway."

Delaney said nothing. He turned and went back to his bunk and started reading a book by the woman they were going to try to kidnap, the woman who obsessed Kellner, the woman who now would obsess them all.

# PART 5
## Mongla and Rangoon

# Chapter 11

Delaney had fallen asleep soothed by the gentle words of Aung San Suu Kyi in her letters from captivity. He awoke to the sound of six drunken mercenaries whooping and swearing and slamming doors.

He had no idea how late it was because they had not given him back his watch, but he sensed from the look of the night sky outside his window that it was not long before dawn. It took the soldiers a long time to settle, and he lay in his bunk listening and waiting for morning to come. He tried unsuccessfully to not think of Ben Yong.

Delaney did not sleep again. Eventually, as the sun rose above the trees, Dima came into his room, carrying a set of car keys.

"Let's go," Dima said. "We've got to get your things out of your hotel. We pull out tonight. When these other guys sober up."

There was no noise from the other rooms. Delaney pulled himself upright.

"Where will you go?" he said.

"Where will *we* go, you mean," Dima said. "Burma. All of us. Like we told you."

"You're crazy."

"Like we told you."

197

Delaney got dressed. Dima went into the room next door and roused Tom, the American. He looked very bad as he came out, tucking a crumpled T-shirt into his jeans.

"Where we going, Dima? I'm messed up," Tom said. "I need a beer."

"We're going to this man's hotel. You go in with him and play U.S.A. tourist while he gets his things and his driver's things. I watch from outside."

Dima turned to Delaney. "We don't want those hotel people to start worrying about you," he said.

"They probably already are," Delaney said.

"Not in Thailand. Not yet," Tom said. "They probably figure you got lucky with one of the local ladies of the night." He belched and scratched his armpit.

As they went out, Tom stopped in the kitchen and came out with some sweet rolls. He tossed one to Delaney and one to Dima and they went out into the morning air. They stood eating silently before climbing into one of the vans.

As they bounced down the rutted driveway, Delaney said suddenly: "I want to see where you buried my driver."

"No way," Tom said. "What's the point?"

"He was my driver. I've known him for years," Delaney said.

"He's dead, that's it, that's all," Tom said.

"I want to see where you put him," Delaney said.

"In the ground, where we'll all end up. No big deal."

Dima drove in silence. He looked over at Delaney, then at Tom.

"Two minutes," he said.

"For Christ's sake, Dima," Tom said.

Dima drove another few metres and stopped the van. He gestured into the trees to their left.

"In there," he said. "I'll go with you."

He and Delaney got out. Tom glowered in a rear seat, and then got out as well, carrying a 9-millimetre Glock.

"He's not going to try anything, Tom, put that away," Dima said.

"No fucking way. He's going to get all blubbery and try to make a run for it. You watch," Tom said.

Delaney said nothing. Dima led him a short way into the trees, with Tom walking a few paces behind them.

"There," Dima said, taking off his wire spectacles and polishing them with the end of his shirt. "Two minutes."

Delaney saw a mound of fresh red earth in a tiny clear area just ahead. He walked slowly forward and stood there in silence with his back to the mercenaries. Insects and bright yellow butterflies swooped around. Tears came, for the first time since Ben was shot.

Delaney stood silently for a while, and then his grief gave way to anger. He swung around and shouted at his captors: "There's not even a marker. He's a human being for Christ's sake and you killed him."

Tom came round from behind Dima and pointed his pistol at Delaney's chest.

"Easy buddy," Tom said. "Take it easy."

Dima watched Delaney calmly, saying nothing.

"I told you he'd freak out, Dima. I told you he'd freak out," Tom said.

Delaney turned back to the grave.

"Let's go," Dima said.

"Yeah, let's get going," Tom said.

Delaney stood a few moments more by his old friend's grave and then turned to walk silently back to the van. They drove all the way to Mae Sot without a word exchanged. Tom sat in the last row of seats, his pistol laid out beside him.

Dima pulled over in front of the Mae Thep Guest House and turned off the engine.

"Let's not make this complicated, OK?" he said to Delaney. "You go inside, you explain to the people there that you are checking out and that you want your driver's things as well. Tell them you're off on a trek. Pay the bill in cash and come out." He threw a wad of Thai *baht* onto Delaney's lap. "Keep it simple. Tom is nervous today."

Tom pulled his T-shirt out of his jeans and tucked his gun into the back waistband. "Very nervous and very pissed off with your little display back there, and very, very hung over," he said to Delaney.

They climbed out and went up onto the balcony and inside. The young Thai man at the front desk gave them both a wai and smiled.

"I'm checking out of Room 14," Delaney said. "My friend who was in 15 is not here but I will pay for his room and take his things too."

The desk clerk looked troubled about this idea.

"Where your friend is now?" he asked. "He can come for his own things later maybe."

"He's on another tour," Tom said, gesturing over his shoulder at the van waiting outside. "We'll meet up with him after."

The clerk still looked dubious, but his Thai politesse and experience with the unpredictable ways of Western tourists prevailed. He reached for two keys from a row of hooks behind him, and Tom and Delaney went upstairs to the rooms.

"Don't start blubbering when you go into your guy's room, OK Delaney?" Tom said. "Just get his shit and your shit and we go, all right?"

Delaney said nothing. He tossed his few things into the small bag that he had left in his room, and found his passport and some other papers where he had hidden them. When he went into Ben's room, the emotions were intense and he fought tears. Ben had placed a small framed photo of his wife and two children on the bedside table. Delaney looked silently at it for a few moments before putting it into Ben's bag.

"Easy, easy," Tom said.

Delaney said nothing. He went downstairs, paid both room bills and walked back out with Tom to the van. Dima slid open the rear door, as a tour operator should. The desk clerk watched them from the balcony.

"Well done, Delaney," Dima said.

"Very professional," Tom said.

On the ride back, Delaney fought grief and regret. But he did not fight the anger. That went into a special place he had developed over the years, for possible use later.

The plan was for them to drive by night in two vans from Mae Sot all the way to Mae Sai, the northernmost town in Thailand, at the gateway to the Golden Triangle, and then cross over into Burma at Tachilek. Apparently, there was to be a rendezvous with the Burmese military, or some faction of the Burmese military, there. This much Delaney learned from snatches of conversation as the mercenaries, late that afternoon, roused themselves and prepared for what would be a drive of at least 11 hours.

They did not take Delaney into their confidence, nor did they appear to be trying to hide much from him. One of the vans was to tow a covered trailer onto which they loaded their small but impressive cache of weapons and equipment. How they intended to get that gear all the way up Highway One, where police checkpoints were common, Delaney had no clue.

By nightfall they were ready. Delaney could see, as he watched them from the window of his room, that despite their carousing and their lack of formality amongst themselves, these were well-trained and experienced soldiers. They moved efficiently around, preparing the vans, securing equipment, loading supplies for the trip. Dima and Stefan, however, were clearly in charge.

They pulled out after Stefan had made a slow final walka-round of the compound, making sure doors were locked and everything was in order. Bobby had roared off earlier on one of the trail bikes, returning with a wiry, unsmiling Thai man in his thirties. This was to be the watchman, apparently. He was assigned a sleeping place on a cot on the open area of the barn, with the motorbikes. Bobby showed him how to start the bikes, and where the electrical switches were and a small fridge in the barn, and then led him to the table on the balcony with the radio.

Again, in the vans, there was military discipline and no complaints about the long journey ahead or the lack of comfort. Delaney was in the lead van, placed in the back row of seats by himself. He rode with Dima, who drove, and the two British mercenaries, Clive and Sam. Stefan drove the other vehicle, with Tom, and with Bobby and Abbey, the two men who had argued most strenuously against Delaney being allowed to come along.

Just outside Tak where Route 105 joins Highway One, the little convoy slowed and then stopped at a roadside restaurant and bar. A middle-aged Thai in a brown police uniform came out of the shadows of the parking lot and climbed in beside Dima, who shook his hand. The policeman looked like a veteran of much trouble.

"Welcome, Sergeant," Dima said. "We thank you for this."

The policeman did not smile. "Long way, long way tonight. Many stops for us, many police stops. Let's go, let's go."

"Sergeant, we have the magic formula for that," Dima said, turning to smile at Clive and Sam, "Magic baht." Dima held up an enormous bound brick of local currency and the three mercenaries laughed.

"I hope this is enough," the unsmiling policeman said. "We need very much baht tonight."

"And much baht for you tonight too, Sergeant," Clive said. "Much, much baht for you."

For most of the way, Dima drove. He did not seem to get tired or need sleep at all. About halfway, Sam drove for a couple of hours, but even then Dima did not sleep. Clive dozed most of the way, as did Sam when he was not driving. Delaney tried to sleep when he could, bracing himself against the constant swaying and the incessant bumps. In the other van, it was the same. Dozing mercenaries, with Stefan driving most of the way.

Their rented personal policeman proved useful. Half a dozen times on the narrow highway, they were stopped at checkpoints. Each time, their policeman got out of the van and spoke for a long time in Thai to the local officers. Money was exchanged, as predicted. At one checkpoint, a baby-faced policeman seemed to insist on seeing what was in the trailer pulled by the rear van. There was a long discussion in Thai, watched warily by Stefan and the three other soldiers in his vehicle who were instantly wide awake and alert.

"Come on Sergeant, come on now," Clive said softly as he watched the scene through the window of the first van. "Show us you're worth it, my lovely."

Eventually, after much debate and much gesticulation and much baht, the baby-faced cop waved them on, profoundly unhappy either with the situation, or with his personal takings, or both.

They stopped for rice and dumplings at a roadhouse outside Lampang that was frequented by truckers and local whores. A teenager with wild eyes came up to their table, selling amphetamine.

"You want *yaa baa*? Drive all night, no sleep. Be with woman all night maybe," he said.

"Piss off, kid," Bobby said.

"Thai stick maybe?" the kid said.

Their policeman said something rough in Thai and the dealer fled.

They pulled into Mae Sai precisely at 8 a.m. That was clear because in most provincial towns in Thailand all activity ceases at 8 a.m. while the national anthem plays at full volume on dozens of scratchy loudspeakers and radios. Dima and Stefan stopped the vans and waited for this brief outburst of national pride to subside.

"Jesus Christ," Clive said.

Highway One, a fairly good road in this part of Thailand, ends abruptly in Mae Sai. It gives way to a vast, dust-choked open space that looks like a chaotic, slowly shifting parking lot for big trucks, vans, cars, motorized rickshaws and motorcycles of all sizes. Cheap restaurants and bars and guest houses surround the area.

But all attention focuses on a narrow two-lane bridge over a muddy tributary of the Mekong. Halfway across this bridge, past Thai checkpoints, is a set of forbidding iron gates, with the words "Welcome to Myanmar" in English, Burmese and Thai. Beyond that, past the Burmese checkpoints and visible through a copse of tall trees, is the tense little garrison town of Tachilek.

Their policeman directed them to a guest house on the edge of Mae Sai, with parking for the vans out back under high trees. They checked in to rest for the day. It was to be another night journey that night, it seemed. Dima spoke quietly in the lobby to their policeman, both of them looking over at Delaney who was sitting, bone weary, in a rattan armchair.

The policeman made a call at the desk and about 15 minutes later two young uniformed officers arrived and saluted him. He gestured toward Delaney and they looked over at him suspiciously.

"These men are going to make sure you don't get delusions," Dima said. "They will be outside your door while you rest."

Delaney lay down immediately after his door was closed. He lay flat on his back in his clothes and tried to ignore the sensation of swaying after the long drive. For him, the journey had been 12 hours of troubled reverie—half-sleep, half-nightmarish assaults of sorrow, guilt and regret about Ben Yong. Into that mix were folded the clearly remembered feelings Delaney had had for all the years after Natalia was killed, the same gut-wrenching certainty that his bad judgment had cost someone else's life.

He slept eventually. When he woke up, the light was already changing. It was late afternoon. He stripped off his dusty, foul-smelling clothes and took a long shower. While the water ran over him he thought of escape, but immediately realized such thoughts were futile—delusions, just as Dima had said. He had no money, no cards, not even his passport; the only thing he still had with him was his international press ID.

He would have to see this situation through, no matter how insane and dangerous it proved to be. And, he realized, there was still an element of reporter's curiosity as to where such an unlikely scheme as this might eventually lead.

When he opened the door to his room, the two young Thai policemen got up immediately from their chairs. They spoke no English at all, and so could not understand his questions about where the others might be. Stefan, however, came out of another room down the hall and saw Delaney in his doorway.

"Food now," Stefan said. "Come on with me." The policemen understood Stefan's sign language and let Delaney pass.

They joined the others already in the guest house dining room. Dima had a map spread out on a table. All except Dima were drinking Singha beers out of big, sweating bottles. A teenaged waitress was bringing plates of noodles, chicken, peppers, rice.

"Reporter man," Abbey said, raising his bottle.

"Asshole man," Bobby said. "Trouble man."

Delaney sat with Dima and Stefan. At the other table, the rest of the men hove into their plates of food.

Delaney sat looking directly at the Russian and South African mercenaries before him. They sat quietly looking back.

"Question?" Dima said.

Stefan laughed, ordered a beer.

"You can't be serious about going ahead with this," Delaney

said. "You're going to bring weapons into Burma, and go ahead with this crazy plan?"

"We have powerful friends on the other side. And some rich Aussies just waiting to get ripped off," Stefan said.

"And a beautiful lady to rescue," Dima said. "Like in a fairy tale."

"Why would they let you?" Delaney said. "Why would they let you do anything? Why would the generals let you bring arms into the country? Why would you bother anyway? The place is lousy with guns. You could get anything you want over there."

"Questions, questions. Always questions," Dima said, smiling.

"Nobody does anything over there without a general saying it is OK," Stefan said.

"Why would it be OK?" Delaney said.

"Which part?" Stefan said

"Any part."

"The Australian part is good for business," Dima said. "Or so the Australians think and also our military friends over there. The Australians think they are buying independent profession- al protection for their compound and their little bungalows and their wives if they are stupid enough to bring them into Burma. They get to build their next casino in Mongla and the road that will lead Chinese tourists to it and they'll all sleep well think- ing they have professional guys like us hanging around at night with their own weapons and nobody to answer to but Australians."

"The generals," Stefan said, "or our generals anyway, think it's worthwhile to show the Aussies we can bring our own gear into the country, that we don't need anybody else to do our work. They think the more secure the Western moneymen believe they are, the better it is for business. The generals also find it amusing, an amusing little experiment, to see if we can bring our gear all the way up through Thailand and into Tachilek. They like to know that these things can be done."

"They've got a giant border with China to bring AK-47s across, anytime they want," Delaney said.

"It's an experiment; they like experiments. Some of the generals like to have little private experiments going on all the time, just to keep their options open. But it is mainly a show for the Australians," Dima said. "Kellner's idea, actually. Everybody liked it."

"And now Kellner is almost certainly dead," Delaney said.

"Maybe," said Stefan. "On the other hand, we may see him tomorrow in Tachilek, or Kengtung or Mongla. He's a good operator."

"And at Mongla, what happens?" Delaney said.

"We make our Aussies happy, we make them feel secure," Stefan said. "We take their five-hundred-thousand-U.S.-dollar retainer and we promise them, promise, promise, that we are at their service. Then we take the money and spend some of it on other expensive fun and games in Rangoon instead."

"And which general is going to let you do that?" Delaney said.

"The one who thinks it is actually money to back his own nice little Rangoon project, another one," Dima said. "You see, Delaney, all of these generals have their own little projects, their own little business deals. They are businessmen. They have their own bits of turf; they have their own factions. They need to have their own support systems, foreign ones and local ones. They put on little shows for each other, little demonstrations of their power or independence or how they have backing from here and backing from there. But by the time this particular general and his people find they have been ripped off too, by our little band of foreign fun seekers, we are all on a chopper heading back to Kellner's farm with the lovely Madame Suu Kyi aboard."

"They are going to kill you all," Delaney said.

"And you too, I suppose. Correct?" Dima said.

Much of the two-way traffic across the bridge linking Mae Sai to Tachilek is pedestrian: Burmese fruit-and-vegetable hawkers walking in to Thailand to sell their wares at little stalls for the day; young Thai men and an assortment of cripples, beggars and a very few backpackers going the other way. Some big trucks occasionally lumber slowly across in either direction.

The mercenaries had loaded their trailer cargo of gun crates and other equipment onto an aging Bedford truck, covered with a tarpaulin at back. The vans were left parked and locked behind the hotel. At dusk, everyone piled into the back of the Bedford as well, leaving just Dima and the Thai police sergeant in front. At the last Thai checkpoint before the bridge, the sergeant disappeared inside with a small sports bag. Delaney and some of the others watched through a flap in the truck's tarp.

After what seemed a long time, the policeman emerged from the guards' hut looking tense and hot. He stood with the border police, smoking a final cigarette and joining his countrymen in a ritual of spitting and smiling. Eventually there were wais all around, handshakes, a bit of backslapping and it was over. The Thai police sergeant leaned inside the cab and said to Dima: "You go."

Dima went. With a crashing of gears he moved the old Bedford forward while their policeman stood with the guards at the border post and watched. Dima drove slowly through the iron gates, under the "Welcome to Myanmar" sign, and into no-man's land. He pulled up at yet another guards' hut, this one staffed by cheerless Burmese soldiers who looked like they would do anything that night for a bit of trouble to pass the time away.

But parked next to this hut was a small black Mercedes 190, not new but immaculately waxed and aging gracefully. Small sets of black Venetian blinds had been installed in the back and side-rear windows. Delaney had seen many cars like this in his career. Their cargo was always power.

Out of the back of this vehicle stepped a Burmese general

straight out of Central Casting, sporting the requisite wide-brimmed officer's cap covered in scrambled egg embroidery and other heavy insignia. He was in his mid-fifties. On his chest were rows of tiny square decoration patches, more insignia, more trappings of power. The aviator sunglasses, not at all required in the failing light, were standard issue as well. On a small rectangular patch on his chest, in black letters, were also the words *Kyaw Thein*.

The man, Delaney could see immediately, was to be their guide and protector for the next stage of this elaborate and increasingly dangerous game.

Dima climbed out of the cab, and the rest got out of the back of the truck. The border guards and the Mercedes driver watched impassively, well accustomed it seemed to mysterious assignations at the border at nightfall. "General Thein, good day to you, sir," Dima said.

General Thein smiled and shook Dima's hand, "Welcome to Myanmar." He looked over at the rest of the group and nodded. "Welcome to Myanmar. You have arrived well and with your cargo intact," he chuckled happily.

"Yes, intact. All is well," Dima said.

"Good. We go to Kengtung now, tonight. I apologize in advance for the quality of the road. It will take six or seven hours for 150 kilometres, I am afraid. But my government is seeing to road works, and other public works in this region, as quickly as we possibly can, as you all know. With some help from our foreign investor friends." This prompted more throaty chuckles from the general as he pondered ironies.

"And our friend, Kellner?" Dima asked. "Is he well?"

"Ah, Kellner," the general said. "Have you no news of him? We had expected to see our good friend by now. Perhaps to arrive with you."

"No, General. No news."

General Thein did not look particularly troubled by this.

"Perhaps Kellner will join us in Mongla then," he said. "There is a newly arrived troupe of Russian exotic dancers there, at the Myanmar Royal Casino. Perhaps we will find him drinking vodka in his usual spot in the front row."

Dima rode in the Mercedes with General Thein. A Burmese soldier drove the Bedford. It was to be another bone-crushing nighttime journey on winding roads. They travelled through dense forest, interspersed with tiny villages of thatched houses on stilts, which Delaney could just make out as they passed in moonlight. He wedged himself between a spare tire and a wall of the truck, but rest was impossible.

"This is one shit detail," Tom said eventually as they lurched along, the only complaint Delaney had heard in two days. The others, wedged as best they could into various corners of the truck and its load, said nothing.

Well before sunrise, they pulled into Kengtung. Delaney knew little about the place, except that it was the last Burmese town of any significance before travellers entered the remote region of northeastern Burma that had been virtually handed over by the Burmese dictatorship to a powerful ethnic drug warlord, Lin Mingxian, on mutually lucrative terms.

They passed Kengtung's police station, a forbidding place except for the strings of sparkling fairy lights for some unknown reason slung through the barbed wire atop the compound walls. The town centre was a maze of narrow winding streets full of traditional shop houses with tiled roofs and dark wooden balconies. Eventually, their vehicles stopped outside a giant concrete-rendered building with a sign in Burmese and English identifying it as the Kengtung New Hotel. Two military policemen standing directly in the doorway saluted when General Thein emerged from his Mercedes, a car now far less grand with a thick coating of dust and mud.

"This is a government hotel. No problems here. Rest now,"

General Thein said to the mercenaries as they unfolded themselves from the back of the Bedford. If he removed his sunglasses, Delaney imagined the general would look as tired as anyone
else. "Talk is for tomorrow," Thein said.

There was much talk the next day, most coming from General
Thein, who was holding court at midday in the cavernous hotel
dining room when Delaney came down, accompanied by Tom. It
appeared Tom was to be his minder for this part of the trip.

Thein was in full uniform again, but now without sunglasses. Delaney saw that he was even tougher-looking without
them. This was a career military man, someone who had nego-
tiated his way through the dangerous shoals of the Burmese
military to reach his fifties and a position from which he could
direct his own little patch of Burmese turf. Delaney wondered
which of the military's many lucrative business ventures had
been awarded to him. This close to Wa State, the Mongla
casino scene and Lin Mingxian's notorious private militia,
Delaney thought, it could be any combination of timber
concessions, gems, drugs, gambling proceeds, people smuggling
and prostitution.

Thein was seated with Dima and Stefan. The others, and
Delaney, sat at a table nearby, listening as they ate.

"The Australians are fools," General Thein said. "Kellner will
have told you this. They have too much money for their mental
capacities, and they have business ideas that are fine for Sydney
and Melbourne and Perth but that do not apply here. They prefer not to know the whole story of how business gets done in
Burma, but that is fine for us. For me and for my usual business
associates.

"They are involved in building another casino in Mongla.
The Myanmar Royal is already doing very well. Other Australians
have a partnership with the Chinese for this, and it is in Lin
Mingxian's region and it is doing very well. So this group wants to

do the same thing. They are at the stage of road building, and the foundations for the casino are going in. But they are nervous, they are nervous in my country, so you are here to help them and make them calm and make them feel safe and happy.

"I will not go with you tomorrow," Thein said. "This is not how things are done in the northeast. That is Lin's region; his people are in charge. But he knows and the Australians know that my associates are in this game, always in such games."

Stefan said: "They are not going to be calm and happy when they find out that their money for security gets them nothing much at all."

General Thein looked over at Stefan. "That reaction has been anticipated. It will in the end be good for these Australians to realize exactly how things must be done here. It will be an expensive lesson for them and we, my side and Lin's, will make sure they think they have what they need after this unfortunate mistake on their part. Of course, we will promise to pursue you, and retrieve the money. Some of it. Of course."

The general practised his malevolent chuckling again and drank milky tea from a gold-rimmed china cup.

The afternoon was for resting. Delaney was given reasonable room to manoeuvre, if only because everyone knew escape in this part of the world would simply bring him to dense jungle or into the custody of the Thai military, who were everywhere. He sat in the hotel lobby for a time, processing all that had happened since he set off for Mae Sot with Ben.

It was now Monday. He'd been away from Montreal for two weeks. He wondered how long it would be before Rawson realized something had gone badly wrong. He wondered what Rawson and Company could be expected to do to help. He realized, however, that the correct answer to that, in Burma, was nothing at all.

The mercenaries played billiards in a games room and drank beer by a filthy-looking swimming pool for their afternoon of rest and recreation. Dima had disappeared—the quiet man of the squad. General Thein had gone off somewhere in his car. There didn't appear to be any other guests in the establishment at all, despite dozens of staff and a small group of pubescent prostitutes flicking through Thai movie magazines in the bar.

Stefan came over to where Delaney was sitting.

"The soldiers' life," he said, sitting down in a tattered leather chair. "Not all action. Not all the time."

Delaney would have preferred to be left alone. The grief for Ben Yong was bad today.

"No questions for us today, reporter man?" Stefan said.

"I get the picture," Delaney said.

"It's a good story, no?" Stefan said, and let go a sharp burst of laughter. "You'll get a good story out of this. Put us on the cover of *Newsweek*, like Tom says."

"I have to make it back to write it," Delaney said.

"Start writing now, my friend. Make a start while you still can," Stefan said, laughing again. "Someone will find the papers on your body, maybe. Send them to *Newsweek*. Bingo, you're famous. We're all famous."

"Dead and famous."

"We all agree, Delaney, that alive and famous is better. Every mercenary agrees with that."

Stefan called out to Clive and Sam, who were heading in from the pool to the bar. "Hey, my brothers. Delaney the reporter man and I are talking philosophy here. What's better? Alive and famous, or dead and famous? What do you prefer?"

"Right now, I prefer a cold beer and one of those tight little schoolgirls over there in the corner," Clive said.

"You got it," Sam said. "In about an hour from now I'll already be famous around here."

That night, before they set out for warlord country, Delaney dreamed this:

*He is an action hero, a soldier, a mercenary, surrounded by an audience of women. He is no longer troubled by doubts or hesitation or regrets. He takes on all challenges, all enemies, with power and grace. There are no failures, no negative consequences, and there is no pain. Usually in his dreams there was Natalia, sometimes Kate. Now, watching him in his manly contests and combats are Natalia and Kate and Mai and Ben's wife and Aung San Suu Kyi and all women, everywhere, always. They form a wide circle around him, a sacred circle. He lunges and thrusts and gesticulates in this circle, then begins a sacred circular dance. He spins round and round, faster, faster and faster. He drills himself into the very earth, deeper and deeper, until finally, he is completely swallowed up and, yes, disappears.*

# Chapter 12

The next morning, Delaney could not resist using the aging yellow telephone beside his bed to see if he could get an outside line. Even a 30-second call to Rawson's people in Ottawa could be helpful now.

Direct dialling was impossible. Delaney hit zero and after a half-dozen rings the desk clerk answered in Burmese. His English was minimal, almost non-existent, but he seemed to understand Delaney's request.

"Overseas call, international call," Delaney said.

"No, Burma, Burma," the clerk said. "Myanmar."

"Canada. Canada," Delaney said.

"No sir, sorry sir. Burma yes," the clerk said.

Delaney hung up. A wasted effort. *Risky*, he thought.

He found out how risky a few minutes later. Someone pounded on his door and tried to turn the handle. Pounded again. "Delaney. You scumbag, let us in or we'll break it down," someone said on the other side. A South African accent.

Bobby's voice. He and Abbey stood outside the door when Delaney opened it. Abbey levelled a .45 at him, glowering. Bobby pressed his way in, pushing Delaney hard with both hands on the chest so he fell back on the bed.

"You scumbag. I told them you would try to mess us up. We should blow you away right now."

Delaney said nothing.

"You think that clerk man stupid too?" Abbey said. "You think we don't already wise him up about you?"

Dima and Stefan rushed into the room, with the rest of the group not far behind.

"Bad move, Delaney," Stefan said. "Who were you trying to call?"

"My editor. Anybody. Nobody knows where I am."

"That's bullshit. Who were you trying to call?" Bobby shouted.

"What do you expect?" Delaney said. "You expect me to go along on this crazy mission with you just like that? You guys are all going to be killed, you must know that. I'm trying to let people know where I am, for Christ's sake. You think this regime's going to let you trail all over the country with weapons and some crazy plan, just like that?"

"They're doing it. The ones who know," Dima said.

"Come on," Delaney said. "They're not stupid."

"I told you we shouldn't have brought this asshole along," Bobby said. "He's going to mess us all up good."

"Delaney, you are in Burma now," Dima said. "We have General Thein and his people behind us. There's no place for you to go in this region. When we eventually get to Rangoon, you'll have no passport, no media clearance, no money, nothing. We tell Thein you've pissed us off, and you're finished. They'll whip you into Insein Prison faster than you can turn around. Reporters aren't welcome in this country at the best of times."

"Not welcome anywhere," Bobby said. "Not here, not Rangoon, nowhere. You in particular."

"You better hope Kellner backs you up, man. You'd better hope he tells us Delaney his friend," Abbey said.

Bobby came over to the bed and slapped Delaney hard across the side of his head. He was about to deliver another backhanded blow when Dima stepped forward.

"Easy, Bobby," he said.

"This guy is trouble. We're crazy to have him along. We don't need this scumbag."

"Easy," Dima said again. "Easy."

General Thein stayed behind when they went to Mongla. They rode this time in a small Toyota bus, as if on a tourist outing, Delaney in the rear seat, with the Bedford following. The road out of Kengtung was bad, but the closer they got to warlord country, the better the roads became. The proceeds from drugs, gambling and women were being liberally spent it seemed.

The Burmese soldier driving the bus seemed to get more nervous as he approached Mongla. Delaney could see why as they got nearer. At the Nam Loi River, they stopped at a Burmese police checkpoint. Their driver went inside. When he climbed back into the bus he drove slowly over a bridge to a more military-looking checkpoint manned by Burmese troops in battle fatigues. The guards waved the bus and the Bedford through.

The next checkpoint told the story of the region. The soldiers there did not wear Burmese Army uniforms but National Democratic Alliance Army gear—they were Lin Mingxian's private militia. Their driver got out and a NDAA man got in and took over the wheel.

As they drove on toward Mongla itself, paddy fields and grazing water buffalo gave way to cleared areas and parked earth-moving equipment. The last few kilometres of road were international standard blacktop, the best Delaney had ever seen in Asia. The better to carry busloads of Chinese tourists and gamblers from Yunan Province, just a short drive away.

Mongla was a sprawling town set in a valley surrounded by dark hills. Even in the old town centre there were small night-clubs and girlie bars and transvestite bars and brothels. As the bus headed outside town on the northern side, they passed more nightclubs, bigger ones, and a hilltop casino with a parking lot jammed with Chinese registered minibuses. Small crowds of middle-aged and elderly Chinese climbed in and out of the vehicles.

The mercenaries' destination was a modern walled compound of tidy townhouses and other buildings set among bougainvillea and high whitewashed perimeter walls. It could have been an upscale expatriate community anywhere in Asia or Africa where serious money was being made, where big deals were made. They stopped at a low building that looked like a community hall: white stucco with stained wooden window frames and smoked glass everywhere.

Inside it was ice cool, over air-conditioned and spotless. A Burmese girl in a long skirt offered them a tray of cool fruit drinks in tall frosted glasses with straws. An Asian man, looking more Chinese than Burmese, in a white shirt and tan slacks approached them accompanied by an NDAA soldier.

"Welcome my friends, welcome to Mongla," he said. "I am Pao Yuqiang. How was your journey?"

They sat for a time making small talk, the mercenaries on their best behaviour, sipping juice like schoolboys on an expedition. As usual Dima and Stefan took the lead.

"Perhaps we could see our Australian clients this morning," Dima said eventually. "It would be good if we could head back to Kengtung today."

"Yes, yes of course. They are waiting for you," Yuqiang said.

They were led into a meeting room with rows of tables arranged in a square. Again, a room that could be anywhere in Asia where deals were made. Bottled water and glasses were set out on stainless steel trays. A basket of fruit sat on a sideboard.

Yuqiang came in shortly afterward with two tall, slim, ruddy-faced Australians in identical dark blue golf shirts and tan slacks. On each shirt were a small crest and the words *Great Southern Investments Pty Ltd*. The men were in their early forties, Delaney thought. All smiles.

"G'day, g'day, thanks for coming up here, it's a bugger of a drive," one said. "I'm Rod Foster and this is my partner Dave Hilyard."

They took the time to shake hands with each mercenary in turn, getting all their names, with non-stop smiles all around, before sitting down.

"Now gentlemen, I reckon you want to get straight down to brass tacks," Foster said. "We all know why we're here, so let's get on with it. Great Southern, that's my lot, are working as you know with the local authorities here and some Chinese partners on a very exciting casino and road project. And as you know, we're keen to beef up our security operation, for our senior staff."

Hilyard broke in: "Now that's not to say we're not happy, very happy, with what our local friends here have been doing for us from Day One. We just want to have that little extra, for the wives and some others when they come up here from time to time. Just for the compound and driving around. Like that."

He smiled over toward Yuqiang, who bowed his head slightly.

"No worries generally, Pao, right? Just that little bit extra for the wives, right?" Hilyard said. "Make the insurance blokes happy back down in Perth."

"Understandable," Yuqiang said.

"So we welcome the opportunity to work with you lot here, and some others who'll come in later, I understand, to make that happen," Foster said, looking at Dima and Stefan.

"We have experience in all parts of the world. We have done this many times before," Dima said. "On similar projects."

"Right, right, we know that. Your mate Kellner told us all about you lot," Hilyard said.

"Where's Kellner anyway?" Foster said. "I reckoned he'd be coming up this way with you."

"He's been delayed," Stefan said. "We expect to meet up with him in Rangoon."

"Ah, too bad, mate. He's good value, Kellner is. He's good

fun, he is," Hilyard said. "We had some times in Bangkok with that one."

"He sends his regards," Dima said.

"Well now, we're probably about done," Foster said. "No use mucking around. Maybe we could have a little look at what you lot brought along, have a fast look at some of your gear and then we can do business, right?"

"Of course," Dima said.

They went out into the blinding sunshine. It was intensely hot. Stefan and the two Australians went around to the back of the Bedford and climbed up inside. Delaney could hear the sound of a crate being opened, and some other movement. The driver stood looking in as well. The rest of the mercenaries stood in the shade, drinking yet more iced fruit drinks. It was all very civilized.

"Impressive, impressive. No worries," Foster said as he got down from the back of the truck.

"Very good, fine," Hilyard said. "Always good to have your own gear."

Yuqiang looked on in silence. Delaney couldn't read his face, couldn't tell whether he approved the arrangement the Australians thought they were entering into or whether he, too, knew it was a charade.

Everyone except Foster went back inside. He went off with the NDAA soldier and came back into the meeting room a few minutes later carrying an aluminum attaché case. He placed it on the table in front of Stefan and Dima.

"For you, sirs. Down payment. Great Southern Investments looks forward to working with you," he said.

"In cash as agreed," Hilyard said.

Dima opened the case. Neat stacks of U.S. hundred-dollar notes lay inside.

"Nice," Tom called out from the side of the room.

"Very nice," Dima said.

"You want to count it?" Hilyard said. "Half a mill."

"That won't be necessary, I think," Dima said.

"Kellner told us you lot would be all right," Hilyard said. "Straight shooters."

"Exactly," Dima said.

As with all business deals in Asia, toasts were drunk. Their tireless waitress struggled in to the meeting room under a huge circular tray of iced Victoria Bitter beer in cans. "Direct from Oz," Hilyard said.

Yuqiang said: "To future cooperation." He raised a glass of beer.

"Here, here," Foster said.

"To mutually advantageous arrangements," Dima said.

"Right on," Hilyard said. "Mutually advantageous arrangements."

"And U.S. dollars," Tom said, raising his beer can.

That raised a hearty laugh from the Australians. Yuqiang nodded and smiled. They all drank beer and stood amicably around for a few minutes. Dima eventually made the move to go.

"We'll see you fellas back here in about a fortnight then," Foster said as they boarded the bus.

"Yes, exactly," Dima said. "You can now count on our services right through to completion of the project."

"Two years, minimum, that'll be," Hilyard said.

"Yes," Dima said.

"Look after that gear for us now, won't you?" Hilyard shouted as they pulled away.

"Of course. We are professionals," Dima called back.

"Too right," Hilyard said.

Delaney half expected the Australians to wave at them as the busload of mercenaries pulled away from the compound. They did not wave, but watched until the bus had turned out of the driveway and out of sight behind the perimeter wall. The mercenaries immediately let out wild whoops. Even Dima was grinning broadly.

"Rip-off!" Tom shouted. "Assholes!"

"Party time!" Bobby said. "Tonight we party."

"Kellner's a fucking genius," Clive said.

The bus driver looked grave, trying to steer and watch them in the rearview mirror at the same time.

General Thein was waiting for them at the Burmese checkpoint on the Kengtung side of the river. Dima climbed into his Mercedes with the aluminum case. The little convoy bounced back down along the winding road to Kengtung, the mercenaries launching into rowdy soldiers' songs and drinking cans of VB liberated from the meeting room.

At the hotel, Dima got out of the Mercedes and walked over to the group where they waited in the parking lot. General Thein got out, saluted them and went inside with his driver.

"Did he take his cut right away?" Stefan asked.

"He did," Dima said gravely.

"One hundred thousand?"

"Yes. As agreed."

"And now he has to produce," Sam said.

"He will produce," Dima said. "And then we will produce, and our people in Mae Sot will produce for us, and we will be taken out of there and back to the farm and this operation will be one for the history books."

"And a story for reporter man, eventually," Stefan said, looking over at Delaney. "If we can keep him with us on this thing."

"We shall see," Dima said.

General Thein took them that night to an officers' club on a hillside outside town. Delaney had been in many such police and soldiers' clubs before, on assignment in Nigeria, in Philippines, in El Salvador, elsewhere. They were all designed to do the same thing. They were to leave no doubt in the minds of those lucky enough to use them that being a senior man in a particular army was so beneficial, so lucrative, had such pleasant fringe benefits, that lifelong loyalty to the soldiering tribe was the only sensible, the only consistently rewarding course.

Delaney was invited along, if only, apparently, because it was easier to watch him there than at the hotel. And also, he started to realize, because this mercenary band really did want a scribe along with them, someone to witness their lifestyle and their heroics. He drank and ate like the others that night—exhausted, resigned, he saw no sense in any further futile acts of resistance.

As always at such officers' clubs, the food, the liquor, the surroundings, the women, were top of the line. In this one, there were tables laden with Western and Asian dishes, heavy on imported beef and other expensive protein sources required for fighting men. Waiters in white jackets grilled and barbequed and sliced for them. Wine was opened, and beer, cognac, creamy liqueurs—in no particular order, for no particular meal course.

Eventually, in such situations in Asia there was karaoke—in this instance on long, curved sofas in a small private low-ceilinged lounge. General Thein in civilian clothes, a floral-patterned shirt, casual trousers and immaculately polished black Gucci loafers. Young, very young, Thai girls in cheap Western-style party dresses were shown in.

"Singing partners, choose one, choose one each gentlemen please," Thein said.

The girls, exuding perfume, sat with their soldiers, snuggling close and calling out the names of songs as they came up on the karaoke screen. General Thein and his girl, who was no more than 18, delivered the first duo, a heartfelt rendition of "Feelings." The general drank from a large tumbler of Remy Martin cognac, and nibbled at small skewers of barbequed chicken.

"Congratulations, congratulations my friends," Thein called out again and again. Sweat poured from his face, despite the blasts of air conditioning on all sides. His girl kissed him repeatedly on his weathered cheek and whispered in his ear. Soon, Delaney knew, Thein and the others would begin to disappear from the karaoke room with their girls, some for longer than others depending on what services they required elsewhere in the building.

Delaney's girl was called Meg, after Meg Ryan, the Hollywood star, she told him.

"You are a quiet man," she said.

"Yes," Delaney said.

"You are not happy with me?" she said.

"You're a nice girl," Delaney said. "No problem."

"You want to make nice now, maybe? Whole body massage for you, maybe?"

"No thanks."

"General Thein says to make nice with everybody tonight."

"That's kind of him."

"You have a special sweetheart girl somewhere?" she said.

The liquor and the heavy food and the stale air had started the room spinning slowly on an axis Delaney could not see.

"Somewhere," he said.


No matter how many times Delaney rolled the problem around in his mind, he could not imagine why the Burmese military, or Thein's faction anyway, would allow a group of mercenaries to move at will throughout the country with AK-47s and other deadly gear in tow. No matter how persuasive Kellner might have been, no matter how much money Thein and others thought they were going to be paid in some other scheme, the whole thing just did not add up. And if anybody at all in the Burmese military knew anything about the wild plan to take Suu Kyi, Delaney was sure they would not have allowed the mercenary team, or Thein himself, to get even this far.

Delaney thought things through one more time as he stood

late the next day on the steaming tarmac of Kengtung's small military airport, watching the mercenary gear being loaded onto a wide Spanish built turbo-prop for the flight to Rangoon. His travelling companions, even the normally level-headed Dima, all looked very much the worse for wear after their night of R&R at the officer's club.

Delaney, too, had had far too much to drink. He vaguely remembered being helped down from the little bus that ferried them back to the hotel; he could not remember who had given him a helping hand. He vaguely remembered the two British mercenaries slapping him on the back throughout the evening and saying what a fine chap he was after all, that he mustn't mind Bobby and Abbey, that they were all proud and delighted to have a journalist of his excellent, no, extraordinary, stature along with them on this adventure. Et cetera.

The night of drinking and male bonding seemed to have defused the tension somewhat, for all except Bobby. Even Abbey seemed more relaxed around Delaney, at the hotel and later at the airport as they waited to board their plane. Only Bobby still scowled at Delaney, displayed menace. The beating Delaney and Ben had given him back at Mae Sot would never be forgotten, it seemed.

The flight to Rangoon took them over the rugged hills of Shan country, where the army was doing its best to wipe out a long-standing rebellion and, if other accounts were to be believed, the entire ethnic Shan population as well. Most good reporters in Bangkok had written about the massive relocation of Shan civilians, the forced labour, the packed refugee camps on the Thai side of the border. Kellner would have filed his share of such stories too.

They landed at dusk at a military airport on the southern outskirts of Rangoon. Yet another Toyota bus took them through the city, heading north. A small truck followed with their crates.

The hot claustrophobic streets of the Burmese capital were teeming; corner teashops everywhere were crammed, the streets were crammed with aging Chevrolet buses, motorcycles, bicycles, bicycle rickshaws. The crumbling pavements were crowded with stalls, each selling only one or two items; perhaps soap, matches and lighter fluid in one, packets of rice and noodles in another. No one seemed to be buying.

At every intersection stood teenage soldiers with AK-47s and fixed bayonets, clearly under instruction to crash down on the slightest hint of trouble. Since the riots and the arrests and killings after the 1990 elections, and since Aung San Suu Kyi was placed under house arrest, the Burmese capital was tense, with only a chipped varnish of normality.

They left the buzzing city centre and moved through quieter colonial era-suburbs of dark dilapidated mansions showing no signs of life within. Aung San Suu Kyi was closeted in just such a mansion, near the University of Rangoon, on a lake that dominates that part of the city. Their driver did not take them anywhere near Suu Kyi's household, which had become the focus of the pro-democracy movement and where squads of soldiers were always at the ready in nearby troop carriers in case one of the rallies outside Suu Kyi's fence ever got out of hand.

Into that scene, the mercenaries now riding with Delaney on a small bus intended soon to thrust themselves, to extricate Suu Kyi and ascend out of danger in a blast of testosterone-fuelled glory.

Their driver pulled up outside a six-story apartment building in a grim cluster of concrete blocks north of the capital. The government had relocated thousands of people, potential troublemakers they argued, from the city centre to the northern suburbs where they would have a far less easy time fomenting revolution. Rangoon was a city of passbooks and curfews and police checks; even visits to family were tightly controlled. In these forlorn modern apartment blocks lived many of the opponents, and victims, of the military regime.

It was an odd place for a band of mercenaries to be left off as night fell. After unloading their crates, they manhandled them up to a sprawling first-floor flat, with four bedrooms and a couple of dark enclosed balconies and little in the way of furniture except mattresses, a fifties-era kitchen table and a few rattan sofas. Their driver, and two other soldiers who had materialized when they arrived, did not offer to help them. They saw no one else in the silent neighbourhood.

The entire building, dying of concrete cancer, and the surrounding streets were virtually deserted. Eventually, a lone ancient lady in a broad straw hat made her way unsteadily along the hot pavement in front of their building. She took no notice of the activity there, too frightened or perhaps too wise to do anything except to make her way past them as quickly as she could.

Tom stood at the filthy kitchen sink and turned on a tap. The faucet coughed and wheezed and spat out a dab of copper-coloured paste.

"Guess it's room service tonight, boys," he said. He opened a sorry-looking Kelvinator refrigerator and felt one of the racks. "Cool, not cold," he said.

"Empty anyway," Clive said.

"We're out of luck for beer," Sam said.

Their driver and the two soldiers had come up the dank concrete stairway to the first floor. The driver spoke reasonable English.

"General Thein says you must wait here," he said. "He will send you supplies tonight, they are on their way. He says there will be meetings as soon as possible."

"How long?" Stefan said, looking at Dima.

"He did not say, sir," the driver said.

"We are waiting for one more man on our team," Dima said. "Kellner. When will he come?"

"Sorry sir," the driver said.

As he spoke, two impossibly young-looking soldiers in wraparound sunglasses and olive green T-shirts, but unarmed, came inside with cardboard boxes of food and drink. They went back downstairs several times for more. Sam and Clive unpacked, stowing tins and small sacks in kitchen cupboards, water and beer in the fridge. For a moment, it was a disconcertingly domestic scene.

"That beer will barely last us the night," Tom said.

"Shit, man," Abbey said. "How long we got here anyway?"

Stefan and Dima both motioned to him at the same time to be quiet.

After the Burmese soldiers left, Bobby and Abbey smoked some marijuana they got from one of the bar girls the night before. No one else smoked. The humid Asian night closed in and they could hear, finally, the sounds of life and meal preparation from apartment windows nearby. But the neighbourhood was still far from busy.

"We've got to find Kellner," Bobby said. "We can't do this thing without him. Where the fuck is he?"

Delaney sat off to one side, watching and saying nothing.

"We all know the plan," Dima said.

"Yeah, but it's Kellner's plan. We can't go ahead without him."

"We can," Dima said.

"What is the point, man? It is his plan, his lady he wants to take," Abbey said. "I don't give a shit for no Suu Kyi."

"That's the job we're here to do. That's what we're getting paid to do," Stefan said.

"Without the man himself," Bobby said.

"We'll get General Thein to track him down for us. Relax. Just relax," Stefan said.

Clive and Sam, the Brits, tough but never talking about it, drank beer quietly, taking everything in.

"Maybe someone took him out," Bobby said, exhaling smoke and passing the joint to Abbey.

"Then we'd be toast too," Tom said.

"Toast," Abbey said dreamily.

"We'll find out what's what with Kellner tomorrow," Stefan said. He looked over at Delaney. "Where do you think he is?"

"What the fuck would Delaney know?" Bobby said.

"I think it's obvious someone's got to him," Delaney said. "Kellner's been missing for well over a month now. Almost two months. No one has seen him. His girlfriend hasn't seen him, Cohen, no one. His editor hasn't heard a word from him. This is Burma. If they had so much as a hint he was going to try something crazy with Suu Kyi, they would kill him."

"He has the military onside," Stefan said.

"All of it?" Delaney said. "And what do they think he's going to do? I don't care what faction he thought he had onside, there is no way he could mess with Suu Kyi. She is off limits, absolutely off limits, to everybody. They simply won't care who it is or who thought they were onside, or not."

"Back off, Delaney," Bobby said.

"We'll locate him tomorrow," Dima said.

"And we have to contact our chopper pilot in Mae Sot," Stefan said. "That's the priority."

Dima went to his pack and pulled out an ordinance map. He spread it out on the kitchen table and everyone except Bobby, Abbey and Delaney crowded around to look. Delaney just shook his head. Bobby saw him and flicked the last glowing stub of marijuana across the room at him.

"I told you to back off, Delaney," he said.

"Don't you be shaking your head in this house tonight," Abbey said.

"The chopper can put down right there, beside the lake," Dima said to the soldiers at the table.

"Tricky," Clive said. "I'd say the backyard is the way to go."

~~~

Dimitri Prokupchuk, mercenary, sat on the balcony of a decaying concrete apartment block in the northern suburbs of Rangoon smoking a late-night cigarette. The soldier's life had brought him here. From the sadism of Russian boot camps, through dirty wars in Afghanistan and Chechnya and two marriages and a variety of children to here, Rangoon, Burma, Myanmar, in the middle of the world.

His colleagues snored and stirred in alcohol- and drug-induced sleep. It might have been tents near Kabul or bombed-out factories near Grozny or any number of uncomfortable, dangerous places. This time the bivouac was mattresses on concrete floors in a bad apartment in Rangoon.

He only felt true feelings, soldier's feelings, when he was in a situation such as this. Calm, smoking a cigarette, men under his command, dangers to be faced, rewards on the horizon. He knew that night, like many other nights, that there was no life for him but the soldier's, the mercenary's life.

He flicked his cigarette off the balcony. It trailed tiny embers through the night, like a tracer bullet seen from a kilometre away. He heard the butt hit and hiss briefly in the parking lot not far below. He would have preferred it if it was distant mortar fire, or distant flares, or distant aircraft overhead that made him feel uneasy that night. Unease was normal. The soldier's life was full of fear and uncertainty and unease.

This time, it was different. With all his experience, all his hard-won experience in battles large and small, he could not shake the feeling that this time something was fundamentally wrong.

Was it because Kellner had gone missing? Not really. Things often went wrong in the days and hours before an operation. There was nothing terribly unusual about that, and a good tactician such as he would know how to allow for such events in the field. No, this time the situation felt fundamentally, irretrievably wrong, as if some basic piece of planning had been forgotten, or not done at all.

He could not think what that might be. He trusted Kellner, had known him for years, valued him as a good contact for freelance work like this.

No, it was not Kellner. And Dimitri Prokupchuk, mercenary, was at ease with ruthless men like General Thein, had had much experience with men like that, whose true motives were never clear, for whom money was one important thing but never, ever, everything, for whom an extra victim here and there was the cost of doing a soldier's business.

No, it was something different this time. Perhaps, Dima thought, as he felt the velvet caress of an Asian night on his skin, it was just a matter of age. He was lucky to have made it to 51, lucky indeed. Maybe this should be his last adventure. Maybe that was what his superstitious Russian soul was telling him that night. Maybe this would be his last adventure.

Delaney couldn't sleep and went out to the kitchen, lit now only by yellow street lights from outside. He saw the glow of someone's cigarette on the balcony, smelled tobacco smoke, but said nothing. He took a beer from the fridge, hoping that this might help him relax enough to doze off until morning.

He saw a red cigarette butt rocket briefly off the balcony and then Dima came in, startled to see anyone else awake.

"Delaney, what is your problem?" he said.

"What is yours, Dima?" Delaney said. They were the two oldest in the group, and stood looking at each other from the vantage of men with no illusions.

"I miss my *dacha* tonight, Delaney," Dima said. "I'm getting old. Maybe that is all."

"You know that this is all going to go bad, don't you Dima," Delaney said.

"Possibly," Dima said. "Yes."

"Then why bother?"

Dima waited a long time before he answered. Perhaps too long.

"Ask me that again tomorrow," he said.

# Chapter 13

No one except Dima was in the main room when the knock came the next morning. Delaney was awake, but still lying down in the small back room where they had put him. It was just past seven. He heard Dima call out "Yes, wait" and move to the front door.

Delaney heard the door being opened and the sound of men moving into the living room. A number of men, in heavy boots.

"General Thein," he heard Dima say. "Welcome to our humble abode."

Delaney got up, dressed quickly, listened from his open doorway. Down the dim hallway, he could see Dima and the general, with at least three or four uniformed soldiers behind them carrying AKs. The other mercenaries had not stirred yet, or were perhaps listening from their rooms, as Delaney was. There was no apparent reason to think that this morning visit was trouble. They had all been expecting Thein to come that day. But Delaney knew this was trouble.

"You will ask your men to come out," Thein said. "We will go to the city now. There is a vehicle waiting outside."

"To the city? Today?" Dima said.

"Yes, now please," Thein said.

"We haven't discussed our next arrangements with you yet,"

Dima said. "We must talk of many things first. And we have not seen Kellner, we have not briefed him on the Mongla outcome."

"That will not be necessary now," Thein said.

"Why not?" Dima said.

"Prokupchuk, you take me for a fool," Thein said. "I have played fool for you for several days and I am tired of it now."

"I don't know what you mean," Dima said.

"I am a soldier. You are a soldier, but I think now not a very good one. Please do not insult me."

Dima now apparently decided to say as little as possible. He was silent and waited for the general to speak again.

"Did you really think we would let you interfere with Suu Kyi and put this revolution at risk?" Thein said.

Dima still said nothing.

"Did you?" Thein asked again. "And did you really think you could persuade a general in the SPDC to take part in any of your other little business plans? Did you think we would let you interfere in our business in the north, or anywhere else? That you could buy me like that? Do you think we would put an important investment arrangement like the one in Mongla at risk and anger some international partners for a few dollars from a band of mercenary soldiers like yourselves? You Westerners think we are fools. We are not fools. All of these little schemes of yours, and Kellner's. You are the fools to think that Myanmar is just a target for people like you. The SPDC watches and learns and we wait and then we strike back at all our opponents. Like today."

"Where is Kellner?" Dima said.

"Kellner is dead," Thein said.

"Dead," Dima said.

"He was uncooperative and then he cooperated and now he is dead," Thein said. "He was a rash man, and inside he was weak. Two things dangerous in combination."

Dima was silent.

"Wake your men," Thein said, drawing his side arm. "We will go now."

Bobby burst from a bedroom between Delaney and the scene in the living room. He was shirtless, but carrying an AK-47.

"Down Dima," Bobby shouted. Dima hit the floor rolling to the right. Bobby opened fire, two brief bursts. The noise was deafening in the enclosed space. General Thein was not even able to raise his pistol. He and the four Burmese soldiers were flung back against the wall and the entrance door, smearing blood as they slid to the floor.

Dima was instantly on his feet again, professional, in charge again.

"Bobby, secure that stairwell," he said. He reached for his .45, which was on the kitchen table. The other men raced into the main room, shrugging into shirts, zipping combat pants. Clive and Sam carried AKs, passing them to colleagues.

"Tom, secure that back doorway," Dima said. "Clive and Sam, take the front balcony and pull down those shutters."

Delaney could hear shouts in Burmese and children's voices coming from other apartments now, above them and from the adjacent buildings.

Clive took a short look over the low concrete wall of the balcony before pulling a metal rollerblind almost all the way down.

"Army van, one driver, at the wheel. Two men with AKs moving this way," he shouted back inside. "And a Mercedes, tinted glass, can't see who's inside."

"I got the stairs," Bobby said from the outside hallway. Delaney heard him shout, apparently up to the landing above. "Back, back, back, go back inside." Burmese voices. A door slammed.

Delaney moved into the living room area, keeping low.

"Out of the way, Delaney, stay down," Dima said. Delaney squatted to one side, back against the living-room wall.

"Get the hell out of here, man," Abbey said. "Back in that room."

"Leave it, leave it, leave it," Stefan said. "Watch that window on the left side."

Abbey moved fast to the left-hand-side window. Stefan moved into the side covered balcony, to the right, looked briefly over the wall and pulled the rollerblind down most of the way as Clive had done.

"Clear on this side," Stefan said.

"Back stairwell clear," Tom shouted out.

Dima and Sam put down their assault rifles and pulled the five bodies over to the corner of the living room between the two exterior balconies.

"Jesus Christ," Sam said, sweating heavily in the morning heat and humidity. He had a Glock tucked into his back waistband. He took the side arms from the dead Burmese soldiers and placed them on the kitchen table in the back corner of the living room. Then he gathered up the soldiers' AKs, pushed plates and glasses to the floor, and laid them on the table as well.

"What's up?" Tom called out from the back stairwell after the crash of plates. "What's up?"

"OK, OK, we're OK in here," Sam shouted.

"We're going to have to get out of here and take that van," Stefan called out from the side balcony.

"And before anybody else comes," Clive said from his lookout on the streetside balcony. He peered through the horizontal gap in the shutters. "Driver on radio, driver on radio," he shouted suddenly.

"Take him, Clive," Dima said.

Clive rolled the shutters up slightly and let go a burst of AK-47 fire into the street. Then another. He rolled the shutter almost all the way down again and crouched below the wall. "He's out," Clive said.

Through the entrance doorway, Delaney heard shouting in Burmese. The other two soldiers had clearly seen the driver go down. They fired up into the stairs. Bullets ricocheted around in the concrete well on the first floor. Bobby took aim downward and fired off a long burst of his own.

"Cocksuckers," he shouted out. He let go another burst.

"Easy, Bobby," Dima shouted. "We've only got limited ammunition in here. Short bursts, short, short."

"We have to get out of here before any others come, Dima," Stefan said.

"We'll go, we'll go," Dima said. "Sam, get what gear we'll need, get it ready. Bobby and I will clear the stairs and then we're out. Head for the van. Delaney, you stay with Stefan."

"We're not bringing that piece of shit with us, no way," Bobby said from the stairwell.

"No time for this now, Bobby," Dima said.

"Leave him, fuck it," Bobby said.

The soldiers below fired blindly upstairs again. The ricochets pinged all around.

"Christ," Bobby said, firing downward again.

"Sam. We'll need a smoke grenade in that stairwell," Dima said.

Sam raced into a bedroom and came back with two smoke bombs. Dima tossed them to Bobby outside the main door.

"Stand by, Bobby," he said.

"Vans, vans," Clive called from the front balcony, peering through the shutters "Troops."

"Jesus Christ," Dima said. "Bobby, hold back, hold back. Tom, you clear? Clear at the back?"

"Clear," Tom called out.

"Van at the side," Stefan called out from his balcony. "Troops out. Six, eight in the alley."

"Van this side, van this side," Abbey called from his window.

"Christ," Dima said. "Stefan, what do you think?"

"The back way," Stefan said. "No choice."

"Blind here, no window," Tom said.

"It's got to be the back, Dima," Stefan said.

Suddenly they heard a voice on a loud hailer from outside, shouting something in Burmese.

"What are they saying for Christ's sake?" Sam shouted.

"They don't know who's here," Clive called back.

"They know, they must know," Dima said.

"They know five Burmese came in here and they haven't come out yet, that's all they know," Stefan said. "They know someone's killed a driver from the balcony up here and someone's firing at their guys from the stairwell. That's it so far. They don't know what's going on."

The amplified shouting continued. No shots were fired from the street.

"They've got to figure some of their guys are still alive in here," Bobby said.

"Yeah," Clive said.

"If they are professionals and they think some of their men are still alive in here, they'll go with tear gas," Dima said. "That is how it is done."

"Right on," Bobby called inside. "And I hate tear gas."

"We got no masks," Abbey said.

"No masks," Dima said.

"Back door," Stefan said. "Has to be. Tom, you think there might be an alleyway back there for vans?"

"Can't tell, Stefan," Tom said.

"It's got to be the back," Dima said. "We'll go out whatever door there is downstairs and take one of the vans from the alley on the right-hand side. The right side as we go out. OK?"

"OK," said Stefan. "Everybody got that? Down the back, we cover each other and take a van in the right-hand alleyway and we go."

"Bobby, we'll need those smoke bombs for the back now," Dima said.

Bobby tossed them in to Sam, and Sam ran with them to the back of the apartment. There was more shouting in Burmese from the loud hailer outside. Clive pulled up the rollerblind on the front balcony to have a look and immediately there was heavy fire from the street. Bullets ricocheted inside the enclosed space.

"Christ," Clive shouted, pulling the blind all the way back down and slumping to the ground. Blood gushed from his face. "I'm hit," he said.

"Go Delaney, check him out," Dima said. "Everyone else stay in position. Stay where you are."

Delaney moved quickly to the now-darkened balcony. Clive had been hit by bullet shrapnel and bits of concrete in several places in the face. Not a direct bullet wound but deep shrapnel cuts, all bleeding profusely. One eye socket was gushing blood, too.

Clive was lying quietly, conserving energy, a professional soldier with a wound.

"I don't think it's bad, Delaney," he said.

Delaney looked around for something to wipe Clive's face.

"Is it bad?" Dima called out.

"Face," Delaney said. "Shrapnel, I think. There's a lot of blood."

"I'm OK," Clive said, trying to sit up.

"Can you move, Clive?" Stefan called out.

"Yeah," Clive called out. "Can't see too good, though."

Everyone went silent for a moment. Then Stefan said, "We've got to go."

Suddenly there was a whoosh and a clattering from the front stairwell. Bobby cursed and fired downward. "Tear gas, tear gas," he shouted.

He grabbed a canister from where it hissed and whirled at his feet and hurled it back downstairs. Two more canisters rocketed up and landed nearby, pouring out stinging billows of fumes. Bobby kicked at them and tried to fire down the stairs. Bursts of AK fire ricocheted around him from the soldiers below. He raced coughing and gagging inside the flat and slammed the door.

"I need a mask," he shouted, falling to his knees and coughing.

The stout entrance door did not appear to be letting fumes inside.

"This getting hot now, brothers," Abbey said from his vantage point at the left-hand window.

The closed metal blind in the front balcony clanged like a big out-of-tune cymbal; once, twice, then again.

"They're firing tear gas canisters at the fucking blind," Sam called out from the back. "Delaney, get Clive out of there."

"Everybody stay in position," Dima said. "Delaney, get out of that area, get Clive out of there."

Now AK fire hammered at the front balcony rollerblind. Some bullets pierced the slats, letting in slim tracers of sunlight. They heard the sound of a helicopter hovering above.

"Chopper," Clive said as Delaney helped him into the centre of the living room. Blood still flowed from his cuts and his left eye was closed.

"Tear gas, tear gas," Tom shouted from the back doorway. There was another whoosh and clatter as canisters came up from below. Tom fired downstairs and then he too came gagging and coughing into the apartment, slamming the door behind him.

"This is looking very bad, Dima," Stefan said.

"It's bad," Dima said. He looked over at Clive, who was lying quiet and still. He looked at Delaney, who was mopping Clive's wounds with a dishtowel. He looked around at the rest of the men.

"Delaney, you better make a run for it," Dima said finally.

"No way," Bobby said.

"He's no good to us," Dima said. "He doesn't know what he's doing. Suddenly you want him to stay. What's the use?"

"No way," Bobby said, standing up and rubbing his streaming eyes with his left fist.

"Where's he going to go anyway?" Stefan said.

"Upstairs," Dima said. "We've only got a few minutes."

"So we go upstairs too," Abbey said.

"Abbey, you know they won't let any of us get out that way," Dima said. "They're sure to have guys on the roof by now. You heard that chopper. We fight our way out down the stairs or we're finished. Jail or dead."

"We're finished, man," Abbey said.

"Delaney, you have one chance to get into an apartment above us. One chance, maybe a few minutes, that is all you've got. Go," Dima said.

"No way," Bobby said. "We die, he dies too. We do jail, he does too."

Tom called out from the back. "What's the point, Bobby? He's not with us. He's a reporter."

"Reporter man, I think you going to die," Abbey said quietly from the window.

"He goes," Dima said. "We haven't got time for games now. Bobby. Stand by on that front door."

"No way," Bobby said, raising his .45 and pointing it at Dima.

"Easy," Sam said, levelling his AK at Bobby. "Relax."

"Delaney, come, come, come, hurry up man," Tom called from the back. "Run."

Delaney left the standoff in the living room and raced to the back of the flat.

"Come on, come on, come on," Tom said.

Delaney hesitated for a second at the back door.

"You make us look good, you hear?" Tom said. "Front cover of *Newsweek*, right? Fucking heroic figures, right?"

"Yeah," Delaney said. "Front cover." He looked briefly down the long hallway to the front. Dima raised his hand. Delaney raised his.

Tom opened the door. The fumes had subsided but lingered still. Tom stepped out into the back stairwell and fired downward. "Go, go, go," he shouted.

Delaney covered his face with the bloody dishtowel and raced up to the next landing and then the next. His eyes stung and mucous ran from his nostrils as the tear gas did its work. He tried the door of an apartment on the third floor, rattled the handle, pounded, but it was locked and no one came. The door had a big panel of glass in its upper half, for light in the dim stairs. He rolled the dishtowel around a fist and smashed the glass. He reached inside and opened the flimsy handle lock with trembling fingers.

Below, Tom stopped firing and slammed the door to the mercenaries' refuge. Gunfire came from the ground level of the stairwell and Delaney could faintly hear more firing from the front of the building. In the distance, a helicopter beat the air and someone on a loud hailer shouted instructions, warnings, exhortations in a language none of them could understand.

Delaney hurled himself into the neighbour's apartment and hit the floor in the hallway, lying still and listening intently. His eyes and nose streamed from the tear gas and his heart was pounding ferociously in his chest.

He thought he heard the sound of children crying somewhere in the flat. It was identical in layout to the flat two floors below he had just escaped from. He got cautiously to his feet and began to look around, not knowing what he wanted or needed to find. *Slow*, he said to himself. *Go slow.*

All the bedroom doors were open except the one nearest the living room. He turned the handle on this one and immediately a woman's voice began wailing, screeching, beseeching, in Burmese. He opened the door and a middle-aged woman cowered on the bed, with two toddlers, a boy and a girl, clinging to her and crying.

She raised her right hand to him, imploring him in Burmese, drawing her children closer to her with her left arm.

"It's OK, it's OK, it's OK," Delaney said to her.

He stepped her way and she cowered even farther back. The children wailed louder. Delaney retreated, closing the door behind him. The apartment seemed otherwise empty.

He half crawled onto the enclosed balcony, behind its low wall. The rollerblind on this one was up, all the way. From one corner of the opening he raised his forehead and eyes high enough to see out. On the street below, he saw clusters of vehicles; army vans, police cars, a troop carrier. Away in the distance, he saw a tank lumbering up, clearly about to be placed in position in front of the building.

There was no firing now. The Burmese soldiers all seemed to be waiting for the arrival of the tank. An officer with the loud hailer kept shouting in Burmese. Whether he was shouting to the mercenaries or to the building's residents was not clear.

Delaney knew there was not much time now before the mercenaries were captured or killed. Then there would be a house-to-house search, if the Burmese soldiers were professional, and he would be taken, or possibly killed. But there was nothing to do but wait. Escape was impossible.

He found a glass, took some water from the kitchen tap, drank. He rinsed his face. The children had stopped crying in the bedroom and all was quiet inside.

On a small table near the entrance door was a telephone. Delaney went over and picked up the receiver. There was a dial tone. He decided he would try to call Rawson in Ottawa. He knew only a few other numbers in Canada by heart and Rawson was the only one in any position to help him in some way, even from afar.

He had no idea whether the phone in the apartment was set up for international calls and he did not know the international access code for the Burmese phone system. He tried 00 and Rawson's mobile number in Canada. A recorded voice in Burmese came on the line. He tried the 0011, as in Britain. He tried 011, the Canadian code. No connection.

He tried zero. A Burmese operator came on.

"Long distance, please. Long distance, international," Delaney said. The operator replied in rapid-fire Burmese. The helicopter swooped overhead, very low.

"English, English, please," Delaney said. "International call."

The operator carried on in Burmese. Then she paused. Delaney heard her speaking to someone else off the line, and then she came back on the line, speaking to him once again in Burmese. The line clicked, appeared to go dead.

"Christ," Delaney said.

Then an operator speaking very basic English came on the line.

"International, yes please," she said.

"I need to call Canada," Delaney said. "Urgent call to Canada, please."

He was sweating, thinking that at any moment a 50-millimetre tank shell would crash into the building just two stories below. He had been in enough places where tank fire had gone astray to know how much danger he was still in

"Number, sir, please. Number sir," the operator said.

Delaney gave Rawson's mobile number, looking at his watch. It was 8:30 a.m. in Rangoon, 10:30 p.m. the night before in Ottawa. A Tuesday or a Wednesday night, if his calculations were correct. Rawson would surely be at home getting ready for bed.

Rawson answered on the second ring. "Yes," he said quietly. "Rawson here."

"Jonathan, it's Delaney. It's Delaney. Listen to me, OK, I've only got a few minutes. I'm in Burma and I'm in an awful jam."

"Delaney, for God's sake," Rawson said. "Where the hell have you been? Everyone is frantic over here."

"Jon, just listen to me, OK? I'm in serious danger here. I'm under fire from government troops in a building outside Rangoon. I've managed to get to a phone."

"For God's sake, Francis. Rangoon . . ."

"I'm somewhere in the northern suburbs. Kellner's dead. He was in on some crazy scheme to kidnap Aung San Suu Kyi with some mercenaries and they were found out. The army is hammering away at the mercenaries two floors below me and there's a tank coming into position as I speak."

"A tank, Francis, for God's sake. You get out of there," Rawson said.

"I can't get out, Jon," Delaney said.

"I'm in Ottawa, Francis, I can't get anyone to you in Burma fast, you know that. If at all. I'll make some calls, I'll make some calls . . ."

"Jon, I just want you to know I'm in Rangoon. Either I'm going to be killed right here, or they will arrest me after the fighting's over. I want someone to know I was in Rangoon."

"Where are you exactly?" Rawson said. "What time of day is it?"

"It's after eight in the morning here. I'm in one of those workers' suburbs the government built after the election. North of the city by about 20 minutes."

"Francis, you have to get out of there. Get out and go to the Australian embassy. We don't have an embassy in Burma anymore. The Australians handle things for us over there. Or go to the Brits. I'll alert them both."

"Jon, I'm not getting out of here unless I'm arrested. Either I'll be killed in this firefight or arrested. That's all there is."

Suddenly the helicopter swooped very low. The soldier in the loud hailer began shouting instructions again. AK-47 fire sounded from inside and outside the building.

"What the hell's that?" Rawson shouted down the phone line.

"It's heating up again here, Jon. It's getting very bad. I'm two floors above the mercenaries, flat, there's heavy fire again."

"Jesus Christ, Francis," Rawson said.

There was a roar from the street outside and a *whump* and an aftershock and the building shuddered.

"Tank fire, Jon. They're going to take the apartment now. I've got to get away from the window. I'm on the third floor."

"Stay down, Francis, stay down," Rawson said. Delaney hung up and hit the floor. From the main bedroom, the Burmese woman and her children wailed in utter panic.

Delaney lay prone on the floor in the living room, hands over the back of his head and neck. The tank fired three more rounds into the building, then there was heavy AK-47 fire from inside and out, on the front side. There was a lull, then more firing from front and back and then from the stairwells. The helicopter made periodic low passes.

Finally the firing stopped. Delaney heard yelling in Burmese, not from the loud hailer this time. The sound of vehicles roaring in and out of the area, soldiers' boots running on pavement and in gravel. The helicopter appeared to land somewhere close by.

Delaney rolled over, crawled out onto the balcony and lay still for a long time, not daring to get up yet or to peer over the wall. He knew, however, that for the mercenaries it was finished. Firing had stopped, the shouting outside had stopped. The Burmese soldiers, he knew, would be mopping up, starting a house-to-house search. He wondered if any of the mercenaries had survived.

Eventually, he crawled to the balcony and ever so slowly raised his head above the low wall. There were ambulances now and bodies and wounded being carried out of the building on stretchers. Three bodies lay on the grass beside a van parked away from the other vehicles and marked in Burmese and English "Military Police." One of the bodies had a shaved head; Bobby. A black man lay beside him; Abbey. Delaney couldn't see who the third man was.

Eventually he heard boots running on stairs, heavy pounding on doors in the hallway, shouts in Burmese. The soldiers were coming now.

After about ten minutes he heard boots outside the door to the apartment where he was hiding. He pulled out his international press card and sat with his back to the balcony wall, trying to control his heartbeat and his breathing.

Someone pounded on the door and shouted in Burmese. Delaney did not move to answer. The soldier pounded again, harder this time, and shouted again. Delaney did not move. Inside, the door to the main bedroom opened slightly and he saw the woman peer cautiously out. She did not want to go to the entrance door either. Then she spotted Delaney on the balcony and slammed the bedroom door shut again.

The soldier outside shouted again, then shouted what sounded like instructions to his comrades. Booted feet began to kick at the door. It heaved but did not immediately open. More kicks, the sound of wood cracking. Finally the door gave way.

A squad of six soldiers rushed inside, all carrying AK-47s, covering each other as they secured the apartment entrance. The lead soldier revolved expertly around with this weapon, checking all open areas, then pointed the AK at the balcony. Down the short barrel, he saw Delaney. He shouted to his comrades.

"Press, press, press," Delaney shouted, holding up his red international pass. "Media, TV, TV."

He threw the pass out into the living room and put his hands over his head. The soldier, AK poised, advanced slowly and kicked the red booklet behind him. He shouted at Delaney in Burmese. One of his colleagues picked up the pass and opened it. It had a picture and identified Delaney in five languages as a foreign correspondent, but none of the languages was Burmese. Delaney prayed the young soldier knew a bit of English or French.

The lead soldier shouted at Delaney again, motioned for him to lie flat. He came over and kicked at Delaney with his boot and knocked him from his sitting position sideways onto the floor.

Then with his foot he stretched out Delaney's legs. Two other soldiers came onto the balcony and trained their guns at Delaney as the first one searched him for weapons and papers.

"Media," Delaney said. "Media. Canada, Canada."

The lead soldier went to the balcony opening and shouted something down to the street. Shouts came back up. In the living room, a soldier with a radio spoke in rapid-fire bursts of Burmese and a crackling voice replied.

The rest of the squad searched the other rooms in the apartment. They pulled the screaming woman and her children out into the living room and she let loose with a volley of Burmese, pointing at Delaney, pointing at the balcony, pointing all around. The children simply sat on the floor and cried.

Then an officer rushed into the apartment from downstairs, followed by another small squad of young troops. He was carrying a pistol and looked very angry indeed, enraged.

"What language, what language," the officer shouted to Delaney. "*Quelle langue?* English, French, what? Quick, quick, quick."

Delaney thought the officer was going to beat him with the gun, so enraged did he look. The name patch on his uniform said Hla Min.

"English, English," Delaney said. "Press. Media, Canadian media. I'm a journalist."

"A journalist?" Min said. "No. No. Not possible."

"There's my press pass over there. The red booklet. Your man has it," Delaney said.

Min looked over at the soldier holding Delaney's press pass, motioned impatiently for it to be brought to him. He thumbed it open, read what was inside.

"Not possible, not possible," he said. "*Montreal Tribune*. No. Where is your passport, where is your visa?"

"They are lost," Delaney said.

"How are you here? How are you here? I have many men

dead today. You were with the Western soldiers down there. Now you try to escape. Where is your weapon?"

"No weapon, no weapon. I'm doing a story, a story for my newspaper," Delaney said. "I'm a journalist. I came from Bangkok."

Min walked over to where Delaney lay, pulled the action on his pistol and pushed the muzzle against Delaney's ear.

"There are many Burmese soldiers dead today," Min said. "Too many men dead. I could kill you. I want to kill you now, now."

Delaney said nothing, trying to control his fear.

"Journalist," Min said, pushing the gun muzzle harder into Delaney's ear. "No."

Eventually, Min pulled the gun away. "We will see," he said. "You will answer and we will see."

He barked instructions at his men and two of them pulled Delaney to his feet. Min glared at him and pointed his weapon at Delaney's chest.

"Now we go to Rangoon city, to Insein, Insein," Min said. "You will tell us everything there."

He motioned for his men to take Delaney out and they half dragged, half carried him down the dim stairs into the brilliant sunshine of the street. Delaney could see no sign that any of the mercenaries were still alive. But only three Western bodies lay near the military police van. He thought the third one could be Stefan—a hideous head wound made it impossible to tell for sure. Burmese soldiers shouted and pointed when they saw Delaney being dragged outside, all enraged at what had happened that day, all mourning lost comrades and looking for someone, anyone, to blame.

# PART 6

## Rangoon, Bangkok and Ko Chang

# Chapter 14

Rangoon's Insein Prison is notorious among Burma's democracy campaigners and also among local and foreign journalists. Scores, hundreds, of opposition activists have been detained there—interrogated, tortured, half starved there by the military regime. And journalists who fall foul of the regime also find themselves there, all interrogated, many tortured, some executed. Some, the lucky ones, usually the foreign ones, are deported from Burma and barred from returning for life.

Delaney's cell was small, airless, but better, he knew, than many others in the prison where important enemies of the Burmese Way to Socialism were held incommunicado for years. Delaney, for the first days of his stay—he calculated it was about a week—was also incommunicado. Not cut off from just the outside world but from everyone except for a few guards who manned this section of the prison.

No one came to interrogate him; no one spoke to him at all. He was given two small meals a day, mostly rice with some bits of meat or vegetables, sometimes with a murky soy broth. He was given no explanation about what was planned for him, what charges might have been laid, when he might be able to see anyone in a position of authority or any foreign officials. It was a common technique in totalitarian regimes, he knew, and he accepted that he would simply have to wait.

Another widespread practice to weaken opponents of such regimes is the deliberate use of illness, even poisoning. This, apparently, the jailers also employed in Delaney's case. After two days in his cell he was literally floored with stomach cramps, diarrhoea, vomiting, fever, chills. The cause was of course the food and water, or maybe an additional substance added to them, but whatever it was, it worked its dark magic. A severely ill and uncomfortable prisoner soon loses the capacity to resist or make plans or attempt to escape. For days, all Delaney could manage was to lie in his bunk and try to control his bowels.

His fever became severe. Even his guards began to look concerned as he lay sweating and trembling for hours. Eventually, through the haze of fever and delirium, Delaney saw what he thought was a more senior man arrive outside the cell and look in through the bars alongside the guards. This officer left, returning shortly afterward with a Burmese civilian, clearly a doctor.

The medical man came into Delaney's cell, speaking slow but exact English.

"Your illness is worrying to us," he said. "I am a doctor, Doctor Kyaw Ba."

Delaney shifted onto his side and said weakly: "I need medication and good water."

"Yes," Ba said. "I will arrange this. Even enemies of the country are well treated, as you will see."

Ba left the cell and returned about half an hour later. He carried an old-fashioned doctor's bag this time and some bottles of mineral water. He set these down on Delaney's small table and began preparing a syringe.

"What's that?" Delaney asked, knowing that whatever it might be it would be administered anyway.

"Antibiotic," Ba said. "Another one like this tomorrow. And a third day." He expertly swabbed Delaney's upper arm and gave him the injection. He poured some water into a glass and stirred a sachet of powder into it, stirring it for a long time.

"Drink this slowly, very slowly at first," Ba said. "I will leave you some other packets. It is for rehydration. Soon your sickness will go."

His captors had clearly decided he had been sufficiently weakened and tamed by the bout of dysentery. In a few days, Delaney was feeling well enough to sit up and take tentative steps around the cell. The guards let him shower in a cubicle at the end of the cellblock. They gave him fresh clothes, khaki prison issue. They gave him something to read: *The New Light of Myanmar*, the official English-language newspaper. The story of the firefight in the suburbs and his arrest did not appear.

The fever lingered. It intensified his dreams:

*Of course he dreams of Natalia. But just of Natalia now, no other women, no other female figures. They are swimming together, diving together, deep in an aquamarine lagoon, through which rays of sunlight undulate. There are dolphins with them, making wise noises, which he tries to understand. Above them floats his beloved sailboat, the hull dark against the bright sea and sky. Natalia swims ahead, at ease under the water, never surfacing, never needing to surface. Delaney feels no regret in this dream, no grief, no guilt anymore at his role in Natalia's death. She pauses occasionally, looking behind to see if he is still with her on their underwater journey. Delaney swims closer, closer, overtakes her, and suddenly she is gone. But again there is no regret. He feels the warm wonderful certainty that at last he and Natalia have become as one, that no matter where he goes, what dangers and troubles he encounters, they are swimming together as one.*

His interrogator identified himself as Lieutenant General U Maung. His English was very good.

"You are feeling better now," Maung said. It was not a question.

"Yes," said Delaney, sitting on his bunk. "Almost better."

"We have helped you to get better," Maung said. He sat in the cell's one chair. He was in his late fifties, still soldier-straight, with close-cropped salt-and-pepper hair and an extremely well-tended moustache. "Now you must help us to understand some things you have done. I am with the Directorate of Defense Services Intelligence."

Delaney knew, as any foreign correspondent in Southeast Asia knew, that the DDSI is the major player in a vast security apparatus that keeps Burma's population, and its opponents, under control. The methods were tight restrictions on contacts with foreigners, media censorship, surveillance of government employees, harassment of political activists, intimidation of families, confiscation of property, arbitrary arrests, detention, torture and extrajudicial executions.

The DDSI came under the direct control of General Khin Nyunt, the military intelligence chief known throughout the country simply as Secretary One. Other generals were above Nyunt in the SPDC hierarchy, but it was he who held sway. Delaney wondered how direct a connection there was between his interrogator and Secretary One. The more direct the reporting arrangement, the more danger he was in.

"You claim to be a journalist," Maung said.

"I am a journalist," Delaney said.

"Journalists do not simply come into this country and do as they like. Everyone knows that. If you are a journalist you would know that, too. There is too much false reporting about our country already," Maung said.

"I entered illegally," Delaney said.

"If that is true, you are in serious trouble with my government at least for this. If it is true and you are a journalist," Maung said. "We do not believe that this is true."

"What do you believe is true?" Delaney asked.

"We believe that you are a member of the band of foreign

mercenary soldiers sent into Myanmar to encourage the over-throw of our government," Maung said.

"I'm not a soldier," Delaney said.

"We believe that foreign interests were part of a plan to sow discontent and agitation among the population, those in the population who oppose this government. We believe, we know, that your mission was to enter the home of the lady, Aung San Suu Kyi, take her away from Myanmar and create agitation in the population."

"That would be an extremely foolish plan of action," Delaney said. "Impossible to carry out."

"Impossible without major support and complicity from certain foreign powers who oppose my government," Maung said.

Delaney said nothing.

"You are aware that Madame Suu Kyi is free to leave Burma at any time?" Maung said.

"So she is told," Delaney said.

"She can leave at any time. She chooses to stay. She is confined to her house for her own safety. Do you think she needs mercenary soldiers to rescue her?"

Delaney said nothing.

"Even when her husband was dying in England she did not go, she chose to stay," Maung said. "What does that tell us? She wishes to remain in Burma. She does not need soldiers to rescue her."

"That plan had nothing to do with me," Delaney said.

"Do you know of another foreigner, who also claimed to be a Canadian and a journalist, named Mr. Nathan Kellner?" Maung asked.

"Yes, he is a friend from many years ago. I knew him well when we worked in Montreal. He is the reason I am here," Delaney said.

The admission unsettled Maung, it seemed.

"You admit to knowing Kellner," Maung said.

"Yes. I was asked by his editor in London to try to find out where he had gone. He disappeared from Bangkok. They asked me to try to find him."

"And you joined a band of mercenaries who entered this country illegally, carrying weapons, knowing they were enemies of this government with evil intentions," Maung said.

"I entered with those soldiers because they forced me to. I had found them in a house Kellner used in Thailand, in Mae Sot. I was trying to find out where Kellner was, what he was doing. They took me with them into Burma."

"You were working with them, helping them."

"No. I am not a soldier."

"You are an agent."

"No."

"If you are a journalist, you were to write about their plan, help them sow agitation and opposition to this government."

"No."

Maung himself was becoming agitated.

"Do you know what happened to your friend Kellner?" he said.

"Yes, I think so," Delaney said. "I was told Kellner was dead."

"Who told you that?"

"General Thein. When he came to arrest the mercenaries in the apartment that day."

Maung stood up suddenly and put on his officer's cap.

"That day, General Thein and many of our good soldiers died," he said. "Your comrades killed many men before they were killed themselves that day."

"They were not my comrades," Delaney said.

"We believe they were. But only you crawled into another apartment when the fighting started and hid there like a rat in a corner while brave Burmese soldiers fought to defend this government against evil foreign interference," Maung said.

The initial interview, it seemed, was over.

Lieutenant General U Maung returned each day for almost a week, asking Delaney questions, pressing for details, usually rejecting or debating the answers he got. One day he brought with him an extremely thin man in civilian clothes who was from the Press Scrutiny Board, the country's chief censoring body and overseer of the policy that severely limits reporting about the regime inside and outside Burma.

"You are aware that every foreign journalist is required to make application before entering Burma for a media visa, and to register with our representatives abroad their intentions and the articles they intend to produce?" the press man said. He introduced himself only as Myint. He chain-smoked all the time he was in Delaney's cell, extinguishing his spent cigarettes on the bars and throwing them into the seatless toilet.

"Yes," Delaney said. "I have told General Maung that I entered the country illegally."

"You admit to this," Myint said.

"Yes," Delaney said.

"This is a serious offence," he said.

"I have told General Maung that I want to speak to an embassy official about all this. This is my right, surely," Delaney said.

Maung, standing to one side, laughed out loud.

"Please, Mr. Delaney," he said. "Do not speak of rights when you are in detention for serious crimes against our country."

"I should be allowed to speak to an embassy official."

"Which country are you from? Which one will it be today?"

"Canada. I have always said Canada. You know that."

"Where is your passport then?"

"It was taken from me. You know that already. Look at my press pass. It says where I am from."

"Canada does not have consular representation in Burma," Maung said.

"Australia's embassy will deal with Canadian issues; they do this," Delaney said. "I want to speak to someone from that embassy. Any Western embassy."

Delaney began to lose track of days. He was not ill treated, never tortured, but the repeated visits by General Maung and others occasionally accompanying him began to dissolve into each other. Delaney thought he had been in custody for almost three weeks when Maung, arriving at the usual hour, told him he would be escorted elsewhere in the prison.

Three armed guards went with them down a series of corridors and stairways. Maung walked ahead. On the way Delaney saw some other Westerners in cells, some looking very bad indeed, and he saw many Burmese, also looking haggard and unwell. No one spoke or called out.

Eventually they stopped in a damp sub-basement outside a heavy double door.

"This is our morgue," Maung said, and waited for Delaney to react.

"What do you expect me to say, General?" Delaney asked. "That I am frightened?"

"I want to show you something in here. Come," Maung said.

He pushed open the swinging doors and spoke briefly to an orderly wearing a green smock and surgeon's cap. The orderly consulted a clipboard at his small desk and led them to a row of large stainless-steel drawers at the back. He pulled open one drawer, revealing a body covered in a muslin shroud.

"This is where Mr. Kellner's story ended," Maung said.

He motioned for the orderly to remove the shroud. Kellner's body was the pale yellow-green hue of those long dead—not decomposed because kept very cold, but the wrong colour altogether, a morgue colour. The body bore a number of marks: scrapes, cuts, bruising. The face was badly bruised, one corner of the mouth had been cut and a scab remained.

"Shall I tell you when I am sufficiently frightened?" Delaney said.

"You are arrogant, Delaney," Maung said. "This is no place for arrogance. Here, or anywhere else in this prison."

They stood looking at each other over Kellner's body.

"I know it is in your power to put me in one of these drawers beside Kellner," Delaney said. "I know that already. But I tell you, I have told you, that you are wrong about me. And if I disappear, my country will know it was at the hand of your government. That is all I can say."

Maung stared at Delaney for a long time. The orderly stood at ease, hands clasped behind his back

"No one has come for Kellner," Maung said.

"Someone will," Delaney said. "You and I are not the only ones to know he died in Burma."

Back in his cell, Delaney thought for a long time about Kellner. About his crazy life and the way he had ended up in a cold prison morgue somewhere very far from home. Delaney tried to understand what would have prompted the man to embark on such a wild and dangerous scheme.

He thought of the safe house in Mae Sot, with the special room dedicated to Aung San Suu Kyi. Everything carefully assembled and laid out, everything she could possibly want, except her freedom. An insane private shrine to the lady of Kellner's dreams.

He thought of Kellner's study in Bangkok, of the photographs of Suu Kyi carefully pinned up, of the bizarre love letters that never got mailed. The notebooks, the planning, the obsession with one woman, the image of one woman.

He thought also of Mai, Kellner's daylight woman, his real world woman. She would grieve for Kellner, miss him terribly. She was young, beautiful, bright, articulate and kind. Why was she not enough? Why was any real world woman never, apparently, enough?

The Australian embassy official was Bruce Jopson. He looked extremely hot and flushed when he was escorted into Delaney's cell. His short-sleeved shirt was damp with sweat, his necktie was as loose as it could be and still be called a tie.

"I've been trying to get these bastards to let me see you for two bloody weeks, mate," Jopson said. "Your lot have been driving me mad with phone calls and emails and diplomatic pouches. You must be a bloody media superstar over in Canada."

"I'm glad to see someone at last," Delaney said.

"You look bad. You look like death warmed over, mate. You're one lucky lad your government knows you're in here, or you'd probably never get out," Jopson said. "This is a nasty bloody place."

"I'm pretty keen to get out," Delaney said.

"Well, you've pissed off a lot of people, mate. An awful lot of people. It's going to be a bit tricky, this is. You'll be lucky to get off with no jail term. They don't like journos here, they just don't like journos. And the bit of bother the other day with the mercenaries, well, that's really pissed a lot of important people right off."

"They buy into me being a journalist?" Delaney said.

"Oh yeah, I suppose. Yeah. Your lot have been telling everybody that over and over. And me too. Now you are actually a journalist, you're sure about that, are you?" Jopson said with a conspiratorial smile.

"Lifelong, card-carrying," Delaney said.

"No other freelance activities?" Jopson seemed to need something, anything, more, just to know where he stood. "For your lot back home?"

Delaney paused. "Hardly any," he said.

"Right, then we better bloody get to work and get you out of here," Jopson said.

"How are you explaining your side of things?" Delaney said.

"What side might that be, mate?"

"Up north, in Mongla. The mercenaries and their deal with the casino guys. The security arrangement."

Jopson straightened up.

"Very sensitive stuff, that is. I wouldn't go too far down that road if I were you. In here or when we get you out. Sensitive stuff, that. It's a tough place to do business, Burma. Really tough. Our people do what they have to do to make an honest buck out of their investments."

"An honest buck," Delaney said.

"Absolutely," Jopson said.

"With some pretty nasty partners," Delaney said.

"Welcome to the world of international business, mate. Welcome to the real world."

"Mercenaries. On the payroll of an Australian business doing work in Burma."

"Nothing to do with me. A business transaction. Their choice. Nothing to do with Australian policy over here. Business."

"But you knew about it."

"We know a whole lot of things about what our business-people get up to in this part of the world. That's our job."

"Right," Delaney said.

"Those mercs are history anyway," Jopson said. "The whole idea's dead, if you'll pardon the expression."

"Right," Delaney said.

Eventually, they let him make a phone call to the Canadian side. They let him call the Canadian embassy in Bangkok. Jopson gave him a name to ask for. It was Rawson.

"Delaney, for God's sake, are you all right over there?" Rawson said.

"Not bad, OK for now. I was sick for a while. Hoping to get out of here soon. How's that looking?" Delaney said.

"Hard to talk about properly on the telephone, Francis. We're doing all we can. We are making a strong case for you, trust me on that. From the highest levels. But you've broken some national laws over there. Your newspaper is not too happy with you about that either, by the way."

Delaney knew this was for the benefit of the DDSI people surely also on the line.

"The paper knows all that's happened?" Delaney said.

"Most of it, Francis," Rawson said. "Details later, OK?"

"You coming over to Rangoon?"

"Best if I stay here in Bangkok. I can get more done here, I think. The Aussies are making strong representations on our behalf."

"There's an Australian angle to this story too, Jon," Delaney said. "Up in Mongla."

"We're aware of that," Rawson said. "All sides are aware."

"Can you call someone for me?"

"Sure, who?"

"Kate Hunter," Delaney said. It felt good to have a woman to ask about. A daylight real world woman.

"Already done. I'll call her again."

"She OK?"

"Very worried about you, Francis."

That felt good too.

A few days after his phone call with Rawson he was taken out of the prison in an army van. There were no windows in the back, but through an air vent in the side he could see the crumbling streets of Rangoon sliding past. They went to a colonial-era building inside a fenced compound. There were many army vehicles and motorcycles moving about.

His destination, it turned out, was General Maung's office. Maung was there, surrounded by the trappings and memorabilia of a career in the Burmese army.

An enormous, highly polished glass-topped desk. Water decanter and glasses neatly set out near a black telephone and intercom. Glass-fronted bookshelves jammed with awards, medallions, small commemorative flags, banners, paperweights. Diplomas and certificates of appreciation and commendation on the walls.

Two other senior officers in uniform sat on leather armchairs in a corner opposite Maung's desk. Maung motioned for Delaney to sit on a leather sofa. He looked very much out of place in his prison khakis.

"Mr. Delaney, these men are my esteemed colleagues," he said. "Senior General Thun Shwe and Major General Sein Ye Aye."

The two generals nodded briefly at Delaney. Shwe was the oldest, a man with a very puffy face and drooping sacs under his eyes. Ye Aye wore tortoise-shell sunglasses even though indoors.

A young secretary wearing a tight shift dress came in carrying a tray of tea already poured into floral-design cups. She placed the tray on the low table in front of the sofas, looking furtively at the Westerner sitting in his prison garb. The two generals picked up cups and added sugar and milk to their tea. Maung stayed behind the desk.

"You may drink tea," he said to Delaney. Delaney reached for a cup and set it down on the table in front of him.

Maung spoke briefly to the secretary as she left. She nodded. A few moments later, she came back in with Bruce Jopson, looking impressive now with a tan summer suit, sky blue button-down shirt and a carefully knotted tie. He was wearing wire-rimmed spectacles, giving him a professorial appearance.

"G'day, my friends," Jopson said, shaking hands with the three military men. "Delaney, I hope you are well."

"Well enough, thank you," Delaney said.

Jopson sat beside Delaney on the sofa, helped himself to tea, nibbled on a biscuit.

"Let me say that my government is extremely pleased and

grateful to all of you for your cooperation on this important mat-ter," Jopson said. "My ambassador has asked me to convey to you his personal thanks and best wishes."

"Thank you, Mr. Jopson," Maung said.

"The government of Canada, whom we are representing in this, also sends its thanks and warmest wishes. The Canadian ambassador in Bangkok has asked me to do this as well."

Maung and the other generals nodded.

"Serious matters," Shwe said. "Most grave."

"Indeed," Jopson said. "Indeed."

"Mr. Delaney," Maung said, "the State Peace and Development Council of Myanmar has, as you have probably gathered this morning, decided to release you into the custody of the Australian embassy. In the interest of our relations with Australia in particular and with your country also we have decid-ed to release you, even though you are clearly guilty of a serious breach of the laws of Myanmar, for which you would under normal circumstances have been given a term in our jails."

"We thank you once again," Jopson said, looking sternly over at Delaney.

"I am grateful," Delaney said.

"There are questions that remain unresolved," Shwe said.

"Yes, there are many questions that we choose to leave unresolved in the interest of harmonious relations with the inter-national community," Maung said. "We have decided that we will do this in your case, Mr. Delaney, as a gesture of goodwill."

"But you are no longer welcome in Myanmar," Ye Aye said. "You will go immediately and you will never be allowed to return."

"We have satisfied ourselves that you are a journalist, that is why we have spared you further time in jail," Maung said. "But you have displayed a reckless lack of regard for our laws here, Mr. Delaney, and you will be deported from our country immediately."

"This is a generous and far-sighted solution to a difficult problem, General Maung," Jopson said.

"We are hopeful, Mr. Delaney, that on your return to Canada you will compose newspaper reports that reflect the true situation in Myanmar and the generous way in which you were treated," Maung said.

"I always strive for accuracy in my reporting, General Maung," Delaney said.

Maung looked at him for a long time.

"We are hopeful, Mr. Delaney, that your reports will show clearly how Myanmar is constantly under threat from those who do not share our view of how to best meet the needs of our people. We hope that your reports will describe the evil plot by foreign soldiers to destabilize our government and put Madame Aung San Suu Kyi at grave risk. She does not need rescue. She is safe here and can leave this country at any time. We are hopeful that you will write of this dangerous plan to kidnap the lady, the plan which you became aware of and which brought you into this country illegally."

"Mr. Delaney is a respected journalist. What he writes always generates significant interest," Jopson said.

"I will do my best to write something that reflects what I have learned here," Delaney said.

"We are not monsters here. You have been well treated. You will tell that in your country," Shwe said.

"I have been well treated," Delaney said. He looked at Jopson, could see Jopson was willing him not to say too much, not to mention Kellner, to just ride things out to the end.

"There are those in the Western media who spread lies about Myanmar, Mr. Delaney," Ye Aye said. "This generates bad feelings about this country. It hinders our development, and frightens investors and foreign experts who could help us. We are a poor country, in a development stage. The State Peace and Development Council of Myanmar takes decisions that are not always well understood outside the country. But always we have the interests of our people at heart."

The other generals nodded and looked at Delaney for a reply. Delaney looked at Jopson. Jopson said: "May I have some more tea?"

The Australian embassy car was parked in a small patch of shade near the entrance to Maung's office building. It was a black Toyota. The muscular young driver looked far more like a Special Forces man than garden variety embassy staff. He had left the car idling with the air conditioning on; he got out to open the back door when Delaney and Jopson came into the sunlight.

"Clear?" the driver said to Jopson.

"Almost," Jopson said. "Let's go."

The leather seats inside the car were ice cool. Delaney slid into the back. Jopson came in afterward.

"Go," Jopson said.

The driver headed to the gate of the compound, headlights on. A small Australian flag fluttered on a standard attached to the right-front fender. A soldier at the gatehouse came out and pushed up the metal barrier. The car glided into the swarm of Rangoon's afternoon traffic and the barrier went back down.

"Just like that. Not going back to Insein, nothing?" Delaney said.

"That's how it works. No fanfare. You're out with just the shirt on your back. And that's bloody lucky. Let's get you onto a plane and let me start playing tennis again."

They went to the Australian embassy on Strand Road. The doorman and the receptionist looked startled and then amused as Jopson and the driver hurried Delaney up the stairs and through security in his prison overalls.

"Special guest, Bruce?" a young clerk in a golf shirt called out from behind the glass of the visa section.

"Too right," Jopson said.

They hustled Delaney into a reception room on the first floor. The driver stayed with him, clearly more than just a driver.

"Tim Scott," he said, shaking Delaney's hand. "I'll be going with you to the airport."

"One of our tough guys," Jopson said. "There's a Thai Airways flight out to Bangkok tonight at 21:00. Timmy's going to fly over there with you. There's a shower in the room through that door over there. Get yourself in there and have a shave and clean yourself up a bit. There are some clothes in there for you too."

As the warm soapy water cascaded over him, Delaney began to relax for the first time in many weeks. When he got out of the shower, he regarded himself in the bathroom mirror. He had lost weight, 10 kilos at least. His hair was long, too long. He had big dark circles under his eyes.

*Media superstar*, he thought.

Jopson had organized some lunch. Delaney sat on a couch eating from a tray on a low coffee table. Salad, fruit, sandwiches, juice. Things he had not seen for weeks. Jopson and the driver sat watching him eat hungrily.

"That's bloody pathetic, mate. Oliver Twist stuff, that is," Jopson said.

"More gruel, please sir," Scott said.

"Can I make a phone call?" Delaney asked when he had finished eating.

"Best if we just get you out of here, I think," Jopson said. "Rawson is aware in Bangkok. And they tell me you've got the world's smallest family. Not many people to call anyway. A sister in LA and that's it. Plus some Mountie girlfriend. Bloody pathetic."

Delaney said good-bye to Jopson on the steps of the embassy.

"Glad to see the back of you, cobber," the Australian said.

"Thanks, Bruce. Really," Delaney said.

"Don't get soppy now," Jopson said.

"Thank the ambassador for me," Delaney said.

"He doesn't want to know anything more about you, mate. Sick to death of you and he hasn't even met you."

"Thank him for me."

"He will be scanning the world's press, of course, for your excellent forthcoming articles on Myanmar," Jopson said. "And on Australia's fledgling business interests here. Investor confidence. Very sensitive stuff, that."

The Canadians had sent over a new passport for him. Delaney thumbed through it as Scott manoeuvred the car through darkened streets to the airport. The picture of him was perhaps ten years old, a press ID photo they had retrieved from somewhere or other. He was no longer the person in the photograph, hadn't been that person for a long time. But he liked his new passport very much. His old one had been battered and beaten, full of the stamps and stickers and remnants of years of solitary travel. This one was crisp and fresh and full of possibility.

# Chapter 15

Rawson was waiting for him at Bangkok Airport. He was accompanied by another tired-looking CSIS man who said nothing at all. They took Delaney and his Australian escort into a shabby VIP waiting area with bad drapes and low wooden coffee tables strewn with an assortment of cups, saucers and multicoloured metal tea flasks. Thai policemen and a haggard Thai government official hovered nearby.

"Mr. Rawson, on behalf of the Commonwealth of Australia I hereby turn over the prisoner to your good custody," Tim Scott said with a huge smile. He winked at Delaney. "Good riddance."

"My government thanks you and your colleagues very much," Rawson said.

"I'm going downtown to get pissed," Scott said. "Can you blokes organize some transport?"

"Of course," Rawson said. He motioned to the other CSIS man, who went over to have a word with the Thai official.

"Delaney, I won't say it's been a pleasure," Scott said, offering his hand.

"Thank you very, very much," Delaney said, getting up. "Really."

"If you are ever in Canada . . ." Rawson said.

"Never, mate. No chance," Scott said. "Too bloody cold."

He headed off with a Thai policeman. Rawson and Delaney sat back down.

"Are you all right, Francis?" Rawson said.

"Yes. Now I am."

"Was it bad?"

"At the beginning."

"You are very lucky to be alive. Lucky just to be out of that damn jail. It took everything we had to get you out of there. You know that, don't you?"

"I would imagine it did," Delaney said.

"We were all dreadfully worried."

"I was too."

In the car, moving through the midnight traffic and heat haze, they said surprisingly little. Rawson was leaving Delaney alone with his thoughts, but also clearly thinking about damage control, information gathering, next steps. Delaney simply watched the city slide by; resting, giving thanks.

Rawson was not a Royal Hotel sort of man. He had booked them instead into the Oriental, one of Bangkok's best, in Thanon Silom on the river front. The parking lot entrance was gated, manned by uniformed hotel security. The lobby was palatial, ice cool, all but deserted in the early hours. All surfaces gleamed, all was peace and safety and elegance.

"Breakfast debrief," Rawson said. "Too late for any of that now. We've put some things in your room for you. From back at the Royal, and some new stuff. You should be all right for tonight. I'm in 2107."

Delaney was in 2118, with a view of the river and the gilt-covered *wats* and snow white pagodas on the other side. Rawson had put them both on the same floor but had spared them the unease of rooms side by side.

His suitcase was placed neatly beside the bed and there were a few plastic bags with new shirts, underwear, toothpaste, shaving gear. His laptop bag was on the desk.

Delaney knew he would not be able to sleep for hours, if at all. He took a long shower in the five-star surrounds of the bathroom. He put on the hotel bathrobe, helped himself to a miniature bottle of Jameson's from the mini-bar, munched on overpriced cashew nuts, stared out the window at the scenery.

As he was cracking the seal on a third tiny whiskey bottle, his laptop was booting up. He connected to the Internet through the hotel's data port on the desk, logged on for email, and his life cascaded back out to him on the computer screen.

Dozens of messages: from Rawson, then Kate, O'Keefe, *Tribune* people—many from the newspaper. A couple from his sister, one from the Jung Society, more from Kate. A trail of connections and obligations that he had, for more than a month, been forced, or in some cases fortunate enough, to neglect.

Kate's messages ranged in tone from routine inquiries and chitchat to the concerned, then to the gravely concerned. The newspaper's messages went though that range as well, but ended with the profoundly displeased. There were many loose ends for Delaney to untangle or re-tangle. That would be for another day, however. Tonight, he would only call Kate.

She picked up the direct line phone at her RCMP desk.

"Hunter," she said.

"Delaney," he said.

"Oh, Frank, for god's sake, where are you?"

"Bangkok. Safe and sound. In a very fine hotel looking out over the city. No problem."

"For god's sake, Frank. Are you all right? I've been so worried. I got some calls from Ottawa with news but no one really seemed to know what was going on at all. They said you had been arrested in Rangoon, no one knew exactly where you were, no one knew when they'd let you go or if they would let you go. What on earth happened to you? Did they hurt you? What were you doing in Burma anyway? You said you were in Thailand."

"I'm OK, Kate. Really. I'm OK now. It's a very, very long story and I will tell you all about it soon."

"All?"

Delaney paused.

"Probably," he said. He paused again. "You're the first person I've called."

"I'm so glad to hear your voice, Frank," she said.

"I'm glad you're glad to hear my voice. I'm glad you're the first one I wanted to call." The Australians would accuse him of getting soppy.

"I missed you, Frank. I was very, very worried. More than you deserved."

"Thank you for your worry, Ms. Hunter. I will make it up to you."

"When are you coming back to Montreal? When will you tell me about all of this?"

"I can't come back right away. There are still some things I have to do."

"Frank, for god's sake."

He surprised himself by saying: "I think you should come over."

"Where, to Bangkok?" Kate said.

"Yes."

"When? You mean right away?"

"Yes. Come stay with me in this terrific hotel while I tie up some loose ends and then we can go to the beach somewhere for a while. Ko Chang is good. Come over."

She paused at the other end of the line.

"Nice idea," she said.

"Can you get away?"

"Probably. They know I've been worried about someone, that I've had some troubles."

"Tell them it's a family thing," he said, aware how soppy that sounded.

"Nice idea," she said.

"There are flights every day," Delaney said. "Vancouver, then Bangkok. The bathrobes are good at this hotel. Fluffy white ones, with a nice monogram. I'll get them to send one up for you."

"You should get yourself arrested by the Burmese police more often, Frank," she said. "Seems to do you good."

"Something they put in the water over there," he said.

The next morning Delaney and Rawson had a very long breakfast in the Oriental's gigantic main dining room, busy with international business types hurrying back and forth to the buffet table for their scrambled eggs. The hotel hubbub gave them privacy.

Delaney filled Rawson in on almost all he had discovered on his latest CSIS assignment. Rawson, as always in these matters, looked on impassively, giving no sign of how much or how little he already might have known. Every bit the CSIS spymaster now.

"A real shame about your driver, Francis," Rawson said eventually.

"I'll try to see his wife later today or tomorrow."

"Who actually killed him? Which of the mercenaries?"

"A guy named Abbey. Nigerian."

"And you're sure that one's dead? You're sure all members of that group are dead?"

"Yes, very sure. No one could have got out of that apartment alive. Not with all that firepower and not with how angry the soldiers were that day."

"There's not a lot we can do about your driver now, Francis."

"I know that. I'll handle it," Delaney said.

"We can't do much for Kellner's girl either," Rawson said.

"I'll handle that too."

"You are absolutely sure that was Kellner's body you saw in Rangoon."

"Absolutely."

"Not sure if they'll ever release the body back to us," Rawson said. "They haven't even officially acknowledged they had him, let alone that he's dead."

"Jon, my best guess now is that your guys knew he was dead before you even sent me over here," Delaney said. "But as always, I get only the minimum information required and then you set me loose."

"Not quite like that, Francis."

"Did you know Kellner was dead before I came over?"

"We knew he was in some serious trouble."

"Did you know about his crazy idea to kidnap Suu Kyi?"

Rawson did not answer.

"Jon, I almost got killed on this assignment for you. My driver was killed. He had a wife and two kids. You can't just sit there now and play spy. You send people out on these things—they need to know what's what. Preferably before they go, but absolutely they have a right to know afterward exactly what's been going on. Who knew what. I keep being sent to places where people get killed because I don't know enough about what I'm involved in."

"Easy, Francis."

No one mentioned Natalia's name. No one needed to.

"Did you know about the Suu Kyi angle?" Delaney asked again. "Kellner got himself killed with that stupid idea. Did you know about it? And did you just let him carry on to see how far he was going to go?"

"No, Francis. If we had been sure what he was up to we would have stopped him before it got out of hand."

"It was out of hand the minute he started planning for such a crazy thing. You should have stopped him right away."

"We weren't sure. We were never sure. We only had reports he might be going down that path."

"Who from?"

"You know I can't tell you that, Francis."

"You can if you want to. Someone owes me the full story. Or I'll get it myself."

"Francis, there can be no stories about this. Never. You know that."

"I'm a journalist, Jon."

"Not always. Not on this assignment."

"Either I'm a spy, or I'm a reporter. If I'm a spy, you tell me the whole story, so I know."

"All anyone needs to know is that a Canadian citizen with delusions of grandeur was, thank god, not able to intervene in Burmese politics. His wild scheme would probably have gotten an awful lot of innocent people killed, including possibly the best hope that country has for a democratic leader, and maybe started a civil war in a country he had no business being in in the first place. We couldn't have allowed that to happen and we wouldn't have allowed that to happen. No matter how we might originally have found out."

Rawson went silent, stirring coffee.

"Who tipped you off to the Suu Kyi plan? When?" Delaney asked again. "Who told the Burmese? I need to know that."

"Why? So you can go after someone? That's not your job, Francis. That's not even your style. And we were never quite sure what the plan entailed until you found out for us. We just had indications."

"Look, Jon, we both know Kellner was crazy; he was addled by drugs and booze and the whole idea was literally a pipe dream. But he got himself killed doing it and in a crazy way I think he honestly thought he was doing something good. He thought he was going to save Suu Kyi and start a process in Burma that would be a good thing for the people there. He was completely off his head, but I believe he thought he was doing a good thing. I want to know how it all fell down and whose fault it was that the Burmese found out and killed him. He deserves at least that much."

"That's not how we see it," Rawson said. "He's no hero in my eyes."

"He might have ended up a hero," Delaney said.

"You can't be serious," Rawson said.

"If someone gets killed doing something he believes in, even if it's crazy, even if it's some drug-induced pipe dream, if he's trying to do something he thinks is a good thing for someone else, then he at least deserves to have people around him know what exactly went on. Maybe he's no hero, but he deserves a little bit more than a drawer in some Rangoon prison morgue and no marker."

"So how many people get to know, Francis? Where do you stop with something like this? How far does the story go? Who needs to know? Who else may get hurt by it?"

"Whoever spilled this to the Burmese, no matter whether it was direct or indirect, got Kellner killed. He almost got Ben Yong and me killed in Bangkok that day outside Kellner's apartment. He eventually did get Ben killed. We would never have blundered into Kellner's place in Mae Sot like that if we had known everything we needed to know."

Rawson looked very thoughtful. He lit a cigarette, a rare thing for him to do at this time of the day.

"Let's just say, Francis, that Kellner had some indiscreet friends. At least one very indiscreet friend. Word can then get around fast in a place like Bangkok. That's all I am going to tell you and it's far more than I should be telling you."

"Cohen," Delaney said.

"No comment," Rawson said.

Rawson had to go. There would be other debriefings, meetings, consultations later, Delaney was sure of that. And the Thai police still wanted to interview him about the circumstances of Ben's death. Rawson and others would accompany him for that, when the time came.

He went back up to his room to rest and regroup. He was still weak from his time at Insein and he wanted to gather his strength. He slept a dreamless sleep until early afternoon and then started to tie up some loose ends and to make a plan. Today he was feeling far more journalist than spy.

He called Ben's wife to arrange a meeting for later that day. She was monosyllabic on the telephone, still overcome with grief. He had told the Australians early on that Ben had been killed and where and by whom. They had told the Canadians before he was released. Someone had already had the job of telling Mrs. Yong.

"Yes, Kuhn Frank," she said. "Come. It will be good if you come. Ben liked you very much. Always."

He called Mai. She was also paralyzed with grief. Again, news that her man was dead had preceded Delaney's return to Bangkok.

"Oh Frank, please, please tell me it is not true what they tell me now," Mai cried out to on the phone. "Please tell me Nathan is coming back to me. Please."

"He's gone, Mai. I'm very, very sorry."

She wept quietly at her end.

"I'll come to see you. Tomorrow, OK?" he said.

"OK, Frank," she said "That will be OK."


Delaney sat on his terrace for a while, drinking Jameson's and daydreaming; resting, making his plans. The river far below buzzed with boat traffic and horns and muffled shouts. He, too, was paralyzed for a time.

The phone rang. It was Kate, calling very early Montreal time to tell him she was on a flight that night bound for Bangkok. His heart raced like a schoolboy's.

"Vancouver to Tokyo then Bangkok overnight tonight. You'll already be in bed when I fly. I can't believe I'll be seeing you tomorrow," she said. Like a schoolgirl.

"Any trouble getting the time off?" Delaney asked.

"None. Professional reasons. A Mountie always gets her man."

Rawson had organized a car for him, with a Thai driver. No uniform, but almost certainly a policeman or special services. The driver said nothing at all, just drove slowly through the heaving main Bangkok boulevards and then on to smaller and smaller back streets to Ben Yong's neighbourhood.

Ben's wife was waiting for him on a straight-backed chair set up outside the cinder block wall that surrounded her modest house in a dusty soi far from downtown. A large courtyard space where Ben used to park his car was now empty and forlorn. Cans of motor oil and plastic containers of turquoise windshield washer fluid were stacked neatly to one side.

She had made Delaney an elaborate Thai meal. The children had been sent to her sister's for a while, she said. The house would be too sad for children to live in for a while yet. She would have to burn many more offerings of incense and put many more offerings of flowers and oranges in the small Buddhist shrine in the garden before the children could be expected to come back.

"Ben was one of the most reliable people I have ever, ever met," Delaney said awkwardly as Mrs. Yong stirred furiously in her sizzling wok. She put down her spatula and gave him a slow wai.

"Ben said he could depend on you too."

"I should not have taken him where we went, Mrs. Yong," Delaney said.

"He went many dangerous places with reporters," she said. "It was his job. He said he liked his job. He liked all the foreign reporters."

"I made a mistake, Mrs. Yong. We should not have been there."

"You did not kill him, Mr. Delaney."

Delaney was not so sure.

"He is not the first person who has died because of me and the work I do," Delaney said. "A woman I loved also died because of me, because of a mistake I made. I never wanted that to happen again."

"The souls of the dead are at rest if we love them," she said. "It is your own soul, and mine, that now must seek rest in this lifetime."

They ate silently for a time, looking up at each other occasionally and smiling.

"What will you do now, Mrs. Yong? You and your family."

"My family is very large, Mr. Delaney. We will be OK. We will stay here and my family and Ben's family will help us."

"I would like to help too," Delaney said.

"You have come to talk. That is enough."

"Please tell me if you need anything, anytime. Even a long while from now," he said.

"I will."

They drank tea.

"There is one thing. Two things," Mrs. Yong said.

Delaney looked steadily at her.

"Did you see where they buried him?" she said. "Shall we leave him there?"

"His body has not been brought back?"

"Not yet. They are saying it is still a crime scene. But if it is nice there maybe he should stay?"

Delaney thought of the small clearing in the trees where Ben had been hastily buried. He thought of the birdsong and the butterflies and the heat and light. But it was not the right place.

"I think he is in a good place but it is not right for his final place. I think you should bring him back closer to his home and family," Delaney said.

"And what happened to his car? We were wondering. My son especially. Ben loved his car."

"It was left near where Ben was killed, Mrs. Yong. I can try to find out where it is now if you want me to."

"Please. Yes. My son has been asking. He wants to be a media driver too, when he grows up."

That evening at the hotel there were drinks and more debriefings with Rawson and an embassy man named Franklin. The Thai side had still not indicated when they wanted to see Delaney but he was expected to stay in the country for a time. Rawson was clearly worried Delaney planned to write a story about Kellner's plot to take Suu Kyi. Delaney did not reassure him.

Rawson wanted also to talk about the Australians in Burma. Not the embassy Australians—the casino Australians.

"They contracted for some private security through Kellner," Delaney said. "He and his guys and the generals ripped them off. Then the generals double-crossed Kellner's guys in Rangoon."

"There is too much of this private militia stuff going on everywhere these days," Rawson said. "Every two-bit mining project or building project or dam project or whatever it is tries to hire a private army to take care of things for them. It's easy money for mercenaries and it never works out without problems. The Australians aren't the only ones going that way. Canadian companies are doing it too, in Africa and other places."

"Well, those Aussies were well and truly ripped off," Delaney said. "They'll be looking for payback in some way. Money, or political payback. They aren't just going to sit around and get taken like that."

"They seem tough?" Rawson asked.

"Not particularly. Probably in over their heads in Burma. They'd be better off back in outback Queensland somewhere, where they know the rules of the game. Their embassy in Rangoon seemed to know all about them. They want to keep it quiet. An investor confidence issue was how the embassy people put it. Not keen on the story getting out.

"None of us are keen on any of these stories getting out, Francis," Rawson said gravely.

In his room alone later, Delaney finally began to address the issue of work and the fact that his editors at the newspaper were distinctly unamused. The last email in a series from Patricia Robinson and Harden, the editor-in-chief, said it all.

*"Frank,"* Harden wrote, *"I'm told now that you have been arrested in Rangoon on an assignment. I have no idea when you might eventually see this and I, like everyone at the paper, fear for you and hope you will return safely. But the minute you do get this email, we will need to talk about a number of issues. The first and most important of which is how you ended up in Burma in the first place. Neither I nor anyone else at this newspaper assigned you to Burma, nor to Thailand for that matter. Patricia tells me you simply announced one morning you were off to London to research a column. London is not Bangkok or Rangoon. And even so, I did not assign you to or approve of your travel to London or anywhere else. Once again, we all pray for your safe return and we are doing all we can to help the embassy and External Affairs to negotiate with the Burmese authorities. But for the record, and for any legal issues that may arise later, this newspaper did not assign you to Europe or to Asia and can bear no responsibility for your situation. As soon as you are safely out of Burma, I must insist that we speak immediately about a number of important issues."*

Delaney saw that the email had been copied to Patricia, to the newspaper's lawyer and to someone at External Affairs in Ottawa whose name he did not recognize.

He looked at his watch. Still too early in Montreal for him to call, thankfully. He would reply by email for the time being.

*"Dear Mr. Harden,"* Delaney wrote. *"I appreciate your concern and the concern of all my colleagues at the paper. I am sure you are already aware that I am safely back in Bangkok. I also very much appreciate the effort you and everyone else made to have me released. I am being debriefed by Canadian officials, and the Thai side wants*

*to see me as well to give them details of what happened. I will call you as soon as possible for a full discussion of all of this."*

*Suicidal*, Delaney thought, as he clicked on the Send icon and watched the email go. *Delaney is no longer at large. Delaney may soon be looking for work.*

He called O'Keefe, knowing he would wake him up.

"Delaney, for God's sake, where are you man?" O'Keefe said groggily.

"Did I wake you?" Delaney said.

"No, of course not, I was just coming in from my overnight shift at the 24-hour vigil we have all been keeping for you at Notre Dame Cathedral. A cast of thousands. Your picture on placards, locks of your hair in reliquaries."

"I'm back in Bangkok now."

"Well, that's a good thing. We were all worried at the press club someone would have to go all the way over to hellish Rangoon and retrieve your body."

"No need."

"You all right, Francis? They treat you bad?"

"Yeah, a little bad at first."

"Even I started to get a little bit worried there for a while."

"Thank you."

"What the Christ were you doing in Burma anyway?"

"I think I've got a good story going, Brian."

"I hope to hell you've got something. I'm not sure you've got a newspaper to write it in anymore. Harden is some pissed off, my man. Royally pissed off."

"It's more of a magazine piece anyway," Delaney said.

"That's the spirit. No loyalty to the *Tribune* whatsoever. Good career move."

Mordecai Israel Sebastian Cohen was always a trifle paranoid.

The drugs and the alcohol and the dissolute life he led had made him so. But today, lately, his paranoia was extreme. As he went about his appointed rounds, delivering small stashes of dope here and there to the media and expat crowd in Bangkok and environs, he was sure he was being followed.

This was not the world-stopping, heart-stopping paranoia of the cokehead, in which sufferers imagine helicopters, rocket ships, hovering overhead with surveillance cameras and recording equipment monitoring the thoughts inside your very head. This was instead the creeping, nagging paranoia of the merely addled—a paranoia nonetheless worrying, because, in contrast to the cocaine-fuelled variety, there was always the possibility that someone, indeed, was watching, that some menace was indeed imminent.

Cohen darted in and out of taxis and tuk-tuks and various buildings, sweating profusely in his Hawaiian shirt while out of air-conditioning range; shivering and freezing while inside. He glanced incessantly over his shoulder, certain, persuaded, that he would see any number of police or hulking civilian assassins about to swoop.

He broke one of his own unshakable rules and smoked a fat joint of choice Chiang Mai gold outside, in public, while standing on a busy street corner near Patpong. His nerves were bad, very bad, had been getting worse each day since he got news that Delaney and his driver had disappeared. That, along with Kellner's disappearance, had left him more shaky than usual. Far more.

There was that, and there was also the very strong possibility he had upset any number of players in Bangkok, northern Thailand, Burma and elsewhere. This was the most worrying aspect, he thought as he finished up the last of his outdoor joint. *Not cool, not cool, not cool*, he thought.

The Australians had been in touch, yelling at him in shifts down a bad phone line from Burma, demanding to know where

Kellner was, where their security detail was, where their money was. To their entreaties he played dumb, and deaf. Kellner's gig, not his, he said. He was just a helper, a messenger, a small player. Kellner's gig, he said.

The Burmese side did not call him or approach him, however, and he could not decide whether this was worrying or not. He was just a helper, a messenger, a small player, but this time, for once, he was on his own gig, a freelance gig. Not Kellner's. On the contrary. And this was now becoming most worrying, unbearably worrying. It had all, clearly, gone terribly wrong.

What had started out as a nice little sideline—a nice source of pocket money and, if he were honest, a nice source of pride that he, too, not just Kellner, could pull levers, run a scam, command respect—had now turned very sour indeed.

The Australians had at first been delighted with his little bits of information, his hints and allegations about Kellner's plan for a rip-off. Services rendered for cash that would, Cohen had thought, also prevent Kellner from getting himself killed up in Mongla. Doing a friend a little service, saving his ass, and getting paid for it by grateful parties on various sides; it didn't get much better than that. And if that meant that Kellner ended up with no money for his Suu Kyi thing, his even crazier thing for the lady, so much the better.

Or so it had seemed. Then Kellner disappeared and it had all started to unravel. Everyone suddenly on his case, questions from all sides, people passing through Bangkok at all hours of the day and night, Delaney dropping out of sight, the driver out of sight, hassles, worries, perturbations of all kinds. Uncool times, decidedly uncool. Now, stoned, paranoid and petrified Cohen went about his appointed rounds persuaded that soon, very soon, some heavy consequences would come crashing down around his aching, spinning head.

# Chapter 16

Delaney had been followed many times before, both as a journalist and as a CSIS operative, and he knew the signs. The signs this time were glaringly obvious. It did not come as a surprise; Rawson himself warned that they would both very likely be followed by any number of players right up until they left Bangkok.

The morning Kate was to arrive, Delaney left the hotel early, told his waiting official driver he was taking a walk and that he would be back soon. He walked through the parking lot to the back automobile gate, away from the river, and saluted back at the white-uniformed gate attendant.

He walked up a curved side street heavily shaded by giant mango trees and put his head in at various small overpriced shops that sold brass dinnerware and chess sets and basketry to the wealthy who, like himself, occasionally deigned to walk somewhere rather than take an air-conditioned car.

This made it complicated for whoever had been assigned that morning to watch him. It would involve either a conspicuous walk behind him across the broad parking lot or a clumsy tail operation in a car, stopping and starting conspicuously as Delaney moved in and out of shopfronts.

They chose the car method and made a very poor job of it.

Two solid-looking Asian men in suits, barely visible through the dark tint of the window glass on their white Land Cruiser. He'd seen the car on the first day he got back to Bangkok. Possibly plainclothes Thai police, Delaney thought. Possibly Burmese, but very difficult to know for sure. As he was already to travel with a Thai police or special services driver, he thought it more likely they were Burmese.

They parked up the street from where he window-shopped, not really making much attempt to conceal themselves anymore because they might lose him entirely if they allowed him too long a leash. Eventually, buying nothing, Delaney sauntered back through the hotel parking lot and into the back lobby. Through the plate glass he saw the Land Cruiser roll back through the gate and across a series of speed bumps to sit idling again near the back entrance.

Rawson was in the lobby, talking to some other Westerners in suits. He spotted Delaney and hurried over.

"I'm going out to the airport to get Kate," Delaney said. "That white Land Cruiser out there is my tail today."

Rawson went to the glass and looked out.

"Saw it yesterday. Pretty big vehicle for close surveillance," he said.

"Could be Thai, because they don't seem to care too much about whether we know they're there or not," Delaney said.

"But you've got one of their drivers anyway," Rawson said.

"Yeah. No matter who they are, I'm not keen on having them with me at the airport when I meet Kate."

"This idea of bringing Kate out here is not good, Francis. You know that. I don't see why you don't just wrap up the loose ends here and head back to Montreal. We don't like the Kate idea at all."

"Holiday, Jon. Some R&R after a tough assignment."

Rawson looked worried.

"I'd much sooner see you out of here altogether," he said. "Kate's going to make things even more complicated."

"We won't need an escort where we're going, Jon. We would in fact very much prefer no escort at that stage."

"Well, you'll have one anyway. My guys, the Thais for sure, maybe even the Burmese, depending on who owns the big four-wheel drive out there. No chance of a romantic getaway. That's exactly my point."

"We'll see," Delaney said.

He went back up to his room and called the airline to make sure Kate's flight was on time. He checked his email. Only one message of consequence, this from Harden at the *Tribune*. Delaney had still not called in and had not told the paper which hotel he was staying at. Email was the only way they could express their extreme displeasure. Harden, an ex–wire-service man, did this in very few words. Each message was getting shorter.

This one read: "Delaney, insist you call in ASAP. No excuses accepted. Regards, Harden."

Delaney wrote back, wire-style: "Got yours. Apols but still in debriefs. Best to give you full situationer when clear. Phone may not be secure. Please stand by. Thanks and bests, FD."

He normally avoided confrontations with editors, but in this case he was also still not sure how he wanted to play the Kellner story. If at all. And, if he were to file something, for whom and how much of the story to actually tell. He was not at all sure that the *Tribune* was the proper medium for the Kellner story or if they would run it anyway. He sensed another bad career move on the horizon.

Rawson was not in the lobby, but one of the CSIS or Canadian-embassy types still was. He looked about 30 years old; on a first overseas posting, probably, and determined not to mess up today's assignment. He came over when Delaney came out of the elevator carrying a sports bag and his laptop.

"You off?" he said. He sported trendy tiny rectangular glasses and precision sideburns. "I'm Ted Green. I'm based here." He offered his hand. Delaney shook it.

"I'm going out to the airport," he said.

"Your driver's outside," Green said.

"And my tail."

"Yes. White Land Cruiser. Two guys inside." Green looked very pleased with himself.

"Thanks for that, Ted."


Delaney wanted no company whatsoever at the airport—Thai, Burmese or Canadian. He told his driver to take him to the Regent at Siam Square, the Oriental's arch rival for the title of best hotel in the city. The driver looked surprised.

"No airport?" he said, lowering his sunglasses to look at Delaney over the back of the seat.

"No. I'm going to the Regent."

The driver pulled out and the Land Cruiser pulled out with them, making very little pretence now of not following. It stayed back five or six car lengths. Their little convoy moved out of the parking lot, down the curved side street at the back of the hotel and into the morass of Bangkok morning traffic.

When his driver pulled up at the Regent, Delaney got out quickly and said: "I'll be about an hour, maybe two. Meetings." The driver still looked dubious. He pulled his silver Peugeot into the shade of the hotel's entrance archway. The Land Cruiser sat in the intense sunlight across the street.

Delaney went directly through the lobby, around the main ground floor restaurant, past some function rooms and out onto the back terrace. He hurried past sunbathers sipping morning cocktails at the pool, past the pool attendant and the gardeners and the lawn sprinklers to the employee parking lot hidden behind a high row of hedges far out at the back. A security man at a gated break in the hedge looked startled when Delaney asked to be let through.

"Staff parking here, sir," he said. "Do you need a car, sir?"

"No, I want to go through this way. I'm getting the Sky Train."

Bangkok's elevated light rail train had been installed a few years earlier and had failed to make much of a dent in the city's world-renowned traffic problem. But it was fast and efficient and cheap and it transported thousands of workers each day who would otherwise have driven to their jobs in the city at hotels, offices and construction sites.

"I think car is better for you, sir. Taxi is better. I will get you a taxi," the security man said.

"No, thank you very much. I will go out this way and get the Sky Train."

Delaney moved through the gate. He could see the security man was weighing up whether it was worth offending a hotel guest or best to let this eccentric Westerner get lost on local mass transit and lose his wallet to pickpockets. He opted for the latter.

"Please watch your belongings on the train, sir," he said.

Delaney hurried through the parking lot and out onto a narrow back street. He turned left toward a main street and then hurried up the steep steps to the elevated station platform. There was a long queue for tickets so he simply walked straight on through the barrier area and onto a waiting train. The gate attendant did not even bother to ask the sole Westerner if he was carrying a ticket.

The train headed west to the National Stadium. Delaney got out there and moved quickly down to the street. Lines of Toyota taxis waited there and he climbed into one.

"Airport," he said.

Delaney had not actually waited in a crowd at an airport arrivals gate to greet anyone for a very long time. He allowed himself to enjoy this slightly domestic experience, along with all the families and drivers waiting with him. He found himself, like many in the midmorning crowd, craning his neck eagerly to see who was emerging next with laden baggage trolleys, to see who would be greeted with hugs and smiles and cries of delight.

Kate looked concerned as she came out, pushing a trolley with one small bag on it. Her hair was tied back and she wore a denim jacket, white T-shirt and a brown-and-white floral print skirt. An undercover Mountie, far undercover.

She scanned the heaving crowd, looking anxiously, as do all arriving passengers in a strange city, for the familiar face that would instantly humanize and soften the first moments. When she saw Delaney waving from far at the back, her broad smile locked onto his broad smile and the magnetic pull drew them swiftly together, parting the throng.

They kissed and embraced unself-consciously, like student lovers.

Delaney had reserved a room at the Amari airport hotel. It was just a short indoor walk away, no cab ride required, nothing to alarm or annoy them, nothing to delay their coming together.

As Kate showered, Delaney sat enjoying the upmarket order of their room, the absolute anonymity and comfort of a good business hotel. The intense quiet, the immaculate carpet and linen, the basket of fruit, the silver ice bucket, the booklets and menus and guides carefully laid out on tables and desk. The promise of peace and safety and ease.

Kate looked terrific in an oversized, over-luxurious white hotel bathrobe.

"Welcome to Asia," Delaney said.

"I think this is going to be all right," she said, towelling her hair with a huge white towel.

"No one in the world knows where we are," he said.

"That is a lovely, lovely feeling," she said. "How long can we stay here?"

"As long as we like," he said.

Kate draped her towel on a chair. The robe, too, she draped on the chair. Her skin glowed from the steaming hot water of the shower. Her face glowed. He couldn't take his eyes off her.

"Is this too much like a scene in a movie, Francis?" she said.

"This is the part I like the best," he said.

"She stands naked. They fall hungrily into each other's arms, do not emerge from the hotel room for hours, days even. They survive on ferocious, passionate, perfect sex and occasional room service meals."

"Exactly," he said.

It was, in fact, almost exactly like that. They began to think about emerging from their room only late the next afternoon. They did not act quickly on the idea. Kate lay in the bed with her right ear to Delaney's chest and her left arm around his hips as he tried to read the *Bangkok Post*.

"Did you think they were going to kill you, Frank?"

He put the newspaper down.

"I thought I might end up dead. But I didn't think they would purposely kill me."

"And your friend, Nathan Kellner?"

"They never told me what he died of and I didn't ask. He looked like he had taken a few beatings."

"You saw his body?"

"Yes."

"Where?"

"In a morgue in Rangoon. They took me there to show me."

"Did it scare you?"

"Yes, it did."

"Oh, Frank."

"Everything's OK now. Everything's fine. A few loose ends to tie up, then we can have a little holiday and go back to Montreal."

"Should you be scared still?"

"No, not really. Careful, yes. Scared, probably no reason anymore."

"Even after you write your story?"

"Even after that," he said.

He had told her most of it and, like anyone, she could not fathom the craziness of it, the craziness of Kellner's obsession with Suu Kyi, the lengths to which he was apparently willing to go in order to indulge that obsession.

Kellner's other lady, his daylight woman, would have to try to fathom that obsession. Mai was one of the loose ends that still needed to be tied up. Delaney needed to go to her, to tell her the story, to try to help her understand what had happened to the man whose life she thought she was sharing.

Delaney had decided even before Kate arrived that she should come with him to see Mai—because he had no secrets from her anymore, except for his involvement with CSIS, and because the presence of another woman would help.

His mobile phone had rung occasionally as they hid out in their airport hotel room. Rawson had given the phone to Delaney when he arrived back in Bangkok. His own phone had been lost somewhere along the way to northern Thailand. It could only be Rawson calling, so he ignored the calls until he and Kate were ready again to join the real world.

When Delaney did check, he found that Rawson had left a number of voicemail messages, all essentially saying the same thing. Delaney was a fool to drop out of sight like that and forego close protection. Delaney should come back to the Oriental at once. Delaney should finish up his business with the Thai authorities and get himself and Kate back to Montreal as soon as possible. Delaney should write no stories about this whole affair. Delaney should call Rawson immediately.

They reluctantly checked out of the hotel and took a slow city train from the airport to downtown. Delaney could see no sign of anyone following them and no one would expect them to use the local train, which took about an hour for the run from Don Muang, across the highway from Terminal 1, to Hualamphong Station in the city centre. From the train station to Kellner's apartment, Mai's apartment, was a short taxi ride. It was at the apartment that Delaney knew they would have to begin to be very careful.

He had the taxi driver let them off on Thanon Sathon Boulevard at the U.S. Information Agency, far up the long adjacent soi from Kellner's building. They walked cautiously down the soi, Delaney looking ahead and behind for any cars, for anyone following on foot. He saw nothing. No one was parked outside the courtyard of Kellner's building either, when they eventually came up on foot.

The watchman was in his usual place, reclining on the wooden bed frame, reading a Thai newspaper. He jumped up when he saw Delaney and the Western woman approach. He looked nervous. He offered no wai.

"We've come to see Khun Nathan's lady," Delaney said.

"She is inside," the watchman said.

"Is she alone?" Delaney asked.

"Yes."

"Has she had many visitors?"

"Yes, many."

"Western or Thai?"

"Both. Farang and Thai."

"When? The latest ones."

"This morning."

"Who? Farangs."

"Yes. In a big car."

"A tall man, very short grey hair, nice dress-up clothes? Canadian?"

"Yes, this morning."

Delaney knew they were taking a chance coming to Mai.

Rawson had already been by, but the real problem would be the others. He began to wish they had arranged for Mai to meet them somewhere else. He looked over at Kate. She did not seem frightened.

"Anyone in a white Land Cruiser with dark windows?" Delaney asked.

The watchman shook his head. Kate looked back at the entrance to the courtyard. Policewoman now.

"Do you have a cell phone?" Delaney asked.

"Yes," the watchman said.

Delaney wrote down the number of the telephone Rawson had given him.

"Here, take this. If someone comes, please call me fast on this number, OK? We will be inside Mai's house. Let us know who is coming, all right?" He gave the man a U.S. 20-dollar bill along with the piece of paper with the number. "Very important."

The watchman looked at the paper with the number on it and looked at the money.

"Khun Nathan is dead, correct?" the watchman said. "Mai has been very sad."

"Yes, he's dead," Delaney said.

"You know who did this?"

"I think so."

"I know that you tried to find him first."

"I did nothing. It was too late," Delaney said.

The watchman shook Delaney's hand. "I will call you if someone comes," he said.

"Even if it's police," Delaney said.

"Even police."

Mai was where she always was, on the big lounge with her cats, watching satellite TV in the dim light. She cried great streams of tears while Delaney held her, the two of them standing together in the middle of the living room, cats darting to and fro at their feet. She wet the shoulder of his shirt with her tears.

Kate and Mai were instantly close, as women can be in such situations. Kate had probably also had her share of such encounters with grieving loved ones, post-criminal acts. She watched quietly as Mai cried and hugged Delaney and then she went over to hug Mai herself. Kate's shoulder was wet then too.

Kate also watched quietly later as Delaney told Mai most of what he knew. He did not tell her about the morgue.

Eventually, the three of them sat on the balcony with glasses of iced tea.

Mai said: "He went to Burma only because of the lady, didn't he, Frank."

"To make some money first, then because of the lady," Delaney said.

"He was going to be a hero," Mai said.

"I'm not sure about that, Mai," Delaney said.

"He wanted to be a hero for her," she said again.

Kate said: "I think he probably wanted to be a hero for you too, Mai."

"It wasn't my story. It was her story he wanted to be a part of."

"You were in his story too," Delaney said. "For a long time."

"Now you have to write this story, Frank," she said.

"I intend to." He looked over at Kate.

"You have to make sure people understand why he wanted to do this thing, Frank," Mai said. "He was, what have you said, obsessed by her but only because he wanted to do something good, to help her and to help Burma. And then he got killed because of that. That's what you will say in the story, isn't it Frank?"

"Something quite like that, I think, Mai. It is a very unusual story and hard to tell right. Not the usual hero story."

"If someone dies trying to do something for someone else, that is a hero, isn't it, Frank?"

"Yes."

"That's a story, isn't it? People should know about that, shouldn't they?"

"Yes."

They stayed with Mai that night. She made them a small meal and then they drank some icy Thai beer on the darkened balcony in a humid breeze.

Like Mrs. Yong, Kate wanted to know when the body would be returned from afar.

"I don't know if they will ever return it to Thailand, Mai. I'm sorry. They haven't even said officially that he's dead."

She looked stricken. Her attitude was not quite like Mrs. Yong's on these matters.

"I want to see him one last time, Frank," she said.

"You may not be given the chance to do that, Mai," Delaney said. He looked over at Kate. Ever so slightly, she shook her head. Enough.

Kate said she wanted to have a look at Nathan's bulletin board and desk and went inside, apparently playing policewoman for a time. Frank and Mai sat quietly for a while. Mai smoked marijuana from a small brass pipe. They watched the smoke curl up into the night air.

Eventually, Mai said dreamily: "Kate loves you, Frank." She touched him on his leg. "You are lucky."

For some reason, Mai's words sent an alarm through him. He pondered the implications.

"Nathan loved you too," Delaney said eventually. "He would not have stayed with you for so long if he didn't."

"No, farang men don't do that here, do they?" she said.

"They don't, Mai. Here or anywhere. Farangs or not."

"Kate will stay with you for a long time," she said. "If you want her to."

Delaney pondered the implications.

"Take good care of her," Mai said. "Don't let her go away."

In the guest bedroom that night, with their door closed only halfway to catch the breeze from the balcony, they heard Mai moving here and there in the silent apartment as she got ready to sleep. They heard the cats wrestling and tumbling with each other, racing each other across the waxed tiles.

Kate lay with her right ear on Delaney's chest. "Mai loved him very much," she said.

"Yes," he said.

"But he was obsessed with someone else."

"It happens like that sometimes," he said quietly.

They lay in silence for a moment.

"Do you think you can love me, Frank?" she asked.

"I think I can, yes," Delaney said.

"Just me?"

"I think I can."

"I don't need you to be obsessed by me. Just for you not to be obsessed by anyone else. Is that fair?"

"It's fair."

"Would Natalia have thought that was fair?"

He waited for a long time before answering that one. He felt an eyelid blinking on his chest, someone's breath on his skin. It reminded him of something, of a quiet and close and gentle time with another woman a long time ago. He couldn't quite remember anymore exactly when or where that was. That was a good thing.

"If Natalia could see us tonight, I think she would have advised us to fall in love," Delaney said. Emotions gripped him; some happy, some not.

"A wise woman," Kate said.

"Yes."

They all slept very late. It was only the ringing of Delaney's mobile phone that woke them. He lay listening to it ring many times before remembering that it could signal trouble outside, serious trouble. He jumped up and answered, expecting it to be the watchman sounding an alarm. It was Rawson, with a lecture.

"Francis, for Christ's sake, where are you? You can't pull stunts like this on us, OK? We moved heaven and earth to get you out of that scrape in Rangoon and now you're traipsing around Bangkok like nothing at all has happened. This thing is not over yet. I've had the Thai police and the embassy people on my case for two long days. You're not being fair to any of us and not fair to Kate. You don't know who's going to make the next move. None of us do. So you better come back in where we can watch you and get you the hell out of here back to Canada. What are you up to anyway, for Christ's sake?"

"I'm taking a breather, Jon. Thinking things through. Spending time with Kate. Resting."

"Bullshit," Rawson said. "That's bullshit. You better come right back in."

"OK, Jon. OK. We'll come back today."

"Where are you?"

"Kellner's place. With his girl."

"For Christ's sake, Frank. Anybody could be watching you over there. Anybody could come in there."

"I was careful coming in."

"I'm going to send someone over there right now," Rawson said.

Delaney looked over at Kate, still lounging happily in the bed. She smiled at him. He knew Rawson had a point.

"OK, Jon, that would be good. Give us an hour or so."

They had a quick breakfast with Mai and the cats on the balcony. She didn't want them to go.

"Stay with me," she said. "Let's live here all together for a while."

"Nice idea," Kate said.

"Nathan would have said so too," Mai said.

"It's a nice idea, Mai, but not possible," Delaney said. "We've got to get going."

His mobile rang. It was the watchman, agitated, saying a car with two Westerners had pulled up outside. Immediately after Delaney hung up, it rang again. Ted Green this time. Waiting outside with a driver in an embassy car.

They went back into the guest room and threw their few things into bags. Delaney stopped for a moment, looked over to Kate, looked over at the armoire where he had found Kellner's field gear when he first searched the apartment weeks ago. He hesitated and looked back at Kate again.

"What is it, Frank?"

"Rawson's got me worried, with all of his Canadian worrying," Delaney said.

"Should we be worried?"

"I'm not sure I should have brought you over here now," he said.

"It's perfect," she said.

"It's not all finished yet," Delaney said. "I don't think so anymore."

"So, we'll finish it up together," Kate said.

Delaney went to Kellner's armoire and pushed aside the hanging camouflage pants and vests. Hidden down at the bottom among the combat boots and a flak jacket and a helmet and running shoes was a wooden case. It contained a black Walther .38 pistol and a box of bullets. Delaney had seen the gun last time. He pulled it out and checked that the magazine was empty.

"Frank, what's that for?" Kate said.

"I'm going to bring it with us down south," he said.

Kate the policewoman was dubious.

"Those things can make a bad situation worse, Frank," she said. "Do you know how to use it?"

"Yes," he said. "I've been around these things a fair bit." A vision of Natalia lying dead of gunshot wounds in a snowy

Quebec forest flashed before him. And a memory of him using a gun to deadly effect that day in the snow, and again months later in a Rome back street on the rogue Vatican agent who had killed her.

"We may need this, Kate," he said, wrapping the weapon in a T-shirt and putting it in his bag. "You just don't know in a situation like this. Rawson's got me anxious."

Kate looked unconvinced.

"A gun can make things worse," she said again. That was exactly what Ben Yong had tried to tell him outside Mae Sot.

Rawson, it seemed, spent most of his professional life looking aggrieved in hotel lobbies. He was waiting for them when they got back to the Oriental.

"Bad move, Francis. Very bad," he said. To Kate he said: "Officer Hunter, I would have thought RCMP training would have led you to advise our Francis against going to ground like that in this situation."

"I'm off duty, Mr. Rawson," she said, shaking his hand.

"Well, I'm not. My job is to get this man, and now you, it seems, back to Canada in one piece. As soon as possible. We could go tomorrow if the Thais agree they've got everything they need."

"We're going to take a beach break," Delaney said. "Don't get upset."

"A beach break? No chance," Rawson said.

"A short one," Kate said.

"No chance," Rawson said.

"Let's talk about this tomorrow, Jon," Delaney said.

Delaney wanted to find Cohen before they left. He didn't want Kate to come with him. She agreed, reluctantly, to stay in their hotel room to rest. They ate an early dinner and he gave her his mobile number.

"Should I be a true Canadian and start worrying now?" she asked.

"No," he said. "It's just a visit to Cohen, if I can find him, and I'll get the last bits that I need on this. You rest here tonight. Then we go south. Without Rawson and Company."

"OK, Frank. Are you going to carry that gun tonight?"

"No. I'm going to use the Thai driver tonight. He's a cop."

"Will he be in with you everywhere you go?"

"Outside. Close by."

"Is he any good?"

"I'd say. They wouldn't assign him to us if he weren't."

"All right, Frank." she said. "But I'd rather go with you. Mountie escort. The best in the world."

"No chance. You'll cramp my style. And Cohen's."

Rawson started his search at the Chivas Bar. Some of the regulars there said Cohen had not been in for a while. They suggested another small bar farther down the Patpong strip. It was called Lace. Sometimes Cohen met dope contacts there, they said.

The sex show had not started at Lace when Delaney went in. It was too early for a place like that. Tough-looking Thai guys in their twenties were lounging around, waiting for tourist marks to come in later and get into trouble of various sorts. No one had seen Cohen there either.

Delaney's driver took him over to the Dusit Thani Hotel. Delaney went up to the top floor to the press club. He had two things to do there. One was to check for Cohen and to find out where else he might be. The second was to put a notice on the bulletin board about Ben Yong's death. A lot of correspondents had known Ben, had used his services.

Delaney had tapped out a short notice on his laptop earlier and printed it out in the Oriental's business centre. It read: "The foreign correspondents' community in Thailand has lost a valued colleague and a dear friend. Benjarong Yongchaiyudh, known to all here as the best of drivers, was killed in May 2001 while on assignment in Mae Sot. He was 57. He was a journalist in spirit and in deed."

Delaney pinned the notice up, along with an old ID picture of Ben. A couple of early drinkers came over to look. Word would spread quickly around the club and Delaney knew that later, when the usual crowd arrived, there would probably be an impromptu journalists' wake.

Chris Hislop, the Voice of America man in Bangkok and a press club stalwart, said as Delaney turned away from the bulletin board: "That's a damn shame. Ben was a top driver."

"The best," Delaney said.

"What's the story?" Hislop asked. "Was he with you?"

"It's a long one, Chris. I'll tell you another time, OK? Tonight, I've got to find Mordecai Cohen. Something urgent. You seen him around?"

"No, not for days. We figure he's hooked up with some girl or he's scored something special to smoke and he'll turn up eventually."

"Where does he go, when's he's on one of those?"

"He usually just stays home. He's got a terrible little local-style place down by one of the canals way over in Thonburi. Terrible place. No air con. Nothing. Cheap and cheerful. No one bothers him there."

Delaney got full directions. Cohen's place was not accessible by car. He would have to take one of the narrow longtail river boats, powered by huge American automobile engines directly attached to a combination rudder and drive shaft. They raced at all hours up and down the Chao Phraya River and its maze of adjacent canals.

Delaney's driver clearly didn't like the idea at all. He seemed unsure whether it was his duty to stay with the car at the dock or to come along with Delaney in the longtail. He opted to stay with the car. That suited Delaney fine.

Delaney took a boat all to himself. The boat driver manoeuvred the craft as fast as he possibly could through the heavy river traffic, leaving a trail of spray, a V8 roar and a haze of oil smoke behind him. He seemed to know where he was going.

The canals got very narrow eventually and the boatman had no choice but to slow down to a crawl. The huge engine growled and backfired in protest. They passed old teak houses on stilts, with yellow lantern light coming from the windows. Delaney wondered how much, or, more to the point, how little it would cost Cohen to rent one of these sagging canal houses. Surely he would be the only Westerner in the area.

Eventually they pulled up to a house flying a Jolly Roger pirate's flag on a small pole out front. Crates of empty beer bottles were stacked on the deck. Delaney gave the driver 20 dollars and asked him to stay. He climbed up the rickety wooden stairs to the deck. Psychedelic music from the sixties wafted from an open window. Delaney smelled opium and fresh popcorn. Cohen was clearly at home.

Delaney didn't bother to knock. He pushed open the low door and went inside into the lantern light. Cohen was dozing in a hammock hung near a small table laden with beer bottles, smoker's paraphernalia and photography magazines. His eyes snapped open immediately when Delaney shook him, and he tried to leap out of the hammock and head for the door.

"Cohen, for god's sake take it easy. It's me, Delaney."

"Delaney, what are you doing here, man? You almost killed me."

"Why so jumpy, Mordecai?" Delaney said, as Cohen adjusted his sarong and collapsed back into a low rattan chair. He wore no shirt.

"You almost killed me, man, waking me up like that. What are you doing here?" Cohen fumbled for a Marlboro, lit it with a vintage Zippo.

Delaney saw no reason to ease in. He stood next to Cohen in the lamplight.

"Kellner's dead, Mordecai," he said.

Cohen stiffened, took a long drag on his cigarette. His hand was shaking. "No way," he said.

"In Burma. The generals killed him."

"No," Cohen said.

"Yes, Mordecai. I saw his body in a Rangoon morgue."

Cohen suddenly started to cry. He sobbed like a schoolboy, covering his face with both hands, cigarette still grasped between index and middle finger of his left.

"No way," Cohen said. "No way."

"It's your fault, Mordecai," Delaney said. "And Ben Yong is dead too because of you."

"No," Cohen said. "No, no way."

He stubbed out his cigarette and hugged his knees. He looked wistfully over at his table of drugs and beer.

"Who did you tell?" Delaney said.

Cohen lit another cigarette, said nothing.

"Who, Mordecai? The Burmese? Why would you do that?"

"I didn't tell the fucking Burmese anything," Cohen shouted.

"Who then?"

"The Aussies. The fucking Aussies," Cohen said.

"Why them?"

"Because Kellner was going to rip them off. Because the whole idea was stupid and I figured I'd stop it that way. I told them they were going to get ripped off, that's all. They slipped me some cash. I needed the cash and I figured the whole Suu Kyi thing would fall down if the rip-off messed up. That's it. It would have been better that way. That's all I did. Nothing about Suu Kyi."

"You stupid pathetic asshole," Delaney said.

"Then Kellner disappeared and everything fell apart," Cohen said, he hugged his knees and started crying again. "I need a joint," he said.

"You pathetic asshole," Delaney said.

"The Aussies wouldn't have killed him," Cohen said.

"But the generals would."

"I didn't tell the generals."

"But the Australians did. They must have."

"But only about the rip-off, man. That's all they could have said. No way they knew about the Suu Kyi thing."

"For Christ's sake, Mordecai, you know what that regime is like. The generals take Kellner in to ask him some questions and the way they work he would have told them everything, anything. Then they killed him. And stood back and watched it all unfold in Mae Sot, Mongla and then Rangoon."

"Jesus, Frank. Jesus. Give me a break. I never meant for them to kill him. No way. It was just a little gig for me on the side."

Delaney felt anger welling up from somewhere deep inside. He suddenly felt glad he had not carried a gun that night. He understood, as he had on only a few other occasions in his life, the impulse to attack, to injure, to murder.

"And you told those mercenaries Ben and I would be heading up to Mae Sot," he said.

"Give me a break, Frank, come on. I didn't think they would hurt you. I thought they'd just throw you the hell out of there. I didn't want you to get pulled into it, so I told them you were on your way."

"They killed Ben Yong."

Cohen hugged his knees and rocked in his chair. He wiped tears away with the back of his hands.

"And now you're hiding out in this hovel, stoned and worthless and hiding," Delaney said.

"There's guys following me, Frank."

"Good. People are following me too."

"They're going to take me out, Frank."

"Good," Delaney said.

"Come on man, you can't mean that," Cohen said.

"I mean it. You're lucky I don't kill you myself."

# Chapter 17

Rawson warned him as they went by embassy car to police headquarters the next day that General Kriangsak Chatichai was not a happy man.

"He's a cop's cop," Rawson said. "He's been made to understand by his superiors and by the political people that this is not a standard case and that there's an international diplomatic dimension. He knows something very strange was going on in Mae Sot, but he's been told to ease off because most of what actually happened, happened in Burma and because the Thai side simply doesn't want this to blow up any bigger. But he's not a happy man, because a Thai citizen ended up dead at Kellner's place up there, and was buried up there, and no senior policeman worth his salt, even in Thailand, would want to just let that go. So he'll go through the motions today, just for his own self-esteem, but there's not a hell of a lot he can do on this one because he's been told to stand back and because the guy who killed your driver is already dead."

General Chatichai was indeed an unhappy man. He frowned deeply when an aide brought Delaney and Rawson into his large office. He did not get up from his black leather swivel chair. He waved at two straight-backed wooden chairs placed in front of his massive, glass-covered desk. He did not offer his guests any tea, although a large tea flask and an array of cups sat on a tray close at hand.

"I understood that I would speak to Mr. Delaney alone, Mr. Rawson," Chatichai said.

"I am representing the Canadian government during this interview with Mr. Delaney today, General," Rawson said. "I think my embassy has indicated this to your colleagues."

"I have not been told," Chatichai said.

"My apologies," Rawson said. "I am just here to observe."

"There is no need for observers," Chatichai said. "This is routine police business."

"That is not quite how my government sees it, General," Rawson said.

Chatichai's frown deepened. He turned to Delaney.

"Mr. Delaney, I have read your written statement about what happened in Mae Sot last month. I appreciate your detailed description. You are a journalist and used to reporting what you have seen. I need you to talk to me today about what you apparently did not see. Your report is not clear on some matters of importance to the police."

"I'm happy to help," Delaney said.

"You say that a group of foreign mercenaries abducted you when you went to the farm outside Mae Sot. You say one of the men shot Mr. Benjarong Yongchaiyudh and then they abducted you. Is that correct?"

"Yes it is," Delaney said.

"Why did they not shoot you also?" Chatichai said.

"We were separated at the time. Mr. Yongchaiyudh was waiting for me on the road and I was still on the property. The men came back and saw him there and they shot him."

"You were still on the property?"

"Yes."

Chatichai looked at Delaney's typewritten statement.

"With another of the men you say were mercenaries."

"Yes. They were definitely mercenaries, General."

"Why had you not gone out to the road with Mr. Yongchaiyudh? Why did you stay back? Your statement does not speak about this."

Delaney hesitated.

"I was trying to find out where Nathan Kellner might be. That's why I went to his farm. I stayed to look around some more."

"You were searching his place."

"Yes."

"You entered illegally."

Rawson said: "General, Mr. Delaney's statement says clearly that he entered the farm in the hope that his friend would be there. He did not enter illegally. He simply entered the farm property and the house to see if anyone was there."

"And the person you say was a mercenary was there and he attacked you and Mr. Yongchaiyudh and then you, as you say in this report, subdued him," Chatichai said. "You hit him with a chair and tied him up."

"Yes," Delaney said.

"Why did you not run out then, if you had been attacked? Why did you wait so long that the others returned and shot Mr. Yongchaiyudh? Would it not be a normal thing to run away at that point, Mr. Delaney?"

"I wanted to find out where Mr. Kellner was."

"So you asked Mr. Yongchaiyudh to wait in the road, where there might be danger, and you searched the house you say you thought belonged to your friend."

"I didn't think Mr. Yongchaiyudh was in danger," Delaney said.

"Someone you said was a mercenary attacked you and you felt it necessary to beat him over the head with a chair and tie him up. You did not think there was danger that day?"

"We didn't know what to expect next."

"Wouldn't a normal response be to run away to safety?"

"I wanted to find out where Kellner was," Delaney said again.

"Was that so important that you would put your driver in such danger, Mr. Delaney?" Chatichai asked.

Delaney felt anger welling up. His guilt over Ben's death was not police business. He would deal with that privately. Rawson raised his hand ever so slightly, urging Delaney to stay calm.

"What was it that you were actually looking for that day, Mr. Delaney?" Chatichai asked again. "What was so important that a Thai citizen needed to be shot while you searched a farmhouse in Mae Sot?"

"I've answered that question, General," Delaney said.

"And then they took you to Burma."

"Yes."

"They shot the Thai national and they brought the Canadian national with them by road all the way to Burma."

"Yes."

"You are very fortunate to be Canadian, Mr. Delaney."

"Mr. Delaney had a very difficult time in Burma, General," Rawson said. "He was abducted and treated very roughly by the mercenaries and then by the Burmese authorities."

Chatichai threw Delaney's written statement down on the desk.

"And now your government wants me to simply close this file, just like that," he said.

"That would be a police decision, General, not one for my government to make," Rawson said. "We have given you our full cooperation."

The interview did not get any better. Chatichai went through the motions of questioning Delaney and went through the motions of expressing outrage but, in the end, politics and diplomacy prevailed over police work and he showed them the door. No handshakes, no wai. A distinct lack of Thai hospitality.

"I intend to order that this file be left open," the general said as they stood by the doorway.

"That is your prerogative," Rawson said.

"I reserve the right to continue the investigation."

"Again, a police prerogative."

"Mr. Delaney, we may have more questions for you the next time you decide to visit Thailand," Chatichai said. "Any time you come back again."

"Is that a threat, General?" Delaney said.

Chatichai looked like he would explode.

"It is a statement of fact," he said.

Kate was waiting for him at the pool when Delaney got back to the hotel around noon. She was already deep in holiday mode, in a yellow swimsuit and an RCMP ball cap.

"Well, at least they didn't keep you in overnight," she said when she saw him.

"Almost," he said. "You cops are a tough bunch."

"Let's get out of here," she said.

"Right," he said. "Tomorrow. We'll have to shake the embassy guys first."

"Outlaws," she said.

There was one last bit of business before they could go in holiday mode to Ko Chang. Delaney needed to speak at last to his editor, to explain that he was taking some more time off before returning to Montreal. He would leave out the part about his planning to write a long piece about Kellner and the Suu Kyi plot for *Asia Weekly*. The editor there, who Delaney knew well, had been more than delighted, even on the vaguest of descriptions of what the article would entail, to commission something over the telephone from Singapore. They would hold pages open for him in the next issue. With the current edition about to go to press, that gave Delaney about ten days grace to write and file.

Rawson was off somewhere doing spy business. Delaney and Kate sunned themselves for the afternoon and ate an early dinner in the dining room with well-heeled tourists and business types. Rawson found them there as they were finishing and sat down at their table.

"Yes, you can buy me an aperitif," Rawson said. "No, I am not offended that you failed to ask me to join you this evening for dinner. Now that the pressure is off. Gin and tonic, please."

"Our friend General Chatichai doesn't think the pressure is off," Delaney said after the waiter had gone.

"Kate here will appreciate his desire to close the case properly. Imagine how an RCMP inspector would react if he was told to let something like this slide. No police officer would be happy with that."

"The perpetrators are dead, Jon," Kate said.

"Chatichai can't be sure of that," Rawson said. "He wants bodies, motive, murder weapons, DNA, fingerprints, witness statements, chapter and verse."

"He'll just have to let it go," Delaney said.

"You'll just have to get out of his country," Rawson said.

"Soon, Jon," Delaney said.

"Tomorrow," Rawson said. "Thai Airways to Vancouver."

"This time next week. Same flight," Delaney said.

"Bad move," Rawson said. "Very bad."

Harden was very agitated indeed.

"Frank," he said when Delaney reached him by telephone that evening, "you must think we're running some kind of sheltered workshop just for you over here. You drift in and out, filing the odd column whenever you damn well please, ignoring the wishes and suggestions of your section editor. You spend more time on your own book projects than you do on your column. Then you drift over to Europe without my say-so or Patricia's, apparently to do research there, god knows why, for a column that is supposed to be about Canadian politics and issues. I see no story proposal, no forms filled out, no request for air travel, nothing, nothing. You drop completely out of sight for almost a month and then we get an urgent call from External Affairs saying you are in a jail cell somewhere in Rangoon and can we please confirm to the Burmese authorities and the Thais and whoever the hell else wants to know that, yes, you're on assignment for the *Tribune* or you may never get out. Frank, I've been in the newspaper business for more than 30 years. You're in for about 25, or thereabouts. What is your best guess about what an editor-in-chief, and a son of a bitch of one at that, would say to a staffer who messes up like that?"

"Ed, there's a lot more to it than that. I'll explain it all to you when I get back."

"Have you got something to file? What all this about Nathan Kellner? Where's he fit into all this? Can you at least file something after all this nonsense?"

"I'm not sure it's a *Tribune* story, Ed," Delaney said.

"What in Christ's name is that supposed to mean? You're over there and you're working for me and you're telling me whatever it is you've got is not a *Tribune* story?"

"I think it's really more like something for a world readership, Ed."

"Frank, I'm going to ignore that. I'm going to pretend I never heard you say that. You're a *Tribune* staffer . . ."

"I'm a contract columnist, Ed," Delaney said.

"Frank, are you out of your mind? I've been very patient with you for years. Very patient because you're good at what you do. Don't push your luck any further, OK? You are on very thin ice at this newspaper as it is. I want you to come in to see me the minute you get back and we'll thrash all of this out once and for all. Patricia has some ideas for changes."

"Let's sort it all out then," Delaney said.

"Yes, let's do that," Harden said. "When are you coming back in?"

"Next week," Delaney said.

"You really are out of your mind," Harden said.

Delaney had not been dreaming much since his release from Insein Prison. There was never any predicting when he might have what the Jungians would call a big dream. In Bangkok, however, before heading out with Kate, he dreamed this:

*He is deep in Quebec woods, the same place where Natalia was killed. But it is summer, not winter. All the snow is gone and the maple trees and the elms and the oaks provide a green canopy, shading him from the hot sun. Cicadas whine and there is birdsong. All is peaceful. He walks slowly through the trees, knowing exactly where he is to go. He comes into a large clearing and there before him is a round lake, smooth as glass. A perfectly circular mirror. The still water reflects the blue sky and white clouds overhead. There is a long narrow dock heading out to the centre but it does not quite come all the way in to shore. He must make a leap from the water's edge onto the wooden slats of the dock, one last leap before he can walk out to the exact centre of the lake. He is almost at his destination. He hesitates, and the dream ends.*

Rawson had, on the face of it, given up. He was not in the hotel lobby when Delaney and Kate appeared the next morning, ready to set off for Ko Chang. Ted Green was not there either. Delaney expected they would have arranged some sort of subtle surveillance, if not of the six-hour drive to Trat and the ferry ride to the island, then at least of their stay there. Delaney had thought it sensible, given the dangers and the various interests they had offended, to at least tell Rawson where they were going and when they planned to come back.

Delaney and Kate did their best to avoid being followed because there was no telling whose faction might want to come along: Canadians, Thai police, Burmese agents, perhaps even a representative of the much aggrieved Australian businessmen.

There were car rental desks in the lobby but Delaney had

arranged instead to get a car from Hualamphong Station. It might appear to those interested that they were taking a train south, and the sprawling station itself would give them opportunity to disappear into throngs of locals and backpackers hurrying for the platforms.

He looked behind them many times in the taxi as they headed from the hotel to the station but he saw no overt sign of interest. Certainly there was no white Land Cruiser in sight. The absence of any interest whatsoever seemed odd to him, but it would be equally odd to complain of no interest after complaining all week about too much. He settled back into the seat beside Kate and tried to relax.

At the station, they signed out their Toyota Corolla and retrieved it in the station's vast underground car park. The dim coolness there gave them a sense of privacy for the first time that day.

"Alone at last, lover boy," Kate said as they put bags and Delaney's laptop computer into the car. She smiled at him across the metallic roof.

"Looks like it," he said. "We may just be able to pull this off. I would have expected more of an escort."

"Lucky," Kate said.


Getting out of Bangkok by car was always arduous. It was almost an hour before they were on open road heading toward Chon Buri and, beyond that, the coastal highway along the Gulf of Thailand to Trat near the Cambodian border.

It was a typical Southeast Asian highway: narrow, rutted in places, choked with belching trucks and swarms of motorcycles and three-wheeled vans. After Chon Buri and Sattahip, they were truly in the Thai hinterland. Few villages, traffic thinner, heavy rainforest on both sides of the road.

Delaney had always liked a long car journey in rural Asia or South America. It brought you out of the international cocoon of airports and aircraft and taxis and business hotels. The sounds and the smells of a country came cascading over you on a road trip and Delaney revelled in them as he drove. He also revelled in the presence of a good-looking woman at his side, with neither of them in any hurry to get anywhere and problems left behind.

They had lunch at a truckstop noodle house just past Rayong. From there, if they wished, they could have gone over to Ko Samet but Delaney knew the island had been badly overdeveloped. They would carry on to Ko Chang, where they had a reservation at a hotel on at the northwestern tip that Delaney knew would give them what they wanted: quiet, solitude, beach time and a place where he could produce the *Asia Weekly* article by deadline.

They were the only farangs in the truckstop. A dozen heavy vehicles idled outside. The drivers clearly appreciated the presence of a good-looking Western woman, but they expressed their appreciation with restraint. Delaney knew of a lot of cultures where Kate would have caused a stir in a place like that, perhaps trouble. Mexico came to mind.

The afternoon had become very hot. They were both sweating after their lunch and the walk back to the car. Perspiration beaded on their foreheads and they shivered as the car's air conditioning kicked in and cooled their skin. As they waited, a massive khaki-coloured Bedford dump truck moved out just before them, spewing diesel fumes and groaning angrily as the driver changed gears.

"I'll have to get past this guy if we want to breathe this afternoon," Delaney said, sleepy from his pad thai lunch and a large beer.

"No hurry," Kate said.

The truck moved at a snail's pace, even though it carried no load. Delaney tried a couple of times to get around, but the driver, apparently just as sleepy as they were, was swaying back and forth across the middle line, so passing was a challenge.

"Lucky there's not much traffic out here this afternoon or he'd be a road statistic," Kate said.

"The guy really seems to want to drive on both sides at once," Delaney said.

He looked in his rearview before making another attempt to pass and knew instantly they were in trouble. A white Land Cruiser was immediately behind them, appearing as if from nowhere. He could not see the driver through the vehicle's dark windshield, but he had no doubt it was the same one that had been trailing him in Bangkok.

"Kate, I think we're got a problem here," he said. "Our friends in the Land Cruiser are with us all of a sudden."

She saw him looking in the mirror and looked back herself.

"Where on earth did they come from? Do you think it's the same car?"

"I really do, Kate. This is not good."

"Let's go back to the restaurant. There are a lot of people there."

"Hard to turn around here, Kate. If we stop we may be in even more trouble."

"Maybe they're just following us to see where we're going."

"Maybe."

Delaney tried again to pass the dump truck ahead but could not squeeze by. "Christ," he said.

The Land Cruiser drew up closer behind them. The truck ahead slowed even more. Delaney realized suddenly what was happening and knew that trouble had truly come.

"Kate, quick now, get me that gun out of my bag. They're going to squeeze us in, maybe put us off the road."

There was very little shoulder to pull onto and deep concrete culverts on both sides of the road. Kate moved fast, a police-woman in an emergency. She reached back to open Delaney's sports bag and rummaged quickly around to get the pistol and bullets out of a bundled T-shirt. She expertly loaded eight rounds into the Walther's magazine and set it firmly into the handle, slapping the bottom to set it. She pulled the action and placed the gun down on the seat between them.

"Good to have a police officer along," Delaney said grimly.

"This doesn't look good at all, Frank," Kate said.

The truck in front of them suddenly stopped dead. Delaney hit the brakes and skidded to a halt less than a metre from its high hulking cargo box. The Land Cruiser raced up and hit them from behind with its steel bumper bars, shaking them up and shoving their light Japanese rental car right up into the truck in front, wedging them in.

"Let's get out Frank," Kate said.

"No cover between here and the trees. And that ditch will be tough to cross fast."

The passenger door of the Land Cruiser opened and a wiry Asian man in his thirties climbed out, moving fast. He wore a dark blue tracksuit, wraparound sunglasses and a black baseball cap. He was carrying what looked like a vintage Colt automatic, holding it low against his thigh.

"Not good, Kate, not good," Delaney said. "Get down low."

Kate slid lower in her seat, hand on the door handle.

"Careful, Frank, careful," she said. "Let me have the gun. I think I can take him through the glass."

"No, no, not from that angle. And when he sees the weapon he'll start to shoot. I'll wait until he comes around to the side."

The gunman went around behind his car, and came up cautiously on the driver's side of theirs. Delaney cradled the gun. He knew he would have only one chance.

"At that range the rounds will go straight through him, Frank," Kate said. "You'll need to get off more than one to take him down."

Delaney said nothing. The gunman was at the window, gun visible but still held low at his thigh pointing down. He looked briefly behind him to the road and then motioned for Frank to lower the window.

As the electric window wound down, Delaney got ready. As soon as the glass disappeared into the car door, he raised the Walther and fired three quick rounds into the gunman's chest. The man reeled immediately back into the road, one hand clutching at crimson wounds, the other hand firing off a useless round of his own into the blacktop.

"Out out out, go go go," Delaney shouted to Kate.

He leaped with her out of the passenger door and down into the stinking weed-choked drain culvert. They scrambled up the sloping concrete on the other side and ran for the rainforest. Delaney looked back briefly and saw the driver of the Land Cruiser running over to his partner's body on the road. He saw the truck driver climbing out of his cab, carrying an AK-47 assault rifle.

No cars on the far side of the road appeared to be stopping, but a short line of traffic had slowed on their side had to move past what probably looked like an accident scene with a trio of vehicles pulled onto the shoulder.

They plunged, breathless and sweating, into the deep green cover of trees and vines, slipping on the damp red earth as they went. Despite the danger, despite the need to move fast and without distraction, Delaney's mind was suddenly flooded with intense memories of the last time he ran for his life with a lover through trees, seeking shelter from gunmen. The way that time had been heavy with snow and the outcome disastrous.

In the aftermath of Natalia's death in the Quebec woods, Delaney had sworn never to put someone he loved in the way of danger again. He had also, without realizing it quite so clearly, sworn never to fall in love with anyone again, sworn he had had enough unhappy endings for a lifetime. Now, not in the snow of Quebec but in the heat and humidity of Thailand, he had already been responsible for Ben Yong's death and very possibly, if he did not act quickly, Kate would die because of him as well.

She ran expertly ahead of him, head low, arms brushing aside vines and branches as she went. There was no track through this forest as there had been through the snowy woods in Quebec. Delaney tried to devise a plan as they ran, but none, at this stage, seemed as sensible as simple flight.

Eventually, they threw themselves behind a large boulder all but hidden with vines and low hanging branches. They stopped there and listened. They were panting with the exertion and the heat and the fear. Delaney put a finger to his lips. They strained to hear the sound of someone in pursuit.

After a long anxious wait, Delaney said finally: "I never should have brought you over here, Kate. This is craziness."

"It was my choice to come, Frank," she said. "How would you know it would turn out like this?"

"Because it was already like this. Because of what happened before, to Ben and to Kellner and to the mercenaries. These people absolutely do not fool around. This story is not over yet and I should have never gotten you into it."

He brushed damp hair from her forehead.

"We'll get out of this, Frank," she said. "They'd be crazy to come into deep cover like this knowing we have a gun."

Delaney remembered coming to that exact conclusion in Quebec, minutes before Natalia was shot. He said nothing.

They decided to stay exactly where they were until nightfall. Delaney knew now that in such situations it was better to stay put, to listen and to watch, rather than to move into what could at anytime become an armed confrontation. They leaned against the boulder, Delaney's arm around Kate's shoulder, and, despite the danger, fought sleep in the afternoon heat.

It appeared that their opponents had decided not to chance armed pursuit in the Thai rainforest. After darkness fell, after hours of waiting and listening, Delaney and Kate made their way clumsily back the way they had come, to the edge of the trees near the road. They found themselves about two hundred metres back down the road from where they had been stopped that afternoon.

Delaney peered cautiously out. It was very dark but a half-moon lit the scene faintly. Occasionally, a lone car or a truck would move by but there was very little nighttime traffic. He saw their car still pulled over on the shoulder. The Land Cruiser, the dump truck, and the gunman's body had all disappeared.

"I'll have to go over and see what's what," Delaney said.

"They could be watching," Kate said.

"There's no car except ours," he said.

"It's dark, they could be anywhere around," she said.

"We've got to try to get out of here with the car," he said.

They made their way under cover to a break in the trees directly across from their car, probably the very spot where they had broken into the jungle and started their flight hours ago.

"You wait here, Kate," Delaney said. "I'll go see what's happening with the car." He gave her the gun. He'd done that once before in a situation like this, with another woman, now dead. "Watch as I go."

She took the Walther, knowing they had little choice. They could not find their way elsewhere through rainforest at night. The road was the only way and the car was their best option.

Delaney ran, keeping low. Moonlight lit his way. He looked inside through the front passenger window of the car. The driver's side window was still down. Their bags and his laptop were gone from the back seat. The key was not in the ignition.

He cautiously opened the passenger door and the interior light went on. Suddenly, there was a massive burst of automatic weapon fire from the trees on the other side of the road. Dozens of high-velocity rounds tore through glass and ricocheted off metal and asphalt. Delaney flung himself backward into the concrete culvert behind him and prayed for the deadly AK-47 to stop.

He heard nothing at all from Kate. She stayed where she was, too experienced to call out. He lay panting in the wet muck at the bottom of the culvert. No cars passed.

Eventually, he heard footsteps coming slowly across the road. The gunman stopped on the far side of the car, waited for signs of life. Then shoes crunched onto the gravel of the shoulder. From where he lay in the culvert, Delaney could see a man's head slowly appear over the edge, then shoulders and the unmistakable outline of the AK, with its curved magazine.

From Kate's position in the trees, he heard a burst of firing. Five handgun shots in instantaneous succession. Then silence. The gunman fell where he was, unable to get off a single round.

"Frank, Frank," Kate shouted from the trees.

"Alive," he shouted. "It's OK, Kate, I'm OK. Alive."

The sniper was badly shot up. He carried no identification. Delaney couldn't tell whether he was Burmese or Thai. They knew someone could possibly be along at any moment to check up on his all-night vigil and that there was no time to waste. Delaney retrieved their keys from the dead-man's pocket and pulled the body into the drainage ditch. He started the car and they headed out fast, toward Chanthaburi.

They had no bags, but Delaney had his wallet, passport and mobile phone in the photographer's field vest he was wearing. Kate's money and passport were in a small waist pouch she had on. They decided to call Rawson from Chanthaburi but not the police. Suddenly, they craved Canadian company, a little close protection. Delaney held Kate's hand very tightly as he drove.

Rawson was suitably enraged, about the attack and at them for putting themselves into danger. They were more than happy now to tell him exactly where they were and what they planned to do. Delaney also told Rawson, as precisely as he could, where the shooting had occurred and where the gunman's body lay.

"I'll try to sort this out for you, Frank, but for god's sake, please don't disappear on me again," Rawson said. "I'll have someone watching out for you on Ko Chang but the best place for you both is on a plane back to Canada. General Chatichai is going to go absolutely crazy. This is no time for a holiday."

"Just a day or two, Jon," Delaney said. "Then we go. I promise."

It was not really a holiday, just a period of rest and recuperation and a time for Delaney to write his article. At daybreak they checked into the Alyapura Resort on Ko Chang, just outside Ban Khlong Son village. Two plainclothes Thai policemen, stern-faced, not amused, introduced themselves at the front desk.

"We are to escort you back to Bangkok," one of them said.

"Soon. Two days, maybe three," Delaney said. "We need to rest. And I have one piece of work I need to do."

The policemen did not debate this. They spoke to the hotel receptionist, who looked over nervously at the new guests. One of the officers went behind the reception counter and into the manager's office. Delaney and Kate went to their bungalow. It had a wide cool veranda and big teak bed under a fan.

They slept until late afternoon and even then they did not venture out. They sat on the veranda, eating room-service noodles, saying little and needing little. Occasionally, they smiled serenely at each other, as survivors do.

Delaney had been composing Kellner's story in his head for weeks, so when he sat down to write in the hotel's tiny business centre, the words came quickly. He told it all, starting with Kellner in Montreal through to his bohemian expatriate lifestyle in Asia and his incredible obsession with one of the most famous female figures in the world. He told about the elaborate, ill-advised plot to liberate that woman and her beleaguered country, and he told about Kellner's death at the hands of the Burmese generals. He told it all, but left it to readers to decide if Kellner was, in the end, a hero or a fool.

Bangkok airport. Delaney and Kate in the departures area, tanned and browsing in the Duty Free, as lovers do. Items purchased, and then celebration drinks. A toast is proposed. To Benjarong Yongchaiyudh. To Nathan Kellner. And to a newsstand brimming with foreign and local newspapers and magazines. The latest edition of *Asia Weekly* on display. Kellner's picture on the cover; outdoors and squinting against the sun, in full foreign-correspondent mode. Banner headline, for all to see:

# EXCLUSIVE.
# Special Report.

## THE BURMESE DAYS AND DEATH
## OF NATHAN M. KELLNER.
### One Man's Quest to Bring Down a Military Regime.

# EPILOGUE

# Opposition Party Calls for Inquiry into Journalist's Death

OTTAWA, June 15, 2001 (Newswire) – The New Democratic Party's External Affairs critic Roger MacNaughton called on Friday for a public inquiry into the reported death in Burma of Canadian journalist Nathan Kellner and for a full explanation from the Burmese military regime of the circumstances surrounding the incident.

MacNaughton also called for an explanation from Burma of the arrest and alleged mistreatment in a Rangoon prison of another Canadian journalist, Francis Delaney. An article by Delaney in a recent edition of *Asia Weekly* magazine about Kellner's death and a bizarre plot to bring down the Burmese regime has created an international furore. Delaney, a well-known political affairs columnist for the *Montreal Tribune*, was recently expelled from Burma while on assignment there and is now back in Canada.

"The Canadian government cannot stand idly by while its journalists are killed or mistreated in Burma or anywhere else," MacNaughton said during a raucous House of Commons exchange with External Affairs Minister Bill Hodgkins.

"We know, we have known for years, what is going on inside Burma and the way its people are mistreated and murdered by the military. The government of Canada has done too little to end the reign of terror in Burma. Now at least, the government should stand up for our own journalists who, as they go about their important work, run afoul of the generals running that country."

Hodgkins told reporters outside the House of Commons that he would immediately look into claims made by Delaney in the *Asia Weekly* article and take whatever action was required. Hodgkins said he would summon the Burmese ambassador for a discussion of the article's allegations and Kellner's whereabouts.

The minister refused to commit his government to a public inquiry.

"We have as yet had no official acknowledgement from the Myanmar State Peace and Development Council that Mr. Kellner has in fact died in their custody," Hodgkins said. "We are making urgent inquires. It would be premature to go down the public inquiry road."

Kellner, a Bangkok-based correspondent for the prestigious *Defence Monthly* magazine, has been missing for many weeks, according to a spokesman for the magazine in London.

Delaney's article in *Asia Weekly* alleged that Kellner was killed by the Burma regime after officials uncovered a plot to abduct National League for Democracy leader Aung San Suu Kyi from Rangoon, where she has been under house arrest since September 2000.

Previously, she was detained under house arrest from 1989 to 1995.

Delaney's article claims that Kellner was "obsessed" by the charismatic Burmese democracy activist and planned to use mercenaries that he himself had hired to bring Suu Kyi to safety in Thailand, an action that he hoped would foment a popular revolution in Burma.

The Burmese military refused to accept the result of the 1990 election in that country, which, according to the NLD and international observers, Suu Kyi's party won by a large margin.

The *Asia Weekly* article claims that Burmese authorities got wind indirectly of the plot via a Canadian informer in Bangkok, whom Delaney named in his article. Acting on that information, Burmese soldiers reportedly stormed a safe house in Rangoon where a small band of mercenaries from a variety of countries was awaiting orders from Kellner. All the mercenaries died in that operation, the article said.

Delaney's article claims that some time before the mercenaries were killed, Kellner was arrested and interrogated in Rangoon's notorious Insein Prison, where he later died. Delaney himself was arrested by the military in the vicinity of the mercenaries' safe house as he was gathering information for his magazine report. He was released after intense diplomatic pressure from Canada via the Australian embassy in Rangoon. Canada no longer maintains an embassy in Burma.

A spokesman for the Burmese ambassador in Ottawa had no immediate comment on the Asia Weekly article or on the call by opposition MPs for a public inquiry into Kellner's alleged murder.

Diplomatic observers in Burma say the *Asia Weekly* article has outraged local democracy activists, some of whom now accuse the military regime of fabricating a story about the plot to abduct Suu Kyi as a pretext for causing her to disappear. Anticipating unrest from activists who fear for Suu Kyi's safety, the regime has stepped up security around her house in Rangoon and put additional troops on the streets throughout the capital.

Supporters of Aung San Suu Kyi in Ottawa, Toronto and Montreal say they plan to march on the Burmese embassy this weekend to demand a response to the *Asia Weekly* report and to underscore their ongoing demands for the release of Suu Kyi from house arrest and for the military rulers to accept the 1990 election result.

Human rights groups say hundreds of pro-democracy activists, students and intellectuals have been imprisoned, tortured or killed by the military regime over the past two decades.

# Expatriate Canadian Murdered in Bangkok

BANGKOK, Thailand, July 1, 2001 (Newswire) – Thailand police confirmed on Monday that Canadian freelance photographer Mordecai Cohen died after being shot several times at close range in his house on the outskirts of Bangkok.

Initial reports said Cohen, who was from Montreal, had died in a fire in his traditional-style house on one of Bangkok's remote canals in the city's Thonburi district. After repeated requests from Canadian authorities, results were released of an autopsy report that indicated Cohen had been shot before his body was badly burned in the house fire.

Cohen had lived in Thailand for almost ten years, making a living as a freelance news photographer. His work appeared occasionally in magazines and newspapers in the region. He was a well-known and flamboyant figure in the foreign correspondents' community in Bangkok.

Cohen was named recently in a controversial *Asia Weekly* magazine article as the indirect source of information which the military regime in Burma used to storm a safe house in Rangoon and kill mercenaries whom they said were going to abduct pro-democracy leader Aung San Suu Kyi and bring down the government.

Canadian journalist Nathan Kellner, a close friend and colleague of Cohen in Bangkok, died in Burmese military custody shortly before the attack on the mercenary hideout, according to *Asia Weekly* The magazine claimed that Kellner was the mastermind behind the bizarre plot to rescue Suu Kyi from house arrest and bring democracy to the country.

The Canadian government has been trying unsuccessfully since publication of the article to get a full explanation from Burma via diplomatic channels of the circumstances surrounding Kellner's death, but has so far refused opposition demands in Parliament for a public inquiry.

Burmese authorities have refused to comment on the *Asia Weekly* article or to confirm that Keller was ever in their custody. Kellner has been missing for almost four months.

*Montreal Tribune* columnist Francis Delaney, author of the *Asia Weekly* article about the alleged Burma abduction and mercenary plot, has insisted that he stands by his report. Delaney repeated that when contacted by News Wire for comment after the first reports of Cohen's death in Bangkok.

"The answers to any remaining questions about the death of Nathan Kellner and of Mordecai Cohen can only be answered by the Burmese military regime," Delaney said when contacted by telephone in Montreal.

Delaney was himself arrested in Burma and expelled as he gathered information for his *Asia Weekly* article.

# Leading Columnist Quits Newspaper

by Fraser J. Harrelson, *Tribune* Media Writer
*July 8, 2001*

MONTREAL – The *Tribune*'s own Francis Delaney, a columnist with the newspaper since 1998 and a former investigative journalist and senior editor at *Forum* magazine, has resigned effective immediately.

Delaney, who is 49, said in an email message yesterday to *Tribune* editorial staff that he and senior management of the newspaper had agreed it was "time for him to move on."

The "Delaney at Large" column was widely respected and often broke new ground on political stories, nationally and internationally. Delaney is a former foreign correspondent whose assignments for *Forum* magazine and other Canadian publications often took him to trouble spots around the world. He is the author of several well-received books on political topics.

Delaney recently caused controversy with publication of an article in *Asia Weekly* magazine about an alleged plot by another Canadian journalist, Nathan Kellner, to bring down Burma's military government by hiring mercenaries to rescue pro-democracy leader Aung San Suu Kyi from house arrest.

Canada is still investigating claims made by Delaney in his *Asia Weekly* article, including the allegation that Kellner was murdered while in Burmese government custody.

It is widely known in Montreal media circles that management of the *Tribune* was deeply unhappy that Delaney had sold his Burma report to another publication.

*Tribune* Editor-in-Chief Edward Harden said he had no comment to make on Delaney's departure from the newspaper, other than to thank him for his services. Harden refused to comment on speculation that the *Asia Weekly* article had sparked calls for Delaney's resignation.

A spokesman for the Canadian Newspaper Guild union said that as a contract columnist with the *Tribune*, Delaney had the right to sell material to other publications but would "normally" be expected to offer the newspaper right of first refusal for a breaking news story.

Delaney, a well-known sailing buff, said that in the immediate term he would go with a companion on an extended cruising holiday aboard his beloved 30-foot sailboat, which he recently re-christened *Daylight Woman*.

MICHAEL E. ROSE is a Canadian journalist
and broadcaster whose reporting and travel
have taken him to Latin America, Europe,
Africa, India, southeast Asia and Australia.
He has worked for major media organizations
around the world, including the CBC,
*Maclean's*, UPI, Radio France International,
the *Sydney Morning Herald* and Reuters.
From 2003-2006, he was Chief of
Communications and Publications for
Interpol, based at the agency's
headquarters in Lyon, France.